THE LARKS

JEM SHAW

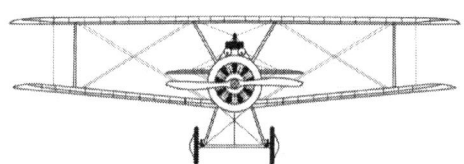

The Larks
A Novel of the First World War

:: PENKHULL

Copyright ©2013 Jem Shaw
Jem Shaw asserts the moral right to be identified as the author of this work
ISBN: 1484060830
ISBN-13: 978-1484060834
All rights reserved. No part of this publication may be reproduced, stored in a retrieval system, or transmitted in any form or by any means, electronic, mechanical, photocopying, recording or otherwise, without the prior permission of the author.
This book is sold subject to the condition that it shall not, by way of trade or otherwise, be lent, re-sold, hired out or otherwise circulated without the author's prior consent in any form of binding or cover other than that in which it is published and without a similar condition including this condition being imposed on the subsequent purchaser

Contents

Foreword	ix
Prologue	1
The Larks	6
Epilogue	369
Glossary	375
Acknowledgements	380

Jem Shaw became fascinated by words in a small primary school in Sutton Coldfield and by the age of five and a half had consumed all of the available Dick and Dora stories and moved onto a child's edition of Homer's Odyssey.

His love affair with aviation came a little earlier. Brought up close to Castle Bromwich aerodrome in the early post-war years, he would pursue his father and elder brother into the back garden to watch Spitfires, Walruses and, later on, Vampires and Venoms as they swept over the chimneys.

Nowadays he spends as much as possible of his time aloft in venerable aircraft. He earns part of his living by writing articles and designing and developing web applications for one of the world's largest flyable vintage aircraft collections.

So given these ingredients it's inexcusable that he reached the age of sixty before it occurred to him to put them together and write his first novel.

He lives in Staffordshire with his long-suffering wife and enjoys the peace that results when the kids grow up and leave home. He has been heard to threaten the creation of a sequel.

August 2014 sees the release of "It Never Was Worthwhile", an anthology of stories about the Great War written in collaboration with fellow Penkhull Press author, Malcolm Havard.

For Frank Shaw

FOREWORD

by Martin Shaw

From our earliest days my brother and I have been fascinated by aeroplanes. The mutual association began early; at eighteen months of age, in an attempt to determine the flying capabilities of my favourite model, he contrived to land it with commendable accuracy in the living room fire. I have only recently forgiven him.

We were brought up in Birmingham almost within sight of Castle Bromwich aerodrome, where so many Spitfires made their first flights in World War 2, and where I made my first flight at the age of ten in a de Havilland Rapide. My father and I had contemplated the silver biplane offering pleasure flights during an air show, I with longing, he with the mental arithmetic associated with subtracting the required ten shillings from next week's budget. Any financial adjustments that were required are long forgotten, along with any explanations demanded by my Mother. What remains is the memory of the world seen through the wings of a biplane, and the wonderment and intense satisfaction of answering the question: "What's it like up there?"

This is a question I've had the privilege of answering many times since as a pilot and owner of vintage aeroplanes. Jem was my first passenger when I achieved my pilot's licence, a flight in which I distinguished myself by getting lost and running out of fuel. The engine stopped on final approach and we landed dead-stick. To this day I remain unsure which I found more disconcerting, the stationary propeller or Jem's implacable calm (and uncontrollable laughter at our survival). He has become a considerable expert on all matters aviation, and wins most quizzes with disarming ease, so it should have come as no surprise that this book is so accurate in its ability to put the reader in the cockpit with the pilots.

There is much of the Birmingham of our youth in these pages, and when Andy goes home on leave, it is to the house in Erdington where Jem and I grew up. In fact there are many places and incidents that I recognise, from the living-room range to the lavatorial habits of the idiot dog.

Prepare for take-off, laugh out loud, and perhaps shed a tear for those Larks of a century past.

Martin Shaw

PROLOGUE: AN END TO WAR

Even with the engine off the vibration threatened to pull the little Sopwith apart. The broken propeller was windmilling at a speed that would be impossible were there any compression resisting it. *Engine's well and truly buggered.*

The morning was sharp and bright. The haze had already cleared from the cold, thin air, but grey tufts still clung in the wounds of the seared, Bisto-brown wasteland. Somewhere down there life huddled in those damp pockets, waiting for the feeble warmth of the thin sun. Somewhere down there was a flat area large enough to accept a disabled aircraft; large enough to let it roll safely to a standstill; large enough to let its pilot live as long as it took to be taken prisoner.

The pilot was leaning far out of his cockpit, scanning for space among the greenish, stinking shell holes. He winced as a trick of the wind drove an icy blast under his earflaps and he waggled life back into his numbed fingers.

He glanced up at the swirling machines spiralling above him. They'd been alerted by black puffs of Archie bursting around an RE8 on patrol over the German howitzers. Too few and scattered for a concerted attack, the shrapnel bursts were clearly a signal to nearby Hun aircraft.

They'd seen the attacker, a two-seat Halberstadt, as it opened fire from its forward gun. The Harry Tate, caught by surprise, had managed to buy a few seconds more life by flopping out of the killing line, turning down towards its climbing attacker and causing the Halberstadt to break sharply away to avoid a head-on collision. By the time the

German had turned back to the attack the five Sopwiths were on him.

They'd divided to attack from each side and split the German observer's fire. This pilot had followed close behind the flight leader, guarding his tail. Suddenly the lead aircraft had pulled sharply away without firing, its pilot already hammering the cocking levers of his jammed guns.

Up to me then. He'd closed to within fifty yards of his prey before squeezing his trigger. The two Vickers blatted satisfyingly for two seconds before the interrupter gear failed and a chance shot removed a large chunk from the propeller. Even before the pilot had cut the power, a sharp metallic clank, felt as much as heard, announced the internal destruction of the unbalanced engine. A flying fragment of the airscrew tore a large hole in the trailing edge of the right upper plane, dismounting the aileron, which flapped awkwardly in the slipstream.

Six miles back to the front line, against the wind. Fat chance.

The altimeter showed 500 feet and the pilot leaned further out into the biting wind to find a safe path through the shell holes and truncated trees. The landscape was bereft of life, deserted by humanity and nature. *There.*

A scant 200 yards ahead of the descending biplane was a stretch of reasonably clear ground. The pilot kicked in a hard sideslip to shed height, causing the broken aileron to bang repeatedly against the right rear strut. *Come down you old cow.*

He unfastened his safety strap. Preferring, like most pilots, the swift pain of broken bones to the wracking agony of burning. *Hold it off, hold it off, hold it off.*

Nose-high, the Sopwith rapidly bled off airspeed, settling sedately on to the churned ground. An unseen tree stump snatched at the right wheel, jerking the aircraft around and digging the left wingtip into the frozen ground. The machine swung back to the left, tearing off the undercarriage and skidding to a halt, leaning drunkenly over a flooded shell hole. The pilot, dazed and bruised from hitting the dashboard and cockpit coaming, climbed painfully from the cockpit.

He squatted on the ground for a few moments, cherishing his throbbing head, before returning to his machine to retrieve the dashboard timepiece. He tore a length of fabric from the wing and twisted it into a wick before letting it down through the fuel filler into the petrol tank. He pulled the fabric out and re-inserted the dry end, then took a box of vestas from his pocket and applied flame to the cloth. *Goodbye you evil old bitch.*

Seated on a mound of earth at a safe distance from the pyre, he saw that his squadron mates had already dispatched the Halberstadt. He glimpsed its death-dive, a line of white vapour streaming behind it as it arrowed into the ground.

«*Bonjour monsieur, ça va? Êtes-vous blessé?*»

Startled, the pilot looked around. A young girl of twelve or thirteen was standing uncertainly a few yards away. She held the strap of a heavy bag over her shoulder. «*Oh, bonjour mam'selle. Non, je suis tout, je vous remercie.*»

She looked at the burning wreckage two fields away and laughed bitterly. «*C'est bon ! A bas les Boches! Ils ont bien fait, vos amis!*»

Apparently satisfied of his harmlessness, she came and seated herself beside him, looking up at the scattered British aircraft. The leader, marked out by the streamers on his rear struts, was highest. He was high in his cockpit, working at the breeches of his guns.

She pointed higher up. «*Et les autres, qui sont-ils?* »

The pilot looked, saw, and stood up, hands clutching his head. "No, no, no!" A cloud of dark specks was cascading from the eastern sky. From the viewpoint of the British machines they'd be exactly in the Sun.

One of the Sopwiths flashed by at low level, its pilot waving as he passed. The downed pilot barely saw it. He ran forward, impotently waving his arms and pointing. "No, no, no!"

The remaining three Camels were still scattered. One, displaying a deputy-leader's streamer, was flying erratically as if its occupant was injured. It was heading north-east, exactly away from safety. A second Sopwith pulled in alongside to check on him.

The plunging wolf pack was approaching killing range when the lowest Camel returned from the west, climbing hard. A crimson flare arced from its cockpit and finally the others reacted. The number-two aircraft turned sharply and climbed head on to meet the attackers just as their leader opened fire. Tracer criss-crossed between them and then they were past, flashing by at a closing speed of nearly 300mph. As the next two pulled into line to exchange fire with the climbing Sopwith they touched and locked together. The Camel bunted sharply downwards to miss the descending tangle and was almost through when the two aircraft broke apart. One pulled into a more gentle dive, apparently under control; the other continued down for a second before its wings crumpled. Its airscrew severed the British machine's rear fuselage just ahead of the tail. Both broken aircraft flashed in the early sun as they tumbled to earth.

The pilot tried to count the German attackers, but gave up as they split. *Twenty at least. It's a massacre.*

One group pulled up to attack the leader, the energy of their 200mph dive taking them vertical to regain a height advantage. The leader had put his nose down to run for the lines, but the Huns still retained a speed advantage as they levelled out slightly above his tail. Their faster Albatros and Pfalz machines closed the distance in seconds and the Camel dived full-power into the ground just fifty feet below.

When the stranded airman looked back to the east he saw a falling comet. The other group had found the injured deputy leader and killed him as he flew helplessly in the wrong direction.

The pilot became aware that the girl was tugging his sleeve. She pointed wordlessly at a patrol of field-grey infantry approaching. Though they were still out of rifle range he stood and raised his arms above his head.

He turned his back on them as his eyes returned to the war above. The one remaining Camel had clawed its way to 1,000 feet. As he stood, hands raised by his own burning aircraft, the pilot could hear its engine note stutter. *That bloody engine's been dud ever since he got that kite.* He saw it turn in little more than its own length, dipping its nose and diving to start its hopeless dash for home.

A voice behind him called in almost accentless English: "You are our prisoner, Englishman. Please keep your hands up and turn towards us. You do not want to see your last comrade die."

CHAPTER 1

June 1916

Andrew Douglas Palmer, 2nd Lieutenant, Royal Flying Corps was two weeks shy of eighteen and proud of his new pilot's wings. He waved to the mud-coloured motor omnibus that had dropped him in the village square and looked around him. Away from the noise of the 'bus and the ribaldry of his fellow travellers he became aware of the grumble of distant thunder. Occasional louder thumps identified the noise as man-made; he felt a small lurch under his ribcage. He had joined the War.

The day was hot and the dusty flagstones were warm through his boots. An elderly farmer sat and swung his legs over the side of a battered wagon, a horse of apparently similar vintage to its owner sagging between the shafts. It studied the water trough, undecided whether drinking was worth the effort of extending its neck. The farmer puffed his pipe into activity and looked up.

"*Bonjour! Vous êtes l'aviateur anglais?*"
"*Oui, m'sieur. Je m'appelle Andrew Palmer. Qu' il y a un... er...* Crossley tender *ici pour moi ?*"

The farmer gave an eloquent shrug and nodded towards the cart. Palmer, his fund of French exhausted, climbed to take his place among a collection of ammunition boxes, crates and petrol cans; presumably the farmer was augmenting his income by delivering freight, both live and inanimate, for the British Expeditionary Force. He arranged two anonymously agricultural sacks against a Royal Aircraft Factory crate and accommodated his long, angular body to their crackling softness. The farmer returned to his leg-swinging. Flies buzzed. Somewhere nearby, a clock chimed the half-hour.

Palmer's doze was interrupted by a rapid flow of French. He lifted his head and blinked against the glaring brightness of the square. Another RFC-uniformed pilot officer was chatting easily with the farmer. He looked around Palmer's age, round-faced and no more than average height. His uniform fitting him in a way that suggested expensive tailoring. Palmer glanced down at his own RFC-issue tunic; it contacted his body at neck and waist, standing out everywhere else in rigid folds. The issue quartermasters obviously expected six-footers to carry more poundage. He glanced back at the sleek newcomer and silently cursed his relative poverty.

The stranger pushed his bag over the tailgate and pulled himself aboard the farm trailer.

"Morning, you headed for 128 Squadron?"

"Yes, you?"

"Yep. Colin Hingley. You're…?"

"…bloody terrified to be honest, but you can call me Andy. Andy Palmer. Take a sack, make yourself comfy."

The newcomer settled into an angle between two boxes and fumbled for his cigarettes, passing the packet over to his new companion.

"Thanks. Can't say I think much of the squadron transport."

Hingley struck a match and nodded.

"Apparently the Crossley's broken down, so they've asked Robert here to ferry us to the 'drome. Still, beats Shanks's I suppose. Done much flying?" Palmer eyed the new RFC wings on Hingley's tunic. "Got twenty-five hours, mostly Avros. You?"

"Forty-eight, but most of 'em on Longhorns. I got my hands on an Avro for four or so. Nice machine. But I did get a go in a Nieuport at Omer."

Palmer's estimate of the newcomer's experience climbed rapidly. The Maurice Farman Longhorn was an antiquated box-kite reminiscent of the Wright Brothers' Flyer. But the Nieuport... the fast, tricky weapon of choice for the great flying aces, that was a real pilot's machine.

"A Nieup? Wow! What was it like?"

"Bloody impossible. Damn' thing nearly killed me. Fast as hell, but I choked the engine climbing out and thought it was all over. Then it kept trying to nose-up all the way round the circuit. You're pushing on the stick the whole time to keep it flat. Made me wish I'd joined the infantry to be honest."

Another reassessment of Hingley's flying skills. *OK, so he's not that far ahead after all.*

The French farmer climbed onto the front of the wagon. He called a cheerful warning and whistled the horse into a gentle, unhurried stroll. The resulting pace was barely faster than walking but, as Palmer said, it beat Shanks's pony. Just.

Hingley fashioned the available ordnance and agriculture into a comfortable easy chair and sprawled in the sun, drawing gratefully on his cigarette. "Where d'you hail from Andy?"

"Erdington, just north of Birmingham. How about you?"

"Suffolk. Father's a bishop, so the war came just in time to save me from the family business. What about you?"

As the fields ambled by, and the questions of origin, schooling and flying experience were answered, silences began to grow. First one, then the other began to nod, and the two new pilots delivered to No 128 Squadron needed a firm shake from the gate sentry to recall them to their duties.

*

They were met by a small, bird-like captain, leaning heavily on an ivory-handled stick. "Pleased to meet you, I'm Acting Major Barrington-Holt, Recording Officer. I like to meet new chaps in person. Come with me and I'll show you your hut. The private will bring your bags."

He executed a sharp about-face and started away without waiting. Even his limp displayed a military precision.

Colin raised his eyebrows at Andy and flicked a grin, then started after Acting Major Barrington-Holt's erratic progress as he limped across what appeared to be a farmyard. The recording officer waved his stick at a large, dilapidated house that lowered over the wide, walled space, whose uneven cobbles treacherously twisted ankles under a century's encrusted manure.

"OC's office in there. He'd like to see you once you've settled in."

The field beyond the open farmyard gate revealed two rows of low, corrugated iron constructions, a few of which boasted small, carefully tended front gardens. Acting Major Barrington Holt led them to a neglected, briar-grown hut and opened the door. "Here's home for you. Just the two of you for now. We're struggling to keep anyone who lives in this one for long. Ha Ha. Get yourselves settled in, clean yourselves up a bit and pop over to see Major Tiverton. Do something about that bloody straw in your hair, Palmer."

As the RO's stick clacked into the distance, the boys took in their new residence. A grubby table stood disconsolately amid three sagging straw-bottomed chairs. Flies circled a stained tin mug. The stove, made from an inexpertly adapted oil-drum, rocked unsteadily on its uneven stand of broken bricks as Colin inspected its workings. "He's going to be a bundle of laughs ain't he?"

Andy looked out from a tiny cubicle in which he'd found a wood and chicken wire platform. "What d'you make of this? It looks like half a rabbit hutch, but these blankets are giving me a bad feeling." He picked up a shapeless grey bag. "And you don't think this is meant to be a pillow, do you?"

The Officer Commanding stood as his new pilots entered his office, new boys shuffling nervously into their headmaster's study. "Morning; Henry Tiverton. Sorry about the horse and cart, but Depot keeps sending the wrong crankshaft for the Crossley. You must be Palmer and Hingley. Which one's which?"

Colin awkwardly adjusted his half-finished salute to meet the OC's handshake. "I'm Hingley, sir. This is Andy Palmer."

"Welcome to 128 Squadron. You've got straw on your back. Drink?"

Andy took in his new surroundings as Colin chatted easily with the OC. The liquid in the dusty glass he'd been presented with turned out to be a half-gill of gin, and it combined with Tiverton's relaxed informality to calm his first-day nerves. He began to drift, gazing through the window as a dun-coloured Nieuport 11 settled expertly onto the grass strip, the chequered band around its rear fuselage showing sharply in the June sunshine. A brace of mechanics ran out to take the wingtips and guide the taxiing biplane. He noticed tattered fabric hanging from the upper wing. Acting-Major Barrington Holt's voice spoke in his mind: *We're struggling to keep anyone who lives in this one for long.*

An outburst from Tiverton brought him back. The OC was talking to Colin, but it was clear that Andy was now the topic under discussion.

"Twenty-five hours? For God's sake, I thought they'd sorted the bloody training hours! What in Jesus' name are they doing sending him out here with twenty-five hours? Baxter!"

A greying, ink-stained sergeant appeared at the office door. "Sir?"

"I just saw Captain French land. Ask him to pop over, would you?"

"Yes, Sir."

Captain French was tall, softly-spoken and appeared little older than Palmer and Hingley. His coat, helmet and face were smeared with oil, all except for clear skin where he'd removed his goggles. He wiped his mouth with a piece of cotton waste, revealing a sandy moustache. "Call me Arthur. You'll be in A-Flight with me, Lord help us all."

"They've shipped this one over with twenty-five hours and nothing on type. Thought you'd want to know as soon as possible." said the OC.

"Oh joy." French turned to Colin. "What about you?"

"Er, forty-eight, sir. Two in a Nieuport."

"OK, well added together you're half way to being right, so let's make the best of it. Either of you put in any time on a 2c? Oh, and it's Arthur."

"No sir... Arthur."

"Nor me sir."

"Well let's do something about that toot sweet. You need these chaps for anything else, Henry?"

Tiverton raised a hand in agreement. "No, you carry on with it. Good luck, chaps. Stick with this man here and you'll be fine. See you for a couple of gins later."

French led them from the control hut across a short apron of cracked, grass-grown concrete, darkened by a layer of some hard-packed, dark material of indeterminate colour. "This used to be the farmyard. Don't get that stuff stuck in your boot soles, it stinks to heaven when it warms up."

Rounding the corner of a corrugated iron hangar they discovered a neat row of Bristol and Nieuport scouts with, here and there, a mechanic working busily away. At the end, unloved and unlovely, slouched a weary BE2c.

"Don't be put off; she might not be pretty, but at least she'll never do much to hurt you. Anyway, it's the only two-seater we have, and I'm not letting you loose on a scout until I've seen what you can do."

Hingley and Palmer tossed a penny and Andy, having lost, sat down on a packing case and watched as an Ack Emma swung the prop. The captain seated himself comfortably in the front cockpit while Colin, looking less confident, climbed into the pilot's seat behind him. The engine started without excessive reluctance and the battered two-seater rolled out towards the strip. Hingley's take-off was distressingly expert. The tailskid came up neatly and there was no discernible tail-wagging in the blustery wind. Andy tried to be charitably pleased that his new friend was already such a competent pilot. He failed and lit a self-conciliatory cigarette.

"Mr French showin' a new boy round is he?"

A short, approximately-shaved man in dirty overalls appeared at Andy's shoulder, a soggy roll-up hanging from his lower lip. "Morning sir, Hughes, sir, sergeant rigger. Everybody calls me Hughie."

Hughie's salute spared Andy the duty of shaking the grimy hand. "Palmer, Second Lieutenant. Pleased to meet you Hughie."

Hughie squinted up at the BE2c, now performing lazy S-turns. "Needs to watch that, he does. Can't put much stress on those wires. I said to 'em, I says 'them wires need changin' sir or I won't answer.' But nobody listens to Hughie do they? You remember when you gets up there sir, keep it level whatever you do. That old kite ain't safe."

Andy stared more intently at the 2C. "How unsafe is unsafe?"

Hughie sucked his teeth. "Well, she should be alright if you're gentle with her, but I wouldn't answer if you do any fancy stuff. If you see any flapping from the fabric on the bottom wing, get down quick or you'll be down even quicker."

The two watched in silence as the 2C settled onto a downwind track. Hughie broke up the remaining stub of his rollup and crumbled the mummified tobacco into a fresh paper. He swore softly to himself as the wind repeatedly defeated his attempts to marshal a miniature compost heap into something vaguely cylindrical. He inserted the sagging construct between his lips and applied a match; the resulting flash fire singed his eyebrows but drew no comment as he inhaled gratefully. "Here 'e comes."

The 2C glided quietly in, its big four-blade prop windmilling. A brief float, and tailskid and main wheels kissed the ground almost together. Hardly a bounce. *Bastard.*

Colin was elated as he climbed out of the rear cockpit. "Beat that mate! I love it here!"

Andy looked worriedly at the lower wing as he took Hingley's place. Should he say something to French? Presumably the captain knew about Hughie's misgivings; better to keep quiet and fly carefully.

The captain turned in his seat. "OK, nothing much to know. She's a forgiving old thing, but she climbs like a carthorse. Oil pressure no lower than 20, and temperature no higher than 90. Bit of rudder to keep her straight but she doesn't swing that much. She needs a bit of stick to get the tail up, then just let her fly when she wants to. Keep her level when she comes off and wait for the pitot to come up to sixty, then keep it at 60-65 as you climb. I'll give you a wave to level off, then show me a couple of turns. Don't bank more than thirty degrees. Nothing too flashy, I just want to see how you handle her."

Colin swung the prop and the machine trundled back to the downwind end of the strip. *Check the gauges, look around, then open the throttle.* The BE began to gather momentum and Andy soon felt the tail go light. He forced his attention away from the lower wing and eased the stick forward. *Too far! The prop's going to hit! Pull back! Damn!* A slight thump as the tailskid bounced. French grinned over his shoulder. The bumps from the undercart faded and the aircraft lifted. Level off and wait for sixty. *Are those wrinkles in the left wing?*

The pitot staggered unenthusiastically to 60mph and Andy eased the stick back. *Take it gently*. French waved two hands above his shoulders. *I know, I'm already climbing.* French's gestures became more emphatic and Andy applied a little more back-pressure. *Watch those wings.*

The corrugated roof of an airfield hut flashed by a few feet below the wheels. *Pull up!* As Andy pulled back on the stick he felt his eyes drawn again to the lower wing. The inner panel on the left was beginning, unmistakeably, to flap.

*

Colin settled himself comfortably on the recently vacated packing case to watch Andy's take-off. He taxied competently enough, and the burst of throttle he applied to help the tail round at the end of the strip showed a judgement beyond his meagre flying hours. *So far, so good.* The take-off roll wasn't too tidy, but anyone can bang the skid on an unfamiliar kite. The 2C was a little late lifting off, but there was plenty of airfield left as long as he started climbing now.

When the 2C did begin climbing, it quickly became obvious that it was going to run out of room. Acceleration, even for a BE2c was disastrously slow – some sort of engine trouble for sure. Shouts from the hut at the end of the strip heralded a mass exit of khaki-clad figures as the machine laboured over, barely clearing the roof. The aircraft's nose came up as the climb steepened.

There was a slow-motion inevitability about the stall. The wings wobbled briefly, and then the aircraft nosed over, disappearing behind the scrubby trees that marked the perimeter.

Colin began to run.

*

By the time Colin reached the perimeter trees there was already a crowd around the crashed machine. All he could see was the tail slanted skyward as he ran breathlessly across the rough meadow. Panting furiously, he shouldered through the onlookers in time to see French hanging on to the rear cockpit coaming with one hand as he reached in to attend to Andy, who appeared to be slumped in the rear seat. As Hingley climbed up to help, Andy looked up, dazed, a bright welt blooming above his goggles. He grinned vaguely at Colin. "Oh, hullo, can't get my bloody strap undone."

Andy's first night in the mess proved a good deal more expensive than he'd intended. The 128 Squadron High Court found him guilty of murdering fifty worms belonging to the loyal French farmer whose meadow he'd inadvertently ploughed. A sentence was handed down ordering him to buy a drink to commemorate each one. Colin, defending, appealed for clemency on the basis that this was a first offence. This was viewed sympathetically and the Court ruled that Andy wouldn't have to drink them all himself.

The evening was a blur of introductions, most of which were forgotten in seconds. Henrik Doke, the C-Flight commander, was a stocky, dark-moustached pilot with an unrecognisable accent. He seemed to be permanently laughing at the world. Robière was a tiny, birdlike Canadian who clasped scuffed records in tattered covers against his chest. His handshake was cut short by the need to stop them sliding from their sleeves as he reached forward. A tall, aristocratic captain with a scarred, piebald face, melted and burnt hairless, extended a similarly patched hand;

"Humphrey Page. Don't be put off by the fizzog, afraid I cooked a 504 and forgot to get out first."

Page had crashed in training in 1915 and spent six months in hospital recovering from burns to his face and right hand. His sight saved by his goggles, he'd re-volunteered on discharge and now had three confirmed kills to his name. He and Colin were soon deep in conversation, their hands tracing complex aerial manoeuvres, fingers sketching positions in spilt alcohol.

Andy looked around the mess, clouded by pipe and cigarette smoke. Robière was carefully positioning one of his prized records on the turntable of a gigantic electric Victrola, standing on tip-toe to place the needle. The first strains of the Prince's Orchestra brought a noisy protest from a large figure slouched over the piano.

"Oi Robbie, If yer going to interrupt my genius, at least do it with something other than fuckin' *Chin-Chin!*"

A chair leg scraped and Andy looked up to see Captain French pulling up a seat and slumping next to him, raising his eyebrows to summon the mess servant.

"Evening, Farmer Palmer; how's the scourge of French agriculture settling in?"

"Feeling a bit of an idiot, sir. How bad's the damage?"

"Could be years before anything grows properly. Plane's not too bad though; needs a prop and some carpentry on the undercart. Hughie's gone propeller hunting – Lieutenant McConnachie telephoned St Omer and found him a good one."

French was philosophical about Andy's disappointing introduction to operational flying. He'd handled the stall well, avoided a spin, and they'd both walked away.

"First question to ask yourself is 'am I getting full power?' If the answer's 'maybe', give it up right then. Even a 2C should accelerate faster than that, so something was obviously broken. If you see me waving my arms like this again, be a good chap and shut the engine down.

"Oh yes, and I'd keep away from Hughie for a bit, it's only a week since Cubby made him work all night rewiring it to tighten up the lower plane."

A commotion distracted them. A wavering human pyramid was assembling near the piano. Doke, the short pilot with the strange accent called across the mess,

"Hey you, the skinny new boy! Get down here, you're seconded to "C" Flight for tonight. We need somebody with a bit of altitude for scaffolding. You're about to learn the art of Bok-Bok!"

*

"Morning sir, cup of tea?"

Andy squinted at the hideously cheerful corporal, accepted the proffered mug. Morning, er... Mossley?"

"Mossley, sir, yes. How are we feeling this morning?"

"Bright-eyed, bushy tailed and lying through my teeth, Mossley. You wouldn't have an aspirin there would you?"

"Thought that might be it sir. Here you go. The Major would like to see you when you've had your breakfast."

Sergeant Baxter gave Andy a knowing look as Palmer entered Major Tiverton's outer office. Possibly he was just recognising the effects of excess on an unaccustomed drinker. Possibly.

"Major Tiverton and Mr McConnachie are waiting, Mr Palmer, you can go right in."

Andy recognised the officer slouched opposite the OC as the frustrated pianist of last night. He appeared to have been poured into the battered leather chair. He sprawled bonelessly; a sagging, inch-long finger of ash fell unheeded from his cigarette and added to the small pile already on his breeches. The Major stood by a scratched bureau, holding a dusty bottle.

"Morning Andy, hair of the dog?"

"No thanks sir. Bit fragile to be honest."

"I'd like you to meet Lieutenant Cuthbert McConnachie. Cubby, get up and shake hands you ignorant bugger."

The stranger unwound himself from the chair and extended a dinner-plate hand to Andy. "Pleased to meet yer, mate. Heard about what you did to my old 2C. Hope yer gonna pay for it."

The accent was strongly Australian. McConnachie was over 6 feet tall, his wrists protruding too far from his slightly dog-eared RFC uniform jacket. Andy took in the two pips, the purple-and-white MC ribbon, but no pilot's brevet. *His* 2C?

"Sorry, Cuthbert, it didn't really look as if it belonged to anyone who cared much."

"Ah, no worries. Needed a pilot to drive me around any way. Now I got you; just need an aeroplane. And it's Cubby."

"Cubby's done some flying himself," said Tiverton. "Came out here before he'd finished his pilot's ticket to get a go at the Boche before we'd finished them all off. I'd like you to have an experienced man as an observer, and Cubby here's short of a pilot since Smith-Wright went home with TB."

So that explained the sergeant's knowing look. "Observer? Sir, I thought I'd be flying single-seaters."

Cubby caught the Major's eye, nodded at Andy and left the office.

"Sit down Andy." He inspected his glass; looked up. "You're not going to understand why I'm doing this, but I want you in a two-seater for a while at least. Cubby's one of the most experienced men I have, and I think that's what you need for now."

"Look sir, I know I came a ball of snot in the 2C, but I do know how to fly. I just…"

"You just let yourself get dragged into one of Hughie's little games. That's exactly what I mean, my lad. You're, what, eighteen?" A nod. "I want you to see a few more birthdays, and to do that you need to understand a bit more about how the world works. Arthur French thinks you'll be a decent pilot – when it all went to little reels of cotton, you turned a nasty crash into a rough landing. A lot of pilots would have tried to turn back, and you'd both be dead. It's not your flying ability that needs work, it's your brain. So I'm putting you with a good teacher."

Andy's protest was stilled by Tiverton's raised hand, and the Major's voice hardened slightly.

"I'm sorry, Lieutenant, this isn't up for discussion. Apart from anything else, I need at least one spotter – just now we don't even have that. Command's sending me single-seaters and missions for two-seaters. You and Cubby are my recce crew from now on. Give me a few weeks' worth of good obs and we'll see about giving you a scout. The 2C will be back in operation tomorrow, and there's plenty of work for you to do. I need you on art. reg. yesterday, and Intelligence are going bananas for some more of Cubby's snaps. So sod off and get to know your observer."

Andy avoided the sergeant's look as he left the Major's office. But worse was to come outside when he saw Colin approaching. Hingley seemed a decent bloke, but sympathy from an instinctive pilot wasn't what he wanted just now. He was spared by the arrival of Cubby, who pulled a dented Thornycroft lorry to a halt in a cloud of petrol fumes.

"Hop up mate, let's show you round."

The French countryside rolled gently in and out of sight as the Thornycroft growled towards Terramesnil. A donkey and cart rattled comfortably ahead, the driver as apparently oblivious to the olive-drab truck behind him as he was to the repeated thump-thump of heavy guns in the distance. Birds twittered contentedly in the hedgerows.

Cubby gestured with his cigarette. "Coming in from the east there's not a lot to help you. Terramesnil's pretty hard to spot from the air, so you need to look for Beauval. If you get overhead of that you've gone too far. You need to look for the rise before the woods, and get that wood over there on your left. The corner of it points straight at the strip. If you're in trouble you can get down in pretty well any of these fields, but watch for ditches. Help yourself."

Andy accepted Cubby's open packet of Scouts and tried to ignore the smell of petrol as he lit one. Artillery rumbled constantly.

"How far from here to the front?"

"You'll see in a bit, though I doubt we'll be able to get close in the Thorny – there's something big going on I reckon. It's about ten miles in a straight line east, by Ocean Villas."

The French farmer turned into a yard on the outskirts of the tiny village and Cubby picked up speed. At the crossroads beyond the few houses they saw the first signs of war. A whistle-blowing infantry corporal gestured to them to halt to allow a column of artillery to pass through, the horses plodding stoically as their limbers and howitzers bounced on the uneven road.

"Bloody great. So now we get to drive at five miles a bloody hour through a mountain of fresh horseshit." He leaned out of the cab. "Oi, yer dung-spattered moron, pull those guns over and let a motor lorry through!"

"Who the fuck's asking?"

"The fuckin' officer who's ordering you to clear the fuckin' road before he gets out of his fuckin' motor lorry and shoves the startin' handle up a gobby fuckin' corporal's arse!"

"One moment please, sir."

Andy grinned at his companion. "So, what brings an Aussie to the RFC?"

After thirty seconds, Andy decided the older man hadn't heard the question. "What brings…"

"Long, boring story." Another extended pause. "What about you?"

"Short, boring one. Out of school, into a drawing office. My Dad was an office manager at Hercules, and he put in a word for me. Believe me, nothing the war can do to me can be worse than trekking to Birmingham every day to draw pictures of push-bike pedals."

"Your Dad still alive?"

Andy thought for a moment. "Last I heard he was. He's with the PBI up at Ypres. Sergeant-major. He re-enlisted last year. My older brother's a pilot with the RNAS."

"And you didn't follow him?"

"Bit of a family scrap about that. Dad wanted us both to join the Royal Warwickshires so's he could look out for us, but Rob's always had his own way of doing things. I toed the line for the sake of peace."

Cubby laughed. "Not a lot of peace up around Wipers from what I hear."

"Not a lot of peace when I put my name down for pilot training as soon as I joined up, either." He glanced across at Cubby. "You married, Cub?"

Cubby gestured to the right. "Look out here. You try to get down into either of those fields and you'll come a right ball of snot. Power lines and holes everywhere. The one to the left is OK from here up to the wood. About the best emergency field between here and the front. Look for the triangle the two roads make and turn up the hill towards the trees. There's usually PBI at the crossroads, so they'll wait till the fire goes out and send your ashes to your Mum."

"Lovely."

"Yeah lovely. And I'll be the innocent bystander cookin' in the front seat, so let's hope you do better than yesterday."

"Aye. Afraid you drew the short straw, getting the new boy as a pilot."

"No I didn't. I asked for you."

"You asked for the oik who pranged your 2C?"

"You prang one in training?"

"No. Couple of rough landings that's all."

"Thought so. You'll do for me. That crash yesterday was Hughie's fault, not yours. I saw him talking to you before you went up. The Ack Emmas love to play games with the new quirks. Don't worry, I'll put the little toad right. Oh, and just so's you know, they found a sticky valve in the 2C – that's why it wouldn't pull. You concentrate on keepin' me alive and we'll get on just fine."

Progress slowed as the truck ground closer to Auchonvillers. Infantry lined the verges, sprawled around small fires with bubbling mess tins. Stops became more frequent and prolonged; horses shook their heads and whisked their docked tails in attempt to discourage the ever-present flies. The warm air thickened with the smell of horse sweat, dung and petrol. Traffic NCOs became ever more furious, blowing their whistles and shouting for a lane to be left clear for officers' horses and bicycles.

Eventually Cubby pulled to the side and switched off. "No point going any closer in the motor; even if we could get forward we'd never get back against the traffic. Might as well leave it here and walk on a bit."

Abandoning the congested road for the rolling fields, Andy found himself in a world of contradictions. The sun was warm, the fields green, the mad burbling of a skylark ringing clearly now that the sound of artillery had subsided to an intermittent grumbling. The occasional sharp *smack!* of small-arms signalled that some real or imagined target in the German lines had appeared above the trench line. A French poacher saluted them cheerfully with his ancient rifle, proudly holding up a brace of hares for them to admire. They re-joined the road as they reached Auchonvillers. Before the war it had probably been a pleasant French village; now it was a confusion of rubble, tents and corrugated iron. The church still stood proudly, though many of its gravestones were broken or fallen. Outside a regimental aid post, a group of lightly wounded soldiers clustered around the inevitable boiling mess tin, their bandages startling white against grimed flesh. People and ordnance swarmed everywhere, emerging from cellars and bustling off on some unknown errand, workers serving their invisible and ravenous queen.

Cubby's Cook's Guide continued as he worked to instil an awareness of the terrain in his new pilot. "This is Rue Delattre. Jerry's not fond of it, so it gets a fair amount of artillery attention. Look for the water tower there. From the air it shows like a shilling on sweep's arse. The cutting there is Beaumont Road. It leads straight to the front. You can't see it at all from above."

As the cutting came to its end, Cubby put a hand on Andy's chest. "OK, that's as far as we go. They don't usually shoot this far, but there's always the chance that some Jerry sniper's bored enough to have a pop. Just keep your head lowish and get a feel for the terrain."

The contrast was stark and disturbing. The green and gold of the Ancre River valley gave way to colourless, baked earth, criss-crossed by the avenues of trenches. To the right, a grubby trench railway chugged its cargo of mortar shells reluctantly forward. On the hill directly in front was a forbidding construction of wire and sandbags. A chance movement up there caught Andy's eye and two or three rifles cracked apathetically from the British lines. "That's Hawthorn Ridge," said Cubby, pointing. "Command's got something big planned for it, no idea what. It's pretty much the anchor for the German front line here. Lots of Archie just behind it – old Hun are a bit shy about us looking at it."

He pointed to the left. "See the white scar up there? That's White City. Big bunch of RAPs and dugouts. It's out of sight of Hawthorn Ridge, and behind those bloody great piles of chalk. They're cramming it with 86 Brigade. Bloody good blokes. You can see the chalk from Berlin, so aim for it if you get lost. You can get down behind it pretty well, and they'll look after you like royalty until the squadron picks you up."

"You've landed there?"

"Believe me, you won't spend much time here before you need the hospitality of 86 Brigade. Best PBI in France. Bloody good blokes."

*

The middle-aged armourer hefted a box of .303 ammunition onto the plank table.

"Thanks Topsy." Cubby handed Andy a brass plate with holes of various sizes drilled through. "OK, you check 'em, I'll load 'em."

Andy dropped the first round into the largest hole. "You telling me all the pilots do this?"

"Not at all. That's why so many of 'em come home with their guns jammed solid. I like it when it makes a nice loud noise every time you pull the trigger."

"But it's the armourers' job."

"Yeah. To check the ammo for twenty machines, plus the guns for the AA pits. Believe me, your concentration will be shot by the time you've done the first magazine. We do three, four of our own drums a day and stay alive."

It was tedious work. Each round had to be inspected and measured before being pushed into the finger-trapping drum. By the third magazine, Andy was already drifting. Then Cubby tossed a round back to him.

"Look at that one again mate."

Andy's mind focused rapidly. The bullet was scuffed on one side, and slightly skewed out of line with the cartridge.

"Fuck. Sorry mate." Cubby's honorifics were contagious.

"No worries. You see what I mean though. Topsy!"

The armourer was already approaching, clutching two mugs of tea. "Sir?"

"You're making us shoot round fuckin' corners again. By my reckoning you're down 7/6d already this week."

"Sorry, Sir." Topsy looked genuinely penitent. "Won't happen again, sir."

"Too bloody right it won't. Lieutenant Palmer spotted it, so no harm done. In fact, as a special one-off, armourers for the use of, he's just offered a ten-bob bonus if we don't get another dud this week."

Topsy brightened. "Thank you very much sir. I won't let you down. Would you like some Nestlé's in your tea?"

Andy returned to checking ammunition with more care. "What have you legged me into now?"

Cubby chuckled. "Investment in survival sonny. I bung Topsy and his mates a quid a week to pre-check the ammo, less sixpence for every dud. Amazing how reliable a Lewis can be."

"I thought a pilot's pay was good; what with buying the squadron's drinks and paying the armourers to let me do their job for 'em I won't have much of it to spend."

"War's an expensive business, son."

*

Colin was sitting at the table writing when Andy entered the hut, throwing his Sam Browne, tunic and cap onto his bed. "Never realised there were so many ways to trap skin in a machine gun magazine. Writing home?"

Colin sat back, tapping his pencil against the table top. "Yeah, doing my sonly duty and keeping the bish and bishopess up to date on the heroic exploits of their only beloved son. There's some fresh tea in the pot. Tin of Zam-Buk and gauze on the shelf if you need it."

Andy examined his fingertips. "No, I'll let it fester and get myself a wound stripe." He poured tea into two tin mugs. "I came here to fly aeroplanes. So far I've flown twenty yards, crashed into a potato field, been for a drive in a lorry, and got pressganged into tearing my fingernails off doing an armourer's job for him – and I'm ten bob down on the deal, thanks to the barmy Ozzie I now seem to be chauffeuring. This job's a bit shit if you ask me."

Colin nodded sympathetically and poured condensed milk into Andy's cup. "Rest your poor young arse and tell your Uncle Col all about it. Make me laugh enough and I'll even fetch you a tot of whisky to put in that."

"Not for me mate, not after last night."

"You did join in with some enthusiasm; what the hell was the human pyramid all about?"

"God knows. It was that little guy with the funny accent started it, what's his name? Doke? Bok-Bok he called it."

"Well you seemed to grasp the rules pretty quick. I'm impressed you can still walk."

"The immunity of the true drunk. God knows what my mess bill will be for that bender."

"Not much – Page and French split a third each onto their tab. Said you'd shown willing, and that was enough."

Andy sipped his tea. "Bloody hell, that's pretty decent isn't it?"

"The job might be shit, but the natives are friendly."

"What's in store for you today?"

"Big day for me. French wants me down at the sheds. Think I'm getting my scout."

"Lucky bastard."

Colin tapped the pencil against his teeth. "I heard about that. You've got the 2C?"

Andy nodded slowly. "I've got the shit, shittier, shittiest 2C. I get a shit plane for being a shit pilot." He looked at Colin; saw him groping for a suitable response. "Sorry, mate. Big congrats on getting your scout. Do you know what you're getting."

"Well it's going to be a Bristol or a Nieuport, 'cause I think that's all they've got here. I'd rather the Nieuport, but either suits me, really. They're both rockets from what I've heard. Really sorry about the 2C. What's McConnachie like?"

Andy walked to the door to throw out his tea leaves. "Entertaining. I think he is a bit mad, but he sort of gets everyone dancing to his tune, you know?"

"F'r instance?"

"Well , he'd borrowed this lorry to show me round the front. On the way back he stopped at this barn and took a huge padlock off the door to get in. There was about twenty bolts of linen inside. He gets us to pick up one each and put them in the back."

"So, what? Is he on the pinch?"

"Well, that's where it gets a bit mad. Yes, he pinched them, but only after they'd already been pinched."

"Go on! Who by?"

"By Hughie. Turns out he'd got a regular mart going. He was nicking all sorts of stuff and selling it on. So much that he'd lost track of his stock. Cubby wasn't keen on that."

"So he nicked Hughie's stock of nicked linen?"

"He nicked Hughie's stock of nicked *and* un-nicked linen, then confused Hughie so much he thought he'd just lost track and accidentally sold all his stock. So suddenly he was up shit creek without a paddle."

"So McConnachie's a bigger crook than Hughie."

"Sort of, but not really. Hughie was shitting himself, and thought he could ask Cubby for help. Cubby promised to find him some linen from somewhere and not tell anyone what Hughie had done. So Hughie gets the riggers to do Cubby all sorts of favours, and Cubby rewards him by giving him enough of his own stock back to keep the machines in fabric, but not enough to black-market the surplus."

Colin whistled softly. "Now that's creative policemanship."

CHAPTER 2

The patched, battered BE2c looked little better than its pre-crash appearance, other than a brand-new, gleaming, laminated airscrew. Hughie was applying a final polish when Andy arrived to do his pre-flight inspection.

"Morning Mr Palmer, Sir. She's all ready for you. What d'you think of that for a prop, sir?"

"Very pretty. Seems a shame to get it dirty."

"Went to Depot myself, sir. Had a right go with old Fuller to get it. Apparently it was earmarked for some Lord Smarty-Pilot up by Wipers. Cost me a few favours to get it lost." The little rigger bobbed uncertainly as he explained, glancing up at Andy for signs of approval. "The fitters couldn't believe it sir. Best prop on the Western Front, that."

"Thank you Hughie. I really appreciate it."

"Welcome sir. I… Well I didn't know you was going to be flying with Mr McConnachie, sir. We all try our best sir, 'specially for Lieutenant McConnachie."

"Yes, I'm noticing that." Andy patted the prop and bent to check the landing wires. He was waggling the rudder when Cubby arrived to admire the new propeller. "Thanks Hughie, couple of bolts of linen for you outside your shed."

"Thank you sir."

Watching Cubby thread his bulk through the maze of struts and wires into the front pit reminded Andy of a contortionist he'd seen at Bingley Hall. The big Australian was surprisingly agile, threading expertly past the gun and settling himself on the observer's bench. He shot a grin over his shoulder. "believe me, mate, I can get out again even quicker."

Take-off was significantly less dramatic than Andy's last attempt. The skid unstuck neatly and judicious applications of rudder kept the machine tracking straight in the tricky wind. The new prop made the machine deliver speed with a reasonable approximation of enthusiasm, and the 2C rose over the enlisted barracks, if not gracefully, then at least without massacring any more French worms. Cubby waggled two hands in a "Lawdy Lawdy" mime; the back of his head appeared to be grinning.

*

Colin's second day with the squadron started well. Captain French walked him down the line of machines to a Bristol Scout with a large white "G" painted on the cowling. "This one's yours." He said, patting the stained leading edge of the lower plane. "She's not too pretty, but the engine's OK. I want you to take her up as often as possible, *this side of the lines*, and get the lie of the land."

Colin admired his new possession. He had his own aeroplane! As French said, she'd clearly seen some hard use: the airscrew was pitted and worn, and the oil-stained fabric was a patchwork of ill-matched olive-dun dope. He'd never seen anything so beautiful.

French was talking again; "She's fuelled up and ready. Go and get the feel of her. Stay to the west and within sight of the aerodrome." He turned and called to a group of engineers; "Ack Emma on the prop please!" Colin lovingly started his pre-flight. The Bristol, his own Bristol, looked sleek and purposeful, from the Lewis perched aggressively on the top wing, to the narrow, racer-like undercart. The

Nieuport 11s were tiny and ephemeral alongside her. *Mine. All mine.*

French helped him with his belt. "You've flown a Nieuport, so this one won't give you any surprises. It's less of a handful, but you'll still need some forward stick to stay level. Careful with that though, she's very sensitive fore and aft. Don't pick the skid up too hard or you'll clout the prop. Good bootful of opposite rudder as the tail comes up.

"Use the fuel lever on approach rather than the blip switch. That way you can get the power back on if you need to take another go. You can blip it once you're committed. Turn the fuel off if you blip for more than a couple of seconds. One hand for the fuel, one for the throttle, and the other two for the stick and blip switch.

"Have fun and don't bend it."

The Bristol was tricky, demanding, and even better than he'd expected. After the training hacks and yesterday's circuit in the 2C Bloater, the Scout felt like the eager, responsive thoroughbred he'd dreamed of controlling. The tiniest fore and aft movement of the stick set the nose bobbing; *have to watch that.* An icy draught on his right cheek told him he wasn't flying straight, and a whisper of right rudder blew cold air under the left flap of his flying helmet. He adjusted his control inputs and hoped his inexperience wasn't too apparent from the ground.

For those without fear of the air, there's little to compare with the sensation of flying. Just five minutes after leaving the landing ground, the first wisps of the cloud base were misting the windscreen. Colin levelled off and pulled into a steep turn, grinning down along his left wing to the chequered fields below. A patch of sunlit meadow a mile or so away caught his eye and he turned towards it. The gap in the clouds, when he reached it, was barely wide enough for the Bristol to spiral up and through. But as French had said, the engine had plenty of power and, barely a minute later, the grey walls rolled away, leaving the Scout and its enraptured pilot in a blazing cloudscape of rolling white. The brilliant Sun cast its grateful warmth from an azure-purple sky. The war, even the earth itself, faded from this existence.

Another aircraft dropped alongside him, causing him to start violently, snatching the stick away. The other machine turned with him and he saw Robière, the tiny Canadian, grinning broadly across the narrow gap. *Right, you cheeky little sod, let's see you follow this.*

Colin pulled the stick hard left and back, kicking in some initial rudder to tighten the turn before easing in some opposite to keep the nose up as the Scout came onto the knife edge. He looked back and up to see Robière's machine turning easily inside him. *Bugger!*

He flattened the turn and aileron rolled level and beyond, pulling back hard again as the Bristol settled into the opposite turn, its radius tightened further by the engine torque. Robière remained glued to his tail.

After expending every trick and misdirection he could conceive, Colin finally admitted defeat and levelled out. Robière dropped in alongside him again and raised both hands to applaud the younger aviator's efforts. Colin shook his head and touched his forehead, waving his obeisance to the Canadian's consummate flying skills.

Robière waved and beckoned, darting away to lead Colin in a neck snapping follow-my-leader through the cloud peaks. The two aircraft dived, swerved and swooped between Himalayan cliffs, flicking over vertiginous chasms that revealed dun patches of surly earth. Finally, the Canadian broke away and settled sedately, nose up, to kiss the cloud tops, waving as he sank from view. Colin throttled back and drifted towards the white valleys below him, solid, peaked, irresistible. A wide plateau beckoned and he set the nose to touch perfectly at its start. He anchored his Aldis sight on his chosen landing spot, and was pleased to find that he could now coordinate the sensitive controls with such precision that it barely deviated. *Committed.* He thumbed the blip switch and the Bristol settled, nose-high, to a perfect three-point landing on the cloud. As the grey-white rose to engulf him he gently moved the stick forward and released the blip switch.

Nothing.

Damn! Forgot to turn off the fuel, and now the bloody plugs are oiled up.

Colin had heard plenty of stories of pilots who'd become disorientated in cloud and dived inverted into the ground. Alone in the cold grey damp, he fought back panic and looked at his ASI. Sixty-five and accelerating gently. *OK, so we're descending, and it's not too steep; keep it about there.* He turned off the fuel and waited for the windmilling prop to clear the cylinders. The fifteen seconds before the exhaust farted white smoke were the longest in Colin's life. He readjusted throttle and fuel and berated himself as an idiot.

When the engine whirred happily again, the young pilot took stock of his situation. He'd never intended to fly through the cloud, but now that he was in it, he decided he'd rather carry on descending than climb back up and try to find the gap he'd entered by. *It's not a problem, just watch the airspeed and feel for the wind on your cheeks. The compass is wandering all over the shop, but nothing unusual about that. Just keep the wings level and the ASI at around eighty and everything will be fine.*

As the cloud began to thin, an orange-pink flicker lit the grey tufts for a second. The Bristol emerged into a fine drizzle, its wings canted thirty degrees from horizontal as it described a leisurely descending spiral. Colin recovered quickly from the disorientation as his eyes directly contradicted what his other senses knew to be true. Somewhere down there was an aerodrome. He righted the machine and dived for a closer look.

The sun caught the wings of an aeroplane below him and he saw Robière's machine descending in a tight spiral. The cinder strip of the airfield resolved itself through the haze. The Canadian's approach was spectacularly unconventional: He spiralled in, descending almost vertically and straightening out only when the aircraft was almost on the ground. Then he somehow pulled everything together and dropped gently onto the cinders almost exactly between the two ack emmas who were running forward to take his wingtips.

Colin's own landing drew unexpected attention from the ground. As he lined up for approach two bicycles were already racing across the field, pursued by running figures and fire trolleys. He concentrated on demonstrating his best-ever landing, this time keeping his hand dutifully on the fuel lever. One bitten, twice shy.

Turning at the end of his ground roll, Colin found his way blocked by the tender; overalled figures ran forward brandishing carbon tet. extinguishers. He recognised Hughie in the lead and heard his shouts: "Out! Out! Out!" Colin's gratitude for the goggles and oil that concealed his blushes was a poor substitute for the congratulatory remarks he'd been expecting.

Humphrey Page pointed at the lowering overcast with his pipe stem. "That was a nice little engine fire you had going when you broke through the clouds. Bloody lucky it went out. Lesson one if you're going to play silly buggers doing cloud landings old chap: turn the sodding fuel off!"

CHAPTER 3

Dear Mum and Dad,

Well, this is the life! I'm settling in well, and your parcel got here before me, so I'm well supplied with socks and cake. The accommodation's not too luxurious, but the grub's not bad and we've got a d____d good piano player and one of the Canadian pilots owns a huge Victrola gramophone, so there's plenty of singing and fun in the evenings.

And now the best bit – I have my own aeroplane! We're not supposed to write down what we're flying, so suffice it to say Gnl Baden-Powell might be found near Bath (7,5)!

I'm feeling a bit silly, thanks to making a bit of a mess of my first mission yesterday and setting fire to my aeroplane! Fortunately I was diving at the time so it went out. The Flight Leader (who seems a good type) said I did exactly the right thing and slapped me on the back. I didn't have the phlegm to tell him I didn't even know I was on fire!

I got here at the same time as another chap, a couple of years younger than me. We're sharing the aforementioned accommodation, and we're busy getting it cleaned up and habitable. He's a good sort too, though he pranged a two-seater on his first day and has been relegated to flying the crate he banged up. Justice here is swift.

The Flight Leader got in yesterday from a patrol with a line of bullet holes in his top wing. But he got an Albatros, which brings him to 7 and puts him back in front of the squadron. I hope I'll get one soon. Who knows, maybe you'll read about me becoming an ace!

So, taken all round, this is a grand place and life is full of laughs. Tell Tabs not to worry, the Hun are on the run now we have the measure of their Fokkers.

Your affectionate son,

Colin.

Colin was collecting his kit for the afternoon job when Cubby banged through the flimsy wood and oiled-cloth door of the hut. "Afternoon, sorry to burst in on you. I need a tall, skinny Pommie who can fly an aeroplane. You wouldn't have one of those would you?"

Colin pointed at the corner cubicle, where Andy's socks were visible, crossed at the foot of his pallet. "There's a tall skinny Brummie in there. Can't make any promises about flying a plane, though."

"Well we do the best we can with the shit we got." Said Cubby, shaking a prominent toe and eliciting a sharp cry of reproof from Andy's cupboard. "Come on, beauty, you'll have to skip the kiss, the Kaiser's missing you."

*

Andy levelled the BE2c out at 1500 feet and banged on the fuselage in front. Cubby made a final scan of the sky and began letting out the wireless aerial, glancing up every few seconds at the Sun. The fact that German incursions were virtually unknown this far behind the British lines was irrelevant to his careful, analytical view of the world.

"Don't assume the Hun will always do what he always has," he'd admonished Andy in the mess last night. "There's always the wild card who'll do something unexpected. Right now, that 2C out there is the last one on the squadron. The others are all smashed up somewhere out there because people made assumptions. Do it my way and you just might be able to tell your grandchildren about it."

Andy promised himself never to make assumptions and squinted round his gloved thumb at the blazing June Sun.

Cubby finished letting out the wireless aerial, fitted the mica registration card into its holder and bent his head over his Morse key, tapping out test signals to the artillery battery below. Andy began the laborious climb to 3,000 feet. As the village of Terramesnil floated under the lower plane, the German Archie batteries began to pay attention to the lumbering two-seater. Black woolly-bears stained the sky ahead, most of them two or three hundred feet above the 2C's height. Cubby pointed up, his voice lost in the engine's clatter, but the lips easy to read; "Take it up!" Andy climbed and watched with some satisfaction as more explosions puffed below him. He climbed again, only to find the next salvo bursting to left and right. Cubby grinned back at him and mimed tossing a coin. The Lines slid below. Time to go to work.

Artillery registration; art reg; hazardous occupation. It involved flying an outdated aeroplane, very slowly and predictably, directly above the targets the enemy most wanted to defend. The enemy who knew exactly what you were there for, and who knew it was your job to bring down a firestorm upon him. And who wanted you dead. Archie had found their height before even the first British salvo landed, and greasy smoke wisped past the windscreen; the acrid, metal stink of the gunners' work stung Andy's nostrils. Then a sharp buffet, and a giant's shadow flickered at the edge of sight. A grey cloud puffed from the criss-crossed earthworks behind Hawthorn Ridge, a pink-orange flower bursting at its core. *Too long*. As Andy shrank from the sensory assault he saw Cubby, standing up in the front pit and leaning far over the side, his eyes fixed on the fall of shot below. He bent quickly to his wireless, tapping out the results of the salvo. Somewhere to the west, the Royal Artillery were adjusting their range.

As one salvo followed another and the BE2c continued to plod its untouched course up the ridge and back, Andy began to settle to his work. He guiltily remembered that he wasn't simply here to fly the plane, and began scanning the sky above and to the east. All clear at the moment.

At last the ordeal was over. Two consecutive salvoes landed almost exactly on top of the German redoubt, albeit with no visible result. Cubby signalled to head home and began to reel in the antenna. Freed at last, Andy dropped the nose and wheeled to the west. A loud *crump* and shrapnel shattered the right windscreen panel, striking a splash of bright metal on the frame. Up front, Cubby waved a torn glove for Andy's inspection, the severed wireless aerial dangling from bloodied fingers. He shook the wrist and mouthed "Fuck it!" Then the other hand appeared, pointing behind Andy, and this time Cubby's voice wafted over the blustering wind; "Shit, shit, shit!"

Andy was already kicking right rudder as he swung round to look behind him. Nothing to see. Empty sky. He recoiled in shock as the Lewis barked from the front pit. A look back to the front to see Cubby leaning far to the left to play the machine gun, still on the left mounting, just above Andy's head. Each bullet whined as it passed, audible even through the racket. He looked over his shoulder again. Cubby had taken exception to something, but what the hell was it? He banked hard and pulled the stick into his lap; felt the aircraft complaining as it took up the unaccustomed strain of a steep turn. In front, Cubby had turned the gun back and was firing straight down the left side of the fuselage. He pointed urgently down, but by now the 2C had lost too much speed in the turn; Andy felt the controls slacken and the cumbersome aircraft flopped into a spin. The nose dropped and dull brown earth, pocked with shell craters, filled the starred windscreen.

*

It was Colin's first patrol with A-Flight. For the thousandth time, he checked his position behind French's left wing. He'd spotted early on that he could hold formation by keeping the tailskid of the flight leader's Nieuport lined up with its right wing. The summer air was bumpy, but by now the Bristol's good manners had become second nature. It was a little slower than the Nieuports, but judicious zooms kept it in place. Colin tracked his leader with an accuracy that drew an approving nod from Page, cruising on his right.

Colin scanned the sky to left, right, behind and above. He glanced across at Page, who waved a glove. *Decent bloke, that, even if he has got a face like a map of the Underground.*

Beasley's Bristol appeared suddenly between Colin's aircraft and Page's. The fourth man was alternately diving and climbing, signalling a dud engine. Page nodded, gave a thumbs up and swooped forward to alert French as Beasley turned back to the west. Two Nieuports and a Bristol Scout, the last struggling slightly to keep up, crossed the lines at 5 pm. on a blazing summer's day.

The wings of the leading aircraft waggled almost immediately, and French pointed down to the right. Colin dipped a wing to look, but could see nothing other than a few dirty puffs of Archie above the baked, crenellated lines of earthworks. French's and Page's Nieuports rolled into a steep dive. *They've seen something, buggered if I know what.* Colin threw the Scout after them. The dive reversed the speed differentials as the Bristol's narrower wingspan and greater weight took effect. The wires screamed as he darted between the two Nieuports and chose his attack spot in the German trenches. *So we're ground strafing. Wish someone had told me.*

A flick of light dead ahead resolved itself into a rolling biplane. *Jesus, I'm going to hit him!* Colin pulled on the stick, heavier than worlds under the pressure of 140mph winds pressing on the elevator. Two options: lose the tail or smash two kites. Personal outcome: identical.

A third option manifested as the buff-coloured aeroplane flopped out of the Bristol's line. Colin glimpsed the British roundels on the top wing; saw the observer half out of the front pit, his arms flailing to find purchase; saw a dark iron shape falling away; a Lewis gun, shaken from its mounting, tumbling earthwards.

Danger past. There would be no collision today, but the possibility of augering into the ground still loomed, with hideous literacy, ever larger. *Still got 2,000 feet or so, don't pull the tail off getting level.* The controls were solid stone; all his strength sufficed only to pull the stick back the merest fraction. His arms were agony. Slowly, so slowly, the nose began to come up. A giant's hand compressed his head into his shoulders. Colin forced his head back to look up for his flight mates, but could see only the BE2c he'd so nearly impaled. It was spinning quite slowly, and after another half-turn flattened into a shallow dive. The observer appeared to have regained his cockpit. *Looks like he's got it under control.*

A dark speck above and behind the 2C resolved into a diving Fokker Eindecker. Tracer drew a curved line, sagging below the two-seater's tail. Whoever the Hun was, he was fairly green; he'd opened fire far too early on a sitting target. Colin's pitot still showed 140; lots of lovely energy for a zoom climb. Forgetting that his own inexperience at least matched the German's, he pulled the nose up to cross the Fokker's path. Speed bled off rapidly as the Scout climbed to intercept the Eindecker. This was going to be tricky; his Bristol lacked an Aldis gunsight, relying instead on a simple pair of cross-hairs mounted ahead of the windscreen. His visions of pouring devastating fire into a helpless enemy had never included this twisting, impossible dance. The briefings had told him that his Bristol was faster and more manoeuvrable than the Fokker. Clearly, the German pilot had attended different briefings.

*

Andy wrestled with the 2C's controls, the stick so slack that it felt unattached. The big, numb aircraft flopped its nose towards the ground and continued to rotate. Cubby, standing to switch the gun to the right mount, was caught off guard by the spin. The massive weight of the Lewis pulled him almost out of the front pit and he grabbed at the coaming with his injured hand. Andy watched helplessly as the big Australian abandoned the gun to gravity and reached down with his other hand. Ailerons and elevator were dead, pointless, the stick limp in Andy's hand. But the rudder still sent messages to his feet. He pushed hard on the left bar. The spin stopped almost immediately, leaving the 2C in a fairly gentle, undramatic descent. Cubby gratefully pulled himself back into his cockpit. Life returned to the stick.

Andy barely had time to guess at what had just happened before his wondering was partly answered by a shimmer-line of tracer below his left wing. He glanced back as he side-slipped and this time saw the humped black line of the diving Fokker. He pulled again into a turn, remembering to feel for the stall, the Hun turning easily inside him. The cumbrous, slouching 2C was dead meat to the tiny, prancing killer.

It was the 2C's miserable flying speed that saved them on this pass. The British aircraft flopped into the turn barely above the stall, and the inexperienced Boche overshot with no more success than a bullet hole in the 2C's upper plane. Andy straightened to the west and put the nose down to coax whatever remaining pace the Royal Aircraft Factory had failed to eradicate from the hopeless two-seater. Off to the left, the Eindecker pulled a steep turn to start its next attack. Cubby beat the fuselage in frustration, hoping his falling gun had at least brained someone in the trenches below. A Bristol Scout came in fast from behind the 2C. The German pilot made a diving turn to the right to clear the line of fire, put his nose down and turned tail to the east. The Scout pulled high and dipped sharply left to drop onto the Eindecker's tail. Two Nieuports dived in from the right, the leader hosing fire into the retreating Fokker.

The Hun's right wing caught the westering sun, flashing brilliant yellow as it tore away from the fuselage. The Fokker broached sharply, flinging its pilot into space, a dark, wriggling shape plummeting fast away from the fluttering, dying dragonfly.

CHAPTER 4

Andy stared at the report form, absently chewing a flaking pencil. He'd seen other pilots' patrol reports, but writing his own was a greater challenge than he'd imagined. The image of the falling German twisted incessantly against the blurred white paper, interspersed with the sight of Cubby grabbing desperately at the cockpit rail. How to write that?

"Cracked the bone and took me fingernail off. Didn't even need stitches. Bollocks, just when I thought I'd managed to cop a nice cushy Blighty." Cubby's tocsin entry, like a blundering, likeable sheepdog, dragged Andy back to the present. "Get that bloody report scratched out. Nothing fancy, just scribble it off and come on. Your mate Hingley's been credited with half the kill – not bad on his first patrol. Frenchy's standing us dinner in Beauval."

Dinner turned out to be tough roast chicken at a dusty estaminet in a large white house in Rue Charles Cagny. The five young aviators consumed it with enthusiasm, repeatedly toasting one another in the proprietor's acidic but plentiful – and cheap – wine. Murky mirrors faced one another across four oilcloth-covered tables, reflecting halos around the pungent candles that flavoured the gloom. The restaurateur fussed around them, stooped and cheerful, while his thin-lipped wife glared at the pilots from the kitchen door and exchanged whispered, rapid rebukes with her husband. The wind blew sudden rain against the misted window.

Page stood and raised his glass to the blustering elements. "Here's to a thoroughly dud day tomorrow so that we can all get riotously pissed tonight, and so honour our fire-eating new champions of the sky."

Shouts of "Hear, hear!", "Bless 'em all!", "Dumb luck!" and "Sit down, you bacon-faced prat!" greeted the dedication and another bottle was summoned.

Colin laughed and drank. He raised his glass in response. "Thank you, Humphrey, on behalf of Lieutenant Palmer and myself. May I also point out that I thought we were attacking the trenches right up until I nearly cut Andy in half, and that I missed the Fokker by a mile."

"I saw you hit that Hun's wing, no question. My gun jammed as soon as I fired it, so that one's between you and Arthur. Absolutely no question."

French chimed in; "With the gun sight on that Bristol it's a miracle you got within twenty feet. I'm going to find a way of getting you a proper set-up. I think you're going to be a Hun-getter."

He grinned at Colin's mumbled, flattered response. "Don't get too sentimental. If you hadn't got lucky you'd be on a disciplinary for ropey observation, breaking formation, endangering the lives of your countrymen, and being a jammy little tit."

Another round, another refill, another bottle.

"How's the hand, Cubby?" asked French.

"Hurts like a bloody gympie gympie, mate. Didn't do it any good when I was hanging on for dear life while Adolphe Pegoud here did his stunt routine."

It was Andy's turn to be embarrassed. "Sorry Cub. I panicked a bit and forgot you'd undone your belt."

"Fuck that mate, it was bloody good flying. Didn't think a 2C could do a stunt like that - fooled that Hun a treat. If you hadn't done it we'd a been dead meat anyway. Made my arse go like the battalion bugle, but you got us both home."

The rain raised a mist on the soaking pavement. Lightning flickered. "We're going to get bloody wet walking back." Observed Page.

"Well we can be pretty sure tomorrow will be dud, so we might as well get a bit more waterproofing down us," replied French, beckoning the maître d'. *"M'sieur! Quatre cognacs s'il vous plaît! Apportez la bouteille! "*

"What's a gympie gympie, Cubby?" asked Andy.

"One of the many joys of God's own country mate. Stinging tree. It's like a cross between a nettle and a howitzer. We had em outside the back of the shop. Nasty buggers, but they mostly kept the snakes away."

"The snakes are the worst are they?"

"Well, you've got the spiders and the scorpions too, so it's hard to say. Then there's the crocs and the white-eared elephants."

"What the hell's a white-eared elephant?" asked Andy, wondering why Page and French groaned at the question.

"I'll show you." He rose, swaying slightly and turned away, pulling his pockets inside-out. He fumbled with his fly-buttons and turned back. "Behold the greater Australian white-eared elephant!"

Andy fought the cheap red wine out of his nostrils and spluttered a respectful acknowledgement. "Lieutenant McConnachie, you are a very, *very* big man."

Cubby clinked Andy's glass. "Why, thank you, Lieutenant Palmer."

Andy drained his wine and reached for the bottle, missing it by an inch or so. "It's just a shame you've got such a tiny cock."

Outside, the rain had stopped.

*

"Oh Christ Mossley, you've got to be kidding!"

"Sorry sir, OC's orders. And I thought you might like some aspirin with your tea."

The rain-washed aerodrome was fresh and new, green and startling; mist clustered in the hollows of the perimeter hedges. Skylarks shouted their tumbling joy. Andy swallowed bile and thought black thoughts.

The morning Contact Patrol was thankfully uneventful. A distant Hun two-seater seemed happy to stay well away, and even Archie did no more than throw up a token welcome. The PBI failed to show their Bengal lights, so Andy was forced to swoop low and check that the huddled uniforms in the forward positions were khaki, not grey. He understood their reluctance to display lights that could attract a sniper's bullet, but bit back resentment as two or three rifles cracked spitefully at the stooping 2C. *Can't they see the bloody roundels?* Head throbbing, he felt a rush of relief as Cubby leaned out to drop his report bag onto the infantry headquarters groundsheet. Andy turned gratefully for home as the big observer snuggled deeper into the front pit to doze and recover from the night's excess.

Colin was already in the mess, nursing a mug of Eno's. His morning offensive patrol had been similarly undisturbed, and the soothing liver salts were calming his embattled digestion. He began to believe he might even survive. He waved and footed a chair out from under the table as Andy and Cubby entered. "Morning, men. How goes the war?"

"It's a gigantic pile of shit mate," growled Cubby. "Which, coincidentally..." He dropped his flying coat on the back of the chair and headed for the back door, softly singing "Keep the home fires burning, though your bowels are churning…".

Andy ordered Bovril from the mess servant and sagged into a chair. "How's the head?"

"Not too bad now. Yours?"

"Getting worse. I'm not sure I can cope with this amount of alcohol. I've been here three days and I've had two death-dealing hangovers already. I was still half pissed when we took off this morning."

"Aye. At Heyford you'd get a disciplinary for a pint of shandy. They do things differently here."

Andy accepted a steaming mug from the servant and inhaled deeply, the rich, savoury fumes wafting him back to Erdington Municipal Baths; the feel of warm clothes; the chlorine sting in the eyes. Was this the same boy, alcohol-bruised in a corrugated shed in France, while ten miles away, thousands were killing one another? Did the lad who cycled home with his bag chafing his neck really watch a stranger fall to his death yesterday, his dark leather coat fluttering?

He looked over at Colin. Not yet twenty: a bishop's son, absorbed in yesterday's Daily Mail, smiling at the Teddy Tail cartoon. He killed a man yesterday. "How did it feel?"

Colin looked up. "what?"

"Shooting that Fokker down. Seeing that pilot fall out?"

Colin shrugged. "I'm not sure it felt like anything. I mean, I thought I'd missed anyway."

"But you were shooting at him. You meant to kill him."

"Well… yes, of course. He was trying to kill you, wasn't he?"

Andy shook his head, uncertain of his own point. "Yeah, sure. But that was… it wasn't him and me… there was a Fokker, and it was shooting at us. And Cubby was shooting back." He sipped his Bovril, looked into the mug. "And then there was a man waving his legs in the sky. Not a machine. He'd... he'd had his breakfast that morning, same as us. He wrote to his girlfriend the night before. He got pissed with his mates, got into arguments, talked bullshit, moaned about the government..."

"...went for a shit that was unlikely to compete with the enormous darkie I've just unloaded. Who we talking about?" Cubby thumped into the vacant chair and nodded his thanks to the mess servant who laid a heaped plate of sausage and egg in front of him.

"Andy here's getting a bit tearful about yesterday's Hun." Said Colin.

"And why would you do that?" asked Cubby, plunging bread and margarine into a grease-speckled yolk. Seeing Andy groping for a reply, he made a negatory gesture with his free hand. "There's no such thing as people up there. If that Hun had blown your head off yesterday he'd a' put another spot on his fuselage and forgotten you existed."

Cubby paused, took a breath, pushed his plate away, throwing his fork into the spreading egg-yolk. "Anyway, better one Kraut takes the long dive than you or me." He stood abruptly and walked out.

Andy and Colin shared a puzzled look. "So, better all round not to let it get to you then," said Colin.

Andy pulled a napkin over Cubby's congealing breakfast. "By the way, we've got roommates."

"Really?"

"Yeah, just met one of them in the hut. Tony something or other, and there was a bag on the other bed. He was off to meet Henry; asked me how to behave in front of him."

"So what did you tell him?"

"What you'd expect: salute every time you answer him; insist you're a strict teetotaller, especially if he tries to trap you into accepting a drink; oh and I may have said something about the Recording Officer liking to be called Bazzer."

"These children should count themselves lucky to have a veteran to advise them."

"They should, they should. You up again this pip emma, Col?"

"Yes. D.O.P. Raincheval-Arquèves-Vauchelles-Marieux."

" How far behind is that ?"

"Maybe six-seven miles. Furthest I've been in. We're going over at 15,000, which is also the highest I've been."

Page walked by, ruffling Colin's hair as he passed. "Wrap up warm, laddie, it's also the coldest you've been."

*

The climb to 15,000 feet took over half an hour, by which time Colin was, indeed, colder than he'd ever been in his life. He shivered incessantly, and the ninety-mile an hour wind that grabbed his arm when he reached out to warm his gun lanced through three layers of gloves to jet bitingly up his coat sleeve. His cheeks stung and froze round the chafing edge of the face mask. He resolved to take Page's advice and opt instead for a liberal application of whale fat on the next patrol. A pale cruciform shape far below caught his eye, seemingly motionless against the brown and tawny geometry of France. A British spotter plodding its relentless beat, possibly even Andy and Cubby doing their unglamorous, unsafe work. Archie was giving them plenty to keep boredom at bay, and it probably still felt like June down there. Colin found himself briefly wishing for a BE2c.

The loose bunch of eight mixed Nieuports and Bristols rumbled over White City. Ahead, A-Flight, with French leading, flanked by Colin and Humphrey Page and with Geoff Beasley bringing up the rear. Behind and slightly above, Doke's Nieuport led C-Flight. Colin groped for the names of the South African's wingmen; Robière, the little Canadian with the big Victrola, sat comfortably at the rear of the group. The night before he'd terrified Colin by landing almost vertically into the gusting wind, holding the nose high in the air until his ground speed dropped to walking pace, As the Nieuport finally stalled he deftly blipped the engine, picked the tail up and settled the wheels on the cinders exactly as the tailskid touched. The aircraft was stationary on the ground within ten feet. A burst of grudging applause came from the handful of pilots slouched outside the mess; clearly the Canadian's antics were something of a trade mark. Between Robière and Doke were the two new pilots, whose identities escaped him completely for now.

He puffed and inhaled the thin, biting air. What little sustenance it contained seemed to be stifled by the facemask, which he pulled aside for a moment, wincing as the breath of a Norse hell drilled his teeth. He looked at the dashboard watch. Ninety minutes of this still to go.

French dipped his right wing and turned gently south. The patrol adjusted and settled on the new heading, propellers facing towards Raincheval. As the patrol passed overhead Marieux, Page suddenly dived alongside French, waggling his wings and pointing down. Below and to the right, above an unnamed village were two or three puffs of Archie. Colin saw French acknowledge the signal and after a moment a red Very light arced from the leader's cockpit. Seven scouts followed the lead Nieuport into a shallow dive.

Colin peered ahead, eventually making out the whirling specks of a dogfight over Thièvres. Diving closer, the picture resolved into three circling Sopwith 1½ Strutters, beset by a Brownian tumble of Eindeckers. The Sopwiths had adopted the defensive spiral, their gunners defending each other's tails, and spraying any importunate Fokker that approached too closely. As long as their ammunition held out they stood a chance, but the gusting west wind was pushing them slowly deeper into Hunland.

French's Lewis opened up at extreme range, more in hope of scaring off the Germans than of damaging them, and three of the tiny monoplanes twisted to meet this new threat. Colin chose the one to the left and began to nose to the right to bring his own Lewis to bear on the fast-approaching Fokker. A harsh chatter, and a line of holes stitched across the Bristol's centre section and a dark shape blinked through his eye line. The scout bucked hard in the buffet of dark wings that crossed his nose less than ten feet away. He pulled hard up and right, kicking in right rudder as another fleeting shape howled out of the sun, the wind of its passing slamming his ears like a blow. The air was full of aircraft.

Colin pushed into a dive and tried to make sense of the tangled sky. Tracer smoke made geometric gashes across a confusion of twisting, unidentifiable machines. A brightly-painted wing stall-turned through his gun sight and was gone before he could reach for the trigger. He glimpsed a Bristol Scout spiralling out of sight, pursued by a pair of Black-crossed biplanes.

He saw French, identifiable by his leader's streamers, pull onto the tail of an Eindecker, and nosed over to follow. A thin mist of petrol sprayed from the Fokker, igniting almost immediately and engulfing the cockpit. At the same moment a pale green biplane pulled into the killing line on French's tail. Colin yawed to bring his Lewis to bear only to see the Hun pull sharply away. Page's Nieuport flashed through, the spat-spat of his gun biting through the confusion of sound.

Colin kicked into another knife-edge turn as a whip-whip-whip of tracer tore the fabric of his wing. He twisted to find the new threat and found a silver biplane barely fifty feet away. He slammed stick and rudder hard to the right, pulling back to roll sharply into an inverted dive. He saw the crosses on the enemy's lower wings flash by as the German overshot. He crouched behind the windscreen and strained forward against his belt, urging every last mile per hour from the Bristol. The silver Hun nosed over into a similar dive and reclaimed a hundred yards of lost distance within ten seconds. The German pilot followed Colin's frantic aerobatics with disdainful ease; making little attempt to mimic the Bristol's erratic twists, he simply held back and loosed off short bursts whenever the British Scout crossed his sights. Colin had little doubt of the outcome of the fight. Not only was the Hun's plane far faster, it was clearly being driven by a more experienced pilot.

He pulled back into a stall, hoping to make the German overshoot. No good; the enemy simply dropped below, pulled his nose up to near-vertical and hosed the Bristol as it hung motionless in the air above him. The young pilot felt bullets tug at his clothing; saw his pitot and altimeter shatter; felt the stick jerk as an aileron wire tore loose.

Heard the sudden silence.

He looked around. Below him, the German aircraft had flattened out, its pilot leaning forward in his cockpit to hammer the cocking lever of his jammed gun. Further down still, Colin saw the bright green wings of French's pursuer fluttering earthwards. He pulled the battered Scout onto the tail of the silver biplane.

The German pilot turned in his seat and looked up straight at the diving Bristol. Without apparent haste he dropped his nose and cleared to the east, easily outdistancing the Scout. As he receded rapidly, Colin was almost certain he saw him wave. The world was impossibly quiet. He was alone among the scattered, unheeding clouds.

Turning west, Colin began to climb back to the safety of height. The machine seemed to be flying reasonably well, despite the flapping rents in wing and centre section. The starboard aileron flapped uselessly in the slipstream, but the port one proved adequate to keep everything reasonably level. As long as nothing else broke, there was a decent chance of making it home. As the Bristol crossed the lines a Nieuport pulled up alongside and Colin looked across as Page pushed up his goggles and grinned across the gap, theatrically wiping his scarred forehead.

*

The riggers found twenty-nine bullet holes in Colin's machine, one of which had almost severed the upper main spar. Hughie brought him a flattened slug that he'd extracted from the cockpit floor. Inspection revealed a matching scratch on the ankle of his fug boot. There were four bullet holes in his coat.

He sat with Page and warmed his chilled bones in the sun, sipping lime juice and awaiting the return of the remainder of the patrol. Beasley and Doke had landed safely before him, and Page had seen the two unnamed new pilots shot down in the first attack of the German biplanes, now identified as Halberstadts. That left French and Robière. Page had lost sight of French as his own stream of tracer blew a mist of red around the cockpit of the bright green biplane that was pursuing the flight leader. Robière was last seen heading east after a damaged Halberstadt.

Andy and Cubby were also overdue.

CHAPTER 5

Andy's instructions were to observe a suspected howitzer battery in the woods behind Pas en Artois. Cubby had been typically profane in his condemnation of orders that put an outclassed, unsupported aeroplane two miles inside Hunland, and Andy's head quartered the sky with relentless conscientiousness. So far the only airborne activity had been the passage of A- and C-Flights over White City. Archie lodged a desultory protest at their intrusion as they passed Orville, and showed increasing interest in their progress as they approached Famechon. By the time they reached Pas en Artois, the 2C was being rocked by an unusually enthusiastic expenditure of hatred. Cubby signalled for a low-level inspection of Bois du Châtelet. Happy to get below the bursting woolly-bears, Andy put the machine into a crossed-control sideslip, dropping over a thousand feet in no more than ten seconds. Straightening up he dipped the left wing and the two airmen scanned the billowing woods two hundred feet below.

Flashes from a rhomboid clearing to the east caught his attention and Andy followed the lines of tracer to their source. Three machine gun nests were raking the low-flying machine. *Something there worth defending.*

He swung to the right and weaved towards the clearing. Cubby, leaning from the scant shelter of the front pit peered into the woods' edge and pointed emphatically. A narrow road ran south alongside the east side of the woods and, lined up in the narrow margin of clear ground, half-obscured by camouflage netting, the ugly snouts of a battery of 150mm howitzers poked skywards. The Germans manning the battery demonstrated unanimous disapproval at their examination by spraying the 2C with rifle and machine-gun fire. The British machine shuddered repeatedly and rents appeared in wings and fuselage. Metallic clangs signalled strikes on the engine and a worrying vibration shook the airframe. Cubby responded with a drum of Buckingham tracer from the Lewis as Andy clawed for height, out of the range of the ground fire and into the relative safety of Archie's domain.

Climbing at full throttle, the vibration became worse. Pressures and temperatures were normal, and no unwelcome mechanical clatters were audible; Andy suspected propeller damage and kept the apparently undamaged engine pulling for all its meagre worth.

At two thousand feet, Andy felt something break, and the 2C began its death shake. He saw a large chunk of propeller blade whirl away and he cut the engine before it could tear loose from its mountings. He pointed the nose west and flattened the glide as much as he dared, eyes fixed on the impossibly distant front line. He called to Cubby to crouch and leaned forward behind his own windscreen. Every fraction of streamlining was vital now. The west wind plucked at rags of fabric fluttering from the upper plane, an invisible hand tugging them back. The chalk scar of White City loomed tantalisingly closer. Behind those earthworks lay the safe landing field Cubby had pointed out on Andy's first day. He watched the friendly lines crawl up his windscreen. They weren't going to make it. He inadvertently pulled back on the stick, feeling the tattered wings tremble as the 2C approached stall speed. *No good. Have to try something desperate.*

He dipped the nose and allowed the machine to gather speed in the dive, pulling flat at a thousand feet and sixty miles per hour. White City held steady in his windscreen and then, thankfully, began to drop slightly below.

By 600 feet, the 2C was again descending too rapidly. With just 50mph showing Andy didn't dare pull back any further, and no more height remained for a repeat attempt of the zoom manoeuvre. Then the heat rising from the sun-baked mud bumped the wings and he dared hope again. They crossed the enemy lines at a little over 100 feet, the German troops too surprised by the silent stoop of the stricken 2C to fire more than a few quick shots. Andy surveyed the confusion of wire and craters on no-man's land for a place to put down. He undid his belt and saw Cubby doing the same in the front pit, also preferring the risk of being flung from the wreck to being incinerated with it.

At the end it was the headwind, which had tried so hard to kill them on their desperate glide over Hunland, that finally relented and saved them. The 2C settled at a ground speed of less than thirty miles per hour and decelerated rapidly over the rough ground, finally nosing gently over into a shell hole.

Picking himself up from the treacly mud at the crater's centre, Cubby grabbed at Andy's arm "Stay low and run for it!"

"They'll shoot us to pieces if we stick our heads up!"

There's fifty trench mortars'll blow them off if we don't! Come on!"

As the two fliers appeared above the crater rim, a deafening crescendo of small-arms and machine-gun fire made Andy flinch back. Cubby bellowed in his ear; "That's ours! Keep going, they're keeping the Huns' heads down!"

Heads low, stumbling in their thigh-length boots, they threw themselves towards the British trench, just ten yards away. An officer waved his pistol, guiding them to a gap in the wire and they dived headlong, landing bruisingly on the duckboards. A shower of dirt, gravel and fabric announced the complete destruction of the 2C as the German trench mortars found their mark. The thunder of covering fire faded to sporadic cracks of anger and a continuing frustrated rattle of machine-guns from the other side.

The infantry captain helped Cubby to his feet and extended a hand to Andy, winded by the impact of a fourteen-stone Australian landing on his ribcage. "Afternoon Gentlemen. Alan Higginson. Either of you need medical attention?"

Establishing that the fliers were relatively undamaged, Higginson led the way to a bunker in the support trench and summoned mugs of gunfire – the weak, sweet tea that has fuelled the infantry since somewhere before Waterloo.

*

Robière landed as dusk fell, his petrol exhausted and ammunition spent, for once eschewing his famously flamboyant landing stunts. He'd chased the Halberstadt nearly ten miles into Hunland; the German was trailing black smoke, but seemed have full engine power. Using the terrain cleverly he contrived to stay well ahead of the pursuing Nieuport. The little Canadian had finally decided on discretion as he emptied his last drum of .303 at the distant biplane, took a long look at his dwindling petrol level and turned for home.

Page and Colin hung around the Squadron Office until a phone call came in from an artillery battery at Puchevillers. French had crashed into a field a few hundred yards to the east of their emplacement. The artillerymen had heard a misfiring engine and seen a Nieuport stagger over the trees, dropping sharply to clear a power line stretched across the pasture. An undercarriage strut crumpled as the biplane pancaked hard and a wing dug into the soft ground, flipping the tail high and releasing a flurry of electrical sparks as it touched the cables. French's aircraft cartwheeled, the engine breaking away and spinning across the field. A disintegrating cloud of wire, wood and fabric spread itself across the pasture.

Running towards the wreck, the gunners had been more than surprised to see French rise to his feet and limp towards them. Nursing a sprained ankle and an assortment of bruises, he was expected back at the Squadron in an hour or so.

The battery confirmed French's burning Fokker and Page's Halberstadt down out of control. The two new pilots, neither of whose names could be recalled by anyone in the squadron, were both observed crashing vertically and unsurvivably just behind the German lines.

A minor smash-up broke out in the mess that night to celebrate French's escape, as well as his eighth – and Page's seventh – confirmed kill. Colin was uncharacteristically quiet and when Doke implemented the inevitable Bok-Bok tournament, he wandered outside to sit on a mechanic's trolley. Gunfire flickered the eastern horizon. Andy and Cubby were somewhere out there, but for them to be still airborne was no longer a possibility. Still, he jumped to his feet at the sound of an approaching engine but sank back as he heard the characteristic organ-chord hum of an FE grinding over to drop its nightly hate on the Germans.

*

The atmosphere in the bunker was an assault on the senses. It was stiflingly hot, and the fug of cigarette smoke, stale food and six occasionally washed infantrymen fused into a hellish melange that was sour on the tongue. The canvas flap at the entrance was pegged back, admitting a scant breeze and a ravenous squadron of midges. Higginson darkened the doorway and entered. "Sorry chaps, the telephones are no-go. I've sent a runner back to let your squadron know you're OK. Looks like you'll be our guests for tonight, though."

"That's fine. Thank you." replied Andy. Cubby had been uncharacteristically taciturn, abrupt to the point of impoliteness. He shifted position repeatedly, his left heel bobbing to a rapid, inaudible rhythm.

Dinner was bully beef, fried in its own fat with sliced potatoes. As a special treat for their guests, the infantrymen produced a large tin of fruit. The chef, a burly Welsh sergeant, held out the tin for Andy's inspection. The label proclaimed '*Aprikosen in Sirup*'

"That's German that is. Gift from Jerry. All thanks to little Eddie here. See, he's out playing…"

"Oi, let me tell it, Stan. It's my story," interjected a small, wiry corporal. "Come to that, that's my bleedin' apricots, excusing my French sirs."

The sergeant nodded acquiescingly to little Eddie and turned to opening the tin.

"We had this sap going out into no man's land," began the little corporal. "And it turned out that Jerry's got the same idea, and we end up twenty feet apart, listening to each other. Well their balloons can see us, and ours can see them, so what's the point of keeping quiet?. So Sarge there shouts out, 'Evenin' Jerry. Tell you what, you don't throw anything nasty at us, and we won't throw anythin' nasty at you.'

"Well we might of forgot to mention that we was fraternising with the enemy, and for the best part of a week we got to be good muckers with the Krauts, and one night I'm sittin' on the firestep playing me trumpet, and Jerry starts shouting out his favourites. You know, 'Play us a sad one, Tommy,' that sort of thing. Well, they always applauds and shouts 'That was a good one, give us another,' and you'd think there wasn't a war on.

"So I've played a couple and Jerry shouts out, 'Play us de factoreim!' or some such Kraut lingo. So I shouts out, 'How's it go?' and this Jerry starts singing. Lovely voice he had. Beautiful. Anyway, the tune was 'The Watch on the Rhine,' and we used to play that at band practice before the war, so I plays it and Jerry sings it in German, and then they all joined in, and there was even a couple on our side who joins in in English.

"So we finishes, and Jerry claps and gives us three cheers, and we give the bloke with the voice three cheers, and then Jerry shouts over, 'Thank you Tommy, here's something sweet to go with your supper.' And something heavy lands in the trench, and I'm shouting 'Grenade!' and trying to tunnel into the wall when I sees what it is. It was that tin of apricots there."

The thoughtful silence was broken by Cubby pushing through the flap, muttering; "Got somewhere to go."

Higginson looked out after him. "He OK? If he's looking for the latrine trench he's going the wrong way."

Andy shook his head. "Dunno, something's up certainly. I've only known him a few days to be honest, but nothing seems to faze him normally."

Higginson, concerned that Cubby could wander into danger, went out after the Australian, but returned after a few minutes. "Couldn't find him. Couple of chaps saw him heading to the rear though, so he should be OK."

The apricots, sweetened further by a coating of Nestlés milk in lieu of cream, were cloying, slippery and utterly delicious. After dinner, Higginson tactfully withdrew while Stan, the Welsh sergeant, produced a canteen and poured fiery, illegal, homemade spirit into seven tin mugs. "Drink up lads, we've got a special visitor to host tonight."

The start of the evening barrage drowned his toast to Andy, and the candle guttered almost to extinction as a shock of air flapped the canvas at the entrance as Higginson returned, sat and quietly picked up the seventh mug. An hour passed. Stan left the bunker and returned with a fresh canteen of poteen. Higginson gave up all pretence of non-complicity and extended his mug to be filled. Andy realised that, yet again, he was getting pissed. He shook his head at the unexpected corollaries of war and paid attention to another of little Eddie's fabulous stories.

"See, I was a cab driver before I joined up, sir. And Saturday nights in the West End was always busy. I'm driving up Shaftesbury Avenue when I gets a hail from this toff. He's got some fine lady on his arm, and she's lookin' a bit off. Anyway, I stops, and this gent says, 'Take this lady home please, she's feeling unwell.'

"Well, I looks and it's easy to see what's made her unwell, and I'm not keen on her puking up in me cab, but the gent gives me a sov and I thinks, well, what the hell." He took a long pull on his mug and smacked his lips. "So she gets in and gives me the address and I turns to look, and you'll never guess who it was."

"Go on."

"It's only bloody Mary Pickford, sir. Sittin there in me cab, with 'er 'at on!"

"No!"

"True as I'm ridin' this bike sir! So she says goodnight to the gent and I starts off to take her home, and she starts to sober up and gets quite chatty. She sees me trumpet in the front and says, 'Are you a musician, cabby?' Well, next thing, we're chattin' away like old pals, and she asks me me name, and I keeps glancing back, and she's got these big eyes, and long eyelashes, and I'm thinkin' 'Bloody 'ell, if only…"

Andy glanced at the other infantrymen, all of them grinning, nodding and following Eddie's every word. Clearly, this was a story they never tired of. He looked back as the little corporal took another swig, wiped his mouth and continued.

"So we gets to this big house in Regents Park and I pulls up outside and says, 'Here we are, Miss Pickford,' and gets out to open her door. She says, 'But I haven't paid you, Eddie,' and I says, 'It's all right, the gent at the theatre give me a sovereign, miss.'"

"Well I started to get this queer feeling, and then she said, 'But that was just a tip, Eddie. You must let me pay you properly.' And then, well you're not going to believe it…"

Enjoying his moment, Eddie held his mug to the sergeant for a refill and raised his eyebrows at Andy. The true professional waited for his prompt.

"Yes, go on, go on."

"Well sir, she's got this skirt that splits up the front sir, and she pulls it to the side and opens her legs, and she's got no drawers nor nothing on sir. And we're just there, you know, gapin' at each other, and she says, 'Will this be enough?'"

He drank again. Andy's reserve snapped and he shouted; "Yes? And what did you say?"

He jumped as six voices chorused; "Have you got anything smaller?"

Andy's explosion of laughter was joined by his new companions, drowning the noise of the guns outside. He clinked mugs with Eddie and forgot the war for a few minutes. As Cubby had said: bloody good blokes.

*

Andy was shaken from his doze and blinked up at Cubby. In bunks or slumped against the walls, the infantrymen were all asleep. "Come on mate, we've got a lift home."

Behind him stood a middle-aged woman in khaki battledress. A FANY badge on her lapel proclaimed her to be a volunteer nurse. "This is my good friend Captain Hamilton. She's got to run back to get supplies and she can drop us at Beauval."

The nurse shook hands, whispering to avoid waking the PBI, despite the thump of high explosive outside. "Call me Connie. Pleased to meet you Andy. Glad you weren't hurt in the crash."

Connie appeared to be around forty, attractive and with a clipped confidence to her voice that suggested breeding and money.

"Thank you, but we can't go without saying thank you to these blokes."

Cubby was clearly eager to leave. "Shame to wake 'em. Come on, we can telephone back and say it when the lines have been fixed."

Andy found a scrap of paper and a pencil and scribbled an explanatory thank-you, aimed a kick at an importunate rat, missed and followed the observer and his good friend out of the bunker.

*

Colin watched the flickering horizon and slapped away insects. He heard the mess door bang closed and the distant gun flashes showed Page approaching in photo-flash jerks.

"Thought you might want a refill."

Colin accepted the offered glass and felt the trolley move as Page sat down next to him. "Holt just got a call. Battery at Ocean Villas saw a 2C crash in No-Man's-Land. No word whether anyone got out, but they're pretty sure the trench mortars finished it off."

Colin nodded his thanks. "Four of ours for two of theirs. Not good arithmetic is it?"

Page sipped his drink. "The sooner you do see it as arithmetic, the better, because you're going to see a lot more people go. If you survive yourself that is."

Colin nodded again. He sat for a long moment, then tipped his glass at the distant barrage. "Is it usually that heavy?"

"Not usually. They get enthusiastic for an hour or two some nights, but word is there's a really big push coming up. They're going to keep this up for days apparently."

They sat in silence, drinking occasionally. The playground row from the mess slowly resolved into a bawdy sing-song, the clanging piano groping to find the key, chased by a confusion of drunken voices. Colin stood, placing his glass on the trolley. "Think I'll call it a night, Humph. Thanks for the whisky."

"Goodnight chap. Just arithmetic, remember."

*

Andy threaded through the narrow, twisting trenches, occasionally glimpsing the slim figure of the nurse ahead of Cubby's bulk. He found himself craning his neck to see the seat of her khaki trousers move in time to her brisk walk. *Nice arse, that.* The bundled mass of his flying coat, helmet and gloves snagged repeatedly on unseen protrusions and he bunched them higher in his arms. The fur-lined boots chafed his thighs as he began to sweat profusely in the warm night air. He'd long lost track of the turns and branches by the time they reached an RAP. He sank gratefully to his haunches next to Cubby as Connie Hamilton asked them both to wait and disappeared into the darkness.

They sat for ten minutes or so. From the cluster of tents came the bustle and clink of healing, along with occasional groans. From somewhere nearby, a hopeless voice droned; "Oh golly, no. Oh golly, no." Ether wafted on the occasional breeze. Cubby's heel began again to bounce and he stood, fidgeting and peering into the dark.

A whine of gears preceded the unlit shape of a Sunbeam ambulance. Connie jumped from the passenger seat and called the fliers over. "Andy, you sit up front with Stainton. Cubby and I will ride in the back."

Andy caught the infinitesimal emphasis on the word "ride" and climbed accommodatingly onto the wide bench seat. Stainton was a silhouette in the driving seat, who grunted a clenched-teeth "Evening. Hold tight," in an upper-class, but unmistakeably feminine voice."

Andy turned in surprise. "Hello. I'm Andy Palmer. Thank you for the lift, Miss Stainton."

The driver ground the gears and pulled forward with a jerk. "It's just plain Stainton. Stainton Hamilton. You've met my mother I believe."

The tight disapproval in the voice discouraged response, and Andy contented himself with hanging on in terror as the ambulance negotiated the barely visible track that led to the rear. An occasional outburst of laughter from the back of the vehicle caused Stainton to accelerate angrily until the young pilot clung desperately to the front sill, sliding side to side on the slick bench. Dark banks and pale posts flicked by in the darkness.

Arriving at a T-junction, Stainton jumped down to light the lamps. "This is Kilometre Lane. We can use lights from here." The stark acetylene glare revealed a cap of short, dark hair, accentuating the gamine, elfin effect of large eyes and a suggestion of freckles. The shapeless battledress hinted at a thin, slightly gawky figure, the resemblance to Connie unmistakeable.

Stainton looked up, squinting in the light. "It's rude to stare you know."

"Who says I'm staring?"

"Oh, you're staring."

She hopped back into the cab, movements quick and positive. Andy looked at her in the glow from the road as she pulled left and accelerated.

"Stainton?"

"What?"

"Nothing. I just mean... Stainton?"

"Oh, the name. Some grandfather I apparently had. I think they wanted a boy, so when I turned out to have a piece missing they stuck with the name they'd already picked."

"Ancestors sometimes have a lot to answer for."

"True. Have you known Cubby long?"

"No. Few days is all. Seems like longer though."

A flash of white teeth in the dark cab. "Yes, he's like that. He fills a lot of time as well as a lot of space. He's certainly my mother's type."

"Oh, this isn't a chance meeting then?"

"Oh it's a chance meeting. Every chance they get in fact. I could be convicted for operating a disorderly ambulance."

Andy laughed quietly. "How does it make you feel. I mean, your Dad and that?"

Stainton glanced at him. "Me? I'm used to it. My father was killed at Blood River Poort and she took me to Paris. She took up with Isadora Duncan's crowd. Mum's always been a bit mad, and she just fell in with all that Bohemian stuff. Men, women, she flirted with them all and bedded most of them - still does. Your turn's bound to come soon, so be ready." She thought for a moment. "I think I'm probably a bit of a disappointment to her."

Andy grinned. "After Lieutenant McConnachie, I suspect I would be too."

Stainton laughed in response. "You sound as if you're from Birmingham. Whereabouts?"

"Is it that obvious?"

Stainton laughed again. "Not when you speak like that, but it will be when you stop trying to sound posh."

"OK, you got me," Andy grinned back. "Yes, Erdington. You?"

"Not far away actually. Sutton Coldfield. Do you know it?"

"Yes I do. I was at the training camp in Sutton Park when I first joined up. We used to go to the Boldmere for a drink."

"You were just up the road then; we live in Monmouth Drive. Mum probably complained about your singing at some point."

"Probably not mine. I'm not that much of a drinker." He reflected for a second. "Well, not till I got to France anyway. I seem to have managed to get roaring drunk every night since then."

"I know. You reek of the stuff."

Andy was suddenly conscious of the sweaty, poteen-laden odour rising from the open neck of his tunic. He huddled in on himself. "Sorry. Hospitality of the infantry. Dugout was a bit stinky too, so I wouldn't get too close."

"I wasn't planning to, but don't worry anyway – I'm a nurse, we smell things a lot worse than sweaty airmen."

Stainton pulled the Sunbeam to a halt to allow a long column of howitzers to pass along Rue d'en Bas.

"There's something big going on. They've been moving guns up non-stop for days now. Those will be right in the front line. I should think the Jerries will be too close to shoot at."

Cubby's voice boomed from the back; "Shit! We're not there are we?"

Stainton shook her head and replied; "No, nowhere near there yet."

"That's a relief," called her mother. "Nor am I."

By the time the ambulance pulled onto the airfield, Andy was mawkishly in love. He and Stainton stood awkwardly as the engine ticked and cooled. Cubby and Connie were audibly completing their contract in the back.

"Do you get any time… you know… can I see…"

"No, you can't."

She relented slightly, seeing Andy's crestfallen look in the hissing acetylene lights. "Andy, how old are you?"

"Eighteen. In three days."

Stainton smiled. "Many happy returns. I'm a year older than you then." She worried a flint from the tyre tread with quick-bitten fingers. "I'm here because my mother wants me to find a nice young officer like you to settle down with and have fat babies. Either that or to meet an immoral nurse who's queer for a mother and daughter relationship."

She looked up and smiled in apology. "I'm not my mother. Sorry."

The ambulance rocked as Cubby tumbled out, buttoning his tunic. He put his arm round Stainton and kissed her cheek. "Thanks for the lift Stinny, you're a diamond. Come on young Palmer, your squadron needs you."

*

Colin was sorting the new pilots' belongings when Andy entered the hut. He jumped to his feet. "You're OK! We heard you'd gone down in No-Man's Land!"

"We did, but Cubby's bulletproof, and it seems to have rubbed off on me."

"So he's alright too? Hang on. Let me get a brew going." He poured spirit into the primus and struck a match. He indicated the bags on the table. "They weren't so lucky."

"Both of them? " Andy read the name tag on the nearest bag. "A. G. Irvine. Damn, I can't remember his first name."

"Anthony," said Colin, putting a pan of water on the primus. "To be honest I couldn't remember the first or second of either of them until I read their letters home."

"You read them?"

"It was something someone said to me while I was waiting around at the Depot. He said somebody should always check dead men's belongings before they're sent home, in case there's anything they wouldn't want their families to see."

Andy fiddled with a cigarette lighter, noticing an inscription: "To my Tony. All my love, Anne." He flicked it, but it appeared to be broken. "The RO said nobody lasts long in this hut."

"Oh, don't get superstitious on me. It's just a dirty old hut in France. And tomorrow you're going to help me make it a bit more habitable. Jesus, what the hell have you been drinking?"

Andy recounted his adventures of the day and evening, his mind vividly replaying the glimpses of white teeth, dark hair and bright eyes in the glow of acetylene lights.

CHAPTER 6

Acting Major Barrington-Holt, having failed to locate a replacement BE2, detailed Andy and Cubby to collect an FE2b from an issue depot at Amiens. The squadron tender remaining out of action, Cubby summoned one of his endless contacts to drive them to the station at Montrelet, where a shrugging porter confirmed that a train was due *"probablement assez bientôt"*. They lazed on the flower-decked platform, the war once again a distant illusion in the continuing heat wave. It was easy to pretend that the ever-present rumble of artillery was simply summer thunder, grumbling behind the babble of the ubiquitous larks.

They bought fresh croissants from a baker's tray and drank dark, sweet coffee from the station café. The platform slowly filled with travellers who chatted and laughed as children weaved through their legs, arms outstretched, voices imitating machine-gun rattles. Occasionally, one would spiral noisily to his temporary death. Bees investigated the willow herb at the trackside.

The train, when it finally arrived, was a small, wheezing shunter from the last century. The varied gaggle of carriages was already half-full, and Andy gave up his seat to an ample dowager who thanked him politely before squeezing between two young mothers. It was only then that Andy noticed the complete absence of men.

Cubby was already deep in chattering conversation with a pretty governess.

*

The FE2b stood at the end of a line of Morane Parasols, dwarfing the tiny French monoplanes with its fifty-foot wingspan and towering height. The depot clerk had little to offer of advice, having never left the ground. "I know it goes sirs, because I saw it fly in here. It only landed about ten minutes ago. That's all I can tell you really."

Andy and Cubby made their best attempts at inspecting the vast biplane, guessing whether the play in the ailerons was normal. The huge Beardmore engine was still warm, and the reek of petrol suggested that it was still adequately primed. Reasonably satisfied, they contemplated the task of climbing up to the cockpits.

"I'd better go first," decided Cubby, ducking under brace wires and control cables to stand on the left wheel, reaching up to find something solid to hold. He eventually gained the nacelle and swung from the rear Lewis mounted between the cockpits to stretch a foot into the front pit. "Hey, where's me bloody seat?"

Andy attempted the ascent, and finally lowered himself into the pilot's seat. Cubby, with bad grace, tried to find a comfortable position on the floor of the empty observer's pit. From the height of the control cockpit, Andy could see his knees, almost poking above the low coaming.

Andy looked around. The aerodrome seemed deserted. He cupped his gloves and called towards the hangars "Ack Emma please!"

Silence.

"Ack Emma on the prop please!"

Swearing profusely, Cubby stood and swung back past the rear Lewis, engulfing Andy in his leather coat as he struggled through the rear pit to drop onto the wing root and down to the ground. "Read the pilot's notes, mate. I'll find someone." After a brief search of the deserted hangars he returned with the hapless clerk.

"I'm sorry sir, but I'm not trained for propellers. I'd like to help you sir, but it wouldn't be safe. I'm sure there'll be a mechanic here after lunch, sir."

Cubby grabbed the clerk's shoulder and marched him to the front of the wing. He handed him the chock-ropes. "Hold those and pull when I tell you. Duck under the wing and stay clear of the prop or you'll save me the trouble of braining you." He wound his bulk under the rear longerons and contemplated the gigantic four-blade airscrew. "Switches off?"

"Switches off!" came Andy's voice.

"Sucking in!" Cubby pulled the heavy prop through four or five blades and called; "Ready"

He heard Andy call "Stand clear!" and backed against the longerons as the engine kicked, sputtered and then roared into life. Cubby was engulfed in exhaust and castor oil, and peppered with grit and small stones from the apron. He squirmed gingerly from the wood and wire cage he now shared with a whirling guillotine.

Cubby yelled again in the clerk's ear to wait for the command to pull the chocks clear and to remember to duck, then once again completed the human fly performance to regain the front pit. Andy watched for the temperatures to rise and then ran the engine up to 1100 revs. Satisfied, he throttled back and waved a thumbs-up and made a sharp pulling motion to the terrified clerk, who eventually succeeded in pulling the chocks clear and stood transfixed as the engine roared and a wing knocked him to the concrete. Cubby leaned out of the front pit to look back and then signalled to Andy; "He's OK."

After the 2c, Andy found the FE2b instantly endearing. Perched ten feet above the ground, his view uninterrupted by engine and propeller, he applied rudder and felt the big aeroplane turn obligingly to taxi along the line of parked aircraft. Turning into wind, Andy looked around him, exchanged thumbs-ups with Cubby and opened the throttle. As the speed climbed to 40mph, he felt the aircraft detach itself gently from the ground. Lively she wasn't, but clearly she was good-tempered.

Cubby experimented with the gun positions on the way back. He could operate the front Lewis by crouching to fire forward, leaning to aim left or right. To fire to the rear, though, required standing completely straight, facing back to aim the second machine gun over the top wing. Andy felt the speed drop sharply as a six foot two Australian disrupted the slipstream. Cubby found the two-gun arrangement gave him a vastly superior field of fire to that of the 2c, but that it was achievable only by leaning far out over the side of the pit, hanging from the Lewis's spade grip. The cockpit coaming came little more than half way up his calves, leaving him completely exposed to the wind – and an easy target for enemy pilots.

He tightened his grip on the gun and thought of parachutes.

*

Dear Mom,

I'm sorry I haven't written for a few days, but it's been really hectic here. I had a letter from Dad yesterday, and it sounds as if he's doing fine. Have you heard from Rob? All's well here though we had a bit of a crash in no mans land two days ago and had to run for the trenches. Don't worry though, Cubby and me were both fine and had a great night with the infantry. (He's my observer. Australian, foul mouthed and makes me laugh a lot. He's nearly 40 and looks after me as if he was my

Dad.) I met a nurse coming back and she's from Sutton, near that pub where you and Dad visited me in training. Her name is Stainton don't laugh.

We've been on patrol today in my new plane. I like it much better than the old one that I crashed though it's a bit slow and Cubby hates it because he thinks he's going to fall out because 'there's no bloody strap'. Told you he was foul mouthed. There's a strap for me, and two guns for him to hold onto so I'm sure we'll be fine.

July 1st tomorrow! My birthday! I'm hoping we'll have another party – we seem to have an awful lot of parties here – but I think it's going to be a busy day. We've been told to be ready to be in the air all day, just coming back to refuel. Everyone's quite excited to know what's happening. Our guns are kicking up a frightful row. They're saying there'll be no Huns left alive after this barrage, it really looks like we're winning.

Must go now. Colin (he's my roommate) is agging me to go to the mess. Humphrey Page got two Fokkers today, so he's buying drinks to celebrate pulling ahead of Captain French. Those two will win the war on their own!

Please let me know what's happening at home.

Much love,

Andy.

The mess servant brought the third round of drinks just as Major Tiverton entered, Acting Major Barrington-Holt marching rigidly at his elbow. He pulled over an empty chair. "I'd go easy on that stuff tonight, chaps. Busy day tomorrow." He looked up at his recording officer. "Get the weight off that leg Barrie, I think we can do this briefing sitting down."

"I'll stand, thank you sir." He raised his voice to speak to the mess in general. "Gentlemen, you'll have noticed the increased activity from our artillery during the last week. I can now tell you that this has been in preparation for the largest push of the war, and that zero hour is 07:30 tomorrow morning."

"Two million shells have landed on the German positions in the last seven days. Their wire and trenches have been largely destroyed. Field Marshall Haig confidently expects ground resistance to our attack to be minimal. The enemy may mount a desperate air defence as a last stand. This must be destroyed. A-Flight will take off at 05:00, followed by B-Flight at 05:30 and C-Flight at 06:00. You will each remain airborne for two hours, then return to refuel, and resume patrol thirty minutes later. All reports are to be completed and handed in during this break."

Groans and cries of "That's a break?" greeted this last instruction. Acting Major Barrington-Holt blinked once and continued.

"In this way we will maintain at least two Flights on patrol at all times throughout the day. You will be asked to maintain this pattern until ordered to stand down.

"The observation contact patrol will take off at 06:45. You are to patrol the front line between the salients at Gommecourt and la Boiselle. We are assured full cooperation from the ground forces. You should ensure that you are in the region of Auchonvillers by 07:15, and remain close by until at least 07:45. Advances in this sector are to be closely observed.

"All aircraft are to avoid approaching within 300 yards of the Hawthorn Ridge redoubt between 07:15 and 07:30. A large mine under the German bunker will be detonated at 07:20. This will destroy the enemy's main defensive position, and the crater will be occupied by infantry from trenches near White City.

"The main assault will begin at 07:30, by which time the barrage will have switched to the support trenches. The attack will be made in overwhelming numbers along a twenty mile front.

"The scouts' main objective is to prevent German air intervention. In the absence of German aircraft, you are to attack ground targets at low level." He ignored a general groan from the mess. "Confirm that your targets are hostile before opening fire. Entente forces are expected to penetrate deeply and rapidly," this time he ignored cheers and snorts of laughter. "And friendly casualties are to be avoided at all costs. A map has been marked and posted for you to copy, and typed copies of these orders will be distributed. The mess will close in thirty minutes, and no more alcohol will be served from now. Does anyone have questions?"

A buzz of conversation began as Acting Major Barrington-Holt turned smartly on his heel and limp-marched out, his stick clacking on the pitted linoleum. Tiverton summoned a small brandy and magnanimously overruled his adjutant's orders to the extent of one more round on his tab. He raised his glass to Page. "Congratulations Humphrey. Only four more and you'll be level with old peg-leg Barrie."

Andy looked at the door that had closed behind the recording officer and re-examined his opinion of Acting Major Barrington Holt. Tiverton saw his surprise: "The RFC doesn't recruit people with bits missing, Palmer. Barrie donated half his left leg to the war effort in '14. That man could do things with a Blériot that haven't been invented yet – including flying it home with more lead in him than a church roof."

Cubby's natural ebullience had given way to one of his periods of withdrawal. He left the table to stand slightly behind the knot of pilots gathered around the map, he inspected it thoughtfully, absently thumbing a Scout from its packet. He was still there, alone, twenty minutes later, when Andy joined him.

"Picturing the glorious assault, Cub?"

Cubby shook his head. "Picturing a glorious fuck-up, mate." He pointed to the east. "You've seen what they've got here. They've been here years. They're dug in so deep they think this shelling's a bad spell of rain. When the guns stop, they'll have their shops open for business before the PBI have got a foot off the firestep."

"They wouldn't order an attack if they thought that. Haig knows what he's doing."

"It's not Haig I'm worried about. He does what the Frogs tell him to – and they're getting their arses kicked at Verdun. Letting the Hun shoot at the Brits instead would take the heat off them nicely. This is the forlorn hope. It's going to be a fuck-up and everybody from Hunter Bunter to Lloyd George knows it."

CHAPTER 7

July 1st, 1916

Andy's birthday dawned bright and clear. The morning sun was already warm as he taxied the FE out to the cinder airstrip. The effel drooped from its mast. The sky to the east was a vividly violet haze, with dirty yellowish smoke rising almost vertically in the still air as the conscienceless guns continued their destruction of the German positions. A large reconnaissance camera had been fitted alongside the front pit, and Cubby now shared his cramped workplace with stacked photographic plates. Andy had voiced concern about the effect of the extra drag on an already slow aeroplane, but Cubby had welcomed the addition as something to grab hold of when he fell overboard. Slumped in the front pit, his leather boots high on the forward Lewis mount, the observer was singing loudly. Last night's dark mood seemed to have evaporated and Andy grinned in response.

The squadron's morning mood had been infectious: the prospect of a long-awaited break in the stalemate of positional war, possibly even the re-opening of leave, had carried over from last night's early bedtime. Breakfast had been accompanied by Robière's Victrola, and Cubby's morning serenade echoed the insistent melody of Henry Burr's tenor lilt with surprising accuracy. Andy found himself attempting his own wandering harmony.

I wonder who's looking into her eyes
Breathing sighs, telling lies

He checked the surrounding skies and opened the throttle for take-off. The air over the front line was crammed with English and French aircraft, wheeling and swooping and good-naturedly waving in response to repeated near-collisions. Any German incursion would have been suicidal. Archie was surprisingly subdued, given that he could fire in practically any direction and fuse for any altitude with a reasonable certainty of hitting something. A gaggle of circling dots well behind the German lines proved too tempting for a squadron of RNAS 1½Strutters, and they detached themselves east to engage them, testing their guns as they climbed. As more German aircraft appeared through the morning haze, more allied scouts turned towards Hunland, leaving Andy and Cubby to patrol alone.

The British artillery barrage had reached unimaginable magnitude, and the FE2b was rocked repeatedly by the passage of shells, some of them so close that their scream pierced the numbing cacophony. The German lines were invisible under an unbroken cloud of filthy, rolling smoke. If anyone yet lived under that hell of concussion and razored metal, then they must be deaf, blind, crawling things, their fingernails blunted with earth, their lungs seared by acrid fume. Andy shuddered and checked his dashboard watch: 7:18; two minutes to go. He banged the fuselage to attract Cubby's attention and held up two fingers, then pointed across to the Hawthorn Ridge strong point as it crawled by a quarter of a mile to his left.

The guns had shifted their elevation to shell the German support trenches, and the Hun front line began to emerge from the smoke. At first there was no sign of movement and Andy began to believe that the barrage had truly destroyed the enemy resistance. Then, here and there, flashes of movement. Light flickered on bayonets. White faces appeared at fire ports and ducked away. Inconceivably, impossibly, the German trenches came to life. The second hand of the dashboard watch ticked round to zero hour and Andy and Cubby, along with tens of thousands of other watchers around and below them, leaned forward to stare at the squat, ugly fortification that dominated the ridge above No-Man's Land. Five seconds passed, ten...

A brownish dome forced itself through the earth's mantle, thrusting upwards like a huge, monochrome chestnut tree, blotting out all sight of the German redoubt, erasing it from being, turning earth and steel, rock and flesh to blossoming vapour. There was no flame, just this expanding geyser, spewing profanely skyward. As the fountain of stone reached its zenith, an invisible leviathan back-handed the FE2b onto its right wingtip; a gigantic *Whup* numbed the ears and stunned the breath.

Andy steadied the FE and banked to move closer to the subsiding cloud of earth. The wounded landscape, already pitted and torn by months of automaton destruction, now bore a new atrocity. A smoking sore, 100 yards wide, yawned at the brown-stained sky.

Movement on the far rim of the crater caught his eye. Grey figures were pouring from the severed ends of the German trench; he saw the flicker of trenching tools, and a machine gun crew double-timed to set up behind a mound of spoil, even as sandbag teams erected a well-protected emplacement around them. This was no blind panic of unearthed termites, this was the well-rehearsed response of a finely-drilled force to an assault that had been fully anticipated.

Now his eye was caught by a sally from the British trenches. A small force of infantry burst over the top and made straight for the crater. Fire immediately erupted from the newly-emplaced Germans, and the hastily assembled Maxim flashed against the dark soil. A second machine gun flickered from the left. In No-Man's Land, men threw their arms wide and pirouetted to the ground, while others simply ran into the pocked earth, driven down as much by the weight of their packs as by the scything bullets. A second wave flowed over the trench face, crouching low and zig-zagging through the corpses. As they passed, some of the prone figures of the first wave rose and joined the assault. An officer waved his revolver at the crater, exhorting his platoon to keep going as a line of shell bursts, precise as a row of poplars, cut them down.

Cubby was standing in the front cockpit, hosing fire at the far rim of the mine crater. He bawled incoherent obscenities, driving the bullets with the force of his rage.

The officer was on his feet again, rallying a gaggle of survivors to advance a few more yards before falling again. In the dust-stained, sepia light, Andy saw him crawling, one leg dragging behind him, ever forward. A gaggle of brown figures crouched and crawled with him, closing on the crater rim. Half way across they reached the German wire, supposedly destroyed by the week-long artillery barrage. It was barely disturbed. From their vantage along the rim, the defenders poured fire on their squirming attackers.

A dozen or so infantry eventually gained the near crater rim and began to dig in, leaving a hundred men, writhing and still, ripped open or torn apart, huddled in holes or kneeling at the barbed altar rails, gashed faces bent, arms thrown forward in supplication, white hands dangling.

Cubby turned to Andy, ordering him closer to the Maxim on the crater rim. His face was barely recognizable, eyes wide and saliva spraying from his shouting lips. He pounded a fresh drum onto the Lewis and concentrated the force of his hatred to drive its tracer through sandbags, earth and steel to burst apart the murdering flesh behind. At exactly 07:30, a shrilling of whistles and a roar of voices penetrated even to the circling biplane. The British line darkened to a billowing wave of humanity, scrabbling, and heaving, plunging forward or slumping back into the rising surge behind them. Spread-eagled bodies floated on the wave like drowned swimmers. Those still alive stoically followed their bayonet points, plodding forward into a tearing, whining hurricane.

Cubby exhausted his last drum of ammunition and now crouched over the nose, staring at the slaughter below. He held his big, close-cropped head in two open hands, as though forcing it to turn to horrors it wanted not to see. Andy swooped low over No-Man's Land, needing to feel himself a part of the agony of pointless sacrifice. The FE bucked as shells burst; something heavy hit the right upper plane, leaving a bloody splash on the fabric.

The advancing line, what little of it still stood, reached the German wire, and the wave broke as men ran to and fro, searching for breaks in the barrier. Some laboured with wire cutters, snipping away a few futile strands before the snipers found them. Here and there, scattered groups launched themselves at gaps, only to run into the concentrated fire of machine guns and mortars which had long been trained and ranged. A heavy figure with sergeant's stripes led a charge through an opening, barely faltering as bullets ripped his belly open, falling only when his unwinding guts tripped him and his followers.

*

Andy's hands and feet landed the FE without guidance from his numbed, unbelieving brain. As he'd turned the low-fuelled biplane for home he'd seen the Germans emerge from their trenches to stand, disdainful of the scattered, unaimed fire that met their appearance. They stood to hurl grenades and derision at the tattered, dying remnant of their invaders. The overwhelming force that had so bravely mounted the trench ladders lay scattered, turned to nameless mounds of reddened khaki and mud. But Andy's tear-blurred senses watched Big Stan and Little Eddie fall a hundred times on that infernal Saturday, when even God averted his eyes.

Five more times the two airmen returned to watch impotently as the waves broke on the German lines. Here and there, officers could be seen pointing their revolvers at cowering men; they saw the puff of white smoke and imagined the report that drove those spirit-broken groups out of their shell hole, leaving just that one behind. As the attack flagged, eyes in the German line found time to look up, and occasional bullets began to tear holes in the circling FE. The bulk of the machine gun fire played across the bodies spread along the wire, wire that bounced and waved, shaking the kneeling corpses in an obscenely synchronised dance. Andy saw Cubby crumple in the front pit, to lie huddled below the cockpit rim.

He landed at Beauval and pulled his exhausted, cramped body forward to help his fallen observer. Cubby was curled in the front pit, his knees drawn tightly into his chest, his blotched crimson face pressed against the empty ammunition drum clutched in his clawed hands. He squealed, snotted and shook like an infant, alone in cold darkness.

CHAPTER 8

It took three people and a stepladder to lift Cubby's unresisting body from the FE's nacelle. His howls had subsided to harsh, racking sobs that shook his whole body. Two or three shouts of his name would cause his head to turn and the reddened eyes to focus momentarily, only to glaze and slide away. Uninjured but unable to support himself, he was stretchered away to the hospital.

Andy wandered away from the aircraft and squatted in the sparse potato plants bordering the landing field. The noise from the West was an unbroken grumbling, punctuated by sharp barks as larger shells burst. Out there, people were dying in thousands. The same men who sang songs together and exchanged small gifts were ripping each other's bodies apart. And the man who had shown him the way to survive this obscene illogicality had had his mind torn out and trampled. He drove the heels of his hands into his eyes, fingers groping to stop his ears from the screaming which, though ten miles distant, drowned the sound of gunfire.

"Is that you, Palmer?"

Andy returned reluctantly to the present and turned to see the jerking approach of Acting Major Barrington Holt. The Recording Officer bent and lowered himself awkwardly to sit next to the crouching pilot on the clodded earth. "Bad, was it, laddie?"

The sight of the stiff-backed major, squatting among the potato stalks, his clipped staccato softened by genuine concern, added further incongruity to Andy's world and he found no answer. Acting Major Barrington Holt nodded and looked out at the western horizon. "Aye. Bad." He groped for his pipe. "Bad, bad, bad." Andy straightened his cramped legs, wondering how long he'd crouched in the field. "What'll happen, sir? I mean, it was a massacre. Them massacring us, I mean. They were ready, completely ready." He looked up helplessly. "I think we just lost the war sir."

The major puffed his pipe to life and spoke through fragrant clouds. "Don't you believe it, laddie. Field Marshall Haig doesn't gamble everything on one throw of the die. We outnumber the Hun by nearly two to one, so today won't make a dent." He looked keenly at Andy. "Don't look at me as if I were a monster, Palmer. I do understand what tragedy means, and that…" he pointed with his pipe stem. "…is tragedy beyond measure. It's a tragedy; it's not a disaster."

"I'm sorry sir, but that's a bloody callous attitude."

"Callous? It's a bloody war you idiot! What can be more callous than that? What did you think was going to happen, a gentlemen's excuse-me?" He waved away Andy's response. "Bad show about McConnachie. I need your help there."

"How?"

"It's not necessarily a straightforward case. He should be treated for Flying Sickness D, but there are people at Staff who could docket him for LMF."

"Cubby? Are you serious? Have you actually ever met him?"

"I've known him a lot longer than you have, Palmer," replied Acting Major Barrington Holt quietly. "And no, I don't believe for a moment that he's a coward. Anyone who escapes from hell and then walks back in might lack something, but it isn't moral fibre. The problem is that

McConnachie has rubbed a few brass hats the wrong way – you've seen what he's like. He has a few powerful friends, but a lot of dangerous enemies."

"So what do you want me to do?"

"I'd like you to pack up his stuff ready to ship out with him. As his friend, you should be able to spot easily enough which items might be relevant to a review of his case. Quicker the better actually, Palmer."

Andy stood. "Thank you, sir. I'll do it now. Sorry if I was a bit edgy."

"You were bloody insubordinate. Back here in forty-five minutes. I'll observe for you this afternoon."

*

Cubby's hut contained a stranger.

Andy felt no surprise that Cubby had bagged a large, comfortable hut to himself, or that he'd contrived to furnish it with a passable sofa, electric lighting, a gramophone and even a small gas range. But the person who lived here was impossible to reconcile with the loud, shaggy, good-natured clown who drank, womanised and swore his way into the hearts of all who met him. The hut was spotlessly clean and orderly; avant-garde recordings by Debussy were stacked neatly in their dust covers alongside more conventional classics by Brahms and Beethoven. A scuffed bookcase held well-thumbed works by Thackeray and Conrad. A copy of Tolstoy's "The Kingdom of God is Within You" was peppered with bookmarks and annotations. A pencilled note fell from the pages. Andy retrieved it and read; "Do I kill to kill, kill to not be killed, or kill to end killing? If any of these is true, why should I live?" In stronger strokes, Cubby had written over the note; "Fuck it."

A small writing bureau bore a framed photograph of two ANZAC infantrymen mugging extravagantly at the camera. The older was immediately recognisable as Cubby, the younger possibly eighteen or so, tall and skinny, with hair falling in his eyes and his tunic loose around his chest. They grinned from the picture, inner arms entwined and outer palms extended in a carefree, music-hall *ta-da!* A caption on the back read "March Hares at Mena Camp, 2/3/15"

In front of the photograph was a half-written letter bearing yesterday's date. Andy picked it up and held it to the light from the window. Forcing down his instinctive guilt, he read the scribble.

Dear Danny,

> It's still not making much sense here. The dugouts have no oxygen and the sky's too heavy to stand straight. I ran away from the stories – enemies throw presents and I don't know what they mean. The boy's doing good though. Light in the dark. I need you with me. If I can keep him alive then maybe you

Andy packed everything but the letter and the Tolstoy book, which he tucked under his arm and left the haunted hut. Back at his own hut, he slipped them into the oil-drum stove, splashing in methylated spirit from the Primus. He watched the papers blacken and wondered.

CHAPTER 9

April 1915

The rust-stained funnels of HMS *Queen* drew a brownish trail against the clouds. Strewn around her green-painted decks, khaki-clad figures rolled up trouser legs and a few brave souls exposed white chests to the weak warmth of a Mediterranean spring sun that peeped intermittently through pale-blue openings. A corporal in khaki trousers and olive braces hunched one-handed through a companionway exit, his free hand cradling contraband in his faded undershirt. He bare-footed across the deck and distributed his cornucopia to his three mates, slumped around a ventilator. "There you go blokes, freshly scrumped."

"Thanks Snaff – bugger!" The smallest of the trio, a bespectacled private, fumbled his catch and jumped up to pursue his apple across the deck. "Any news?"

The soldier named as "Snaff" prised himself into a space against the ventilator. "Budge up, Macca." He bit into his apple. "Ner, nothing much we didn't know already. One of the swabbies told me we go in at about 3:30 in the morning, but no knowing if that's bullshit. Fer Christ's sake, Macca, how many bloody elbows have you got?"

Macca, a tall, skinny private, brushed a lock of hair out of his eyes and contemplated the wrinkled skin of his apple. "The problem, Snaffles, lies not in the quantity of elbows, but their quality. Conversely, the paucity of space here results not from the quality of your body, but its quantity. Ergo, your discomfort is a result of my quality and your quantity."

"I could listen to him for hours," said Snaff, with affection.

"Mine's already been half eaten by something," said a freckled infantryman, wiping an elaborately tended red moustache and squinting at the browned interior of his apple.

"Well whatever it was, it's left you the best bit, Bluey. You need to get out of the sun, you're starting to look like Jaffas in blancmange."

The large shape of a sergeant cast its shadow over the group. "Bloody hell, if Kirchner was here he'd want to paint the lot of you. Kit inspection in twenty minutes, bathing beauties. Snaff, have you been nicking stuff again?"

"Providing essential anti-scurvy medication for my section, Sarge," grinned Snaff, tossing him an apple. Sergeant McConnachie was alright.

"Well have the decency to lose all your teeth so nobody suspects," replied the sergeant, deftly catching the apple and polishing it on his battledress. "Ah, glad to see you've already started." He glanced down at Macca. "Danny, you got a minute?"

With some embarrassment, the boy unwound himself from the deck and joined McConnachie at the rail. "I wish you wouldn't do this."

"Do what?" He glanced back at Macca's companions. "Oh, them. They're your mates, they're not bothered."

"I am, though. It's embarrassing, and I'd rather you called me Macca like everyone else."

"OK, but I've been calling you Danny for eighteen years, so don't expect miracles." He lit a cigarette and looked at the distant shoreline. "Listen, this show's got every sign of a class-one fuck-up. When we go in tomorrow I want you right with me the whole time."

Danny leaned over the rail and watched a ginger cat conscientiously inspecting its anus on the deck below. "Why d'you say that?"

"For a start, because the Ruperts are so bloody confident. Overwhelming force, element of surprise, all that bollocks."

"I'd heard that we're going in early, while it's still dark; I take it that's the element of surprise."

"Yeah, because the Abduls haven't noticed half the bloody Royal Navy sailing up the fuckin' Mediterranean. The Moon sets about 3:00am. If you were sitting in your nice cosy gun emplacement watching the ships sail in, roughly when would you expect a landing? It's going to be a fuck-up."

"So you want me with you." Danny sounded resigned.

"I want you home in Euabalong. But as you're here, yes, I want you with me. I want the whole platoon to stick close, but you're to stick closer."

Danny shrugged. "You shouldn't have written the permission letter if you didn't want me here."

"If not writing it would have guaranteed keeping you at home, I wouldn't have written it. But the instant I shipped out you'd have written it for me. At least this way I can keep an eye on you."

Danny watched a torpedo boat bouncing through the waves to starboard. He threw his apple core to the cat, which sniffed it, shook a hind leg in disdain and stalked off. "Better get ready for kit inspection then."

But he gently punched his father's arm as he went below.

*

"Fuck me! Mind where you're putting your bloody great boots!"

"Silence there! Sergeant, take that man's name."

There was the sound of an open-handed blow and a muffled "Fuck me, Sarge!"

"Sorry lieutenant, can't see who it was in the dark."

The boat fell silent, other than the sound of crammed soldiery trying to find a comfortable space.

Lieutenant Bebber's voice came quietly in the darkness. "OK men, You've been briefed. I know we're still a good way out, but there's to be no talking or smoking until I tell you otherwise. We're landing a little north of Gaba Tepe, which will be visible to your right when it gets light. The land slopes fairly gently inland and there are no cliffs. Staff is confident that resistance will be minimal, and that we won't meet heavy enemy forces until we push further inland.

"On landing, stay with your platoon. 12 Battalion will dig in to establish a beach head, while we will press on east to take the ridge. We'll have 9 Battalion to our right, and 11 to our left, so your flanks will be secure. Use your canteens sparingly as the availability of fresh water is unknown."

An invisible naval rating in the bow called softly to cast off and there came a gurgling hiss from the steam pinnace detailed to tow in the invasion party. A slight double jerk and a few gentle bumps against the side of the battleship announced the beginning of the invasion of Gallipoli.

The boats beached at a little before 4:30am, just as the eastern sky began to lighten. As the invaders dropped into the waist-deep water, scattered rifle fire broke out from various points along the dark shore line. Sergeant

McConnachie had scrounged a length of knotted rope from a friendly rating; he led his platoon to the shore in good order, each man holding his knot. They stumbled across the pebbled strand to crouch in a gully bordered with scrubby vegetation. McConnachie's hushed roll call confirmed that everyone had arrived safely, and he ordered his men not to fire unless directly attacked. The noise of trenching tools came from left and right.

A shape dropped next to McConnachie and Lieutenant Bebber's voice whispered in the darkness. "Not much resistance at all. Any casualties, Cubby?"

"No sir."

"Excellent. Have you got your cape? I need to look at the map. Can't make head or tail of where we are in the dark."

"Here you go sir."

"Thank you. Join me?"

Huddled under Cubby's cape, the two soldiers examined the map by the light of the lieutenant's torch. Every few seconds, Bebber snapped off the light to look out and around in the growing light before consulting the map again. "This doesn't look right to me."

"Nor me. If that hill is Gaba Tepe, what's it doing on our left?"

As they looked in puzzlement at the silhouetted outcrop, the sky behind it suddenly flashed, followed a couple of seconds later by a thunder of machine gun and light artillery fire.

"We're too far south, Cubby. That must be the 9th catching it. We were supposed to be to their north."

"Good news for us though, Lieutenant, looks like the Ottomans have moved everybody up north. Maybe we can move east and flank them."

"Agreed. Let me make contact with the captain. I'll be right back." He disappeared into the lightening gloom.

A clinking rustle heralded the arrival of a dozen dark shapes in the gully. "Who's that?"

"Flower, Red Platoon. Who's that?"

"McConnachie, Red Platoon."

"What?"

"Exactly. What battalion are you?"

"Ninth. You?"

"Tenth. We're in the shit, mate."

The newcomer squatted next to Cubby. "Too right. You blokes are in the wrong place."

Cubby pointed at the hilltop. "That hill there's in the wrong place."

Flower looked up at the hill, now clearly visible against the grey sky. "Oh fuck." He looked around, distributing an expletive to each of the remaining cardinal compass points. "Fuck, fuck, fuck." He turned back to Cubby. "And double-fuck the Royal Navy."

"Where's your officer?"

"No idea, blue. He was in the other tow. Anybody's guess where they landed."

Bebber slid back into the hollow. "OK, well I found *a* captain, but not the one I was expecting. It seems all the companies are mixed to hell. Most are moving east as originally intended to occupy the ridge."

"Do we know anything about the terrain or enemy positions to the east?" asked Cubby.

"No, other than that the slope appears to be reasonably gentle."

"Well hoo-fuckin-ray for that. We wouldn't want to be all sweaty and out of breath when we get our heads blown off, would we?"

"That's enough McConnachie."

"Sorry Mr Bebber. This is Sergeant Flower, 9th batallion."

"Ninth? Then who's catching it the other side of that hill?"

"God knows, sir. It might be the Australia Day fireworks for all we poor bastards know."

Bebber considered for a moment. "OK, I'll take Gowie with me as runner. I'll try to get a clearer picture and establish where the rally point is, then I'll send him back with orders. If it all goes to hell, move inland and try to dig in on the ridge."

As Bebber and Gowie left, gunfire opened up to the right of the gully and spiteful shards whined over their heads. The two of them dropped into the dead ground beyond the gully and ran away to the north.

Cubby spotted the muzzle flashes coming from a clump of rocks and spiky bushes a hundred yards to the south. His group was in a bad position; the Turks commanded high ground, and the Australians would be silhouetted against the pale beach whenever they raised their heads. "The Abduls are getting organised. If they can close up on our flank they'll start plopping bombs in and this gully will be a bad place to be." He looked around and pointed up the hill. "Snaff; you, Stan, Mick and Bluey. On my word I want you to get up to the base of that tree there. That should give you some elevation on them, and there's a hollow there that'll give you cover. If you go over the rear lip here and keep your heads down you should be in dead ground most of the way, but we'll give you covering fire just in case – they know where we are now anyway. Move fast and eyes open all the way, there could be snipers waiting for you to show.

"Everybody else, get spread out six feet apart just below the near gully rim. On my word, two full clips each right above Abduls' muzzle flashes. Flower, can you watch the beach flank?"

"Will do. When your men break, we'll break back to the beach. I need to find the rest of my platoon, and it'll split the Turks' fire."

Cubby nodded. "Your call, mate. Everybody loaded and cocked? OK, keep your chins on the dirt. Snaff and Flower, I'll give you the word when the second clips open up. Everyone, call out when you reload. Ready? Fire!"

The sudden fusillade of return fire from the gully seemed to take the enemy gun crew by surprise and their frequency and accuracy of fire faltered. As the first calls of "Reloading!" rang out, Flower slapped Cubby's back. "Good luck mate." He and his platoon darted out to run back down the beach, now showing pale and bright.

Cubby's cry of; "Wait for the fresh clips!" was either unheard or unheeded. Encouraged by the slackening of the Australians' fire, the Turkish soldiers resumed their fire, targeting the crouched, running figures. One man fell instantly; two more ran on with spastic jerks before collapsing among the scattered rocks.

"Fuck it!" Cubby fed in a fresh clip and worked the bolt of his gun. "Snaff, go, go, go!" He resumed firing.

Snaff's team rolled over the rear of the gully and double-timed towards the tree, running with knees bent and faces close to the ground. To the right, two of Flower's platoon were crawling across the pebbles. The hidden gunners fired and first one then the other became still. Flower himself was a dark shape huddled behind a larger rock. Whether he lived was impossible to determine.

Snaff's party, having gained the hollow at the base of the tree, opened rapid fire on the enemy. Mick Griffiths, frustrated that the Turks were still invisible even from this elevated position, stepped over the rim of the bowl and took careful aim. A muted crack was heard from somewhere behind the Turkish position and he looked down in surprise, then sank to his knees, clutching his belly. The rest of the advance party dived below the rim of the hollow, a hand showing briefly as the wounded man was dragged into cover.

The Turks resumed firing at Flower's rock then subsided to occasional bursts of four or five seconds, changing targets now and then to subdue the ANZACs in the gully and around the tree. Every thirty seconds or so, the *spat* of the unseen sniper's rifle would draw a wail of profanities from Snaff's squad.

Cubby raised his voice. "Snaff, how are you guys?"

"Mick's gut-shot, Sarge. We've got a field dressing on it but he's lookin' pretty crook."

"Flower, you still with us?"

"Yeah. Got a bit of a scratch alongside my ankle. Bastard spotted my foot hanging out."

"Can you walk?"

"Hard to say. Bullet went right through. That's good isn't it?"

"Search me."

Cubby heard Danny's voice at his elbow. "So this is what we call a fuck-up then, is it?"

Snaff called from up the hill. "Sarge, Bluey reckons he's spotted the sniper. He's moved to his left. If you can, look for the pale, spiky bush about fifty yards behind the Jackos."

Cubby peered carefully through the scrub. "Got it."

"Come left and down. There's a patch of whitish rock."

"Yeah."

"OK, he's right behind that. Looks like he's shifted to get a bead on you blokes. Bluey's got the scope on. If you can get the Jacko to put his head up, he reckons he can get a good shot."

"OK, give me a second."

Cubby considered the best way to draw the sniper's fire. A bush hat on a rifle butt was the obvious ruse – too obvious to fool a sharp-eyed, trained soldier with a telescopic sight. But the unseen marksman would fully expect his opponents to have their own sniper. "Anyone got a spare undershirt in your pack?"

"Yes, what d'you want it for?"

Danny's undershirt was bleached colourless by repeated laundering. When wrapped around Cubby's canteen and capped with a bush hat, it made a reasonable representation of a pale face. Cubby tied it above his rifle breech with the canteen webbing. "Bluey, you got one up the spout?"

"Cocked and ready, Sarge."

"OK, eyes peeled. Here we go."

Holding the end of the rifle butt in his fingertips, Cubby pushed the muzzle of the gun through the scrub of the gully rim. Within two seconds, a shower of pebbles and a sharp crack rewarded his deception. Almost instantly, a second report echoed from the hillside above.

"D'you get him?"

"Dunno. Thought I did, but I can see his barrel still moving."

A sobbing moan came from the white rock. Cubby risked a glance over the gully lip, but could see no clue to the sniper's fate. The noises of pain climbed the scale from groan to shriek, a disturbing, unshaped sound. As if angered by their comrades' agony, the hidden gunners resumed a stream of fire on the bodies of Flower's platoon; they twitched and jerked, pebbles flipping and spinning around them. Cubby saw Bluey crouch-run from the tree and dart from cover to cover to take up station behind the enemy position. He'd removed his hat, and his red moustache showed brightly against his cork-blackened face as he took aim carefully. His rifle cracked and a loud grunt came from the hidden enemy, followed by a babble of imprecations. Two men darted from cover and charged Bluey, who worked the bolt and fired again, cutting down the leader. The other jerked to his right, forward, and right again before falling under fire from the Australians in the gully and around the high tree.

Little Charlie O'Neil whooped and scrabbled up the gulley side. Cubby grabbed his pack webbing and pulled him back under cover. "Wait!" He looked cautiously over the rim. "Snaff, can you see anything from up there?"

"Nothing Sarge. It's as quiet as."

"Bluey? How about you?"

"All quiet Sarge. Think that was the lot."

"OK, I'm going up to look. The rest of you stay down and keep your eyes peeled. No telling where the rest of the Jackos are."

Cubby stood cautiously and looked around. Scattered musketry echoed from the hills above, but all seemed quiet here on the rim of the beach. He walked to the Turkish emplacement, finding a shallow pit, ten feet across and revetted with sandbags. It was empty except for a water can, a small stack of dry rations and an ammunition box. A lidded latrine bucket huddled against the rear wall. He looked up the hill at the bodies of the fallen Turks, tilting his head back further to look higher as another hopeless moan issued from the lair of the invisible sniper. "OK, Bluey, move in on the sniper. Think he's out of the game, but watch your step. Everybody else, cover him if it turns nasty."

Bluey emerged from his cover and started down the hill, dropping out of sight as he reached the sniper's position. "Oh Jesus Christ!"

"What's up mate?"

"I missed Sarge."

"So what does that mean? Is he down or what?"

"Oh, he's down. Get up here, I don't know what to do."

Bebber returned with Gowie to find Stan Farrow and Charlie O'Neil on the beach, Farrow attending to Flower's injured ankle while O'Neil looked for signs of life among his platoon. He bent to each body, one finger restraining the bridge of his spectacles as he extended a hand to check for pulse or breathing. He jerked as Bebber laid a hand on his shoulder.

"What's happened here?"

The small private straightened and pointed up the hill. "Enemy group with a sniper, sir. They got Mick Griffiths pretty bad too before we settled 'em." He indicated the man at his feet. "This one's still breathing, but I think he's got a Belgium. He's hit bad."

The rest of the platoon stood uncertainly around the bodies of the enemy defenders. Mick Griffiths, who was semi-conscious and breathing stertorously, lay alongside the man who had shot him. The Ottoman sniper moaned softly. Bluey's bullet had hit the rock in front of his face and ricocheted through teeth, palate and left eye to lodge in his temple. Rock shards had torn through his cheeks to lacerate his tongue. Danny was kneeling next to their prisoner, wondering how to place the morphine tablet in the ruined mouth.

Cubby sketched a salute to the approaching lieutenant. "Got two wounded here, sir. You already know about Flower's lot."

Bebber turned to Gowie. "Run back down and get stretcher bearers for four men up here." He turned back to Cubby. "Well done, sergeant."

Cubby shrugged' "It was Bluey here who got three of 'em. But they killed four of ours, plus three wounded. I don't like the look of Mick here, and God knows how many bullets Flower's man down there took. Seven for four, sir. That's not a good score."

The lieutenant nodded. "When you're ready, move up the steep path onto the plateau. Watch for snipers, but otherwise the ground is fairly safe. The kiwis are setting up base on the flat ground up there and you'll find the battalion mustering to the right. Get some food and a drink down you, then we're making for the ridge."

"Do we know where we are yet?"

"Roughly. We're not too far south, we're too far north. That high point is Ari Burnu, not Gaba Tepe. Gaba Tepe is a mile or two that way." Cubby followed Bebber's pointing finger. To the south, the beach ended in a wooded hill on which shell bursts were raising grey clouds. "There's a two mile gap on our south flank between us and the British. We don't know what happened to our north flank." Bebber laughed shortly. "You know where we are, don't you Cubby?"

"Yep. In the shit as usual, Mr Bebber."

CHAPTER 10

July 4th, 1916

It was Colin's day for Orderly Dog. Censoring Other Ranks' letters lacked the element of diversion and the morning dragged with listless monotony towards a distant lunchtime. The recent fine weather had given way to a dreary, squalling greyness that scattered smacking raindrops against the oiled-cloth window. He pulled another letter from the pile:

Dear Tilly,

> All is well here how are you in the pink I hope? Thanks for the parsel, I really needed, socks and the boys shared the cake greedy lot!!! Sorry to here, about your leg again but, keep smiling eh…

He concluded that any non-native English speaker who could decode the semi-literate gibberish was welcome to the information that the Royal Flying Corps was clearly drowning under a surfeit of socks and home-made cake. The office door banged, and he looked up to see Andy slouching, stoop-shouldered into the room.

"Morning. You going to be doing that all day?"

Colin stamped the partially-read letter and threw it, uncensored, into the Out tray. "God, I hope not. Why, you got something more entertaining in mind? If it helps, that would include painting a target on my arse and waving it at the Germans."

Andy shrugged, hands buried in his pockets. "There's clearly no flying today, and the Crossley's been fixed.

Tiverton said I can borrow it. Trouble is, I don't know how to drive the damn' thing. Can you show me?"

"I can chauffeur you. I've driven my father's Siddeley; the Crossley can't be that difficult." He stood up. "Where we going?"

Andy nodded at the unread pile. "What about that lot?"

"I'll find somebody to swap with. If God had meant us to censor letters He wouldn't have given mothers the power to knit socks. What's the mission?"

"I want to find Connie Hamilton, that FANY nurse, and tell her about Cubby. She seemed quite fond of him, so I thought she ought to know."

Colin grinned. "I thought you were looking uncharacteristically washed and groomed. Let's have a look at this daughter of hers then."

The rain drove in through the open sides of the Crossley's cabin. Andy huddled as close to the centre as possible and watched Colin expertly manipulate the alien array of pedals and levers.

Colin operated the windscreen wiper, but gave up with a shrug. "It just pushes the water from side to side; does bugger all for your vis."

"How can it be wetter down here with a roof over our heads, than it is up there with nothing?"

"Up there you're doing more than 15 miles an hour. It goes over your head, not down your trousers. Which way?"

"Just keep heading west. There's a turn-off about a mile this side of the lines. Think I'll know it when we get there."

"OK, well if you see someone in a spiked helmet, ask him for directions."

They drove in silence for a few moments. Colin opened the windscreen's top flap to squint ahead through the squalling veils. "How's Cubby doing?"

"A lot of the time he seems pretty much OK, just a bit... withdrawn, you know? And he's got my name wrong now and again. But then a doctor or a nurse comes in and he just sort of floats away. He pulls his elbows and knees in and rocks back and forward. It's as if he's gone somewhere else. Can't even hear you anymore."

"What about the LMF charge?"

"Dunno. It's still on the cards though, I heard one of the doctors mention it. He was pretty bloody disgusted."

Colin stopped the tender to allow a red-crossed ambulance to pull out of a side turning and drive off towards the front line.

"Is this the turning?"

Andy squinted through the rain. "Could be. It looks different by daylight – and it wasn't pissing down last time I was here."

Colin turned into the narrow track. "Let's give it a try. If we have to reverse all the way back, you're outside giving directions."

The tents of the RAP sagged wetly. Wounded soldiers, huddled under oilskins and scraps of canvas, sprawled in lines outside the largest of them. Through the tied-back entrance flap, the aviators glimpsed a group of men and women picking their way through irregular ranks of mud-coloured humps, strewn apparently at random on beds, boxes and the trampled ground.

The air inside the tent was heavy with ether, sweat and the esters of violated flesh. A stained screen near the far end partly concealed three groups of stooped figures, each working alongside a suspended bottle of colourless fluid. Brick-red rubber tubing snaked down to their unseen charges. From the nearest group, a woman straightened to stretch her back and glanced down to where the airmen hesitated. She waved briefly and called over the batter of rain. "Wait outside. Be with you in a minute."

Andy and Colin were sheltering in the Crossley when Connie Hamilton emerged from the tent. Colin jumped out to let her squeeze into the driest part of the cab. She gratefully accepted a lit cigarette as Andy made introductions. Her hands were stained reddish brown, her face smudged, her hair straggled and uncombed. She closed her eyes and inhaled deeply, head bumping gently against the rear wall.

"Lovely to see you, Andy," She opened her eyes and glanced at the young pilot with tired amusement. "Afraid you've just missed Stainton. She's driven up to the front to bring some more cases back. Surprised you didn't meet her on your way in."

Andy's unconcern was almost convincing. "No, we came to see you actually. It's about Cubby."

She sat forward. "Oh God, no! What's happened?"

"Oh he's not injured or anything. But... Well, something's sort of broken in here." He tapped his temple, "I don't know what to do for him."

Connie sucked a further half-inch from the cigarette. She shook her head. "How bad is he?"

"Bad. It was the day of the big push. He saw all that massacre and just sort of folded up on himself."

"Where is he now?"

"At the clearing hospital. There are a few questions being asked."

She looked at him sharply. "Tell me they're not calling it lack of moral fibre."

"It's on the cards."

Connie threw her cigarette end out into the downpour. "Let me out and wait here."

Colin was dozing when a shuffling thump from the rear of the Crossley roused him. Andy was already standing at the tailgate, watching a loaded stretcher being manoeuvred into the rear tray alongside another huddled shape.

"Connie's collecting some stuff. We've been commandeered."

"What?"

"Here she is now, ask her yourself."

Connie motioned at the cab and climbed in. Sandwiched between the two pilots, she issued instructions. "Drive to the clearing hospital, please, Colin. These two cases need extensive surgery as soon as possible." She turned to Andy. "And then we'll see about sorting out Cubby's problems."

"Do you think you can help?"

"My dear, I was married to a Lieutenant Colonel, who was decorated twice, and was MP for Sutton Coldfield. You'd be surprised at the addresses I have in my little book."

Andy gaped at her in admiration. She laughed. "I'd assumed that was why you came to find me. That and the fact that you have designs on my daughter."

"You know, somewhere on the Western Front, there has to be someone who isn't discussing this. All I did was ask her to meet me – and she turned me down."

"And then wished she hadn't." She waved down Andy's sudden look. "Calm down, she didn't say so, but I know Stainton, and if you asked her again…" she thought for a moment. "She'd probably say no again. She's a prickly little thing. But worth the trouble."

Colin waggled the windscreen wiper experimentally. "Maybe she needs an alternative choice. Someone a bit less bony. Someone with a little more *savoir-faire*."

"Someone with a little more lard and a lot more Brilliantine?"

"Sophistication, Palmer, is unlikely to be recognised by one of your lowly upbringing."

"Don't get me wound up or I won't lift you down out of the cab, you posh dwarf."

"That the future of our great nation should be in these hands," muttered Connie, shaking her head.

CHAPTER 11

Andy watched enviously as A-Flight touched down; French, followed by Page, then a short gap before Beasley and Colin bumped onto the cinders. He'd flown little since the weather had cleared; Acting Major Barrington Holt had joined him for a couple of sorties, but without a regular observer he was effectively grounded.

French waved and beckoned as he jumped down from his machine. "Join us for brekky if you're not busy, Andy."

"Sure, I'm not doing anything useful on my own. Anything happening up there?"

"Not a sausage. Saw a two-seater doing art. reg. by Authuille, but he cleared off before we could get anywhere near. How are you doing?"

"Ready to desert to the Germans if they'll give me a flying job."

French nodded as Colin and Beasley joined the group, wiping oil from their faces with cotton waste. "Well we can't allow that, can we? Come on, I need bacon."

The mess was crowded and it was a few minutes before the five airmen could find seats at a table together. Colin repeatedly nudged Andy, inexpertly concealing some joyful secret. Henrik Doke pulled a chair from a nearby table and joined them, sipping coffee from an enamel mug.

French dipped bread and butter into his egg. "OK Andy, you've probably noticed that young Hingley here's unable to keep still, so there's some news I'd like to share with you." He took a swig of tea. "As you know, I was impressed that he managed to put a few bullets into that

Fokker, and I've been trying to get him a decent machine. So this afternoon there'll be a Nieuport arriving for him."

Andy thumped Colin's shoulder. "Congrats, mate."

French paused to shovel bacon and continued, patting his moustache with the back of a finger. "Meanwhile, Henry's been chatting to Group. There's only so much observation we can do with only one two-seater, and none at all when we're missing an observer. So we're becoming exclusively a single-seater squadron. Which means there'll be a Nieuport here this afternoon for you too."

Andy became aware that he was grinning like a simpleton. Doke leaned over and extended a hand. "You'll be on C-Flight with me, bru. Makes a change to see a khaki that's not a doos at Bok-Bok, nè?"

Andy shook the hand enthusiastically. "I haven't got a clue what you're talking about Mr Doke, but I'm ready to learn."

*

The second Nieuport *Bébé* bounced twice on landing, coming down hard on the left wheel and swerving violently.

"I don't fancy yours, mate," observed Colin from his perch alongside Andy on a maintenance trolley.

"After the scrap iron I've been flying, I'll take it if he wipes a wing off." Andy stood as the two little scouts taxied towards them, an ack emma guiding each wingtip. "Take your pick, mate."

"Go on then, I'll take the one with the dodgy undercart – my superior flying skills may be needed if something falls off."

"Good for you, Col. Don't set this one on fire, eh?"

The delivery pilots climbed out, one of them offering an embarrassed smile as Colin climbed up to take command of his new machine. Hughie fussed around, checking rigging wires and tugging ailerons. His opinion of the standard of aircraft preparation at St Omer was little improved by his failure to find any obvious faults. "Let's get a mechanic to look at the engines before you take 'em up sir. I wouldn't trust the Depot to put petrol in a fag lighter."

"Just check the tanks and find us a couple of drums of ammo each, Hughie, there's a good chap." Colin looked over to where Andy was tinkering with his new machine. "Fancy shooting up a few targets, mate?"

Take-off was a high-spot of Andy's short aviation career. Opening the throttle on his third aircraft type of the month, he caught the Nieuport's extravagant swing with a heavy bootful of rudder and followed Colin down the cinder strip.

Airborne, the tiny French aeroplane was as skittish as a canoe. After the listless numbness of the BE2c and the relaxed docility of the FE2b, it was edgy, sharp; eager to please, but quick to punish. Unlike the two-seaters, this feisty mademoiselle demanded attention every second. She wanted to stand on her tail; she resented heavy fingers on her control column; she derisively ignored a gentle foot on her rudder. Her engine torque was a constant hand pushing down the right wing. She was a little bitch, and he loved her already.

Colin pulled a series of capers, grinning back occasionally to see if Andy was hanging onto his tail. Andy willed his machine to obey and sweated to hold position, contriving to be in roughly the right place each time Colin's goggles flashed over his shoulder.

Reaching the practice targets, Colin pointed up and spiralled to gain height. Just two minutes later, and with 1500 feet of clear air below the two aircraft, Colin topped out and pulled over to dive on the targets. Andy watched the tiny biplane gather speed and faintly heard the rattle of its gun. As his friend pulled clear of the target, he pulled hard back and right on the column, kicking in full right rudder to wing over into his attack. He leaned forward to centre the target in his Aldis sight, squeezing his trigger at 600 feet. The magazine appeared to be loaded one-in-one with tracer, and an almost unbroken bar of white-gold connected the snub-nosed Nieuport to the sandy ground within six feet of the white disc. He gently pulled the sparkling line to centre the target before pulling back, feeling the wings flex as the pull of a world thrust his chin hard into his chest. He zoom-climbed back to a thousand feet and pulled over into a full loop, whooping aloud at the exuberance of the hurricane that he was privileged to ride.

Levelling out at 500 feet, Andy glanced left as Colin's Nieuport dropped alongside. The two young aviators grinned across the intervening space, then Colin, beckoning, dropped away into a steep dive.

Andy had heard the scout pilots discussing their terrain-hopping exploits and longed to be a part of it. He followed the tail of Colin's machine down, down, saw its shadow growing large on the broken metalling of the road. The two Nieuports levelled out, wheels no more than a yard above the blurred gravel. Hedgerows flashed by at a hundred miles an hour. Andy fancied that he heard a scream of joy from the leading plane.

Colin's plane lifted twenty feet and Andy caught sight of a turn in the road as it rushed towards him. He pulled up and threw his machine over, glimpsing the road racing by, seemingly within inches of his wingtip. He looked forward in time to see the lead plane switchback over an oncoming vehicle, then he was on it himself, pulling up to clear its tarpaulined back and glancing through its windscreen into the startled, angry eyes of Stainton.

*

The Sunbeam ambulance was already parked in the farmyard when Andy and Colin pushed through the sagging gate from the landing field. Stainton emerged from the OC's office, noticed their approach and, with a slight shake of her head, climbed into the cab.

Colin stopped by the wall and muttered; "Yep, I'd call that worth the trouble. Good luck, chap. Keep me informed of any territorial gains." He walked back through the gate, heading for their hut.

Andy stood by the Sunbeam's running board and tried a conciliatory smile. "Permission to come aboard?"

"If you can do it without killing me."

He slid onto the bench. "Sorry 'bout that. Bit excited about my new plane."

"Happy birthday to you. Glad they didn't buy you anything dangerous."

"How did you know it was my birthday?"

"I didn't. Is it?"

"Couple of days ago actually. What does it take to make you actually smile?"

"You could start by not throwing a two-ton aeroplane at me. See? It's working already."

"OK, it's a deal. So, what brings you to see me?"

"And who says I came to see you?" The smile widened a little.

"Ah. So, what brings you here?" Andy rubbed his thumb over the scuffed dashboard.

"I came to see you." Andy looked up as she laughed. "I know, I'm bloody hard work. Let's go for a walk before it starts raining; I want to talk to you."

It was inevitable that Andy would guide their steps back to his Nieuport, now standing under a Bessenau hangar amid a cluster of ack emmas. Hughie accurately judged the situation and earned Andy's undying gratitude by actually saluting and announcing. "We're just getting her how you like her, sir," albeit spoiling the effect by adding; "You shouldn't have to tug the joystick so hard this afternoon."

Stainton smothered a laugh and silenced Andy's pique with a nudge of her shoulder. "I'm sure the Lieutenant is most grateful that so many joysticks have passed through your hands," she pronounced in crystal-glass tones. "Shall we walk on, Andrew? I'm sure your little man needs to be about his own business."

The recent rain had cleansed the air of its July surliness. The sun warmed without burning, and the birds competed ardently from every branch. They walked close enough for their shoulders to bump occasionally; Stainton watched a lark explode from the meadow to bob noisily in the pale blue sky. She quietly announced that she was leaving.

Andy's sunlit afternoon darkened. He watched for the stooping hawk that would clear his sky of songbirds. He looked at this difficult, fascinating girl who had just snatched away the incredible future she'd built only minutes ago. "What? Why? I mean, where are you going?"

"Home. England. With my mother."

"And why?"

She shrugged. "Mum has fads. The war was a lovely hobby, but she's bored with it now. She's going back to buy a few more ambulances for our brave lads, then apparently we're going to put together a concert party. The next time you see me I'll probably be playing a piano."

"So you will be back, then?"

"Who knows, Andy? By the time we get to Dover she might have hatched a plan to explore the Amazon."

"It's just… I thought…"

"Well stop thinking." She worried a thumbnail between her teeth, her eyes following a pale grey spider as it scuttled along a lichened fence rail.

"Andy, you're a nice boy. I liked the ride with you the night that Mum and Cubby…" She examined the bitten thumbnail. "You didn't try to chat me up. You made me laugh. "She glanced up, smiling. "And you didn't have half your intestines shot away, how could a girl resist?"

"Yeah, but you did resist."

"And I still am. That's why I wanted to see you before I went. If we'd met somewhere else…"

"Yes, what then?"

"I don't know. I really don't know. We didn't. We met here in France, in a war. We had a ride in an ambulance for half an hour. I went home. It's hardly *La Grande Affaire*."

Andy leaned on the rail, straightened quickly as the whole fence swayed under his weight. "So are you saying it never will be?"

Stainton's characteristic prickles made their reappearance. "Why do I have to be saying anything? I liked you. I came to say cheerio. You're the one who's making it into a romantic novel. Come on, I need to get back."

She turned and led the way back to the airfield.

CHAPTER 12

May 1915

Danny stirred the spitting mass of sliced potato and corned beef. "Bully's about done. Who's hungry?"

Bluey passed over a mess tin, a puddle of milkless tealeaves swishing in its base. "Ladle it out, Chef. My belly thinks my throat's been cut."

Danny, waving away the swarming flies, spooned gobbets of fatty meat and vegetables into the rapidly assembling row of tins. He leaned back against the sandbagged wall, digging into the remainder of the mess with a tin spoon. A large brown centipede fell from the rippled iron roof, and he spooned it deftly into the primus flame. "Seventeen. You won't catch up now, mate."

"Two more fags say I'll top twenty-five by six."

"You're on."

Charlie O'Neil, perched uncomfortably on the edge of his dugout, wiped his spectacles on a stained rag. "You want to stop betting, Bluey. At this rate, all the fags in Gallipoli will be held by the bloke who doesn't use 'em."

"Why d'you think that is?" asked Danny. "This trench smells like Kamel's khazi already, without you lot smoking it up with camel shit."

O'Neil took his glasses off again and breathed on them, increasing their opacity with the hem of his undershirt. "What's a khazi, Macca?"

"It's what the posh people call a dunny." "No kidding? Well, when I meet the King to get me VC, that's knowledge that'll make me look educated. 'Thank you, your majesty; if you'll excuse me, I need to pop to the khazi but.' Who's Kamel?"

"He's the Prime Minister of England. If you get to speak to any of the Pommie officers, make sure you salute if anyone mentions his name."

Snaff appeared in the semi-darkness, leaning with one hand on the damp metal sheeting of the trench roof. "Anybody got one of those Balkan ciggies left?"

Mac threw him a cigarette. "There you go Corp, now do us a favour and smoke it in the open, eh?"

He leaned back again and looked at his companions in the gloom. Bluey, Snaff and O'Neil were worlds apart from any of his university friends back home, yet after weeks of close confinement, he found himself viewing them with an affection that was almost painful. They'd nursed him without complaint through enteric fever, and he'd cleaned their soiled bedding as the infection tore through the cramped trenches. They shared stolen food, covered each other's transgressions, squabbled swore and stank together in profanely divine harmony.

*

Cubby was negotiating the shallow trenches near the far front of No. 3 Post. An informal truce had sprung up so that some of the blackening bodies in the narrow strip of no man's land could be cleared. The Turks had been friendly and fair, and there'd been much good-natured barter and exchange of souvenirs. Even now there seemed little enthusiasm on either side for resuming hostilities, and there was regular banter between the Turks and ANZACs, their trenches only yards apart. His stomach lurched at the smell of some deliciously spiced dish being prepared in the enemy line.

A New Zealand voice raised in protest. "Oi, Mustafa, you're not going to eat all that yourself are you?"

"Aussie, my friend does not speak your foul language, but asks me to tell you that he would share with you, but sadly our officer says that he must shoot you."

"Tell him he can shoot me if he likes, but ask him to spare us a bite. And don't call me an Aussie."

"I will ask him to spare you a bite if you do not call me Mustafa."

"No offence meant, mate."

"No offence taken my friend. Do not put your hand above the trench when you catch this."

A white package arced accurately over the intervening space, to be caught and unwrapped by the Kiwi. A small chicken leg stained the clean handkerchief with its fragrant sauce. "Bless you, you bloody heathens!"

"And bless you too, you fucking infidel!"

Cubby laughed to himself and headed back along the racecourse trench towards the winter dugouts. The trench walls were littered with scrapes and hollows. Most were little more than shelves, roofed with sandbags and scrap wood. A crumpled blanket, a tin mug and an occasional grubby photograph marked the home of a soldier of the AIF. He hurried past a Tickler's Artillery factory, two of the workers smoking nonchalantly as they filled jam and meat tins with gun cotton and small stones.

Snaff was lounging outside the covered support trench, smoking industriously. Beyond him was a long cave with wooden walls and a sweating corrugated-iron roof under two feet of packed earth. A drainage channel diverted the rains from the entrance, keeping resting infantrymen, as well as unnumbered cockroaches and centipedes secure from weather, snipers and enemy mortars.

"Jesus Snaff, those things are worse than a gas attack."

Snaff blew an aromatic cloud into a bobbing horde of mosquitoes. "I'll take that to mean you didn't get me any more."

Cubby unbuttoned a top pocket and took out four wrinkled cigarettes. "Best I could do mate. Even the Abduls are running short."

"Thanks for that, Sarge. Sounds quiet up there; burial truce still on?"

"Been over for half an hour, but nobody seems too eager to start shooting again. Get the men sorted out, word is that Quinn's coming to visit."

*

The platoon was huddled near the engineers' dump in Seaview Terrace when Lieutenant Bebber arrived, accompanied by a powerfully-built, heavy-browed major. Bebber stepped onto a box.

"Men, we have a job to do. Beachy Bill has been getting too cheeky. He doesn't seem to worry about using up his ammunition or wearing out his barrel, and losses on the beach are becoming unacceptable. So we've been asked to do something about it. Problem is that we don't know where the damn' thing is. It has to be on Gaba Tepe. I need a five-man patrol to penetrate south and try to get a fix on it. Major Quinn has something he'd like to add."

Quinn stepped forward, smiling. "I still keep looking round for a major when someone calls me Major Quinn." He raised his voice. "Gentlemen, you know we've been suffering heavy losses from enemy bomb-throwers. They seem to have an inexhaustible supply of the bloody things, while we're limited by the amount of jam we can eat." He paused for a murmur of polite laughter. "General Chauvel has put in an urgent request for Mills Bombs, but in the meantime, I believe we could obtain a supply from much nearer at hand."

There was a general groan. "Fuckin' trench raid, I bloody knew it," moaned Snaff.

"Thank you corporal, I was just about to ask for volunteers, it's good of you to pre-empt me. Now, if I can have four more…"

Snaff found himself in a widening circle of space. He caught Bluey's eye before the red-moustached sniper could look away. "Good on yer mate, knew I could count on you."

Bluey looked around, easily spotting Cubby's bulk above the crowd. "I'm up for it if the Sarge'll come."

Cubby now found himself in a similarly widening circle. He grabbed a small bespectacled figure from the receding circumference. "OK, and Charlie here says he wouldn't miss it for the world."

Quinn chuckled. "The great Australian fighting spirit." He nodded at Cubby, "Good to see you McConnachie; we must go a few rounds again when things quieten down." He looked around. "OK, one more?"

As Cubby scanned the ranks for a suitable nominee, a voice from the opposite side of the terrace called out, "I'll go, sir."

Quinn peered at the tall, thin figure. "Thank you, private. Your name is?"

"Private Danny McConnachie, sir."

Cubby looked helplessly at his son, who grinned insouciantly back.

"Ah, joining the family business are we? Good for you. Would the five of you come with me please?" Quinn led the way to the command bunker.

CHAPTER 13

August 1916

Dear Andrew,

I've just heard that Dad's been wounded. They say that he will live, but I don't know how badly hurt he is. He is being brought back to a hospital in England, and I will let you know as soon as I know more.
I had one from Rob yesterday and he says he is fine, he sends his best, says to tell you he's bagged two Huns, which is more than your old crates can manage, don't blame me I'm just passing it on.

It is hard to keep smiling here with so many people away at the war. Mrs Appleyard has just heard that her son's been lost on a troopship that got torpedoed.

Do keep writing and pray that Dad gets better. Min's blooming and looking well.

All my love,

Mum

P.S. Just as I was about to post this I got a letter from Dad's captain. He was wounded in the leg and was apparently fighting very bravely. The captain says he should do well.

Andy stared at the blank notepaper and chewed his stub of pencil. The letter from home was already a week old, but still he found it impossible to find anything to write in reply. After a month of flying scouts, he was yet to score his first victory, despite vast expenditure of bullets. At first he'd put his perceived failure down to poor marksmanship, but lately he'd seen his tracers tracking accurately into German aircraft that seemed totally immune to damage. That his brother now had two kills to his name was made bearable only by the fact that Colin remained similarly stalled on his single half-kill.

He rubbed his neck. The last three weeks had been more exhausting than anything in his short life. His log book now showed eighty-five hours' flying, and seven aerial combats. French and Page were now tied on fourteen kills each; their Military Crosses had been cause for celebration two days ago. A dice cup rattled. Wheeler and Lynch-Fowler, two newcomers to C-Flight, were playing the battered *Jeu de l'Oie* set that became the inherited property of the hut's successive occupiers. Andy leaned back to watch them. A. Lynch-Fowler, known inevitably as Alf, had downed his first enemy aircraft two days after arriving. *What the bloody hell am I doing wrong?*

Wheeler looked up. "Want to play?"

Andy stood. "No thanks. Going for a walk."

A blustering, swerving wind masked the sun's warmth and teased the effel to and fro. Andy dug his hands into his pockets and watched his feet tramping the scrubby grass. He kicked to behead an offending dandelion. He'd hoped daily for a letter from Stainton.

The drone of an engine made him look up. A Bristol was turning in from the east, bobbing in the nervous wind. The red and white bands around the rear fuselage identified the pilot as Robière. Andy stopped to watch it. He longed to paint personal markings on his machine, but felt embarrassed to do so until he'd at least broken his duck. The little Canadian was obviously in high spirits, and he shed his excess height in a series of flamboyant side-slips. *I bet the little sod's got another one.*

The Bristol touched down tail-high on the cinders; Robière's unconventional landings had become a showpiece, and Andy watched with interest to see what entertainment was to come. Robière applied increasing down elevator as the machine lost speed, then neatly plucked it five feet into the air with the last dregs of lift under his wings. At the same moment the wind gusted the effel round its pole, tipping the Scout's tail into the air and depositing it gently on its upper wing. Andy saw the little pilot berating the uncaring world with clenched fists as he hung upside-down from his belt. *Serves you right you flash git.* He trotted over to help.

Andy was still fifty yards away when he saw the flicker of flame. Robière was still struggling with his belt, head bowed inside the cockpit. Andy broke into a run, screaming at the Canadian to get out as the fire rippled out along the upper wing.

By the time Andy reached the aircraft, both planes and the front fuselage were burning heavily. His hair crackled and he squinted his eyes against the blistering heat as he ducked under the fuselage to free the trapped pilot. Robière was curled into a struggling ball, pounding and tearing at his restraining strap. His body filled the narrow cockpit, blocking Andy from reaching in to help.

Andy felt a pull on his belt and fought to resist. His throat constricted against the searing heat as he panted and clawed at the writhing figure in the aircraft. The fire was now in the cockpit, and Robière's movements had become frenzied and uncontrolled. The pull tightened and Andy fell backwards, tumbling into the two ack emmas who dragged him from the pyre.

The mood in the mess at tea time was sombre. Andy, his left hand bandaged and face smeared with Vaseline, winced as the whisky touched his burned lips. With Cubby gone, the piano was silent, and Robière's Victrola sat unapproachable in its corner. The Recording Officer from 56 Squadron had telephoned to say that Robière had been seen to engage two Albatros two-seaters over Montplaisir, both of which were confirmed down out of control.

Henrik Doke sat down at the table and reached for the mustard pot. He was silent for a few seconds as he spread mustard on his sandwich, then looked at Andy, a triangle of bread and ham half way to his lips.

"Starting early aren't you?"

Andy examined his glass; "Not really. It burns like acid when I try to drink it anyway. Tongue's a bit burnt."

Doke bit into his sandwich. "Well get rid of it. There's a couple of hours of daylight left; let me finish this and then we'll blow those blues away with a bit of Hun-hunting."

"Normally I'd jump at that, but I'm just not in the mood tonight, Hen."

"Bugger your mood, bru. I've given you an order. And if you don't bag a Hun tonight, you're sacked."

Andy sighed, looked at his glass and nodded. "Aye-aye Captain," He tossed off his drink and spluttered at the pain. "Jesus Christ on a tram!"

*

Doke led the way to 11,000 feet over Raincheval. It was a beautiful spring evening; the sun edged the scattered cirrus with neon, shading to tangerine and purple in the west. An hour's patrolling had yielded nothing more dramatic than a hastily-retracted observation balloon near Beaumont-Hamel, and Andy expected an imminent washout signal from his leader. A movement caught his eye and he squinted again at the patched fields around Puisieux. Nothing there. Then he caught it again: two aircraft, two thousand feet below them, showed up white against a triangle of dark woodland. Doke saw them at the same moment and waggled his wings. With their backs to the westering sun, the two Nieuports were in an ideal attacking position. Doke led the way, maintaining height until they were within half a mile of the German machines, then dived, engine-on, steeply to the attack. Andy tucked in behind and pushed his stick forward, watching the speed build past 140.

Doke opened fire at on the leader, a blue Albatros C1, at 200 yards, keeping his gun flaming to within 50 yards of his quarry. The German observer threw up his arms and fell inside his cockpit, quick blood staining the fuselage. As Andy pulled over to follow the number two Albatros, he saw the Hun pilot's head jerk and glimpsed the blue biplane's uncontrolled roll into a steep inverted dive.

The number two machine had dull green wings and brownish fuselage. Andy found himself absently awarding the German pilot minimum points for artistic flair as he pulled to follow the second Albatros's turn. As the two aircraft began the descending spiral of a turning battle, Andy pulled the stick into his groin to bring his gun to bear. The German observer, meanwhile, took the opportunity to pepper the Nieuport. The little French machine shuddered as several shots struck home. Andy's aircraft was the faster and more manoeuvrable, but the German pilot was holding his aircraft near the stall, making it impossible for the Nieuport to show its superiority.

At 4,000 feet a 7.92mm bullet bit half through a cabane strut, and Andy felt splinters slash his cheeks. The situation was in danger of running out of hand. He pushed the stick forward to turn under the Hun's tail, breathing relief as the German gunner ceased fire to avoid destroying his own tailplane. The enemy pilot reacted rapidly, but his low speed made the Albatros sluggish. By the time he'd rolled out of his turn, Andy was already making energy in a shallow dive. With 100mph showing on the ASI he pulled tightly to bring himself behind and below his enemy.

Now the Albatros dived, desperately building speed from the sitting-duck crawl of the turning battle. With more than 30mph of extra pace already in hand, Andy closed to within 30yds of its belly within a few seconds before pulling back hard, throttle closed, directly underneath. The gap closed as he squeezed his trigger, unloading a full drum into the aircraft's underside. For a moment it looked as though he'd misjudged and the machines would collide, then the Nieuport lost momentum and hung momentarily in the air. Wood and fabric shredded from the Albatros, which suddenly climbed, stalled, and fell into a left-handed spin. Andy kicked right rudder and opened the throttle fully. The Nieuport nosed over and he lost sight of his adversary.

Righting his machine, Andy scanned the space below him for the Albatros. It was tumbling end-over-end, already two hundred feet below him. A limp figure hung half out of a cockpit, but it was impossible to guess whether it was the pilot or observer. He lost it at around 500 feet, but spotted smoke and flame as it struck the ground near the triangular coppice. He saw Doke's machine climbing from below and turned south west to meet him. The flight leader pulled alongside and waved an enthusiastic thumbs-up before looking more closely at Andy and pointing sharply at the younger man's face. Andy pulled off a glove, wincing as his hand encountered wooden splinters embedded in his raw, Vaseline-covered cheeks.

*

"Take the magneto out of my stomach,
And the butterfly valve off my neck,
Extract from my liver the crankshaft, There are lots of good parts in this wreck."

For Andy, Robière's wake was a strange contradiction of emotions. His burned, lacerated face throbbed and blisters were forming on his tongue. Each time he acknowledged a congratulating pat on the arm he saw Robbie writhing in his cockpit, spine bent backwards until his face was to the burning earth, mouth wide in a silent scream. Then the rebel thought would break through: *first confirmed kill. I've broken my duck.*

He searched for remorse for the death of the two German aviators he'd killed and found himself facing a void. He thought of Cubby and was shocked by a reflexive mental shrug. Something fundamental had happened to him today. The new Andrew Douglas Palmer could look back to the nightmare Saturday, when Cubby's mind had fled before the sight of massacre, and feel nothing more than vague regret. He thought of Stainton and was relieved to find that this new armoured integument still had some vulnerabilities.

He sipped his beer – spirits were too painful – and joined in the mournful chorus, the words blurred by his swollen tongue.

"Take the manifold out of my larynx,
And the cylinders out of my brain,
Take the piston rods out of my kidneys,
And assemble the engine again."

CHAPTER 14

May 1915

Quinn's bunker contained a rough table surrounded by wooden boxes. "Take a seat and help yourselves, men." He threw an opened cigarette packet onto the table and beckoned his orderly. "Parkin? Round of tea if you would."

He rolled out a map, weighting the corners with a tin ashtray, a framed photograph and a couple of .303 ammunition clips. "OK, we think Beachy Bill must be somewhere south of here, around the olive grove. The fly boys have had a baby elephant up looking for him, but wherever he is, he's got good cover."

Cubby leaned forward to examine the map. "It's about a mile as the crow flies, so probably three with all the nullahs crossing the line of march. Six hour patrol if we get held up by any sort of contact. It'll be getting close to dawn by the time we get back."

Quinn nodded, "I know. I need you men to find a hidden position with a good view, get entrenched before morning and stay there until nightfall. That's why I asked for volunteers."

Cubby snorted. "I know, McConnachie, there's only one real volunteer here, but that's the way the army works. This bloody gun has caused too many casualties. The beach is crammed with men and supplies; He can hardly miss. I need accurate coordinates to give to the Navy. If you can get eyes-on, you can tell us how deeply dug in he is."

"There's going to be plenty Abduls between him and us, sir. They'll hear us if we fart, let alone try to dig in."

"The Turks have individual snipers dotted around everywhere. Your best bet is to find one, bayonet him, and occupy his possie. When you get the chance on the second night, try to get into a Turkish trench and bring back as many bombs as you can filch."

"OK, we'll give it a birl, sir. But it's bull fodder isn't it?"

Quinn considered Cubby. Close-to he had a slight squint in his left eye. His tone was milder than his words, "Frightened, Sergeant?"

"Permanently sir. Cry myself to sleep most nights."

Quinn smiled. "Thought so. You boxed like a frightened man in Mena."

Cubby grinned back. "Hard to relax when you've got two hundred men watching you trying to punch a captain, sir. Especially when you've just found out he's the North Queensland light heavyweight champion."

Quinn was laughing now. He turned to the others, "McConnachie here went six rounds with me. Gave me a bloody nose and a bloody hard fight."

"You still bloody won though."

"Practice, Cubby. I'm used to fighting with gloves on. I wouldn't fancy fighting you without a referee present. Parkin, get us some more tea and be good enough to put a tot in everyone's mug."

Quinn inspected the dregs in his mug. "Yes, Cubby, it's all bullshit. The only way of getting from here to Gaba Tepe is to walk slowly towards the Turk trenches with your hands up. But we've got to do something about that gun." He tapped the map. "If you can get over MacLaurin's Hill and onto the western side of Second Ridge, you might well get a look at Billy Boy. That's a mile each way. Do that and the mission's a success."

"That and a case of bombs."

"The bombs are my addition so that I can point to something when you don't manage to get near Gaba Tepe."

Danny watched his father's relaxed familiarity with the major and yet again envied this empathy he seemed to engender in superiors and subordinates. There was nothing of calculation or manipulation: simply an instinctive confidence in his own worth. The father fitted the space the world made for him, while the son banged his elbows on life's sharp corners.

*

Cubby led his patrol, crouched low and silent, from the shallow trenches into the wider, deeper openings of Steele's Post. He stood gratefully, stretching his cramped back. In the front of the trench, a deeper blackness showed a tunnel entrance, the sentry seated on the fire step alongside it almost invisible against the sandbags. He nudged the lookout standing next to him and whispered, "Got company!"

Cubby moved closer to him, "Trusting sort aren't you? How'd you know we weren't Turks?"

"'Cos I'm still alive to hear you askin' me. You goin' over?"

"Yeah. Won't be back until tomorrow night. Do us a favour and make sure whoever's on guard knows we're expected."

"Will do, cobber."

"Thanks." He turned to his men. "OK, let's have a last look at you."

The four men shuffled into line. Only Bluey carried his rifle, swathed in cloth and fastened tightly across his pack. Cubby had ruled that rifles would be a liability when crawling through the scrubby thorns. If they met significant resistance, revolvers would be just as effective – or hopeless. But Bluey's sniper's eye and suppressed Lee Enfield were an essential contingency to his loose-laid plans for finding a way through the Turkish lines.

Cubby moved quickly along the short line, tugging straps and rattling pouches. He'd had each man bind his buckles with strips of cloth and pack ammunition boxes with rag or the sharp-edged, leathery grass that clumped everywhere. He nodded and moved softly to the southern rim. A whispered "Good luck you mad bastards!" from the lookout sent them on their way into the dark.

Two hundred yards of worming through the dusty scrub brought them parallel with German Officer's Trench and to the edge of their first barrier. The low voices of Turkish troopers could be heard from fifty paces to their left; a sudden outbreak of laughter was cut short by a sharp rebuke. From the lines a little to the north came a single flash and, half a second later, the crack of a rifle. Danny wondered whether the marksman was Turkish or Australian, and whether the bullet had found flesh.

Cubby was scouting ahead, looking for a way around the deep nullah that barred their way. To the right the ground fell sharply away in tumbled boulders and snagging gorse. A fall there would be death by a thousand cuts as much as by broken bones. To the left was the Turkish army.

As sweat dried, stiffening the eyelids with caked dust, the chill of the spring evening started its creep into cramped muscles, aching from the effort of the long crawl. Danny heard Charlie O'Neil drinking from his canteen alongside him and considered reminding him of Cubby's instruction to conserve water. After a moment's deliberation he carefully uncorked his own canteen and gulped a mouthful of tepid water.

A rustle in the darkness and Cubby was back. "No way round. It flattens out to the left, but kick a stone and the Jackos'll be on us like dogs on a steak. Go right and it's bouncy-bouncy all the way down. The nullah's only about ten feet deep, but it's steep as hell. Slip and make a noise and we're fucked. Go down one at a time, facing the wall. Use your hands."

The climb into the gully was treacherous. Groping hands repeatedly found inch-long thorns, and sharp flints slashed palms and knees. Snaff slid the last five feet in a clatter of stones. They froze, waiting for sounds of alarm from German Officer's Trench. The Turks remained quiet apart from the low rumble of conversation.

"You alright, Snaff?"

"Yeah, sorry Sarge. Got a thorn right up under me fingernail. Made me jump a bit."

"Looks like no harm done. All stay here while I have a look over."

The dark at the bottom of the gully was impenetrable. They felt, rather than saw, Cubby leave and begin to climb the southern wall, moving with a silent fluidity that belied his bulk. Raising his head cautiously above the rim he surveyed the ground ahead.

*

Kerem Sahin glanced up from his work as the sun dipped below the western horizon. He watched for a moment, hoping for the fabled green flash, but saw nothing as always. He returned to the work of cleaning the lair he'd dug with painstaking care, and then improved during the week he'd occupied it. His bedding was folded neatly under a canvas canopy that was anchored by stones on a rough shelf below the lip of the northern wall. Three petrol cans of water stood in its shade. A niche in the north-west housed his latrine, angled to hide it from the mihrab in the opposite wall.

He hurried to make the trench clean for Salah. He had no watch and worried that his maghrib would be late. When he left camp two days ago the Imam had reassured him that Allah would understand: "Kerem, you go into the wilderness; do you believe the Prophet took a pocket watch when he did the same?"

Kerem had smiled in embarrassment; the Imam was a captain of ancient days when viewed from his nineteen years. "No Imam, but perhaps the Archangel appeared to remind him."

The old man had thrown back his head, his grey-streaked beard standing stiffly horizontal from his valleyed throat. A low rumble bubbled from deep inside to gurgle in his throat. He pulled Kerem to him, kissing both cheeks and placing his palm on the young sniper's forehead. "May Allah bestow his blessings on you."

He has still been laughing quietly when Kerem left him.

Satisfied at last with the cleanliness of his trench, Kerem climbed to the fire step below the north wall and looked towards the enemy lines. Reassured that all was quiet he poured a little water into his bowl to wash himself for his early evening prayers.

Darkness fell fast. Kerem leaned on the parapet and fought sleep. Occasional flashes along the ridge to his right revealed that other snipers were looking down into the Australian trenches, loosing off a single round at an incautious match-strike. He hoped that he would see no target tonight. Even as the thought passed, he saw a distant glimmer and bent forward, his cheek against the sleek flank of his rifle. He blinked to clear his vision and peered through his sight. His exceptional eyesight and deadly accuracy justified the name his platoon mates called him: the Falcon. He'd been an obvious choice for sniper training, and the solitude suited his inner stillness. The killing he felt as a physical pain.

Two hundred yards away a careless Anzac was lighting his pipe, his face showing yellow through a gap in the sandbags. Kemel settled his cheek closer to the gun stock and exhaled gently, catching his breath just as his lungs emptied, and squeezed the trigger. A long second passed before the distant soldier whirled out of sight. Faint shouts reached him on the night air. He sat down on the fire step, rocking to and fro as he made a brief, guilty dua'a for the man he'd killed.

After a while he prepared himself for Isha'a. As always the prayer left him refreshed and he returned to his vigil with quiet dedication. By sometime after midnight the darkness was impenetrable. Heavy cloud made the sky barely lighter than the tumbled ground and Kerem slowly lost any accurate sense of where the Australian trenches lay. Relieved that he was unlikely to be required to kill again tonight he laid down his rifle and collected a small canteen and the latrine bucket, climbing out of the trench to empty it into the gully that ran across, twenty feet in front of his position.

A clatter of stones from his left and he froze, straining his ears, hearing nothing but the faint susurration of the breeze through the gorse. He lowered himself to a crouch, squinting at the black silhouettes of the bushes against the dark sky. Kemel cursed the noise of blood pumping in his ears; *was that a rustle?* A minute passed, two. Then something flickered in the corner of his eye. He peered into the darkness, flicking his eyes away to try to catch the movement again in his peripheral vision. A small break in the overcast lightened a clearing in the scrub and he saw the ears of a large buck hare standing alert, searching the night for danger. Remembering to breathe again, Kemel emptied the bucket and rinsed it with water from the canteen before walking back to his trench. The lid clanked softly as he replaced it.

Cubby was leaning on his forearms at the top of the nullah when he heard the splash of water from his left. He rested his chin on the backs of his hands and squinted at the skyline. For a moment the outline of a head showed in a flick of moonlight, then a faint metallic clank rang from 20 yards in front of his position. He waited for a few moments to satisfy himself that no one else was following before lowering himself carefully back to the gully floor.

"There's at least one Abdul dug in about twenty yards ahead, maybe more."

"Shit! How many?"

"No clue. I think it's a sniper, so probably no more than two."

"So what do we do?"

"If it's a sniper, we can use his possie. They usually dig in for two or three days, so he'll have water and supplies. There's a decent chance we can lie up in there all day."

"And what if there's a trench full of the bastards?"

"We snotter as many of them as we can and run all the way home."

"Fuck me Sarge, with military brains like yours around, how come we're losing?"

CHAPTER 15

September 1916

As the ack-emmas guided Andy's Nieuport into line he saw Colin already dismounted and examining an unfamiliar machine near the hangar. Andy banged his feet on the cockpit floor, partly to stamp circulation back into his extremities, but mainly through exhilaration after an eventful afternoon patrol. He and Colin had shared a victory over a too-bold AEG that overextended its luck while observing the British trenches. They'd then been forced to scrap furiously when a large group of Albatros had stooped on them. Another nameless new pilot had paid the price of his inexperience, his Bristol exploding to vapour and fluttering shards in the first second of their attack.

Andy dropped from his cockpit and joined the growing bunch of pilots clustered around the stranger, now recognisable as an RNAS Sopwith. Two mechanics were already unbolting the propeller, perched precariously on wobbling stepladders.

Colin dug Andy in the ribs, "Nice shooting, junior! Was that exciting enough for you?"

"I'll let you know when I've changed my breeches. So this is a 1½Strutter is it?"

"In the fabric. Not bad looking is it?"

"Suppose not, if you like two-seaters. Be better without all that Navy paint down the sides."

Page was leaning into the cockpit, admiring the synchronised Vickers mounted under the windscreen.

"This is the way to mount a gun. Right in your line of sight, and no bloody drums to change."

"And no bloody propeller if the gear goes wrong," observed Colin. "Which, not coincidentally, appears to be why it's here."

"Palmer!" Acting Major Barrington Holt was standing by the farmyard gate. "Couple of visitors for you in your hut. Make sure I have your report before you slope off somewhere!" He executed a regimental about-face and limped back to his office.

Sub-Lieutenant Robert Palmer was helping himself to his younger brother's tea-making provisions when Andy and Colin entered the hut. "Rob! Bloody hell! Rob! What are you doing here?"

"Well if dropping in for tea with my little brother isn't a good enough excuse, we'll put it down to mechanical problems."

They embraced, thumping each other's back. Rob was a couple of inches shorter than his brother, but more stocky, exuding a good-natured self-confidence that the younger man lacked. "This is Cyril Weaver, my gun layer."

Andy shook hands with a fair-haired youth and introduced the newcomers to Colin, who was already sloshing boiling water into a tannin-brown teapot.

"So, Bab, how's your war effort coming along?" asked Rob, commandeering one of the sagging chairs.

"Five and a quarter, if the one Col and I got today gets confirmed."

Rob nodded, "Not bad. I'd have made ten today if the bloody interrupter gear hadn't jammed."

Colin, pouring tea, nodded sympathetically, "I saw. Lucky you didn't lose the whole blade."

"Thought I was going to. The engine nearly fell out as it is. Still, gives me a chance to visit the family. Can you find us a bed tonight?"

"You can sleep in here. The bed over there's empty, and this one…" Andy paused, guilty in his callousness. "This one won't be needed now. Just let me clear out some stuff." Andy moved to the fourth cubicle and began collecting the precious irrelevancies of a young man he'd lived with and barely met.

Rob's voice followed him as he worked. "D'you hear the latest about Dad, Bab?"

"Not sure. Last I heard he'd got an infection in the leg, but Mom said he wasn't in danger. You heard anything more?"

"Yeah. It was gangrene. They had to take the leg off, Bab."

Andy leaned against the frail cubicle wall, eyes closed. "Oh Jesus, no. When did you hear?"

"Got a letter this morning. There'll be one on the way for you. They took it off at the knee."

Andy thought of his father: athletic and ebullient, running his two sons to exhaustion on beaches; leading them in whirlwind slaloms along park paths, three bicycles scything through rhododendroned archways; heard him muttering smutty jokes out of their mother's earshot; felt the lurch of him swinging the baby of the family shoulder-high to balance pennyworths of chips on his father's head. He met Rob's eyes and shook his head, wordless against the brutality of fate.

The moment was broken by Page kicking the base of the door; it had swollen in the recent wet weather and required some force to open it. "Heard you'd got visitors, one of whom seems to have charmed Barrie Holt to near-humanity. Thought I'd come and introduce meself."

Andy groped for an extra cup, settling for a tooth mug he found on a shelf in the cubicle. He wiped it with a stained tea towel and dropped it on the table. "Sure, come in Humph, pour yourself a cuppa. This is my brother Rob, and this is… Cyril?" A nod. "What's the news?"

Page shook hands and mixed condensed milk with the stewed lees from the teapot. He sipped and smacked his lips in appreciation.

"Perfect. So, Rob, I don't know what you said to our fearless adjutant, but he's given these two chancers the morning off tomorrow so that they can entertain the Navy properly tonight."

"The natural charm and authority of the Senior Service. These old-school soldiers can't resist it."

"Well you should bottle it, old chap, we'll buy it by the crate here." He drained his mug and dusted tea leaves off tongue and moustache. "Anyway, I just popped in to let you know I'm on orderly dog tomorrow, so if you've room for a littlun tonight, I'd be much obliged for an invite."

"Glad to have you Humph. Dinner in Beauval then?"

The estaminet had become dustier and the food more Spartan in the months since Andy and Colin had celebrated Colin's first kill, and Cubby had made his presentation of little-known antipodean fauna. The proprietor's wife still harboured some unguessable mistrust of the English aviators, glaring at them around the kitchen door and berating her husband as he passed back and forth with bottles and glasses. Their food was brought by one possible cause of her animosity. The daughter was a smiling, strongly-built student of divinity, recently returned from Paris. She had handed a tightly-wrapped infant to her mother before donning an apron to bring eggs and fried potatoes to the airmen. The matriarch dandled the child, her narrowed eyes accusing all Englishmen of its bastardry.

"So what's it like sharing a hut with my little brother?" Rob asked, plying knife and fork with enthusiasm. "His conversation's not too bad but he's got feet worse than death."

"Could be worse," said Colin. "He knows nothing about politics, religion or the war, so it's actually quite bearable."

"You should get him talking about Aston Villa."

"Really?"

"Yes, he knows bugger all about them as well." He addressed his plate again. "Hey, this isn't bad you know."

"Yes, makes you wonder how these Frenchies do it" answered Page. "This is egg and chips, a dish served in every tea room from Inverness to Eastbourne, and one that I've consumed, pissed and sober, many thousands of times. It normally tastes of nothing until you salt it, then it tastes of salt."

"Herbs and truffles. We English think the first are weeds and the second are poisonous." Colin shovelled a perilously dripping forkful of egg. "And we wash it down with stout or tea, not…" he squinted at the faded label on the wine bottle, giving up in the dim candlelight. "…whatever this is."

"The food's alright," opined Cyril Weaver, surprising at least three of the group that he actually possessed a voice. "But what egg and chips need is a dollop of Daddie's Favourite."

"He speaks! Miracles move among us!" Page raised his glass. "Though you speak only to utter heresy, I applaud the fact you have finally given tongue. Now tell us who you are."

Cyril glanced nervously around. "Well, you know who I am. I'm Cyril."

"No, that's what your parents called you. Who are you?"

"Er, well, that's who I am. Not much else to say."

"He's a man of few words is our Cyril," said Rob. "On account of he doesn't know very many." He nudged his gunner's shoulder. "Show him your picture, that'll keep him happy."

Cyril reached inside his tunic and fumbled out a fold of paper which he opened to reveal a white-scarred photograph. Page held it to a candle to make out a pale blur of face staring from a tightly-pinned cluster of dark hair. Whether the subject was Helen or Hector was largely indiscernible, but Page nodded and puffed his pipe appreciatively. "Ah, so you can be brought to earth by a pair of pretty blue eyes." He handed the photograph back.

"Brown. They're brown."

Page waved a hand, "No matter, no matter. I'm encouraged by this evidence of your humanity, and saddened by my own solitude." He shook the bottle, finding it nearly empty. *"Mam'selle! Une autre bouteille s'il vous plaît! Et un petit baiser pour un aviateur courageux, mais seul!"*

The proprietor's wife swept into the room, Lamashtu in a frilled blouse, hidden talons clicking on the parquet floor, the snorting baby her doomed nourishment. She towered above the flinching airmen and extended a clawed hand. *"Deux francs s'il vous plaît! Les baisers de ma fille sont deux francs!"*

Page rattled the change in his breeches pocket. "Pay up lads, and take your pleasure. I fear we may not leave this place alive else."

The daughter was summoned and dry, close-lipped kisses bestowed on the brave aviators. Fees were paid to the girl's procurer and Page announced himself well satisfied. He ordered coffee and cognac to accompany the fresh bottle of wine and extended an obliging knee when the waitress returned with the tray. She seemed fascinated by Page's piebald scars and nuzzled her broad head comfortably against his shoulder. *"Je m'appelle Josette m'sieur. Ce qui est vôtre?"*

The mother, satisfied that all had been respectably paid for, nodded approvingly from the kitchen door.

*

Rob's departure the following morning was clumsily formal. Neither brother felt ready to display open affection in front of the ack emmas. They shook hands by the fuselage of the Sopwith. "Well, tara Bab. It was good to see you."

"You too Rob. Let's do it again soon, eh?"

"Yeah, let's." He stepped up to the foothold in the fuselage side. "Give Humph and Colin my best, and you take care of yourself, little brother. I don't want letters about you." He swung into the cockpit.

Andy watched the Sopwith climb to a dwindling point, shaking away the conviction that he'd been with his brother for the last time.

CHAPTER 16

May 1915

Kemel made himself comfortable among the blankets under his awning. The night was chilly and he pulled the coarse wool tight around his chin. Many of the other snipers worked in pairs but he preferred solitude, entrusting his brief sleeping hours to Allah and to the secrecy of darkness. He stared through half-closed eyes at a clear patch of sky; an unknown constellation flashed ruler-straight lines up and across his latticed eyelashes. Nightjars churred in the gorse and some small creature rustled through the undergrowth nearby. He dozed, faintly appreciative of the coldly aromatic tang of the night on his nostrils.

A massive weight crushed him under the ruin of the awning. He heard the poles snap and found himself drowning in canvas and blankets. Sharp-edged boots trampled him and he felt a series of agonising stabs to his side, buttock and left thigh. He opened his mouth to call out but found himself too winded to breathe through the waterproofed cloth. Kemel's right arm had somehow come clear of the tangle and he flailed desperately, once again feeling the white-hot stabs, this time slashing his fingers and forearm. A ridged boot sole dislocated his jaw, exploding white flares behind his clenched eyelids. His fingers found a stubbled chin and he grabbed, his clawed grasp sinking nails into yielding flesh. The lancing pains came again, grating against ribs, drawing bubbling froth from his lungs, slicing boiling-cold into his lower back and kidneys. The cloth was snatched away from his face and he glimpsed dark clustered faces as he sucked greedily at the air. He felt a gentle tap at the side of his neck and tried to cough away sudden phlegm. Warm liquid surged into his throat, engulfing his breath; he struggled weakly, finding his arms pinioned by the dark shapes. A harsh rattle filled his ears, closer and louder by far than the nightjars.

Snaff and Bluey were the first to drop into the sniper's trench. Snaff immediately became entangled with some unseen construction of sticks and oiled canvas. A pole dug painfully into his armpit as it broke. Bluey had landed in the clear and was struggling with the writhing swaddled figure under the cloth. Snaff unsheathed his bayonet, holding it like a dagger, and plunged it repeatedly into the heaving shapelessness under him. More figures dropped heavily into the trench and Snaff felt a blade scythe across his knuckles. A hand found his cheek and dug deep, tearing his skin.

A trick of moonlight lit the Turk's face as the blanket fell away. Danny's head was against his face, his arm wrapped tightly around his enemy's forehead. His elbow jerked from left to right and the sniper's gasps turned to a bubbling rattle. Danny held the Turk almost tenderly as he drowned, the splashing blood sounding like someone urinating in the darkness.

Cubby felt the Turk's eyelids as they fluttered a last time and were still. "OK, he's gone." He pulled the dead sniper off his son, surprised to find the body so slight and frail after the desperate strength of its last moments. Danny had rolled under their adversary, his legs wrapped around the sniper's waist while his left arm pulled the head back to expose the throat. Now he lay, exhausted, in warm stinking mud.

Cubby was peering over the far side of the trench at the Turkish trenches a hundred yards away. "Don't think they heard anything. Christ knows how. Anybody hurt?"

Both Snaff and Bluey had received gashes from the flailing bayonets of their allies. Charlie O'Neill's glasses had been broken by an elbow that had driven the metal frame into his cheekbone, raising a swelling that already threatened to close his left eye.

"Fuck me, it's a good job there weren't two of 'em or we wouldn't have stood a chance."

Dawn found them huddled against the trench wall, legs drawn in as though shrinking away from their murdered victim. The Turk was a bloody bag of rags. He lay openmouthed, his torn throat stretched open by his lolling head. As the sun found the corpse, so the flies began the work of the day. Snaff examined his hands. The right middle finger was badly swollen, the dark shape of a half-inch thorn visible under the nail. A deep slash extended across the palm from thumb to little finger.

"That little bastard put up a hell of a fight."

"We were fighting ourselves. The poor bastard never stood a chance." Danny sat a little apart, head down, forearms resting on his elbows.

"You snottered him a treat though. Ear to ear, like topping a sheep."

Danny's head came up and he regarded Snaff for a long moment. "The job was to kill him before he could call for help. I did the job." He looked back to the corpse and stood. "Help me cover him up."

"No way. I've got enough blood on me already."

"He won't bleed anymore. We need to do something about the flies."

Cubby had spoken little since the killing. Now he stood, crouching to keep his head below the trench line. "I'll help."

They carefully unwound the body from the blankets. Danny splashed water onto a scrap of canvas and cleaned the Turk's face. Cubby paused, considering his son for a moment, then nodded slightly and began wrapping the corpse, first in the blood-soaked blankets, then in the canvas from the awning. They crossed Kemel's hands tightly under the swaddling and laid him on his right side, facing the shrine in the south-east wall.

Charlie, Bluey and Snaff looked on, baffled. Snaff snorted, "S'truth, I thought you were going to kiss him goodnight!"

"He's a human being Snaff. And if the Turks find us in this hole, they aren't going to go easy on us once they see what we did to some poor kid from Constantinople. At least they'll see we treated him with some respect; that might make a difference to our chances."

The day grew warm as the sun found their foxhole, dispelling the spring mist. The Turkish sniper had been well-supplied with water, making a reasonably palatable breakfast of their dry rations. Cubby had retrieved the Kemel's skullcap, which he placed on Danny's head. "You're about his build. Just let yourself be seen from the Jackos' trenches now and again; we don't want 'em popping over to see if he's lonely."

The drone of an aero engine made them look up. An aircraft appeared above the ridge line to the south, the black crosses on its wings showing dark against the pale fabric. "Everybody tuck in against the south wall!" Cubby was on his feet, bundling the slow-moving O'Neill into cover. "Danny, grab the Jacko's rifle and get over to the loophole and look as if you're aiming at something. Keep your head down, you don't want a bullet from one of our snipers."

The German aircraft zigzagged along the ridge, slowly gaining height. Danny glanced at it over his shoulder and reported its position to his companions. "He's coming this way. If he sees you lot hiding under the wall he's going to think something's fishy."

"If he sees five of us in a sniper's possie he's going to know it for sure," replied Cubby. "We better hope he's looking somewhere else."

Danny glanced up again. "He's going to pass a bit to the west; probably more interested in the beaches. If you get under the south-west wall you should be OK. Going to be close though."

The aircraft passed almost overhead, going north. Danny watched it go by, wondering whether to wave. "It's a Rumpler."

"S'truth Macca, you know bloody everything."

"I've been reading about aeroplanes, Snaff. First chance I get I'm transferring. That's the life for me, sitting up there away from the flies and the whizz-bangs."

"You're madder than I thought, mate. You wouldn't get me up in one of those, they're not safe."

"Whereas sitting in the middle of a thousand Turks is safer than the Post Office."

"I suppose that's a point," Snaff conceded. "Shit or stingers."

"You got your name down then?" asked Bluey.

"Since Cairo. The Pommies are desperate for aviators on the Western Front."

"And I'm going to be his observer," added Cubby. "The Flying MacConnachies. Maybe we'll become a circus act after the war."

"Yes, well it might not work out like that. There's nothing saying we'll both get transferred, or that we'll go to the same place if we do." Whether Danny thought that good or bad was unclear.

The day became hot. Flies swarmed on the bloody patch where Kemel had slept, and probed the folds of canvas that wrapped his body. Snaff took over on watch, taking the skull cap from Danny. O'Neill was too short – and too short-sighted - to see clearly over the parapet, while Bluey's flaming hair and moustache would flash like a beacon to any Turk looking in the right direction. Cubby's sandy hair might pass unnoticed under the skull cap if the lookout rotation became too exhausting. It was clear that their vantage was worthless for a sighting of any guns on Gaba Tepe. The ridge to their south created a false summit that blocked out all but the hill's peak. The prospect of pushing further under cover of darkness, and the near-certainty of another day spent lying up dampened even Snaff's spirits.

"Anybody know the time?"

Bluey consulted his wristwatch. "A quarter of eleven."

"Christ, it feels like we've been cooking in this hole for hours. Shit!" He flinched as a bullet kicked powdery dust into his eyes, the ricochet whining evilly into the blue.

"You OK mate?" Cubby and Danny reached him simultaneously as he crouched under the trench wall. Snaff was coughing furiously, grinding the heels of his hands into his eyes. They gently pulled his hands away.

"Jesus, I dunno. I think I'm blinded." His face was covered in pepper-dun dust; his eyes blinked uncontrollably.

"I think you're alright mate. Danny, slosh some water in his eyes."

Danny already had his canteen uncorked. He splashed water over Snaff's face and the frenzied blinking subsided. He squinted at his two companions. "Sorry, thought I was blinded. And by a fucking Aussie."

"Teach you to keep your head down. Better fire a couple of shots back to show they missed. We don't want the Jackos coming over to see if Mustafa here is still alive."

Danny was picking up the rifle when the Rumpler found them. It droned over their trench at no more than two hundred feet, banking left. The Australians froze.

"Oh shit. We must have missed the noise in the excitement. Now we're for it."

The German observer was looking straight at them. Danny waved and took up station on the north parapet. He fired two rapid shots towards the Australian trenches, aiming low.

"What's he doing now?"

Cubby's eyes seemed locked with the German's, the intervening space contracting to bring them to mortal intimacy. "Not sure. He's going east, but the observer's still leaning over the side to look at us. He knows something's up."

Danny looked round in time to see a red flare arc from the Rumpler's rear cockpit. The aircraft banked into a hard turn.

Cubby was on his feet. "That's it, we're fucked. Everybody over the side and down the west slope."

O'Neil screamed back, "The Jackos'll cut us to pieces!"

"The Jackos'll be here in person in two minutes. And when they see what you've done to Mustafa they won't be friendly. Keep low and run!"

The flare seemed to have caught the Turks by surprise, and the appearance of five running figures elicited no response for several seconds. Then the air hummed with fury. The gorse twitched and snapped around them. They ran in desperation, half-crouched, thorns tearing at their puttees, unseen holes wrenching at their ankles. O'Neil fell heavily, only to rise immediately and run on, limping slightly. The Rumpler dived on them, the observer leaning far out of the rear cockpit to take potshots with his rifle. Then the ground disappeared. Their blind flight had carried them to and over the edge of the ravine. They slid, bounced and tumbled over rocks and through scrub. The Rumpler's shadow flashed over them and Cubby, floating in slow motion, once again locked eyes with the observer before the rocks and gorse took him again.

CHAPTER 17

October 1916

The afternoon job was uneventful. Scudding cloud at 1,000 feet had discouraged the Germans and the patrol proceeded undisturbed. C-Flight flew through wisps of grey-white, top planes brushing the cloud wrack, safe for now from diving Hun. Rumours of the presence of the fabled Boelcke being in the area had been confirmed a few days earlier; he had taken command of a hand-picked group of pilots, among them the almost equally feared Böhme and Richthofen. They were equipped with the new twin-gunned Albatros D1, a fearsomely fast and deadly steed for these elite knights of a new Round Table.

Archie depleted the Reichsbank to the tune of several million marks, the puffs of black wool reassuring the British airmen that they were alone in the sky. Andy nodded appreciatively when Doke gave the wash-out signal and he turned his nose to follow the leader home.

They were met on the ground by Colin and Page. "Get yourselves a wash and smarten up. Visit from G.O.C. He's speaking to us in the mess in 15 minutes."

The buzz of conversation died rapidly as Major Tiverton tapped his stick on a table. "Gentlemen, we're honoured by a visit from Major-General Trenchard." He turned to the dark-haired, intense officer by his side. "General."

"Long winded as always. Can't stand these long introductions," muttered Page.

Trenchard's deep bass voice contrasted strongly with Tiverton's somewhat uncertain tenor, but his speech was uncertain and halting.

"Thank you, Major. It's… er… fine to see you all. We've heard a lot about… um… a German pilot recently who…" He stopped completely, examining the end of his swagger stick. After a few seconds he resumed, frowning at the stick as though the words were written small on its head. "Whose name is… er… Boelcke. Well, we… that is… my staff and I…" He looked appealingly at his aide, who nodded. Trenchard relaxed slightly and gestured to the staff officer alongside him. "Boelcke. Yes. Important you know more. Captain Baring will tell you…"

Trenchard stepped back, massaging his left side with his thumb.

Captain Baring was a plump, balding man with a heavy moustache and a relaxed, jocular demeanour. He stepped forward confidently. "Well gentlemen, I expect you're all eager to hear me tell you what fine fellows you all are, and that the King, the GOC and I are confident that you'll smash the wily Hun at every opportunity."

A wave of polite laughter rumbled through the mess. Baring nodded, smiling slightly.

"Well as it goes, that's quite true, but I have no intention of delaying your tea by telling you so."

The laughter was more convincing, even accompanied by one or two claps.

"I know there's been a deal of talk about the presence of the dastardly Boelcke and his chums in the area. While it's true that he is around, and that he has a potent new machine, he is not invincible, and nor are his pilots. Immelmann was no immortal, as Lieutenant McCubbin proved. Boelcke will fall as certainly as night follows day."

He consulted a printed sheet in his hand.

"Boelcke's squadron follows a strict modus operandi. His tactics are effective, but predictable." He held up the paper. "A copy of these tactics will be posted on the board. I want you to read and discuss them; adopt those elements that are useful, and develop your own strategies for answering them.

"The Albatros D1 is a formidable aircraft. It is fast, climbs well and has two synchronised machine guns. It is, however, heavy and therefore less manoeuvrable. Your Nieuports and Bristols have the advantage in a turning fight." Baring looked around the room, seeing rapt attention. "One noticeable deviation from the norm is that Boelcke's squadron tends to push home an attack. They don't dive, fire and clear the way other Hun tend to. So if you avoid their first swoop, don't make the mistake of thinking it's all over; turn into them and use your superior manoeuvrability to get a killing shot."

Baring paused, glancing at Tiverton, who nodded, smiling.

"Now, on a lighter note, Major Tiverton has been kind enough to allow us to make some announcements. Would Captain Holt step forward please?"

Acting Major Barrington Holt limped jerkily to Baring's side.

"Captain Holt, I'm delighted to say that your acting rank has been confirmed. Congratulations, Major."

He and Trenchard shook hands with the Recording Officer, who saluted smartly as his hand was released. He acknowledged the mess's dutiful applause with a sharp nod and a twitch of the mouth.

"And now, Captains French and Page please."

French and Page detached themselves from the crowd and stepped forward, glancing at one another. Trenchard accepted two small black cases from his aide.

"I take great, er, pleasure... um... His Majesty's deepest appreciation... and two Military Crosses. Congratulations gentlemen... courage and zeal... an example to us all."

The applause was accompanied this time by cheers and whoops. French and Page saluted, bumping each other awkwardly in their pleased embarrassment. Baring raised a hand for silence.

"Gentlemen, we will impose on your time no longer. I have no doubt that you will wish to congratulate your friends properly, and you can do that with far more alacrity without the looming presence of a red collar. The General hopes you will accept a small offering to your celebrations. Thank you."

Baring placed an opened wooden crate on the table, producing an encouraging clink of glass. He accepted his ovation with the practised wave of a true performer, he and Trenchard shook hands with Tiverton and Holt and exited the mess.

The smash-up that evening achieved Bacchanalian proportions. The cloud had lowered even further, unleashing such torrents as would leave the airfield too sodden to use tomorrow, even should the deluge abate. Trenchard's benison proved to be a dozen bottles of champagne, which disappeared rapidly in toasts. Here's to the G.O.C! Splendid chap! Bit of a pilot himself don't you know? By the time the King's health had been drunk and the speeches begun, whiskies were in evidence everywhere, and the soda siphons scattered copiously among the tables presaged an aqueous battle royal.

Page stood, swaying slightly, to reply to Tiverton's congratulatory speech. "Thank you Henry. I look forward to wearing my decoration with pride, and hope that it will carry me to great victories in my battle against feminine chastity."

Cheers and cat-calls encouraged this auspicious start. Page touched his white-seamed face.

"Only in wartime could a face resembling cured ham represent an advantage in carnal ambition. Wearing this bauble I intend to achieve even greater success than I have previously enjoyed."

"Who with? The farmer's sow?" Doke's boots were on the table, threatening the agglomeration of bottles.

"No, Henrik, attractive as she is, I respect you too much to cuckold you."

Doke snatched the nearest soda siphon and prepared to open hostilities. Page restrained him with a gesture. "Before the evening's festivities transcend into open warfare, I ask you to raise your glasses to our loved and respected Recording Officer. Gentlemen, Acting Major Barrington Holt no longer, I give you *Substantive* Major Barrington Holt!"

The adjutant's reply was brief, but nonetheless incomplete when the first bread was thrown, soda siphons discharged, and the cracks of breaking furniture drowned out his clipped accents.

CHAPTER 18

May 1915

The gorse bush was absurdly comfortable. Cubby looked at his left boot, vaguely disturbed by the way it pointed out to sea. The puttee above the scuffed leather showed a spreading dark stain. He turned his head to look around, blinking as the horizon spun sickeningly in the opposite direction. He closed his eyes: *I'll just snooze in the sun until I wake up properly.*

Danny and Snaff found him fifteen minutes later. The gorse bush that had stopped his fall was rooted in a craggy outcrop, twelve feet above the steep floor of the nullah. Danny climbed up to find his father, apparently unconscious and snoring slightly, a deep gash darkening his sandy hair. Cubby's left foot was rotated to point slightly backwards, his puttee bloodsoaked and fly-infested. He opened his eyes as Danny's shadow fell across his face.

"Gidday Danny."

"Hullo Dad. How you doing?"

"Think I've come a bit of a box of tacks. Suppose I'd better move." He made to get up, making the gorse creak ominously.

Danny put a restraining hand on his shoulder. "Better let us help you, Dad. You've done yourself enough damage."

Cubby came fully awake, his head jerking upwards. "Christ, where's the plane gone?"

"Seems to have gone home. Probably out of fuel after the patrol. He'll be back though; we need to move." He reached under Cubby's shoulders to pull him forward, stopping when the older man gasped in pain. "You hurt somewhere else?"

Cubby nodded, breathing in shallow pants. "Think I've done my ribs as well."

"OK, well we've got to get out of here. The Jackos know where we are, and that Rumpler could be back any time. Get some morphine inside you and we'll have another go." He placed two tablets into his father's mouth and held the canteen to his lips.

It took a further ten minutes to lower Cubby to reasonably level ground, by which time he'd lost consciousness, whether from the morphine or the head wound was impossible to say. They stumbled downhill, tracking as far as possible to the north, Danny holding his father's arms over his own shoulders, the forearms crossed on his chest. He fancied he could feel ribs grinding against his back. They walked for fifteen minutes, stopping to rest in a deep gully that sheltered them from the pulverising sun. Danny took advantage of his father's unconsciousness to remove his left boot and examine the foot. It was blue and cool to the touch, jutting unnaturally from the blackening puttee.

"I don't like the look of this."

Snaff looked over his shoulder. "Christ, he's made a bit of a bugger of that. It can't be getting any blood, twisted round backwards like that."

"I think we should try to straighten it up."

"What? You're fucking kidding me! The linseeds always say leave things be until they get to it."

"Find me one right now and we'll leave it to him. No? So we're going to have to do it ourselves, or I think this foot's a goner."

Danny unwound the stiffened cloth of the puttee, feeling the foot sag ever more loosely in his other hand. He wondered whether it was completely severed under the bindings; began to worry that it would actually fall off. In the event it remained attached, but flopped bonelessly as though held in place only by the blue stretched skin. The flesh was torn away in front of the ankle, leaving a half-crown sized crater that began bleeding again as the puttee was pulled away. They improvised splints from their bayonets, fixing them in place with bindings made from both of Cubby's puttees. After an anxious few minutes, a slight pink flush crept into the dead flesh and the toes twitched slightly.

They started at a sound from outside the gully, shrinking into shadow as a figure pushed through the scrubby bushes. Bluey's carrot hair emerged into the small clearing.

"Found Charlie. He's gone." He lowered himself to lean against the cool rock. "How's the Sarge?"

"Not sure. This foot looks bad, but I don't know about the head wound. He was woozy before I gave him the morphine. What about Charlie?"

"He went all the way down. There's a cliff over that way. Got to be forty-fifty feet. He's at the bottom of that. Broke his skull, his neck, pretty much everything. You two alright?"

"Few sprains and scratches. Nothing much. I think we should stay here until dark."

"You don't think the Abduls'll come looking for us?"

Danny shrugged. "No knowing, but for now they don't know where we are, and we're concealed from the Rumpler. If we move, anyone on the ridge will see us straight away."

Bluey looked at Snaff, who was examining his swollen finger. "What d'you think, Corp?"

Snaff sucked at the thorn under the fingernail. "This fucker's got to be an inch long." He glanced up. "Me? No idea Blue. I think we're fucked either way."

The afternoon plodded towards distant dusk. By mid-afternoon their canteens were empty, and clouds of biting insects found their refuge. They slapped, sweated and cursed away the clumping hours as the sun craned its neck to glower directly into the gulley, glaring away the cooling shadows. Each of them would look again and again at the canteen hanging from Cubby's belt; each would catch another's eye and look guiltily away.

Cubby woke up as the light finally began to yellow. He raised his head and winced in pain. "Christ, that hurts!" He licked his caked lips. "Anybody got any water?"

Danny uncorked the canteen and held it to his father's lips. "Here, we saved you some."

The older man swallowed gratefully. "Thanks. How are we doing?"

"Not so good. Charlie's a write-off, and you're as crook as. We thought we'd wait for dark and try to walk north along the coast."

"No sign of the Jackos?"

"Not a peep. Seems like they've forgotten us. We heard the Rumpler stooging around, but we've not seen him once."

Cubby nodded, grimacing as the movement fired darts behind his eyes. "They probably don't think we're worth the petrol." He handed the canteen to Danny. "Get some of that down you and pass it on."

"No, we're OK, we've been drinking our own." Danny stilled Snaff's gesture of protest with a dangerous look.

"Dare say you have. But you wouldn't all be sandpapering your lips like that if you'd got any left." He tried to pull himself up onto one elbow, gave up and sank back. "I'm not going to be doing much walking, so I reckon you blokes are the ones who need it. We'll find somewhere to fill up when we imshi."

The canteen was passed around and each savoured a mouthful of warm water. Finally, the day slipped into cool darkness.

Snaff, who seemed to have conceded his rank to Danny, merely nodded when the younger man announced it was time to start their march home. Danny placed a morphine tablet between Cubby's lips, upending the canteen to let the last dregs of water wash it down.

"We'll give that a minute to work and then make our move. This is going to hurt like a bastard I'm afraid."

The pain of being hoisted onto Danny's shoulders was worse than any of them had expected. Cubby snorted and swore through clenched teeth, fighting back the need to scream in torment. As they left the gulley, each footstep drew a grunt and a low cry as splintered ribs ground against one another. Every twenty-odd steps, his dangling left foot would strike Danny's boot, sending twanging jolts of agony along overloaded nerves to strike fire in his broken head. They walked in silence, Bluey leading, his sniper's eyes constantly scanning the silhouetted, scrubby ridges. Snaff brought up the rear, rarely glancing up from worrying and gnawing at his injured finger, now swollen and purple.

Bluey stopped so suddenly that Danny, plodding with head down, collided heavily with his pack. He looked up in surprise. "What's up?" he whispered.

Bluey pointed at the darkness ahead. "Think I heard something down there. Talking."

They waited in silence, straining their ears to hear human sounds among the chirring insects. Bluey slid his pack off his shoulders and unslung his rifle. "Wait here." He slid into blackness. Danny lowered his father gently to the ground. Cubby was either asleep or unconscious, and merely whimpered faintly. A rustle in the moon-clouded gloom said that Snaff had sat or lain down. Ten minutes dragged by.

A flash lit the bushes two hundred yards lower down towards the seashore, followed a second later by a sharp crack. A hollower, oddly bell-like ring and a dimmer flash came from closer at hand as Bluey returned fire. Danny was immediately on his feet. Telling Snaff to wait he slipped into the night after the sniper. Bluey was no more than twenty yards on, prone against a rocky rise. Danny dropped next to him and peered ahead.

"What's down there?"

"Dunno. I think it's a lone sniper. I popped one back at him, but then it struck me that he might be one of ours."

"Inconvenient."

"Yeah. Well friendly or not, he pops another one at us and I'll put one up his nose."

Another flash, this time from higher up the slope. Bluey swung his rifle right and loosed off two rapid rounds.

"Shit, he's good. We need to move. He's got us skylined from where he is now."

The grenades came from the slope immediately above them. The first bounced off the rock and clattered fizzing into darkness, exploding harmlessly in a deep nullah. The second fell between the two Australians, lodging slightly under Bluey's body. Danny was rolling away when a numbing concussion blasted his eardrums and a million iron hailstones stopped his breath.

CHAPTER 19

October 1916

It was a foul evening to be flying. The wind refused to commit to any particular point of the compass, nor even to settle on any predictable strength. Clouds streamed in confused tatters, causing the six scouts to bunch up in the poor visibility. The bumps and faults in the wind caused even Andy, by now a practised hand, to grab repeatedly at the stick, his left hand forever adjusting the revs to stay in formation. The newer pilots bounced and swerved unpredictably, constantly threatening to collide with their neighbours and tumble, tangle-winged to their deaths.

Andy, his Nieuport, for the first time wearing a deputy flight-leader's streamer, was out on the left of the echelon. Doke was occasionally visible in the leader's position, while Colin was presumably on station somewhere in the murk beyond him. They were at three thousand and further south than usual; Oswald Boelcke had broken the mould of the Germans' customary caution by leading his Jasta deep into Allied territory to prey on airmen when their watchfulness relaxed with the promise of home. The thread of the main Amiens-Beauvais road appeared fleetingly through the swirling grey below their wings. Andy pulled slightly out of line to warm his gun. The trigger felt stiff under his finger, but a one-second burst of tracer reassured him that, in Cubby's words, it would make a nice loud noise when he pulled the trigger. He wondered how the antipodean giant was progressing, feeling a familiar guilt that he'd done nothing to find out. He'd known him for a couple of weeks, several months ago, had learned from him how to survive the weeks from Fokker fodder to competence. Had seen how courage genuinely did mean laughing at danger; the image of Cubby's huge grin as he shook blood from his shrapnelled hand played across his mind.

Courage. What a capricious mistress she had turned out to be. She was glamorous, admirable, lusted after; wantonly receiving any of those willing to pay her price. And cold as wire when she tired of your springheel dancing on air. She had spent months on Andy's arm, fluttering kohl-black lashes at his victories, shudder-swooning at his macadam-skimming mastery of this fiery scout.

And left him in a moment for a dashing, handsome German. Oswald Boelcke had taken her fancy and she had abandoned him to be wooed by her empty-eyed, grey-haired sister.

White puffs of Archie drew Andy's attention. Dark specks were spiralling above a village three miles ahead. The French gunners had presumably seen the British flight and fired off a few rounds to draw their attention to an intruder. Doke saw the explosions and fired a Very light to command the attack. He began climbing gently, groping for the maximum height at which the scudding cloud would allow visibility of the Huns. Andy raised the nose and followed the others. Two minutes to the battle; possibly two minutes to live; two minutes to wonder how he'd measure against the best airborne soldier the world had ever seen.

The spiralling combatants quickly resolved into a pair of DH2s, being harried by a pack of half a dozen Albatros DIIs. The de Havillands were well handled and manoeuvrable, but hopelessly outclassed as well as outnumbered. Doke opened fire early, hoping to draw some of the enemy aircraft away and split the formation. Two of the sharp-nosed machines twisted to meet the new threat. Andy pulled in behind his leader, feeling the buffet as he passed through Doke's slipstream.

The lead Albatros was climbing strongly to meet them, its power apparently limitless. Andy pulled to the left to clear his firing line and saw seemingly solid bars of tracer connecting Doke's Nieuport and the yellow-brown enemy. Closing at over two hundred miles an hour, the three aircraft consumed the intervening air in seconds. Doke pulled right to avoid a collision and the German pilot rolled left to meet him, raking the Nieuport's belly from its twin guns. The little scout seemed to stop dead, suspended on air, then both right wings crumpled and it fell, twisting, to the greyness below.

The Albatros was already turning to meet Andy's dive, wasting no time to watch the tumble of another foe found wanting in the great contest. Its guns flashed and Andy felt his aircraft shudder. But the zooming momentum of the German machine's great weight had finally expired and it sagged away, dropping its right wing in an incipient spin. Andy peered into his Aldis, squeezing his trigger and watching tracer arc down to pierce the black-crossed wings.

Two seconds of accurate fire, urged and steered by Andy's body as he twisted in his seat, mentally conning the bullets into the German, then the Albatros was gone, diving for the patched greys of the French fields. Andy rolled inverted and pulled back hard on the stick, looking up at the ground and the spiralling enemy. He saw the Albatros roll out of the dive, clearly still under control, and climb back towards the turning pack of DH2s. He pulled back harder into a near-vertical dive, aileron-rolling level and straining forward to urge more speed out of his machine.

The turning battle had split up, and the two DH2s were now fighting for their lives, each with an Albatros in crackling attendance. Apart from these and Andy's adversary, which was now closing on the nearer de Havilland, the sky had emptied. The distance between them closed and Andy's finger hovered over his trigger. He forced himself to wait until point-blank range guaranteed his revenge. The two Albatros were identical, both having yellow-brown patchwork fuselages and random blue-green patterns on their wings. The leader had opened fire on the swerving de Havilland, his tail covered by Andy's intended victim. Satisfied at last with the range, Andy squeezed his trigger, felt that stiffness again. Tracer sprayed towards the German for a second before the trigger went slack.

As the first bullets hit his centre section, the German pilot twisted in his seat and stared into the eyes of the British pilot less than fifty yards away. At the same moment the second DH2 flashed across the nose of the lead aircraft, pursued by the third Albatros, this one a dull brown with red and turquoise stripes on wings and tail. Andy glimpsed the fair hair of its helmetless pilot ruffling in the wind.

The leading German machine pulled up sharply, its top plane striking the undercarriage of the second, whose pilot was still looking over his shoulder. The two aircraft checked sharply, causing Andy to pull hard out of line to avoid joining the crash. When he caught sight of them again he saw his adversary flying level, one wheel dangling. The other Albatros was descending slowly, a long streamer of fabric flapping from its top plane. It dropped into a tuft of cloud and disappeared. Andy side-slipped to lose height, scanning the cloud for the reappearance of the German.

The aircraft that emerged from the cloud had become a monoplane. Somewhere in the murk the damaged top wing had torn loose, taking all four main struts with it. How it had done so without decapitating the pilot was a mystery, but the machine was clearly still under control. *God, that guy's good*.

As the crippled machine neared the ground, the second damaged Albatros reappeared, fussing around its mate like a distraught blackbird. Andy pulled the Lewis gun down to his cockpit, shouting his frustration. The Bowden cable had pulled out of its restraining nipple. He tried operating the gun directly but was unable to move the trigger.

The stricken Albatros remained under control all the way to the ground, touching down surprisingly gently before dropping a wing and ground-looping, finally performing a slow tip-over. There was no fire and Andy found himself hoping that the German pilot had survived uninjured.

As the second damaged Hun cleared to the east, Andy finally accepted that the gun jam could not be cleared and prudently remembered the unseen presence of four or five other Albatros. He turned the nose to the north and home.

It is unlikely that Doke would have approved of his wake that evening. Alcohol had become scarce recently and the mess ran dry before ten o'clock. Andy nursed the warm, flat remains of a particularly sour beer and thought about the day. Colin was cracking walnuts, the majority of which contained the shrunken, mummified fewmets of some midget dragon. He scooped the debris onto a tin tray and stood up. "Sod this, fancy a game of vingty?"

"Not just now, mate."

Colin sat down again. "Feeling low about Henrik?"

"No, not that." He toyed with a fragment of nutshell. "Well, yes, that, but… but just everything. I've just had enough of it. I had wind-up like hell when we went in today."

Colin snorted. "Wind-up? You? Do me a favour!" He sobered quickly. "You're just knackered, that's all. We all are. You can't do two-three jobs a day for months on end and expect to stay 98.4."

"Maybe. But what's the difference? It doesn't matter *why* I've got wind-up, it's *that* I've got wind-up that's the problem. I knew I could be going up against Boelcke and I was shitting myself. I was bloody terrified."

"Well here's a snippet of news to allay your terror m'boy!" Page slapped Andy's back and placed a half-bottle of whisky on the table. "Just liberated that from Henry's stores. Have a swig and listen to my tales of derring-do!"

Page seated himself comfortably and waited for the bottle to complete its rounds.

"I refer to Lieutenant Palmer's report dated 28 October 1916." He consulted a pencilled sheet in his hand. "Engaged several Albatros DIIs over Flers. Captain Doke engaged leader head-on and was shot down. I engaged same but was unable to secure a decisive shot. On re-engaging, experienced a broken trigger mechanism. Two Albatri collided, the leader of which lost its top wing and was seen to crash-land in a semi-controlled condition. The second followed leader down then cleared east with severe damage to undercart."

He put down the sheet, enjoying his moment. "Unimaginatively written and – and this is more significant – missing in essential detail. You fail to mention that the pilot of the crashed bus was none other than Commander Oswald Boelcke, now sadly deceased."

"What? But he didn't even come down hard!"

"All true my boy. His helmet came off and he smashed his square head in." He swigged at the whisky. "Just think, if you'd managed to get a couple of shots in you might have got away with claiming the Huns' number one ace!"

CHAPTER 20

Substantive Major Barrington Holt tapped sharply on the door of Andy and Colin's hut with his stick, entering slightly before the laconic summons from within. Colin was stretched in one of the sagging straw-bottomed church chairs, his feet on the table, the chair teetering on its imperfectly fixed back legs. He was studying what appeared to be a window-cleaner's leather, but revealed itself as a thumbed and tattered penny-dreadful.

"Afternoon, Major." Colin assumed a posture acceptably less casual. "What may I do for you?"

"Came to see Palmer. Is he here?"

Colin pointed to the corner cubicle. "Wandering with Morpheus as usual. I'll wake him for you."

"No need. I'm already awake." Andy emerged from the cubicle, brushing his hair back from his forehead. "Afternoon sir, you wanted me?"

"Afternoon Palmer. Yes. You are, of course, aware that Captain Doke's death leaves C-Flight lacking a leader."

Andy stiffened, his face sudden stone. "Yes."

"Well, as deputy leader you may have expected to move up to that position. However, it has been decided that you do not, at least at this moment, possess the required experience. A new flight leader will arrive within the next few days. Until then you should lead the flight, though you will not receive the additional seven shillings. I trust you find that acceptable?"

Andy's shoulders dropped and he smiled slightly. "More than, sir."

"Very well, though I would have expected more ambition from you. Good afternoon."

He nodded at Colin and marched unevenly through the door. A swirl of sodden leaves gusted in, flickering the oil lamp by whose light Colin had been absorbing the unlikely conquests of Scout Sabre, Scourge of the Skies. Colin stood to coax enthusiasm from the stove.

"You all right, chum? You look bloody awful."

"Rough as a tramp's chin. I've had the runs for two days."

"I know. Hardly surprising with the muck the mess is serving up these days."

Andy shook his head. "No, I don't think it's anything I've eaten."

"So what do you think it is?" Colin rubbed his forehead in exasperation. "Oh, don't tell me it's your wind-up fixation again. You've got wind, not wind-up."

"How would you know? How the hell do you know if I've got wind-up or not?"

"Hey, steady on chap. I'm not the enemy, you know."

"Yeah? Well stop telling me how I feel then! I'm the only one who knows that. The day Henrik died I genuinely thought I was going to shit myself in the cockpit. Then when I thought I was going to have to lead the flight, I couldn't sleep, eat or do anything. Holt's just apologised for giving me the best news I've heard in ages." His voice rose.

"Just stop fucking telling me I'm not scared!" He slammed out of the hut.

*

Robière's Victrola had remained unclaimed and the periodic influx of new pilots had washed away its unapproachability. Lynch-Fowler, recently returned from a brief hospitalisation for concussion, had reappeared with a salutary scar and a dozen new records. The harsh, metallic laughter of the mess was softened by a crooner's recollections of the Swanee River. Andy sat in a corner, barricaded behind a two-day old Daily Mail. The story of some plucky schoolgirl who'd gathered material for fifty comforters for our brave lads refused to hold his interest and the oozing nostalgia of the music touched insidiously on his exposed sentiments.

That's why I'm going back where they care for me.
Every night they say a little prayer for me
Down where the Swanee River flows.

He had a vision of his mother kneeling in her flower-patterned sitting room, a cross in her hands, pictures of himself and Rob propped in front of her. He shook his head: like most English families, they went to church for weddings, funerals and occasional Christmases. The notion of his mother, greying head bent in prayer, was a phantasm brought on by self-pity and the high-pitched sentimentality of Jolson. His disrupted bowels had noticeably improved since the announcement that his flight leadership was to be short-lived. If the present dud weather continued he stood a decent chance of welcoming his new senior without needing to fly at all in God-like command.

"You hiding behind that or building a tent with it?"

Andy twitched the paper down to see Colin smiling slightly uncertainly. He kicked a chair towards him.

"Absorbed in the crucial news of the day. Or at least the crucial news of..." he checked the newspaper's date. "Wednesday. You're still speaking to me then."

Colin sat down. "Yes, look, about that, I'm…"

"No, I'm sorry. Take no notice of me. I shouldn't have had a go at you."

"Feeling any better?"

"Yes, which in a way makes me feel worse." He threw the paper onto the table and stood up. "Come on, let's grab Arthur and Humph and see if there's some decent food in Beauval."

CHAPTER 21

Leave! The prospect hovered ahead of Andy's propeller like a rainbow, constantly receding as he approached. He calculated that fourteen more jobs stood between him and that elusive wisp. Fourteen jobs behind the new flight leader. Ellery was a decent enough type, but his eyes were on a DSO in the shortest time possible.

Balloons were a target of unavoidable necessity, not of choice. But Ellery had volunteered C-Flight to make sure that the enemy balloonists had plenty of winch and parachute practice, and they'd followed him on three attempts to do so. The score so far stood at 3-0 in favour of the Germans. Today's job had been typical. On an ice-bright December day, four allied scouts droning in at 5,000 feet gave the Huns time to finish their lunch before winching the great grey gasbags safely to earth. Archie, meanwhile, enjoyed rare leisure to prepare and choose his targets. One balloon remained enticingly aloft, possibly the result of a jammed winch; far more probably a hunter's decoy, its position zeroed to a centimetre by Archie. Ellery had rejected the bait, diving instead to strafe the winches and machine guns. This meant that all four of the machines needed to be missed something like fifty thousand times in the next five minutes.

The flight was returning now, tattered and holed, having at least spread some alarm and despondency. Lynch-Fowler had lost his engine as he climbed away and crash-landed next to an Archie emplacement. Andy wondered how he would fare: rumour had it that the

Germans shot any pilot found to be equipped with explosive ammunition.

Andy's undercarriage broke as he touched down. The left wing and propeller bit into the cinders at the same moment, throwing the aircraft into an awkward cartwheel that thrust the dashboard in to clamp his legs against the seat. The machine came to rest half inverted. Andy, half-dazed, released his belt and wondered why he was unable to exit the cockpit. The smell of petrol cleared his head and he strained desperately against the wreck's grasp. Running feet pounded behind him and he felt arms under his shoulders. He put his elbows against the fuselage and pulled in unison with his rescuer, sliding painfully from the crushed cockpit.

Ellery dragged Andy to a safe distance from the wreck before bending solicitously to check his condition.

"Are you alright? Think you can walk?"

Andy took quick stock, "Think so. Lost some skin off my legs getting out, but otherwise I'm fine. Thanks for the rescue."

"Must have taken some hits to your undercart. Not surprising with all that stuff coming up."

Andy looked at the open, reddish face, shining through its layer of whale fat and blackened with the ubiquitous castor oil. "You know, Ellery, if you hadn't just pulled me out of a wreck, I'd push your teeth through the back of your neck."

"Me? What have I done?"

"Done? Apart from killing three new pilots? Apart from getting Alf shot down and captured and maybe shot?"

"You've got me mixed up with the Germans, boy. I'm on your side!"

Andy pushed him roughly away. "Well stay off my side, *boy*. I'm not buying your fucking medals for you."

Ellery glared at Andy's slouched back; turned to the gathering group of pilots and mechanics.

"What's his problem? He wants to watch his step, threatening me…"

The remainder of the high-pitched complaint was lost in the roar of an engine under test. Andy thrust his hands deeper into his pockets, pulled his head deeper into his shoulders and kicked the door open to enter his hut. There was no sign of Colin and Andy tried to feel relieved. In reality he'd hoped for a sympathetic ear for his grievances, someone to reassure him that he was not in the wrong. Two envelopes caught his eye. He picked them up and performed that unexplainable trick of trying to guess their content rather than opening them to find out. He recognised the handwriting of the first as Cubby's and tore it open impatiently.

Colney Hatch Hospital
Friern Barnet Road
Colney Hatch
Middlesex

December 7th, 1916

Dear Andy,

I'm sorry not to have written before but things have been a bit changeable at this end, I'm sure you know what I mean. I'm doing well now that the head doctors have stopped telling me it's all because I wanted to do unspeakable acts to my mother. Difficult that, seeing as I can't really remember her. I'll tell you more about why I'm better when I see you (which I hope to do soon.)

I spent a couple of days with Connie and Stainton. They came down to see me and it turned out (surprise, surprise) that Connie knows the governor and they got the VIP treatment. We went out for a couple of drives in their car and had lunch. Stainton asked after you but I couldn't tell her much. That's when I realised I should have written before now. Connie thinks you should be due for Home Establishment soon, so don't be surprised if you get the feeling strings are being pulled!

I've put in to complete my pilot training when I get returned to A.S. If we end up in the same squadron then the war will be over in a couple of weeks.

Let me know how you're doing and keep safe.

Your friend,

Cubby McConnachie

Andy stared at the letter, its unfamiliar formality refusing to sit with his memory of the loud, room-filling Australian. The sight of Stainton's name had spun an icy rotor under his diaphragm and he re-read the paragraph, willing it to reveal more detail. *Stainton asked after you.*

Opening the second envelope, he caught sight of the address and the rotor kicked again, building up revs as he scanned down to the signature.

Gorse Park
Monmouth Drive
Sutton
Warks
Telephone – Streetly 208

December 6th 1916

Dear Andy,

I hope you don't feel forgotten, but life has been rather Nomadic, following Mummy around a thousand army camps. Our concert party is resting now, thankfully, at least until after Christmas. By then she will have thought of something else to do. I hope that it does not entail travel to other planets, but a certain dread remains nonetheless.

We drove down to London to see Cubby a few days ago. He looks quite well, if a little thin, and asked after you just as we asked him the same question. We all looked at each other rather guiltily I'm afraid!

Can so many months have passed since we parted? I hope we didn't part bad friends, though I believe I may have been rather colder towards you than you deserved or I felt. For that I apologise. Mummy believes that you should be due for rotation to England and vows to ensure that you are not overlooked. Please forgive her meddling; she means well. Hopefully you do at least have leave soon. Please do come and visit us!

How are you? Give my love to Colin. I hope you're flying carefully and not trying to be too dashingly brave. Better to live on one's feet than to die on one's dashboard.

Affectionately,

Stainton

The rotor had now entangled most of Andy's organs, which spun and entwined like clothes around the washday dolly. *Colder than I felt. Affectionately.*
Visit us.

The missions between him and England assembled in front of him, the sun dazzling behind their silhouetted ranks. Dashing bravery withered in their pitiless gaze. They knew his heightened desire to be in England; they knew it and sneered. Colin banged through the flimsy door, pursued by a flurry of icy rain.

"Jingo, where did that lot come from? It's blowing a bloody gale all of a sudden!" He rubbed his hair, releasing a spatter of raindrops. "Oh hullo, letters. Anything for me?"

"No, they're both mine. One from Cubby and another from Stainton. She sends her love."

"Stainton eh? Gimme!"

He snatched the letter before Andy could close his grip. Holding it teasingly aloft the looked down at his friend, half way out of his chair. "Anything here I shouldn't be seeing?"

Andy shrugged. "No, worse luck. Help yourself."

Colin read the letter, his eyebrows rising. "She's longing for you, mate. Probably sits at her open window each night, the moonlight shining through her diaphanous nightgown, and dreams of your skilled aviator's hands."

"You've been reading those bloody books again, haven't you?"

"Well there's bugger all else to do now that you just lie on your bed and growl every evening. What have you done to your leg?"

Andy looked at his torn trousers, both calves of which were blood-stained. "Nothing much I don't think. Pranged my bus and got my legs caught under the dashboard. Ellery pulled me out."

"Well you'd better get your kecks off and let's have a go at them with the Zam-Buk. You don't want to spoil your ill-intentioned leave by going home with septic legs."

"Suppose so. Hand me the tin though, I'm not having you that close to my undercarriage."

Andy's injuries were impressively bloody but reassuringly – or disappointingly – slight. He rinsed them with water from the night stand, dried them and winced as the thick ointment stung the scraped-raw flesh. Ellery came in, avoiding Andy's eyes, and began to pack up Lynch-Fowler's belongings. Andy watched him for a moment before pulling up his breeches and going quietly over to help.

"I'm sorry, Jack, I shouldn't have said all that."

Ellery looked up, his big face flushing slightly. His drawling six-towns tones were conciliatory. "That's alright. You'd just crashed. Can't be expected to be at your best after you've just had a Nieuport on top of you."

"Thanks." Andy picked up a thoroughly generic wedding photograph. "Didn't even realise he was married. Any word?"

Ellery shook his head. "Not yet, but he definitely got out of the kite OK, and nobody seemed to be shooting at him. I just hope he hadn't got any ammunition left."

Colin joined them, dragging a frayed suitcase from under the bed. "Balloon party wasn't it?"

"Aye. If he's still got Buckingham in the magazine then Herr Schmitt won't be amused."

"But they use explosive bullets themselves," said Colin. "It's bloody unfair if they shoot pilots for doing exactly what they do themselves. I for one don't believe it anyway."

Ellery nodded. "If it's any consolation, nor do I. I did hear of a Hun who came down at 22 Squadron, loaded up with explosive bullets."

"What happened to him?"

"The Adjutant told him that he must give detailed information about his squadron strength and equipment, or he would be shot."

"And did he?"

"Apparently he clicked his heels, stood to attention and said that, if he answered fully, many Germans would die, while if he kept silence, only one would."

Interested despite himself, Andy paused by Lynch-Fowler's locker. "What did they do?"

"Gave him the best meal the mess could manage and sent him off to the rear too pissed to walk."

"Sounds like exactly the medicine I need." Andy closed the locker door. "Come on you two, I'm buying."

Ellery demurred, reminding Andy that they were on for an 8 o'clock show in the morning. Andy opened the door to look meaningfully at the low, yellowish clouds. A few flakes of snow wafted in on a trick of wind.

"That gets going properly we'll all still be tucked up till lunchtime."

"And if it doesn't we'll be off the ground at 8:00 and hunting balloons by 8:30, and you'd better be sober either way."

The wind was strengthening, blowing stinging wet sleet in their faces as they crossed the farmyard.

"What chance is there that we're going anywhere in the morning? Jesus, Col, what a pompous prick!"

"Trouble is, he's right. We'd better take it easy." Colin pushed open the door to the mess, causing a howl of protest as the icy wind blew through the smoke-blue fug inside. "You know what he's like; if it's marginal in the morning he'll have you flying anyway. You want to be giving full revs, so just a couple, eh?

As it turned out the mess was out of alcohol anyway. Andy berated the hapless servant for being a pointless waste of the King's oxygen and then wandered from table to table, soliciting hidden personal supplies. A foray to the other ranks' mess finally bore expensive fruit when a grinning sergeant sold him two bottles of pale ale from his foot locker. Returning to the officers' mess he placed one of the opened bottles in front of Colin.

"Drink up, lad, these cost me five bob each."

The mess emptied early as unsatisfied airmen wandered out to read or play cards in their own huts. Andy and Colin played a disconsolate game of chess while another of the nameless new pilots tunelessly strummed a mandolin in a corner. Colin won as usual and they decided to call the evening a wash-out. The low clouds had cleared, taking with them the snow. The sky was frosted with stars, ice-bright and oblivious. The hut was in darkness, lit only by a faint glow from the stove. Ellery's deep, self-assured breathing hissed infuriatingly from his cubicle, each breath ending with a tiny whimper that made Andy pick up the poker and look threateningly into the dark corner.

Later, unable to sleep without an adequate dose of anaesthetic, he decided to raid the mess kitchen for food. Colin joined him as he left the hut and they tiptoed into the darkness. By the flame of his cigarette lighter, Colin found a pan containing a couple of pints of cold Irish stew, and Operation Ellery was born, fully-formed and ready for execution.

They filled jugs with the semi-congealed brew and sneaked back into the hut. Andy signalled the attack by bumping heavily into Ellery's bed and simultaneously retching loudly. He deposited a quarter of the jug's contents onto the sleeping form. Colin lurched into the night stand, gagging, coughing and groaning. At each eruption he allowed stew to spill loudly around the cubicle. Ellery was out of bed, tripping over his blankets and demanding loudly to know what the bloody hell they thought they were doing? Andy muttered an incoherent apology and fell against him, releasing an appalling, heaving belch that tore his throat. He upended the remaining stew on the writhing body on the floor and he and Colin staggered to the door, banged it loudly and then dived for their own cubicles in the darkness.

Colin lit his candle and sat up in bed, blinking sleepily. "What's happening? Oh, I say, Ellery, are you alright?"

As none of the squadron had been drinking that night, the identity of the inebriates was never discovered. The plan backfired slightly as Ellery ordered their batman to clean up his cubicle, but Colin apprised him of the joke and gave him ten bob, so that was alright.

CHAPTER 22

May 1915

Cubby was semi-conscious, wandering between a world where Snaff stood nearby, shifting restlessly, and another where he seemed to be bare-knuckle boxing an endless chain of officers. Each punch he threw was like dragging a paddle through water, pushing against a great dragging weight to touch ineffectually on the adversary's face. Major Quinn smiled encouragingly as his fists connected with Cubby's broken head with a sound like coal sacks on gravel. Voices brought the real world back into focus for a moment. Snaff had gone and Cubby looked around, finding himself alone. He heard shouts, made distant and shrill by the steam engine rush of blood in his ears, then four men emerged from the scrub, their rifles levelled at him. They jerked him upright and he swam backwards away from the light.

"Işte! Içki!"

Cubby felt something hard knock against his teeth and recoiled back. A bearded face peered down at him from the opening of a dark, swirling tunnel.

"Su! Içki!"

The water splashed into his mouth and he choked. Something blessedly cool enfolded his burning head and he closed his eyes again.

"Hayir! Uyanin!"

A dark head shaded his eyes, easing the stabbing ache of the pale sky. A darkly sparkling tube connected him to a world outlined in rainbows. He blinked and forced himself to return.

Sergeant Duyal Korkmaz poured more water onto the bandage he held against Cubby's head. He looked across to his corporal, who was crouched over the bloodied bundle of another Australian soldier who was groaning feebly. This one was very young, ripped apart by the grenade that, in a few minutes surely, would mercifully complete its unfinished work. The other one, with the sniper's rifle, was already dead. Korkmaz had no regret to spare for murderers. The corporal held his canteen to the boy's lips, looking up at a warning from the sergeant.

"Neden olmasın? Zaten şansı yoktur. Ona su atalim." he answered quietly.

Korkmaz nodded. The boy was dying fast; instructions not to give water to an abdominal casualty were meaningless. If water eased his suffering then it would be inhuman to withhold it. The Australian sergeant seemed to be becoming more alert, the cooling bandage reviving him. His eyes cast around, coming to rest on the young private. He released a guttural gasp and looked at Korkmaz.

"How bad is he?"

Korkmaz had little English, but the meaning was obvious. "Bad. Very bad. Die"

The Australian closed his eyes, his face crumpling. "He's my son!"

Korkmaz understood and blinked back tears of his own. He pushed the bloodied hair back from the Australian's forehead."Çok üzgünüm. Bu, Allah'ın iradesidir." He scoured his scant vocabulary. "Excuse me. Is will of Allah. Excuse me. Please."

The Australian was struggling to rise. "Let me get to him."

Korkmaz summoned a private to help him carry the big sergeant to the boy. The corporal had hastily pulled a cape from his pack to hide as much as possible of the red destruction.

Danny's eyes opened as he felt Cubby's hand under his head. He looked up at his father. His lips formed soundless shapes. Cubby leaned closer, trying to catch the words.

"Say it again, Danny. I can't hear."

The lips moved again. A sighing breath gave voice to one word. "Sorry."

Cubby felt agonising pain in his leg. The Turks were replacing the supporting bayonets with wooden splints and clean bandages. They looked up at his reaction and offered him a morphine tablet. He knocked it away, then reached for it and held it to Danny's lips.

"Give me some water."

He took the canteen and pushed the tablet between Danny's teeth. Danny chewed reflexively, grimacing at the foul taste. He sipped the water, spluttering weakly. Cubby looked at the pale face, the ever-wayward lock of hair plastered to the marble forehead. The sparkling tunnel returned to nebulate his sight and a Wallamanian roaring drowned the voices around him. They caught Cubby as he slumped over the boy's face. Korkmaz saw how the Australian sergeant's eyes were bulging, forcing his eyelids slightly apart, and came to a decision. He called to one of his platoon.

"Şentürk, diğer Avustralya getirmek."

Private Senturk brought the other Australian captive. Korkmaz pointed at the sergeant and mimed pulling him onto his back. The Anzac corporal nodded and pulled the big man onto his shoulders. He jerked back as Korkmaz placed a cigarette between his lips, then nodded gratefully as the Turk lit it. Korkmaz unbuttoned the corporal's breast pocket and pushed in three more cigarettes. He pointed to the north.

"Gitmek!"

Snaff looked at the Turkish sergeant, uncomprehending. Korkmaz pushed him gently. "Go! Fuck off!"

Slowly, suspiciously, Snaff turned to the north, shouldered his burden more securely and began to walk home.

CHAPTER 23

December 1916

The abrasions on Andy's thighs were proving troublesome. They adhered to any cloth that came into contact, ripping painfully when movement broke the connection. Climbing into the cockpit was a twice-daily torture. Colin was solicitous.

"You need to get the Doc to have a look at those, pal. I think the Zam-Buk's making them worse."

Andy examined the yellowish mess. "No, I think it's clearing up a bit."

"Clearing up? You've got legs like Florrie Forde! If they swell any more there'll be no room left for your bollocks."

"Well I'm not going to the Doc. I've got leave in three days' time. I'm not spending it in a bloody hospital in France."

"Suit yourself, but don't blame me if they take you back to dear old Blighty on a stretcher."

Ellery came in, followed by McLeod, a pale Scot arrived the day before to replace Lynch-Fowler. "Blimey Palmer, every time I find you and Hingley in here, one of you's got your breeches down. Do you want a few minutes to yourselves?"

Colin grinned. "No thanks, Ellery, the more the merrier. Bring your handsome young friend."

McLeod flushed uncertainly, his pale, watery eyes flicking to each of his new hut mates, searching for clues.

"I'll just get ma cap. I need to go tae…" He cast about for a satisfactorily pressing appointment; failing to find one among the myriad diversions of a temporary forward airfield he finished lamely, "...the lav."

Andy stood, pulling up his breeches. "Don't worry, Angus. Just patching up a bit of damage."

"Fine. But ma name's Colin."

"I know, but that name's taken. It's Angus McCoatup or Jock Strapp, orders from Wing I'm afraid. Sorry, nothing we can do."

"What's wrong with Mac?"

"Mac?" He looked at Colin. "What do you think?"

Colin appeared to consider the matter, then shook his head. "No, not funny enough. Sorry. I think there's a vacancy for a Ben Doonagen though. Will that do?"

McLeod brightened. "I wouldna' mind being called Ben."

Colin raised his palms in regret. "Oh, no, it doesn't work does it? Ben just isn't funny either. Sorry, Angus, you're christened."

"When Naughton and Gold have finished, perhaps the skinny one would be kind enough to get his finger out and kit up." Ellery disappeared into his cubicle, stepping back into the main room as he began donning layers of clothing.

"You're joking! In this?"

Ellery leaned against the partition to pull on a fug boot. "It's stopped raining and the wind's fairly steady. With this cloud we stand half a chance of catching balloons in the air."

Andy took a step towards Ellery. "Tell me you're not thinking about taking Angus."

"He's on C-Flight, so I don't see why not."

"Because he only arrived two days ago. He needs some time to settle in and get the lie of the land. You certainly can't start him on balloons!"

"I'm taking a flight of four, not a flight of three. My decision, and the Major's agreed."

"Tiverton agrees with whoever spoke to him last." Andy's anger was rising rapidly. "There are plenty of experienced pilots who could come."

"I want my flight to be a flight, not a loose collection of individuals. So we go up as a flight."

"So that's you, me, McLeod here and the other new chap; what's his name? Phillips?" Andy paced back and forth, hands opening and closing. "McLeod, what do you think about this?"

"Ah'm fine. It's what I came over here for."

Andy's shoulders dropped slightly and he shook his head. "Ellery, you know you're an arsehole, don't you? I hope…"

"I think now's a good point to stop talking." Colin stepped into the space between Andy and Ellery. "Ellery, you're within your rights, but that's not the same as being right. I suggest you take your kit and finish changing elsewhere. And after the job, have a word with Holt about getting yourself assigned to another hut."

Ellery bundled his remaining flying gear and stepped around Colin. He fixed Andy with a glare and stopped, half way to the door. Andy took a step forward, to be intercepted again by Colin.

"Leave it for later." He looked hard at Ellery. "Just get out."

Ellery turned slowly, still looking at Andy. Then he laughed humourlessly and left the hut. After an embarrassed few seconds, McLeod followed him.

Andy subsided slowly into a wooden chair. "I swear I'm going to bash his bloody face in, I tell you straight."

"And where's your precious leave then?"

"It'd be worth it."

"No it wouldn't. Just bite your tongue and go shooting balloons. Concentrate on getting back in one piece."

"Oh, I'll come back alright. But those two poor bloody idiots won't know what's hit 'em."

"We're all buying somebody's medals, chum. Best not to think about it."

*

Andy's Nieuport was in as foul a temper as its pilot. The replacement for his crashed machine was brand-new and far prettier than its predecessor, but its engine lacked enthusiasm, and today it blatted damp flatulence every time he pulled up and zoomed to try to encourage some of its missing revs. He flew at the rear of the formation, slightly above Ellery's slipstream. The two new pilots straggled unevenly to each side. They had entered yellowish, sodden cloud at 1100 feet, and every smooth surface inside the cockpit was soon covered in droplets of condensation. He allowed his airspeed to fall off a little, preferring to open a buffer of fresh air between himself and his invisible, erratic companions.

The cloud lightened after only 500 feet and Andy caught glimpses of the other three aircraft. *Well at least they managed to keep it under control through that.* He waggled his numb fingers and began to feel slightly happier.

Ellery was flattening out the climb to stay hidden by the wispy top layer. Pink flashes lit the fog as he warmed his guns. Andy zoomed to close back into formation and his engine chugged irritably at the effrontery. A large formation of anonymous machines coasted deep over Hunland; if they were whatever Jasta Boelcke was called these days, then he had no business east of the lines with a dud engine. But the prospect of turning back, and Ellery's likely reaction, prohibited such an action. He dropped his nose and fired off a few rounds into the cloud. McLeod and Phillips both swerved in alarm, twisting in their seats to see where the threat lay. He fired another burst to reassure them.

After ten minutes, Ellery put his nose down and led them back into the cloud. They dropped into drizzly clarity only a quarter-mile away from the three balloons, rippling in peptic sloth on their cables. *He might be a prick, but he judged that to a T.*

The gas-bags began dropping almost instantly, and with remarkable speed. The Germans had recently taken to looping the cables under a bar on a lorry. To bring them down rapidly, they simply drove the lorry along the ground, pulling the balloon down far more rapidly than was possible with a winch. Ellery was closing fast, letting fly with a long burst of Buckingham at the first balloon. The two new pilots split left and right, heading for their own targets. Archie, surprised by their sudden appearance, threw up an erratic protest that was at least as dangerous to the balloon crews as to their attackers. Andy pitched forward to follow Ellery's attack, releasing a stream of tracer as his leader dipped under the balloon. The two German observers were still in the basket, which was pitching violently in the sudden descent. *Jump you silly buggers.* He kicked the rudder to spray an arc of fire along the length of the grey envelope. *Burn, you bastard, burn.*

He threw the stick to the right, pulling back into a hard, knife-edge turn. Looking along his right wing he glimpsed Ellery diving on the lorry, which swerved violently and stopped. He looked back over his head, craning his neck to see what effect this sudden check had had on the balloon.

Round again, and he once more ruddered his Aldis along the balloon's midriff. It now hung helplessly on its cable, see-sawing slowly; the observers had finally made their exit and their parachutes blossomed dirty yellow through the monochrome drizzle.

Just as Andy pulled away from his attack, a pink-orange flower bloomed from a fast-opening gash in the balloon's side. It spread rapidly, turning yellowish as it devoured the shiny fabric. A stinking furnace breath tossed the Nieuport and the blimp collapsed on itself, whirling down to spread fire across the ground below.

The other two balloons were down and safe. McLeod and Phillips had both disappeared. Looking west he saw Ellery's machine, heading home at no more than five hundred feet. Andy's engine refused to give more than 1100 revs, and he sensed an increasing tightness that presaged imminent seizure. If he dived to Ellery's level then he'd have no margin to glide over the lines if it stopped. But something was clearly wrong with the flight leader, to fly within easy range of the machine guns that populated every square yard of the enemy's territory. He turned to follow at 1,200 feet, diving and climbing to confuse Archie's disapproval.

The lines slid under his wings and Andy started to relax. A Bristol popped up on his left and he looked across to see Phillips manoeuvring into formation, then McLeod taking up position beyond him. He waved and pointed down to where Ellery's machine was bouncing and swerving unevenly homeward.

By the time Beauval came into view, Ellery was down to 200 feet. Andy closed with the leader, pulling alongside to try to establish what was wrong. Ellery was crouched forward, his face inches from the windscreen. He showed no sign of awareness of the aircraft alongside. As they came, side by side, over the perimeter hedge, Ellery pulled up into a three-point attitude, still 100 feet up. The Nieuport stalled immediately, dropped its right wing and spun vertically into the ground.

CHAPTER 24

Andy's swollen legs refused to bend sufficiently to allow egress from his aeroplane. A solicitous ack emma summoned burly assistance and together they lifted him gently from the cockpit.

"Just relax sir, we'll have you out in a jiffy. Can you tell us where you're hit?"

Andy shook his head impatiently. "I'm fine, just a bit stiff. Have they got Ellery out?"

The mechanic looked at the tumble of wood and fabric piled by the hedge two hundred yards away. "They're attending to it now, sir. I don't think he'll be alright though, sir."

"Alright? What's that supposed to mean, you fucking idiot?" He pushed the mechanic roughly away and limped, stiff-legged towards the wreck.

McLeod and Phillips had already arrived there and were standing uncertainly on the edge of the small crowd. A bundled figure on a stretcher was loaded into the tender, which turned immediately and rumbled past him. McLeod and Phillips walked to meet him.

"Are you hit, Palmer? Come on, we'll get you to the Doc."

"No, I'm fine. Is he alive?"

"He's still breathing, but he's broken up to hell. There's a bullet in his chest: came up through the floor and went in just above his left hip. There's blood everywhere. Are you sure you're alright?"

"Yes, I'm… no, I'm not." Andy suddenly felt sick; the world lurched and he fell heavily against McLeod.

"Whoa! Right, it's the Doc for you right away." McLeod pulled Andy's arm over his shoulders. "Get his other arm, John."

Andy waited in the doctor's office for over an hour. His legs throbbed in rhythm with a furiously building headache and he leaned back in the hard chair, hands over his eyes, chin towards the fly-specked ceiling. Eventually the inner door banged and the doctor, a greying captain with a perpetual look of quiet worry, entered, wiping his hands on a stained towel.

"Sorry, Andy. Bit of an emergency there as you'll know."

"How is he, Doc?"

The doctor shook his head. "Well, he's still alive at the moment, but I can't say more. He has multiple fractures, a bullet in his right lung and God knows what internal damage. Let's have a look at you."

The skin on Andy's thighs was stretched tight, the abrasions yellow and sticky. The doctor whistled softly. "My, my, you've made a bit of a bugger of these, haven't you?" He removed the thermometer from Andy's mouth and squinted at its reading. "You're running a temperature as well. It's the hospital for you."

Andy jerked upright, "No, Doc, I'm fine. I've got leave in a couple of days; a week at home and I'll be back on top."

"A week with these legs and you'll be on your back, having them sawn off." He waved down Andy's protest. "You're a daft sod, why the bloody hell didn't you come to me sooner? I could have done something about it and packed you off home; now you've got a roaring infection and a trip to Le Touquet instead."

"But what about my leave?"

"I'm sorry, Palmer. I'm sure you'll be next on the roster once your legs have cleared up."

*

It was the longest night of Andy's life. He lay imprisoned on his back, his bandaged legs raised on improvised pulleys. In the other bed, six feet away, Ellery's rattling, bubbling breaths ebbed and flowed, falling still for endless seconds of suspense before choking and snoring back into irregular life. The smell of chloroform made his head spin but refused to grant him sleep; he watched a spider patrolling its larder in a corner of the clouded sick bay window. For the hundredth time he raised his wristwatch to catch the faint light from the window, but was again unable to establish the time. He hung, trapped like the spider's victims, pinioned in hourless limbo. Ellery's breathing took on a strange, high-pitched descending sigh.

Somewhere between midnight and eternity he began to doze fitfully, coming fully awake when a log spat in the stove; when an owl screeched outside; when Ellery's breathing restarted with choking gasps. His neck ached and his left arm went to sleep. He groaned briefly in torment, wincing in guilt as he thought of the broken man in the bed next to him.

Andy awoke to see the seat of the doctor's trousers as he bent over Ellery. "How is he, Doc?"

The doctor straightened and turned.

"He's gone." He pulled the sheet over Ellery's face. "He couldn't survive with those injuries whatever we did. If we'd operated to remove the bullet we'd have killed him, to say nothing of at least two amputations." He patted Andy's shoulder. "I'm sorry, I know he was your friend."

Andy thought of his last exchange with Ellery; thought of the overpowering urge to punch that supercilious expression off his face; was astonished to find his eyes filling with tears.

"No, he was…" Words left him and he turned his head away.

Colin, Page and French bustled noisily into the sick bay, stopping guiltily when they noticed the shrouded figure on the other bed. The doctor motioned them in, nodded significantly in Andy's direction and left the room.

"That Ellery?" asked Colin, pulling up a chair.

Andy nodded and inspected his bandages. Page perched his backside on the edge of the bed and tugged experimentally at a pulley. "See they got the riggers to work on you. How you feeling?"

"I've had better lifetimes, thanks."

"Can't be all bad. Off to Le Touq and its unlimited inventory of frustrated nursage."

"I'd rather be off to Le Brum, thanks. Like I was supposed to be tomorrow. Any idea who's got my leave?"

French and Page looked at Colin, who flushed uncomfortably. "That would be me, chum."

Andy brightened slightly, "Oh, well that's not so bad then. At least it's gone to a deserving cause."

"I'll have a word in the right ears," said French. "We should be able to get you away pretty soon after you get back."

"Thanks, Arthur." Andy turned back to Colin, "Got a letter off to tell your folks yet?"

"They're in Scotland for another two days. I thought maybe I'd spend a couple of days in the Midlands. I can call in and make your explanations to Stainton."

Andy felt his quick anger rising. "It's good to have trusted friends like you looking out for me," he said with heavy irony.

Colin stood up. "You know, mate, if you picked as many fights with the Germans as you do with your trusted friends, this war'd be over."

He walked quietly out of the sick bay, closing the door carefully behind him. Page and French hovered awkwardly for a few moments before mumbling their good wishes and departing.

CHAPTER 25

Number One Red Cross Hospital was a white painted building that had started life as a casino. The wards were lit by ornate chandeliers that hissed in the dim winter afternoons, casting stark shadows across rows of identical iron beds, their severe angles softened by square-patterned quilts. The nurses floated efficiently between them, administering balm, banter and reprimands to their forlorn or insistently priapic charges. Compared to the chicken wire pallet that had supported Andy's short hours of sleeping for the last six months, the beds were absurdly comfortable. After two days his infection had succumbed to antiseptics and he was free to luxuriate in starched white linen and feather pillows. The food was far superior to mess fare, and the ever-present guns were a distant, almost unheard grumble.

Three days of regular, uninterrupted sleep restored Andy's equanimity and he began reviewing, with rising discomfort, his temper tantrums over the previous weeks. His final row with Ellery rose constantly to rebuke him and he would shift restlessly in the creaking basket chair in which he spent most of his days. His angry parting with Colin replayed in his mind and his guilt was assuaged somewhat. *Cheeky bastard, saying he'd call on Stainton. Rubbing it in that he'd got my leave.*

He played chess and Ludo with an easy-going Canadian sapper who had become too relaxed with his explosives. Frozen rain lashed against the French windows. He felt warm and safe, and sneered at his own cowardice.

On the fifth day he was becoming restless, prowling the corridors or sitting on the wind-blown veranda, huddled in a chequered quilt. He was dozing under the dripping eaves when a friendly but dreary nurse pushed through the French windows.

"You'll catch your death of cold sitting out here like this, Andy. Why don't you come inside in the warm?"

"I'll be in in a minute, Janice."

"Well I came out to bring you a little surprise," she was clearly trying to hide her smile. "You've got a visitor."

"Really? Who?"

The nurse's smile broke free. "It's your wife."

He understood immediately who it must be, despite logic that told him it was impossible. "My…? No! I can't believe it!" That, at least was true.

He followed Janice towards the matron's office, shuffling in burst-seamed carpet slippers, forcing his aching legs to keep up with her efficient heel-clicking walk.

The matron sat resplendent in her throne room, the scarlet mantle of her supreme office draped with meticulous accuracy on her venerable shoulders. She inclined her head graciously and allowed her lips to twitch slightly as Andy was shown in. Stainton was sitting primly in the seat opposite her. She was dressed in a voluminous dark green skirt and tight-waisted brown tweed jacket, a small, brown feathered hat pinned to hair that had grown since he last saw her to curl just below her ears. Her freckles were hidden under a dusting of powder. She stood as Andy entered and walked over to kiss his cheek.

"Darling! It's so lovely to see you!" She took his hands and ventured a tiny wink at his tongue-tied discomfiture.

"Mrs Palmer tells me that you'd been married only two weeks before you came to France," said Matron. "It's quite right that you should want to be together, so I am happy to allow you to leave the hospital each day for the rest of your stay here. You will, of course, be back in your bed by 9:30 each evening. Nurse Wilkes, please arrange for Mr Palmer's clothes to be brought for him."

Janice dipped a small curtsey, gasped "Yes, Matron." and left the room, her eyes sparkling.

Andy gingerly placed his arm around Stainton's waist and grinned stupidly at nothing. His head swivelled between the matron and this well-bred, worldly young woman who rested her cheek against his frayed tartan dressing gown and smiled up at him.

"I'm so glad you're not too badly injured, darling. Matron, thank you for your kindness, it's very sweet of you to allow Andy to visit me."

"Not at all, my dear. Run along the two of you and enjoy your time together. Do give my regards to your mother."

They sat by Andy's bed, knees touching, as they waited the interminable time that all hospitals take to execute tasks as complex as retrieving a patient's clothes.

"How on earth have you done this? I mean, it's wonderful to see you, but…"

Stainton still held his hand in both of hers. "Thank Colin. He telephoned as soon as he got back to England and told me that your leave had been cancelled. He came over and had dinner with Mum and me. He's very worried about you."

"I don't know why. It's not even a proper wound. There are people here with limbs blown off, and I land up here because of a nasty scrape on my leg. Colin could learn to mind his own business."

"He's your friend, so it is his business. He told me you and he had had words. That's what he's worried about: he thinks you're exhausted. That's probably why your legs got infected. And it's thanks to him that I'm here."

"But how are you here? How did you do it?"

"Colin knew where you'd been sent, and he knew there's a hotel here for the patients' families to stay in. He, Mummy and I hatched the plan over dinner. I pretended to be your wife, and Mum pulled the strings that only an MP's widow can pull, and here I am."

"She's in on this too? What does she think of it?"

Stainton laughed, "She thinks we're locked up in a French hotel right now, giving ourselves over to unbridled lust. You have met my mother, haven't you?"

"But… what does it mean? I mean, are we…?"

She became serious. "I don't know what we are, Andy. I just know that when Colin said you weren't coming I felt that I wanted to see you more than anything. Is that alright?"

"Alright? It's… incredible. I feel as if there's a length of bungee connecting my brain and my tongue; I can't even speak properly. And my cheeks are starting to ache."

"You look as if it's the first time you've smiled in a long time. Your grinning muscles are out of practice." She looked up as a nurse brought his kitbag. "It's so good to see you, Andy."

They sat arm in arm on a cold bench by the beach huts, he in scarf and British Warm, she in a dark green coat, her face peeping from black fur. The Channel curled brownly in to splash whitely on the beach. An oystercatcher probed experimentally at a nameless black mound that cratered the grey sand, pink-pinking angrily when a herring gull stooped to claim the prize. She touched the outline of the dressings, visible through his oil-stained cavalry breeches.

"Do they hurt much?"

"Not much now. The swelling went down in a couple of days. I feel a bit of a fraud, to be honest."

"I think they were the excuse for the doctor sending you here, not the reason."

"What do you mean?"

She leaned back to look at his face. "Andy, you should take a look at yourself. You have black rings around your eyes, and you look like a skeleton. What do you weigh now, about nine stone?"

"No idea. We don't go in much for checking the scales."

"Whatever you weigh, it's about two stone too little. I'm going to fatten you up over the next couple of days."

"How long can you stay?"

"It's more to do with how long they'll let you stay. Your legs are nearly healed. But I'll stay until they send you back to the squadron."

He slid his arm around her shoulders, surprised at how natural the movement felt. He felt her hand push inside his overcoat and around his waist.

"So, given that we don't know what we are, and purely in the interests of research, do you think a kiss would be a good move here?"

She put up her free hand to touch his cheek. "I'd say it was bloody mandatory."

They ate fresh sea bass with dark truffles in a warm restaurant facing the sea. Andy insisted on paying the restaurateur's absurdly inflated price for champagne. By the time he began pidgin-French negotiations for the purchase of a cigar, they were both giggling like schoolchildren, their foreheads bumping across the tiny table.

"I keep getting the mental picture of Cubby with his thing out, doing the elephant joke."

"Well get rid of it. I'm not having you picturing another man's thing. Especially that one."

"Well you shouldn't have told me about it. Mum was always complimentary about it and you can't blame a girl for wondering."

"God, woman, is there nothing you and your mother don't discuss?"

"She likes to talk about her hobbies."

He looked at her in the dim light. Her tightly coiffured hair had become tousled and he saw again the huge-eyed elf-girl who had scowled at him from the glare of an ambulance's headlights. She caught his look and raised her eyebrows. "What?"

"Nothing. I was just thinking about the first night I saw you, with Cubby and your Mom going at it in the back of the ambulance."

"And what were you thinking then?"

"Same as I am now. That I desperately want to do the same."

"What, with my Mum or Cubby?"

"Well as they're not here, I was hoping you could, you know, fill in."

She laughed and sipped her cognac. "I seem to remember you saying something about being a bit of a disappointment. I wouldn't want to put either of us through that."

Andy inspected his cigar, trying to cover his embarrassment. "I'm sorry, too far. Too much champagne, sorry."

"Andy, let's find out what we are before we take any steps into the unknown. Is that OK?" She looked at the case clock on the wall. "Nine o'clock. We don't want you grounded for breaking curfew on your first night, and we still have all that kissing stuff to do outside my hotel."

CHAPTER 26

My Dear Palmer,

It is my pleasure to send to you the enclosed, received here today following your successful attack on an observation balloon on 10thInst. Major Tiverton and I extend our warmest congratulations on this well-deserved award.

Confirmation has been received today of your promotion to First Lieutenant. Be advised also that you will take on the role of C-Flight Commander on your return.

Yours truly,

Barr^{n}Holt (Maj)

Stainton put down the letter and examined the purple and white ribbon. "He's obviously missing you terribly, all that lovey-dovey asking after your recovery and such. And he's forgotten to put the medal in the enveloped."

"I think that comes later. You just get the ribbon through the post."

She held it against Andy's chest. "Andrew Palmer MC. It's rather dashing you know; I can see you limping nobly along the sea front, me on your arm, gazing adoringly at my injured hero."

"Yeah, what could be more dashing than septic legs?" replied Andy, taking the decoration from her and dropping it into the envelope.

"Aren't you going to wear it to the party?"

"I'm not, no. There'll be people there who actually deserve one."

Stainton considered for a moment and nodded, a nod that acknowledged his right to such a feeling without condoning its verity. "Well at least let's get your pips sewn on; you're First Lieutenant Palmer now; wouldn't do for a senior subaltern to be out of uniform."

"I'd appreciate a salute when you speak to me, Hamilton."

"My apologies, sir."

Christmas morning had brought an easing of the nurses' cloistral demeanour in the form of necklaces of coloured paper. Even Matron had been heard to emit an undowagerly giggle at some wounded serviceman's ribaldry. Janice fussed happily from bed to bed, singing quietly as she fluffed pillows.

"Why do you call Mrs Palmer 'Hamilton', Andy?"

"It's my middle name," replied Stainton evenly. "My parents weren't fully prepared for a girl."

"Of course." Janice's inability to suppress her smiles re-presented itself and she quickly squeezed Stainton's hand as she moved on down the ward.

"I think she's rumbled us."

"Me too." Andy was unwrapping a ribboned parcel. "Think we're in trouble?"

"I think she can be trusted. Hope so, it'd be a shame to have to kill her."

Andy finished his unwrapping and admired an expensive-looking briar pipe, turning it to enjoy the lustre of the grain in the sunlight slanting through the French windows. "This is beautiful. Thank you very much, I love it."

"I bought it in a bit of a hurry I'm afraid. This whole trip was rather last-minute." She watched as he experimentally fitted the stem between his teeth. "You don't smoke a pipe, do you?"

"Nope." He laughed out loud. "Open yours and then let's go out and buy tobacco."

Stainton began carefully to untie the string binding the inexpertly newspaper-wrapped bundle that lay beside her on the counterpane. Andy watched her nervously.

"It's nothing much, I'm afraid," he said uncertainly. "I was confined to the choice available in the local shops. Most of them weren't even open, but I managed to persuade the lady at…"

"Andy, shut up, there's a dear."

"I will if you'll stop trying to untie it and just cut the knot."

He handed her his penknife and she sawed through the string, pulling back the wrappings to reveal a small, scuffed leatherette box. Inside it she found a single earring. She held it to the same sunbeam that had enriched Andy's pipe; a cotton-thin chain of silver supported a glinting half-inch bar from which three silver bars depended like chimes, each one tasselled by a small diamond. She quickly removed the pearl stub from her left earlobe and ran to Andy's shaving mirror on the bedside stand, turning her head from side to side to admire the flicker.

"I'm sorry, there's only the one, but it was that or an enamel basin…"

"Andy, I thought we'd agreed you'd shut up." She turned, smiling. "It's lovely, thank you. Even better than an enamel basin."

Stainton pulled Andy to his feet. "Come on, let's find a tobacconist's and make a man of you."

"Which will you be doing first?" Janice's voice reached them from behind a nearby screen.

Their feet clattered in the corridors as he stumbled after her, laughing, into the bright, cold outdoors.

*

Christmas evening brought a concert party of sorts. The nurses sang carols and two wheelchair-bound sergeants provided indulgent hilarity with their sketches as two deaf artillery officers.

Artillery officer 1: "Jerry's making a lot of noise tonight!"

Artillery officer 2: "Sorry, it's the food you know!"

Artillery officer 1: "Rude? Who's being rude? I was talking about the damned noise!"

Artillery officer 2: "Well you shouldn't have brought your ruddy tortoise!"

Each sketch would end with the two grumbling, "Deaf idiot. Ah well, back to the dance..." and wheeling themselves to exit stage left and right, pursued by thunderous applause.

Stainton was persuaded to take the piano and she gave a simple, honest rendition of "Keep the Home Fires Burning." Andy had always hated the maudlin romanticism of the song, but sat, rapt and silent, joining in with the rest in the last chorus. The ensuing uproar demanded an encore and Stainton broke the mood with an energetic rendition of "Waiting for the Robert E. Lee". Andy's Ludo partner stood to cross the floor and deliver a courtly bow to Janice, who was seated by the makeshift stage. She simpered and they took the floor, her left hand on his shoulder, her right holding his bandaged wrist. More couples joined them, transforming the asceptic ward into a fluid swirl of starched grey and faded tartan dressing gowns.

Later, they stood in the corridor, he leaning against a clanging radiator, his arms relaxed around her waist.

Rustles and low murmurs from side rooms suggested a general breakdown of discipline. Janice and the Ludo player hurried by, their heads bent in giggling complicity. She halted her partner as she saw Andy and Stainton. Her large, good-natured face was reddened by contraband alcohol.

"Miss… Mrs… Stainton, thank you for a lovely p'formance." She leaned closer, "Matron left ages ago you know. I'll be far too busy to do a bed check, so I'll just have to trust you two won't I?"

The Ludo player tugged her arm and she clicked away down the corridor.

Stainton looked at him for a long moment, her bottom lip caught between her teeth. "Well, I suppose we are married, aren't we?"

"What? Well, of course! I was going to suggest it anyway," replied Andy with unconvincing bravado. "That is, if you're sure…"

"Not sure about anything. But let's take it one step at a time."

*

The elderly night porter who opened the door of l'Hotel des Anglais made no objection to Andy's nervous presence. Andy listened to Stainton's musical French as she explained her husband's presence and was reassured by the porter's Gallic shrug. The wizened Frenchman bowed slightly to Stainton and turned away, darting a wink at Andy and muttering, *"Bonne chance, m'sieur!"*

Stainton's room was chilly, despite a fire glowing gently in the dark. Andy hovered by the door as she circuited the room, lighting lamps. She looked back and saw him there.

"You can at least take your coat off and try to look a little less terrified," she laughed.

He took a step away from the door and began to unbutton his coat. "I thought I was hiding it pretty well. This is all a bit new to me to be honest."

She came over and slid her arms under his coat and around his waist. "It's not exactly familiar territory for me either, you know. Apart from a brief fumble from one of Mum's friends, I don't really know much about how this works."

"Well you're up on me by one brief fumble, so don't expect too much guidance from me."

She became serious for a moment, "Andy, I'm not sure I'm ready to do... all of it. Is that alright?"

"Is it alright?" He put his arms around her and laughed. "You have no idea how alright it is."

He kissed her, feeling her body fold more closely to him than before; her lips parted and he felt the darting tip of her tongue. Her thighs encircled his leg, pushing her pubis against him. She felt him hardening through his airman's breeches and laughed quietly,

"I think I know exactly how alright it is."

They stumbled towards the bed. His hands explored her clothing, losing their way in cul-de-sacs of undiscovered lace. She fell onto the mounded quilts and her quick fingers expertly released the buttons and hooks that had defeated him.

"Are you going to keep yours on then? Come on, you dimwit, I'm freezing."

He stood, immobile, and watched her lithe paleness slide under the quilts, her limbs hiding and revealing glimpses of secrets long imagined. He turned away to sit on the bed, sliding out of breeches and shirt, made self-conscious as much by the sticking-plastered dressings on his thighs as by his own increasingly obvious arousal. He turned quickly, slithering crouched and concealing under the covers. The sheets were icy cold, Stainton a nest of warmth in its centre. As her arms came to meet him he tried to hold his lower body away, gasping as she enfolded him, pulling him against her, her thighs again encircling his leg as she ground against him.

He shuddered, felt the wet heat between their bellies, heard her voice in his ear, "Oh Andy."

The night was endless.

At some pre-dawn hour he came awake to the sensation of her hands upon him. She felt him stir and kissed him. "I'm sorry, did I wake you?"

His thighs moved involuntarily in rhythm. "Please, never apologise for that."

"Andy, I've been awake for a while, and I've been thinking."

He became still. "Thinking? What about?"

"About you and me, and what I feel about you."

"And what did you decide?"

"That I love you. That I've never been so certain about anything. That I don't need to be frightened of anything anymore."

"You mean…?"

"I mean whatever you want me to mean. I mean that I don't want to miss this incredible chance."

Their bodies became warm quicksilver, running over and through each other, fingers exploring regions uncharted no longer. She gasped at a second's pain before the maelstrom drowned them both.

CHAPTER 27

The platform chilled their feet through the soles of their shoes. A wheezing locomotive warmed them with its waste steam as it waited for stretchered and wheelchaired men to be loaded into its peeling carriages. Four endless days of the breathless euphoria of first-time lovers had evaporated to an icy, stone-coloured morning. They stood in a silent embrace, each uttering occasional small gulps and gasps as impossible emotions fought for release.

"You should be home on leave in a few days, surely."

"Bound to be."

"You've been out here for more than six months. You must be due for Home Establishment."

He found no answer, crushing her tighter against him. A short, rounded station master tapped Stainton's shoulder, speaking moistly around the whistle between his lips,

"Madame, le train est sur le point de quitter."

"Andy, be safe, please. Just be safe, and come home." She was crying openly now.

"I'm an old hand now. It's the new pilots who get shot down. I promise I'll be home as soon as they let me."

"Just bloody make sure you do. You have our telephone number, you could even call."

He smiled, "I don't think they'd see that as crucial to the war effort. Anyway, half the time we can't get a line to Wing, let alone England."

He bent to touch his forehead against hers, "I'll write though, and with any luck I'll be with you before they're delivered."

The station master returned, *"Madame, s'il vous plaît, monter le train maintenant."*

A final kiss, a last breathless exchange of devotions and she was on the train, leaning through the window to clasp his hands. She attempted a smile,

"I can't believe how soppy I'm being. I used to hear this stuff from girls at school; never thought I'd find myself behaving this way."

"If it makes you feel any better, I knew damn' well I'd end up behaving like a love-struck owl."

A whistle screamed and the clanking, squeaking train pulled their hands apart. Andy watched it out of sight, tucked his chin into his coat and turned back towards the hospital.

*

Two strangers were playing darts in the hut when Andy arrived back at Beauval. They turned with raised eyebrows and uncertain smiles as he entered.

"Andy Palmer, I live here. Who're you?"

"Rodney Bye. This is Hocking. We arrived today. Major Barrington-Holt put us in this hut, is that alright?"

"It's fine, make yourselves at home. And it's just plain Major Holt, Barrie Holt. He likes you to assume the double barrels."

He took the darts from Bye and threw them with reasonable accuracy at the startlingly new dartboard. "This will brighten up the evenings. Seen Colin?"

"Is that Lieutenant Hingley? No, we've not met him. He was out when we arrived. Hasn't got back yet."

Andy looked at the deepening gloom outside. Occasional wisps of snow wafted past the window. "How long's he been gone?"

Bye shrugged. "Search me. We've been in here about an hour, so longer than that."

Page and French were at their accustomed positions, resting on their elbows on the end of the bar. They stood as Andy approached. "Welcome back, young Palmer. Whisky?"

"Either of you know where Colin is?"

Page nodded at the mess servant and pointed to the two glasses on the bar, cutting his eyes to include Andy in the refills.

"Got separated around Longueval. We jumped an LVG, then got bounced by a bunch of Albatri. Arthur picked up some extra ballast in his rear fuselage, but they cleared off without making a second attack. By the time we'd sorted ourselves out we'd lost sight of Colin and the Ell-Vee."

"How long ago was this?"

French looked at the mess clock. "Nearly two hours. We'd been out for over an hour, so wherever he is, I'm afraid he's down now. Get that down you; you won't be flying until the Doc's had a look at you anyway."

Andy found his eyes blurring and rubbed his knuckle sharply against his nose to cover his discomposure. He reached for the whisky glass. "Thanks."

"Being late home doesn't mean he's crashed. Or even if he has, it doesn't mean he's hurt. We've both proved that – in fact twice in your case," said French. "He'll turn up. "

"What about McLeod and Phillips? I noticed I've got two new hut mates."

"Both gone west. Phillips piled it in while he was practising on targets. McLeod came down Hunside about three days ago; we've not heard any more." French shrugged, "S'what happens to new chaps I'm afraid. How was the hospital?"

Andy smiled despite his anxiety. "Better than expected. Much better in fact."

Page grinned, "Compliant nurses overcome with Christmas generosity?"

"Even better. Let's say I had an unexpected visitor."

"Don't tell me you bedded St Nicholas, you dirty little sod!"

"I'm saying no more."

Page gestured for the whisky bottle to be delivered to this end of the bar. "Oh you will, young man. My methods are relentless."

Despite spirited resistance, Andy revealed more under interrogation than he intended, much to his companions' satisfaction. They toasted him with new respect and delivered him to the bosom of his new hut mates.

Colin had still not returned.

CHAPTER 28

The doctor having pronounced Andy fit for active duty too late for him to join the morning job, Andy mooched around the airfield looking for diversion. He played a listless game of vingty with a group of new pilots whose names refused to embed themselves in his memory. They were irrepressibly cheerful, loudly betting matchstick fortunes with a joyful ebullience that drove him out to sulk around the perimeter track. After twenty minutes of kicking cinders and throwing desiccated potatoes at divers targets he allowed himself to admit to the chill gnawing through his tunic. He pulled up his collar, hunched his shoulders and turned back to the farm buildings. *Better report to the R.O, see what he's got in store for me this afternoon.*

He stopped off at the hut on the way, hoping unrealistically for a letter from Stainton. Colin's stack of tattered penny dreadfuls accused him across the dusty space and he retreated again.

Outside, the noise of returning aircraft made him look up. He recognised French's machine by its chequered fuselage band and watched as he landed smoothly, leading his flight safely home.

"Slides it in like a greasy spoon doesn't he?"

Andy turned, startled by the voice at his side. Colin, still wearing his flying helmet, was looking out at French's taxiing Nieuport. Behind him, its engine drowned by the roar of aero motors, a muddy lorry was already reversing out of the farmyard gate.

"Col! I don't believe it!" Andy grabbed the smaller man's hand, pulling him close with his left arm around his shoulders.

"Woa! Easy there!" Colin's voice was muffled by uniform cloth. "Put me down you great poufter!"

Andy stepped back, still absently shaking Colin's hand. His eyes were moist. "Don't do that to me again, you little tit. Where the bloody hell have you been?"

"Keeping company with the Royal Artillery. Phones were out, so I couldn't call in. I came down somewhere west of Bouzincourt and walked for an hour before I found a battery outside Hedauville. Any chance I could have that hand back when you're done with it?"

"Sorry mate. What happened to you?"

"Engine went sick east of Pozières. Here's Barrie Holt, come in with me and I'll tell you both."

Substantive Major Barrington Holt was waiting outside the squadron office. He nodded as the boys approached.

"Morning Palmer. Glad to see you're back at last, Hingley. Do both of you come inside, please."

The office was warmed slightly by an unenthusiastic pile of greyish coals in the stone fireplace. The Recording Officer sat down behind his desk and motioned the two pilots to the one spare chair. "So, Hingley, where have you been since yesterday afternoon?"

Colin sat down. "Forced landing between Bouzincourt and Hedauville, sir. We engaged an enemy two-seater near to Pozières, then got bounced by a group of Albatri – six or seven I think. I'm not sure if my engine was hit or something just broke, but my revs suddenly dropped to 800. I disengaged and started home, but the engine packed up altogether as I crossed the lines. There was a strong wind from the north-west, so I couldn't make headway home, and I eventually found a field and put down safely. The bus flipped over at the last second, but I don't think there's much damage."

"And...?"

Colin smiled, "And what, sir?"

"And why did you neither return to your base nor report in by telephone until twenty hours later?"

"I walked for an hour before I even found anyone, by which time it was dark. I found an artillery battery next to Hedauville. They sent out a guard for the aeroplane and put me up for the night. The telephones were out of action, sir."

"Convenient. Did you bring your cockpit watch?"

Colin's exasperation was hidden by a tired sigh. "Yes sir, we wouldn't want anything to happen to that."

"Get yourself cleaned up and find some food. You and Palmer are to escort a BE2 on art. reg this afternoon. Take-off at two. Palmer, stay here and I'll brief you."

*

They waited for the BE2 over Beaumont-Hamel, now in allied hands. Andy banked steeply, holding the nose up with opposite rudder and leaning out of his cockpit to gain a better view of the shattered Hawthorn Redoubt and the craters that gaped before it. Clustered round their smoky cooking fire, a group of infantry waved up at him. He waved back and pulled into a tight turn, centring his right wing accurately on the cooking fire to pivot a full 360 degrees on his wingtip. After twenty minutes of stooging around the BE2 had still not made an appearance. Andy waved to Colin and pointed to the south-west, the direction of the reconnaissance machine's airfield. Colin nodded and returned a thumbs-up, and the two Nieuports turned onto their new heading, both pilots scanning the skies for their charge.

The recce squadron's aerodrome was a large field near Allonville. As the cinder strip came into sight, Andy saw a BE2c lifting laboriously into the air. They orbited at 2,000 feet waiting for it to stagger to their height.

By the time it reached them, and its pilot had waved and beckoned them on, the Nieuports had been airborne for forty-five minutes. Andy estimated a twenty-minute flight to the objective and a further twenty-minute flight home. That left an absolute maximum of fifteen minutes over target, with a zero margin of safety. He pulled close alongside the 2c and pointed down at the field, then mimed drinking from a beer mug and pointed at his machine. *I'm low on fuel.* The 2c pilot shook his head emphatically and pointed sharply forward. Andy shook his head in frustration and looked across to Colin on his left wing, exchanging shrugs with his partner. He recalculated again. If the spotter carried out his job quickly they should be able to make it home with a few fumes of petrol left. He shivered, suddenly chilled in the freezing cockpit.

Archie put up an enthusiastic welcome for them when the observer finally let down his wireless aerial and the 2c began its plodding to-and-fro over the target, an artillery battery west of Bapaume. Andy checked his watch and fuel gauge and hoped for a rapid resolution.

The first British artillery salvo finally arrived after ten minutes' orbiting among shrapnel bursts and strings of flaming onions. Swooping and climbing to avoid them, Andy felt each fuel-sapping throttle adjustment as a physical pain. A cluster of black dots appeared from the north-east, well above them. He looked across to Colin, not wanting to wing-waggle and risk flashing a semaphore reflection of the westering sun to the approaching aircraft. Colin caught his look and followed his pointing finger, nodding when he saw the distant specks. Together, they began to climb.

At 5,000 feet Colin pointed down. The 2c had been raked by a skein of flaming onions and was spiralling earthwards, both starboard planes burning. Released from escort duty, Andy gave the wash-out signal and turned for home. 2,000 feet above them, six Albatros DIIs began their attack. Colin saw them coming just before their leader opened fire. He waggled his wings urgently and pulled hard left out of the line of fire. Andy saw the manoeuvre and broke right. The lead Albatros, its fuselage painted a dull red, shot through the empty space, already beginning its pursuing turn.

Andy's machine shuddered as bullets pierced the upper centre section; metallic clangs and whines signalled several hits on his engine. He looked over his shoulder to see the pale blue tail of another Albatros sweep by. He rolled further over, looking up at the ground to see his attacker pulling up hard, exchanging speed for height to return to the assault. He pulled the joystick into his groin to nose over into an attack line. He knew his tail was unprotected; knew that four more enemy aircraft would be choosing their targets behind him, but now his only chance of survival lay in aggression.

Blue-tail had zoomed to slightly above Andy, and now stall-turned back towards him. It was a novice's move that left the German hanging almost motionless in the air for lethal seconds. Andy ruddered his Aldis sight into position and fired.

A searing cold lanced above his right ear and his goggles jerked across his face, bruising his nose and filling his vision with bright sparks. A metallic *ack-ack-ack* filled his ears. Blinded by the impact and the sheepskin padding, Andy rolled right into a spinning engine-on dive. The red-fuselaged Albatros dived to follow. Andy pushed his goggles back into position and looked back. The enemy aircraft closed the distance between them with ease and he saw the flashes of its guns. He pulled level and into a sharp right hand turn, almost colliding with a third black-crossed enemy that flicked across his nose and was gone before he could fire a shot.

Established in the tightest turn he could accomplish, Andy looked around him. To the west he could see three Albatros diving, the number one machine hosing tracer at an invisible target. Behind him, the red aircraft had pulled into a climb to tighten his turn before diving again to the attack. Blue-tail was moving directly away, climbing slightly; presumably he was opening up space to give himself a clear run-in and attack. The third Albatros had disappeared for now.

He touched an exploratory hand to his head. It was impossible to feel much through his layered gloves, but his helmet seemed to be gashed. He looked at his fingers, bright with fresh blood. His head ached poundingly.

The red Albatros dived on him again and he rolled deeper into his turn to spiral under the German's attack line. As he did he saw the third enemy climbing towards him. He held right stick and kicked full left rudder to skid the Nieuport away. The move clearly surprised the German, who turned the wrong way, missing his opportunity. Andy looked behind again to see the red Albatros drop once again into the killing line, Blue-tail flying accurately and protectively behind him. Andy pulled again into the right-hand turn, noticing how the red aircraft made no attempt to try to match the little Nieuport's manoeuvrability, but simply pulled high again. *That Hun's way too good for me.*

Andy knew it was only a matter of time before the one-sided battle reached its inevitable conclusion. The German aircraft were faster, more heavily armed and flown by first-class pilots. Even the apparently ill-judged stall-turn by Blue-tail was now revealed as a perfectly executed trap to line him up for the red leader. *This time you are fucked, boy.*

The zig-zag of the German front line caught his eye and he absently wondered which side he'd crash, just as gunfire barked again behind him. He glanced over his shoulder to see all three Albatros in line behind him and, behind them, a mosquito cloud of more diving aircraft. Tracer snaked among the German machines, which scattered immediately. He saw the flash of tricoloured roundels on the wings of the newcomers as they turned to follow. A full squadron of RNAS Pups pursued the Albatros as they dipped their noses and scuttled away to the east, wolves baulked of their assured kill. Andy turned the nose for home and prayed for a lean-burning engine.

Hoped dared to flicker as Terramesnil slid under his wing. As though sensing his optimism, the engine popped, died, backfired and chugged back to life, dying completely as the airfield came in sight. He set the nose for the best glide angle he could expect and sighted along the Aldis barrel to judge whether he would volplane over the perimeter hedge or crash into the same field that he'd visited ungently on his first operational flight. He caught sight of the tail of another Nieuport, nosed over in a drainage ditch.

The perimeter hedge grabbed at his wheels as the gliding aeroplane settled, its wings near-stalled in the last dying momentum of its descent. The windmilling propeller hit the rutted grass and Andy was flung forward against the gun trigger, further bruising his face. He released his strap and pulled himself clear of yet another wreck, wincing as the effort made the blood pound in his head.

He met Colin slouching towards the office, his helmet dangling from his left hand, his face bloodied and an angry welt growing on his temple. "Bloody hell, mate. You're looking a bit second-hand."

Colin looked up, "You look as though you've just gone ten rounds with the Great White Hope yourself. Glad to see you got down."

"Getting down was always going to happen. Walking away was less of a certainty. We're pushing our luck here, mate. I actually don't know how many times I've crashed now. Have a look at this, will you? Think I stopped one with my head."

Colin's face fell and he carefully helped Andy with his helmet. The wound was impressively bloody but superficial. The surrounding flesh was bruised purple. "I think it just grazed you. You should get the Doc to clean it up. Might even need a stitch, but it's nothing much."

"Pity."

"Yes." They began walking again. "Bloody idiot in the 2c nearly did for us both. Thank Christ for the Navy."

"Yeah, well he won't be telling his kids about it, poor bugger."

"Poor bugger my arse. It's his observer I feel sorry for."

Andy nodded. "I'm asking after my leave as soon as I've reported."

*

"Palmer, you've just enjoyed six days at the rear in hospital. I fail to see how you feel justified in asking now for leave." Substantive Major Barrington Holt was sitting, ramrod-straight, at Tiverton's desk.

"I'm not asking for leave sir. I'm asking after the leave I'd already been given. I've been out here for more than six…"

"How long you've been out here is irrelevant. You do know that there's a war on, I hope?"

Andy gestured at his face, now displaying two black eyes. "I'd spotted that something was going on, yes. But what with the crashes and the people shooting at me, I keep forgetting."

"You'll be insubordinate once too often, Palmer. That tone may be acceptable to Major Tiverton, but use it once more with me and there will be consequences."

Andy breathed deeply. "I apologise, sir. Now I'd like to speak to the OC, please."

"The major is unavailable at present. But you can be the first to know: Major Tiverton has been recalled to Home Establishment; I am to be your new Squadron Commander."

CHAPTER 29

Dearest Stainton,

It was terrific to hear from you. I am missing you too and wish I could be home. Leave has been closed and so I have got no idea when I will see you next. We are getting a new Squadron Commander who is a bit of a stickler. Colin and I both crashed yesterday after running out of petrol, neither of us suffered too badly, though we look like a pair of losing prize fighters! I picked up a bullet to the head in the scrap and thought my number was up, but it turned out I'd only been nicked, it still hurt though and still smarts when I wash my hair.

There is not much else to say here, except that I love you and wish I could be with you. It has become so miserable to get up every morning and fly and fly and fly. We are losing new pilots left right and centre and I don't know when one of us old lags will finally get it. Apparently I've been keeping Colin awake by shouting in my sleep, but I don't think I sleep enough to have bad dreams.

I'm sorry, I just read that last bit again and it sounds a bit self-pitying! I'm just a bit tired.

Please keep writing and, I hope to be with you very soon.

All my love,

Andy.

P.S. Colin sends his love.

Connie entered the breakfast room in a pale-blue dressing gown.

"Letters, dear?"

Stainton nodded, turning the letter over and over. "From Andy. He sounds so tired."

Connie seated herself at the table. "Still no sign of his leave?"

"No. And I keep reading about more and more casualties. There's another piece from Pemberton Billing in the Mail this morning. He says there's a conspiracy to wipe out the RFC. Andy's being sacrificed to earn left-wing financiers even more money."

"A conspiracy to wipe out Billing would be a Godsend. The idiot does more for the left wing than a cupboard full of Bolsheviks. Do you want me to make a few telephone calls?"

Stainton smiled slightly. "Would you? He's had another crash. I'm afraid of every letter that arrives."

"Leave it with me." Connie patted her daughter's hand. "We'll have him out of there in no time."

*

Tiverton's farewell bash started before tea. Fortunately the weather had cooperated by providing horizontal rain, allowing the mess to fill with expectant aviators before the impatient dusk of February had fully descended. French had suggested the early start to try to ensure the OC's reasonably coherent presence before his afternoon's drinking brought the oblivion he so assiduously sought. Now only French was missing from the gathering, having left in the tender after breakfast to collect a new aeroplane from St Omer.

Tiverton entered to a standing ovation and a polite chorus of "For he's a jolly good fellow." He smiled good-naturedly, and Andy was struck by how the major had aged since their first meeting. His hair had faded from light brown to wisps of grey; his eyes were watery and slightly unfocused. He regarded the brimming tankard that Page presented to him with slight puzzlement before tossing back the toxic concoction with a vague shrug.

Page addressed the throng, "Dearly be-buggered, we are gathered here today in the shite of France to witness this man and this bath sponge brought together in unholy alliance against sobriety, which is a pointless state, beloved only of vicars and ladies of tight-lipped temperance. I call upon him now to baptize you all in true devotion to our lord, the almighty Bacchus." He genuflected respectfully to the major. "Draw near now, and be washed in the shampoo of the bath."

A line formed rapidly. Each pilot knelt before the major to be anointed by the bath sponge, which Tiverton dipped into the tin bath at his side before squeezing the whisky-champagne mixture over the upturned face and open mouth of the supplicant. Duly sanctified, the dripping aviator would run eagerly to the back of the line to receive further benediction. The rising hilarity was cut short by the sound of an aero engine. An exodus from the mess assembled a straggling audience, staring upwards through the lashing rain. The ack emmas had all emerged from their unknown lairs to stand in their own group, respectfully apart from the pilots. A dark shape swept by downwind, pressed down by the scudding clouds.

Page appeared at Andy's elbow. "It's Arthur. God knows how he found his way back in this."

Andy looked at the effel, streaming horizontally from its pole, tugging and spiralling in the wind. "God knows how he's going to get in against that. It must be forty-fifty miles an hour."

Page nodded, "If anybody can do it, Arthur can. I've seen him land in far worse than this."

"Really?"

"No."

The sound of the engine disappeared into the gale and forty necks craned forward, trying to pierce the gloom for the reappearance of French's machine. Long seconds passed. A silence fell over the squadron as they listened for the approach of the aircraft. Finally someone shouted, "There!"

A shapeless clump of darkness resolved into the wavering, bouncing wings of a biplane, clawing its way forward with painful slowness. A gust of even greater ferocity threw the machine high, before falling malevolently still. The aircraft hung in the air for a moment, then nosed over. Page clapped appreciatively.

"See? Show me anybody else who could have got the nose down after that!"

The machine dived towards the ground. Page watched intently. "Wait... wait... OK, pull it out my boy, you've got it!"

The aircraft had begun to pull up when another powerful gust hit the biplane from almost directly above the wings, pushing the nose down and robbing the wings of lift. The machine spiralled right to crumple just inside the perimeter hedge; the crunching sound of the impact, known and dreaded by them all, crackled through the gale.

French was conscious and furious when the running crowd reached him. "Bloody wind! I'd have got in if it hadn't dropped at the last second! Somebody give me a hand out, would you? Think I've crocked my knee."

Installed in reasonable comfort in the sick bay, his broken leg elevated, French received regular visitors, each bearing a gift of alcohol. A small satellite party assembled around his bed, its core formed by Page, Colin and Andy.

"You want to watch how much of that you drink," said Colin, "The Doc's bothered about the amount of morphine he's pumped into you."

"Balls to the morphine! Give me shampoo!"

"What price the new Sopwith, Arthur? Any good?" asked Andy.

French fixed him with unsteady eyes, "Bloody wonderful! Goes up like a fart in a bath and it turns on a thruppence. Trust me to catch a Blighty just as we get a decent bus to play with!"

"Trust you to bust up the first one we get, you blithering incompetent!" said Page, refilling his friend's glass.

French died at around 3 a.m. when the blood clot in his fractured leg found and stopped his heart.

*

The tender dropped the three of them at St Omer. Page had been uncharacteristically silent on the three-hour journey, and now trailed behind Colin and Andy, his chin tucked into the collar of his coat, as they reported to collect three brand-new Sopwith Scouts. They dodged the commotion of vehicles that sprayed brown slush as they rattled along the roads of the huge air depot. Several misdirections, either accidental or mischievous, had them walking back and forth from office to stores to hangar until their boots were sodden and their feet numb. Eventually, a taciturn sergeant asked them to wait in a damp, unheated room. They sat, huddled and miserable, watching the afternoon sky darken.

"Sod this for a lark. Wait here." Page stumped out, slamming the door behind him. He returned within five minutes, a nervous private in tow.

"Come on. Frankley here has kindly volunteered to find our aeroplanes while we get some hot food and warm feet."

"What happened to the sergeant who was on duty here?" asked Colin.

"Here, sir? There wouldn't be anybody on duty here. This hut's down for demolition."

"I see. And who would be likely to be around here with three stripes on his arm at this time of day?"

"Could be anybody, sir. There's thousands here, and I reckon half of 'em are sergeants. Sorry, sir, I'd help you if I could, honest."

"Yes, I'm sure you would. Never mind, lead us to this food and you're five bob's worth of forgiven."

*

Andy leaned back from the table, patting his midriff. "Bloody hell, they look after themselves here, don't they?"

Colin was still consuming rice pudding, heavy, steaming and streaked with raspberry jam. "Just a lot, chum. Not eating yours, Humph?"

Page looked up, a match held to his pipe, "No, the beef was a bit rich for this old chap. I've had plenty, though."

"Plenty my arse. You pushed potatoes around your plate and swallowed a couple of forkfuls of cabbage. It's time to return to the land of the living you old bugger."

"I'm fine. Just not that hungry."

"Fuck me! If the Devil should cast his net now!" Standing over them, a heaped plate of beef and potatoes in his hand, was Cubby.

The Australian giant allowed his plate to clatter on the table and delivered a crushing bear hug to each of his former comrades, to the obvious amusement of the occupants of other tables. Andy, laughing, fought free from the rough khaki embrace.

"Cubby! What the hell are you doing here?"

"Returning to increase the numbers and flying skill of 128, mate, what d'you think?"

Andy spotted the new wings on Cubby's tunic. "You finished your ticket? Bloody hell, when?"

"Couple of weeks ago, since when I've been pulling strings to get the posting I wanted. How's things?" He sat down, pulling his plate from its splash of gravy.

"They've been better. Arthur's gone west."

For the first time, Cubby noticed Page's slumped depression. "Arthur? No, I don't believe it. Is he...?"

Page nodded and returned to fiddling with his pipe.

"It was a landing prang," explained Colin. "He was trying to get down against a fifty-mile-an-hour wind and went in hard. Died the same night."

Cubby toyed with his food, looking at Page. "Jesus Humph, I'm so sorry, mate."

Page shrugged. "It happens. At least we had the chance to get him half-cut before..." He stood and walked quickly outside. Colin made to follow but was halted by a minute head shake from Cubby.

"So, who's left? We lost anyone else?"

Andy shivered in sudden realisation. "Nearly everybody, Cub. Doke's shot down, Robbie crashed; there's only you, Col, Humph and me left from the old squadron."

"Well it's not going to be much of a homecoming then. It'll be dark in an hour; might as well get a few down us here." He looked around for a mess servant. "Orderly, get your fat arse over here!"

The evening continued in a reasonable demonstration of conviviality. Page returned after half an hour, chilled and shivering, and accepted the first of several hot toddies that fumed an occasional smile across his patched face. As they left to find their way to their overnight billets, Cubby fell in step beside Andy.

"You and me need to have a chat, son."

"Now?"

"Not now, it's too late. Back at the squadron. But we do need to talk."

Andy looked more closely at his old observer. Cubby's face was paler than he remembered, the cheekbones more noticeable, the eyes shadowed with grey. Pinkish scars were visible alongside each temple. Cubby caught his look and touched them. "These?" he laughed, "Yeah, I suppose they're part of the story. I'll tell you back at Beauval."

*

Cubby cut a strangely incongruous figure squeezing into the cockpit of a smart new Sopwith Scout, now semi-officially re-christened the "Pup". Andy watched his take-off roll with interest. *Nowt wrong with that.* He applied power to follow.

After the battle-weary Nieuport 11s of his experience, the little Sopwith was a revelation. The tail unstuck in seconds, needing only a gentle application of left rudder to keep the eager little machine straight. Less than five seconds later he felt the earthly vibration fall away and his new mount was gaining altitude at a pace that bordered on impossible. Just five minutes later the four aircraft were levelled out in formation at 5,000 feet. Andy looked across at Colin who grinned back, kissing his fingers and waving them skyward. They maintained discipline until Frévent, when Cubby's restraint broke and he dived abruptly on the village's crossroads. The other three dived after him and pursued their least-experienced member on a mad follow-my-leader over the rooftops and out along the south-leading road, trees and telegraph poles flicking by their wings.

The road dived into a wooded tunnel and Cubby pulled up sharply amid a cloud of disturbed starlings. Andy felt two or three strike his wings as he followed through and considered briefly the wisdom of continuing. Then he saw Cubby's machine tip onto a knife-edge and pull into a spine-crushing turn, his wings brushing the bare treetops. Andy grinned and twisted after him.

CHAPTER 30

The new Pups straggled in in ones and twos, bringing delight to those with new mounts and good-natured envy from those still tagging behind the powerful newcomers in their outdated Nieuports. Resentment of Major Holt's irascible, formal leadership gave way to admiration for his staff work as 128 became one of the first RFC squadrons in Northern France to be equipped with the cutting edge fighters.

The contour-chasing race return from St Omer had done much to restore humanity to Page and when, two days later, he downed an Albatros, his recovery seemed complete. The Pups climbed and turned faster than the larger, more powerful German machines, and were unbeatable at altitude. The squadron took to patrolling in force at 18,000 feet, looking for trouble. The news from nearby squadrons was less encouraging. Most were still fielding DH2s and Nieuports, and their losses in the face of this new scourge were crippling.

A new name had emerged to pursue tired airmen through their restless sleep: Manfred Von Richthofen had taken the crown dropped by Boelcke to lead a new elite against the under-equipped, inadequately trained allies. Initially, airmen had reported being attacked by a superbly handled, red-tailed Albatros. Then this new enemy had taken to painting his entire fuselage a dark red. By the time this new nemesis could be given a name, every panel of his machine was the red of congealed blood, the black crosses muted by carmine dope. Page responded by having the ack emmas paint a wide chequered band around his rear fuselage, a tribute to the identification carried by Arthur French. Colin, now officially an ace with five confirmed victories, scavenged the spinner from a crashed Hun machine and had it fitted to his propeller, painted bright yellow. Major Holt, with atypical tolerance, made no objection, and names and inexpert cartoons began to appear on the noses of several aircraft.

Cubby was largely unchanged, once again dominating the mess evenings with his enthusiastic attacks on the clanging piano and loud humour. But Andy noticed how he would occasionally wander away alone, absently rubbing his temples. It was on one such evening that Andy found him leaning against a petrol bowser, his breath a mist in the cold moonlight. He stepped quietly alongside and took out his cigarettes, handing the packet to Cubby.

"Thanks." Cubby struck a match and lit both cigarettes. He inhaled deeply, looking up at the sound of an aero engine. "That's one of theirs."

They scanned the sky for silhouettes, seeing nothing as the thrumming beat of the engine grew louder. "If he's after us he can't miss in this moonlight."

A dark shape flitted across a light patch of sky and one of the perimeter machine gun nests barked ineffectively and fell silent. The German bomber faded into the darkness.

"Looks like it's some other poor bugger tonight. But they know for sure where we are now, thanks to those prats in the nest, so I dare say he'll be back." He ground out his cigarette.

"Might as well be getting in."

"You said we needed to talk."

"Yeah, I did. Not tonight."

"So when?"

Cubby stood for a long moment, looking after the dwindling engine sound. "OK, tonight. My hut." Without waiting for Andy, he walked away.

*

Cubby had reclaimed the solitude of his old hut and restocked it with his own furnishings. He motioned Andy to a chair and busied himself with cups and kettle at the gas ring. He had not spoken since they left the airfield. Andy sat down and waited quietly. Cubby lit the gas ring and stood, hands in pockets, watching the iron kettle. After a few seconds it began to hiss and pop quietly.

"They tried to make me forget everything." He rubbed his temples, his voice little more than a whisper. "This was at Looney Hatch, you know? They'd try to get me to talk about all sorts of other stuff, and there was one bloke who just wanted to know what I was dreaming. He got more and more arsy with me when I kept telling him that I wasn't dreaming anything much. Asked me why I wanted to keep my dreams secret."

He glanced back at Andy. "I made a couple up for him that I thought he'd like, but that just got him more upset. So I asked this other chap I was sharing with to tell me some of his. He had some real beauts. Apparently they were full of sexual metaphor, whatever that is. So this doctor's getting pretty worked up and loving it all and talking about how all his theories were being validated. Then he twigs that he's hearing the same dreams from two people and says he's withdrawing treatment, which was fine by me." He massaged his temples again.

"So they're talking about shipping me back to France when this new doctor comes along. Different story completely. He'd been working with some bloke in Scotland who said that you need to remember, not forget." He shifted the kettle on the gas, swirling it experimentally.

"So we started remembering... *I* started remembering. Not that I'd forgotten. Not that I could."

The kettle began to steam. Cubby lifted it and turned off the gas, waited for the final pop. "Cuppa?"

"Please."

Silent again, Cubby spooned tea into a castle-shaped pot, stirring thoughtfully as he poured in the boiling water. He place cups and condensed milk on the table and hid the teapot's glazed stone walls under a knitted cosy. He caught Andy's look and smiled, "Present from an old friend. Can't stand cold tea."

"So what did you remember?"

"Not sure remember's the right word. Understood, maybe. Faced up to, even. Took a few sessions before I could tell him everything. Some of it I didn't want to say to myself. And he said those were the bits I had to say to you."

He poured tea into tin mugs and pushed his cigarettes across the table. He stared at a blob of froth revolving on the surface of his tea; he fished out a fragment of stem with a finger.

"I had a son," he said.

CHAPTER 31

The scrubby gorse tore at Snaff's ankles as he staggered north. His boots were full of sharp flints and he stumbled repeatedly, the huge weight of Cubby sliding sideways to drag both feet along the ground. The bandages applied by the Turks to hold the sergeant's splints in place unravelled and snagged again and again, jerking the leg backwards and almost pulling Snaff off his feet. Exhausted, he sank to the ground, allowing Cubby to slide down to lie beside him.

"You still alive, Sarge?"

Cubby was unconscious, but breathing rapidly. His eyes were pushed forward in their sockets, forcing the lids apart to show pinkish, pupilless whites.

"Struth, you look like shit, Sarge. Dunno how we're going to get you home, I'm about done."

Snaff uncorked his canteen and upended it over Cubby's parted lips. Nothing, not even the hoped-for couple of drops. "Sorry, Sarge, got no water left. I'll just have a fag and get me breath back, then we'll be on our way back."

The sun was a piercing actinic ball almost directly ahead when Snaff stumbled into view of the Australian trenches. He laid Cubby on the flinty ground and removed his own blouse and undershirt, waving the stained cotton above his head in what he hoped would be recognised as a flag of truce by both sides. Leaving his blouse on the ground, he shouldered his burden once again and staggered forward, the undershirt gripped in his teeth. Every few yards he stopped, gripping both of Cubby's wrists in one hand, and waving the improvised flag above his head with the other. No shots came from either line of trenches. Each time he raised his arm, the big sergeant would slide off his sweat-slippery back.

Snaff's legs gave way fifty yards from the ANZAC trenches and he sank, helpless, to his knees. Cubby slid to the ground and the exhausted corporal bent forward, swaying on hands and knees, coughing and retching. He looked up to see a Red Cross flag being waved above the trench wall and two stretcher bearers stepped into view, one waving the flag, while the other held the stretcher high in the air. Someone shouted something from the Turkish lines, but whether it was a threat or an agreement to truce was impossible to guess through the roar of blood pounding in Snaff's ears.

The stretcher bearers reached him within a few seconds, and handed Snaff a full canteen of water. He sipped and felt new energy rush through his body. He shook his head as the medic asked him if he was injured, then nodded to confirm that he was able to walk to the trench.

They placed Cubby on the stretcher and started back. At the trench wall, the leading stretcher bearer turned and waved to the Turkish lines, "Thank you, Abdul!"

*

The tea was finished. Cubby swirled the leaves, staring into his cup.

"They gave Snaff a bollocking for bringing a deader back and ordered him to report back to his regiment. He copped one about three days later, so I never saw him again. I came to on the ground outside the RAP, no idea how much time I'd been there, but the state I was in says it was a while.

"I saw this officer going by and managed to call him. He came over and was a bit surprised I was still alive. The ones each side of me had already shot through. Turns out the Turks had broken into the forward trenches a couple of hours ago and they were dealing with a load of casualties. When it gets like that, triage means, 'if they look too rough, let 'em be.' There were Turks as well as Ozzies in that same line, and some of 'em were in better shape than me.

"They got me inside and had a proper look. Found a depressed fracture here." He tapped his temple a little above one of the pinkish scars. "There was a bruise underneath that was making the brain swell up, so they opened it up and pulled a bit of bone away and I'm on the mend as quick as." Cubby tapped his ankle.

"Needed a bit of scaffolding in the leg, but there wasn't really that much wrong with me. I get shipped back to Imbros and then the conversations start on what to do with me."

There was a long silence. "Did you find out what happened to your son?" asked Andy.

"I already knew. By the time I got official word I was in England, doing flight training."

The silence stretched to several minutes. Neither man moved, both of them staring at the table. The electric light dimmed and flickered occasionally. The draught curtain over the door ballooned slightly. Finally Andy looked up, his finger tracing the pattern of the linoleum tablecloth.

"And what was it you needed to talk to me about?"

"What we are talking about. I was hoping you'd work it out."

Cubby thought for a moment, then walked to the writing desk, returning with the framed picture that Andy had first seen back in July.

"That's me and Danny in Egypt. Look like anybody you know?"

Andy examined the photograph. "You're not saying he looks like me?"

"Doc in the Hatch reckoned I was making you into him. I'd failed to keep him alive, so I'd fixed on you. If I could keep you alive, he wouldn't be dead."

Andy looked at the photograph for several seconds. When he spoke again there was a slight catch in his voice. "You know, I think I can see it. Sorry Cub, I just didn't know."

"Not for you to apologise son, that should be me."

"What? Apologise for keeping me alive?"

"Apologise for pretending you were somebody else."

"Cub, it hurt like a bastard when you went, when I hadn't got you there anymore looking after me. Now you're back, can you carry on keeping me alive?"

Cubby opened the stove door, peering in at the crackling logs. A dim orange glow illuminated his face and he blinked as he shook in coal from a small shovel.

"If I can, mate."

CHAPTER 32

There was a dog in the hut.

Colin was sitting on the end of his bed, knees drawn up, contemplating the gigantic mongrel that had somehow materialised in front of the stove. It had contrived to wrap itself in the scrap of hearthrug and grinned damply as Andy entered, threads of the ruined braid edging adhering to its tongue. A tattered, greyish rag of a tail thumped good-naturedly against the stove, causing it to wobble perilously on its bricks. Two watery eyes glinted from somewhere under the fringe of carpet and hair.

"What the hell is that?"

"Dunno, but it eats furniture." Colin pointed to an upended chair, one leg of which had been conscientiously chewed, shortening it by an inch or so. "I came in and shooed it away from the chair. So it ate the rug instead."

"Where did it come from?"

"I suspect the new kitbag over there has something to do with it."

Andy walked to the table and reached for the kitbag lying on its top. The dog rumbled ominously and he withdrew his hand.

"He did that when I went to look at it," said Colin. "I think it's his."

"If it is, his name's Sidney Prebble," replied Andy, peering from a safe distance at the bag's label."

He reached again, engendering another rumble from the dog. Which yipped sharply as it met his gaze. The tail rocked the stove again. The door banged open and an unfamiliar figure entered the hut. The dog's claws skittered on the floor as it scrabbled to its feet to launch itself across the intervening space, tripping over the entangling rug. The newcomer, pink-faced and rounded, with a curtain of blond hair falling in his eyes, intercepted the animal's joyous attack, rubbing its ears as he looked up at Colin and Andy.

"Evening. I've just arrived. I'm Sidney Prebble."

"Fancy that, same as the dog," said Colin, standing to shake hands.

"What? Oh, this is Gaston. He's my dog."

"Yes, we were wondering what he was. A dog, you say?"

Sidney looked from one to the other uncertainly. "Yes… he's… a dog." He turned his attention to the animal. "What you got here, eh? Don't want to eat nasty bits of rag, do we? No, we don't!"

Colin raised his eyebrows at Andy. "I'm Colin Hingley, this is Andy Palmer, spinster of this parish and owner of that nasty bit of rag, which until recently was an equally nasty hearthrug."

Sidney held up the tattered wreck and looked suitably contrite. "Oh, look, sorry. He's a bit of a chewer I'm afraid. I shouldn't have left him, but I had to speak to the R.O." He walked over to shake hands with Andy. "I've not got off to a good start here, have I?"

Andy shook the offered hand. "No problem, the rug was here when we took over the hut. I'd keep my eye on the dog though, I wouldn't have put it anywhere near my mouth for a big clock."

"Which bed can I take?"

"Either of those at that end, they're both empty."

"What happened to the previous occupants?"

"What do you think?" Andy suppressed his quick resentment. "This your first posting, Sidney?"

"Yes. I've been stooging around St Omer for two weeks, though, so I've been doing some flying."

"Well that's a start. Do you know what flight you're in?"

"C."

"You're with me then. We'll go up in the morning and have a look at you."

*

Another steel-grey February morning in France. The cloud was solid at 2,000 feet, moved by a thin, steady north-westerly breeze. Prebble was already standing by a new Pup, shivering in his flying coat. Gaston the dog was, in response to some inexplicable canine impulse, trying to force his head and shoulders under the machine's axle. His back legs scrabbled at the ground, throwing up clods of frozen earth.

"Morning, Sidney. You're eager."

"Morning. Yes, well I wanted to be good and ready. Don't want to keep you waiting on my first day."

Andy looked more closely at Prebble's face, seeing blue lips, clamped tight to still the chattering teeth. "How long you been out here waiting?"

Prebble looked embarrassed. "Not long, half an hour or so."

"Right, well it's back to the mess for some hot tea. We're not going up with you freezing to death before we start."

"No, honestly, I'm fine."

"No you're not. Ten minutes won't make any difference. Start off cold on a proper job and you'll get yourself killed. Get hold of that dog before it tips the plane over."

The warm, smoky fug of the mess rapidly stilled Prebble's shivers. He hugged a steaming mug and scratched the dog's ears.

"Here, get that down you," Andy laid a doorstep bacon sandwich in front of him. "You haven't had breakfast, have you?"

"No, didn't feel much like it to be honest. First mission and all that."

Andy sat opposite him. "It's not a mission, it's a check flight. I'll see how you fly today, then you go up on your own as often as you can every day, staying well away from the lines. We'll think about letting you loose on the Germans when you've settled in a bit."

"I thought there was a job on this morning?"

"There is. O.P. at 11:00, but you're not on it."

"Why not?"

Andy spooned sugar into his tea. "Because I want you alive. You'll get your chance when I think you're ready."

Prebble put down his sandwich. "I am ready. I've flown over most of Northern France, waiting for this posting."

"Sorry, Sidney, but you're not. You're not because you haven't got a clue what it's like when an Albatros gets on your tail; you're not because you've never had Archie barking at you," He put up a hand to quiet Prebble's protest. "And you're not, because I said so."

The dog jumped to its feet as Prebble pulled a scrap of bacon from the bread and offered it. He wiped his fingers on his coat and contemplated his tea mug.

"You're the boss, I suppose. Though I don't quite see how I'll ever be *ready* if I never get near a Hun."

Andy thought of his first days and the protecting wisdom of Cubby and French, and suddenly felt the weight of many times his eighteen years.

"You'll get your chance, soon enough. Half an hour's flying now, then I'll introduce you to the rewards of checking your own ammo." He stood and finished his tea.

*

Andy followed Page through the freezing cloud, breaking through into the dazzling blue that still caught his breath with its splendour. In front and below, Page's Pup lead the formation, his streamers fluttering in the brilliant sunshine. Colin and Cubby cruised to left and right.

Prebble's flight had been interesting. In the air he was competent enough, and his firing range accuracy was impressive, but his landing was even worse than his swerving, height-grabbing take-off. The Pup had bounced on alternate wheels, zig-zagging along the cinder strip, forever threatening to bury a wingtip in the potato furrows. Andy had explained his doubts of Prebble's preservation for long enough to be killed in combat to a face blank with incomprehension. He shook his head and shrugged at the recollection. Hughie was going to need plenty of undercarriage spares.

A flare from Page's plane brought him back to the present and he realised he'd been gathering wool. A group of German aircraft was climbing towards them from the north-east. Andy counted at least six before he lost sight of them below his wings as Page took the flight higher. Levelling out at 18,000, Page led them into a spiral, looking down to where the harlequin-painted Albatros and LFGs where still clawing up towards them, the latter beginning to trail behind as they reached their ceiling. *Ten, no, twelve of them.*

As the Albatros contingent of the German pack climbed to within 500 feet, Page winged over into his dive. The three Pups dropped after him in tight line astern, pulling to left and right to clear their firing lines as the Huns scattered. A yellow aircraft flicked across Andy's nose and he raked a burst along its length, flashing by before the result of his shot could be seen. He turned tightly, pulling up to see Page's target, a luminous green skull painted on its black sides, nose up and fall away, its pilot limp at the controls.

Cubby was diving after a blue and yellow Albatros, a similarly painted aircraft plunging after him. Andy turned to help, but saw Colin pull in under the rearmost Albatros's tail, hosing fire into its belly. Both of the blue and yellow aircraft broke apart at the same moment to flutter, in grotesque formation, to the fields far below.

A crackling stutter from behind and Andy turned instinctively, looking over his shoulder to see a red spinner closing in from his right. He pulled into a tight turn towards the enemy, feeling the stick jerk as bullets pierced his elevator, before the Pup's nimbleness shook off the heavier machine's pursuit. Page's chequered fuselage flashed across his windscreen and he heard the flight commander's Vickers crackle as he pulled in behind Andy's pursuer. Andy completed his turn and took up position to protect his leader's tail. The Albatros pilot quickly learned that no manoeuvre would shake the spitting menace behind him and straightened into a dive, no doubt hoping that his superior speed would carry him out of danger. Page also straightened immediately and walked a line of tracer along the German's centre section. An explosion of steam engulfed the enemy pilot as his radiator burst and the Albatros fell away, its upper plane crumpling as it spiralled down.

Andy levelled out and looked around. The remaining three Albatros were clearing to the north east. The LFGs were nowhere to be seen. Below, he caught a glimpse of black crosses on yellow wings. His first adversary was descending slowly, a thin tail of white vapour trailing behind it. As he watched he saw sudden flame spring from the fuselage, rapidly engulfing the cockpit. A smaller ball of fire fell free to sparkle alone to the ground.

*

There was some confusion when the four of them tried to enter the mess four abreast and arm-in-arm. The skies had begun a cooperative downpour of icy sleet as they touched down and they were well saturated by the time the roaring and mutual back-thumping had carried them into the leaking haven, bawling "five-nil, five-nil!" to whatever tune occurred to them. Cubby was first to attract the mess servant's attention, ordering drinks all round on his tab. An enthusiastic crowd quickly formed around the four.

"One each for Colin and Andy, two for Humph, and first solo kill for me!" bellowed Cubby. "Five for no wicket, declared! Chalk 'em up young Palmer!"

Andy marked the kills on the tally board, noting that he was now a clear third in the squadron, with nine kills. Ahead of him were Colin, 12, and Page, 19.

"One more for the full score, Humph!"

The crowd took up the chant, lifting Page to their shoulders and marching around the mess, "One more for the full score! Humphrey gave the Hun what-for!"

Andy caught sight of Prebble, sitting alone with his dog. Sidney met his eyes and clapped his hands ruefully. The dog looked up at the sound, thumping its tail against the table leg.

*

Sidney pulled the FE2b into the tightest turn its cumbersome bulk could manage, causing Andy to stagger precariously in the front pit as he tried to swing the Lewis to bear on the all-red Albatros. He glanced at the ground a million miles below, seeing a khaki line breaking over trench walls; heard the rattle of machine guns and saw the soldiers fall.

"Jesus Christ, save me! Shoot him! Shoot him!"

Prebble's screaming drowned engine and gunfire and Andy swung the Lewis to track the stooping German. The mounting was impossibly stiff and he saw his tracers curving harmlessly behind the Red Baron's tail.

"Shoot him! Shoot him!"

Andy wrenched the gun round, leading his target and squeezed the trigger, only to feel it go slack under his finger. He collapsed to the floor of the pit, sobbing and helpless, Prebble's shrieks bursting his ears.

"Come on! Snap out of it! You're alright!"

Colin was shaking his shoulders, Prebble hovering uncertainly behind him, a moonlit figure in fisherman's jersey and pyjama bottoms. Andy fought off the black fingers of sleep and struggled in the tangled prison of his blankets.

"Is the kite OK?"

Colin patted his shoulder. "Noisy one, that, chum. You back with us now?"

Andy felt a rush of embarrassment. His head was pounding and his mouth tasted foul.

"Yes, sorry. Too much of the pop. I'm fine now." He craned his neck to see Prebble. "Sorry, Sidney. I'm a bit of a noisy sleeper sometimes."

Prebble nodded and turned back to his cubicle. The dog, sprawled in front of the faintly glowing stove, twitched slightly, undisturbed in its slumbers.

CHAPTER 33

"For God's sake, Palmer, I've been here three days! How long before you're satisfied I can fly a plane?"

"I'll be satisfied when I'm satisfied. Maybe tomorrow."

Andy turned to the sheaf of papers on the table. The administrative load of a Flight Commander was nowhere near compensated by the princely seven shillings a week it contributed to his income. Prebble snatched his flying helmet from the hook, tearing the lining on the sharp point.

"Or maybe the next day, or the day after that."

Andy stood up. "Sidney, if you're even thinking about heading east, looking for trouble, forget it now or the trouble will be right here."

"Meaning what?"

"Meaning I've given you a direct order. I'm trying to keep you alive, you prat!"

"What, against Albatri and Pfalz?" Prebble snorted. "If we stay above 18,000, the one can't reach us, and the other can't touch us. You said it yourself. The Pup runs rings around them at that height."

"Yes! As long as you can stay at that height! Get in a real scrap and you're down below 10,000 before you've got a shot in, and at that height you're dead meat, pal!"

"Well, maybe I'm ready to take my chances! Maybe I haven't got wind up, like some people round here!"

"Like which people?" Andy's voice was low and dangerous.

"Pick a cap, see if it fits."

Andy sprang forward, grabbing the front of Prebble's tunic and slamming him against the wooden partition. The dog looked up and wined uncertainly. "If you want to see whether I've got wind up, just push your luck half an inch further."

Prebble was unafraid. "Go ahead, it's safe enough when a chap's not got a machine gun."

Andy pushed Sidney into his cubicle. "Get yourself kitted up. O.P. in twenty minutes. Get in the way and I'll shoot you down myself. And you take off last; I'm not having you wiping somebody out with your lousy ground control."

They patrolled for over two hours without seeing any sign of enemy aircraft. Andy persisted far longer than usual, penetrating deep into Hunland before giving the wash-out signal and leading his flight home. Prebble smirked at him as they stripped off layers of clothing back in the hut. Andy slumped onto his cot and turned his back.

He woke some time later, his head throbbing. Colin was at the table, reading one of his terrible books. His feet were on the chequered oilcloth, his chair tilted precariously.

"Afternoon chum, decent kip?"

Andy sat up, rubbing his face. "So-so. What time is it?"

"2:30. 'Fraid you've missed lunch, but it seemed a shame to wake you."

"It's alright, I'm not hungry."

Colin looked at him for a long moment. "S'truth, chum, you look ghastly. You OK?"

"I'm fine. Bit of a headache is all."

"Another one? You need to have a word with the Doc."

Andy shook his head dismissively and rooted in the cupboard for aspirin. "Where's Sidney?"

"Out taking the idiot dog for a walk. Have you and he been squabbling again?"

"Why'd you ask?"

"No reason, really. But from your answer, I take it that's a yes."

Andy found and uncorked the aspirin bottle, fishing out the cotton wool plug with a little finger. "I've never known why they put cotton wool in aspirin bottles – or why we don't throw it away when we open them."

"Mystery of human nature, chum," answered Colin, "And you're avoiding the question."

"Yeah, I wonder why that is." He threw the bottle onto the table and walked out.

A steady wind blew occasional flecks of snow across the airfield and Andy quickly missed his British Warm. But going back for it meant further exchange with Colin, so he tucked his hands into his armpits, put his head down and walked out towards the perimeter track. Finding some shelter in the lee of the bank and hedge that divided the northwest of the field from the road, Andy stopped to light a cigarette. A Pup flew overhead, heading west, and Andy recognised Cubby's machine by the inexpertly painted animal on the nose. He recalled that Cubby had identified it as a Tasmanian devil, though it could easily have passed as a kangaroo, a weasel, or possibly some species of furry newt.

He stood for a while, smoking reflectively and wondering whether his nerve was really gone. He dreaded every take-off; flew with ears constantly straining for the splutter, creak or crack that would signal some catastrophic failure and send him spiralling to his death. Then enemy aircraft would appear and he would, without hesitation, lead his flight into combat. Fear would leave him alone in the cockpit, returning after the fight to choke his throat, to tremble the joystick in his numbed fingers. He threw the stub away, looking up as he heard an aero engine. Cubby's

Pup was roaring up the field, no more than fifty feet up and parallel with the hedge. As he neared Andy he put his nose down and dived lower still, his right wings almost clipping the leaves. Andy swore, laughed and threw himself to the ground, feeling the blast of the propeller wash as the Pup shot over him. He looked up to see Cubby climbing in a left bank, making gestures of onanism as he pulled away.

"If you ask me, it's more dangerous here than it is over the other side."

Andy looked up. Prebble had emerged through a gap in the hedge; the dog half jumped, half fell down the bank behind him.

Andy stood, brushing dead leaves off his knees. "The difference is, he was trying *not* to kill me." His expression of dislike was impossible to ignore.

Prebble opened his hands in protest. "Hey, I didn't mean anything. I'm just saying is all."

"Just saying you know it all. Just saying you're ready to take on the whole bloody German air force. Richthofen must be shitting himself." He pushed away the dog, which was trying enthusiastically to sniff his crotch.

Prebble stepped forwards to pull the dog back, "Sorry, he does that. Look, Andy, I understand what you're doing and I'm grateful, I really am. But I came over here to fight, not practise. I just want a chance at the Hun."

"A chance is exactly what you won't have. You're getting the same treatment any new pilot would. I'll tell you when you're ready."

"It's not the same treatment, though. Page takes his replacements on patrol inside two days."

"Yes, and Page gets through replacements twice as fast as I do. It's my job to keep you alive."

"Oh fuck off, Palmer. It's your job to kill Huns. If you won't take me on ops then I'll speak to the O.C."

Andy suddenly grabbed the collar of Prebble's tunic and dragged him towards the distant squadron buildings.

"Right, great, let's both go and speak to him now. You can transfer to another flight, or better still another squadron, and someone else can have the responsibility of getting your stupid fucking head blown off."

Prebble fought to free himself as the dog circled them both, darting in and out with sharp, questioning yaps. Their struggles were becoming more violent and the tug of war becoming an outright fight when the roar of an engine distracted them. Cubby's Pup taxied in close to them, blasting them with twigs and dust as he turned the nose away and switched off. Cubby jumped out almost before the airscrew had stopped turning and ran towards them.

"Oi! If yer can't play nice, your friends'll have to go home!"

The two younger men ceased their struggles and turned guiltily to face Cubby, who stepped close, gently restraining the dog's ecstatic welcome.

"What are you two silly buggers playing at?"

Andy looked from Cubby to Prebble. "It's nothing mate, just a bit of a disagreement about…" He hesitated, uncertain how to explain.

"Palmer thinks I need a nursemaid to change my napkins."

"Really? Well maybe Palmer knows more than you do, son. Now be a good boy and run along, eh? The grownups want to talk." He saw Prebble begin to protest and stepped a little closer. "*Now*, son."

Prebble muttered something unintelligible and walked away, whistling to the dog, which continued to gaze adoringly at Cubby until Sidney pulled it away.

Cubby watched them walk away. Two breathless ack emmas arrived by the aircraft and looked enquiringly at him. He tossed the nearer mechanic a packet of cigarettes.

"Much better, guys, thanks. She's running like a watch." He turned to Andy. "OK, time for you and me to have another chat, you reckon?"

Andy buried his hands in his pockets. "Not much to say, really."

"OK, well let's head for somewhere warm while you don't say it. I'm fucking perished."

*

Andy coaxed Cubby's stove back to life while Cubby made hot chocolate for them both on the gas ring.

"You wouldn't have a couple of aspirin there, would you Cub? I've got a real pounder."

"Seems like you've always got a headache these days. You seen the Doc?"

"I wouldn't say always. I get one when I haven't slept."

"What I've heard you're asleep the whole time you're not flying."

"Well, what else is there to do around here?"

Cubby shrugged. "Fair dos. You dreaming much?"

"Has Colin been talking to you?" Andy banged the stove door shut. "Yeah, so I shout a bit. I'm not the only one."

"Here, get that inside you." Cubby handed Andy a scalding mug and slumped into the easy chair. "So, what's going on with you and Sidney?"

"Nothing much. He just has a problem listening to reason."

"Yeah, I saw how reasonable you were being."

"Yes, well it might have got a bit out of hand. But what am I supposed to do?"

Cubby raised his eyebrows and inclined his head. "You could let him fly."

"Let him get killed, you mean. Then what?"

"Then he'll be like a million others. You going to keep 'em all alive?"

"No. Just the ones I'm responsible for."

"Look, Andy," Cubby expelled his breath in a snorting sigh. "You can't take this on. You do your best, course you do, but some people will die. You can't prevent it, and you can't try to do their dying for them. Believe me, I've learned that."

Andy cradled his mug in both hands. His words were barely audible. "Dying isn't what I'm trying to do. Fact all I want to do is stay alive. I'm keeping Sid off ops when all I really want is to keep myself off." He looked up. "I've lost it, Cub. My nerve. I shout in my sleep because I'm bloody petrified. Every patrol I think about getting lost and landing in Holland, spending the rest of the war as an intern."

"You and every other pilot in France. But you don't do it, do you? You haven't lost your nerve, son, or you'd have buggered off ages ago."

"What? I'm brave because I haven't got the balls to run away? That's bollocks, Cub. I stay because I haven't got the nerve to go."

"And what the hell difference does that make? You stay, and you fly, and you make a bloody good flight commander because you protect your men. Whether you do it because you're a hero or a coward doesn't make a gnat's cock of difference."

"It makes a difference because I don't think I can keep doing it."

"So go see the Doc. Tell him about the headaches. Tell him about the nightmares. You're due leave anyway. Five minute chat and he'll have you written up for a nice little holiday in sunny Birmingham."

"And what happens to you lot while I'm gone?"

"We get by, mate. One, two weeks and you'll be back. Or you can do it the way I did and laugh it off with electrodes stuck to your skull." He rubbed the fading scars on his temples. "Come on, it's got to be better than learning Dutch."

CHAPTER 34

Andy dozed on the tram. He'd left Beauval the previous morning to catch the 4pm Boulogne-Folkestone leave boat. Thirty hours of trains, taxis, buses and trams had left him jaded and grubby. He'd spent a few hours in the clean sheets of a London hotel but found sleep impossible.

The doctor had listened attentively, seeming to understand far more than Andy told him. He'd signed off 14 days' leave without hesitation, and Barrington Holt had made no protest, merely reminding him to pay his mess bill before leaving. Andy suspected the guiding hand of Cubby, but was unable to elicit any hint of confession at the farewell binge in the mess the following evening.

The tram's brakes squealed as it stopped near the corner of Erdington Hall Road. Andy woke, realising that his head had drooped onto the shoulder of the large, brown-coated woman who sandwiched him against the window. He apologised, excused himself and threaded his way down the gangway and onto the platform, nodding to the conductor as he stepped off. He bought cigarettes at the Co-op. Cursing himself for forgetting to buy presents, he bought a selection of such treats as the shop had to offer. The shop girl found him a bottle crate to carry them and he staggered out, his purchases balanced precariously like a brown-paper cornucopia. By the time he turned into the Grove he was sweating profusely despite the cold and his arms ached.

He negotiated the side gate and let himself in through the unlocked kitchen door. Burglars, presumably, would find themselves defeated by the securely locked – and seldom used – front door and give up in frustration. He met his mother at the door into the back room. She opened the door to investigate the source of the noise and found herself face to face with her son carrying a beer crate. She stood uncertainly for a moment, giving him time to place his burden on the draining board before catching her as she flung herself into his arms.

"Dad! Dad! It's Andy, home from France!"

"Well bring the silly blighter in here then, I'm not coming in there to fetch him, am I?"

She led him into the back room, gripping his arm tightly. The room was unchanged other than a neatly-made camp bed under the window. Three children, a girl and two boys, forced wooden smiles from a blurred photograph on the sideboard. The fireplace range gleamed in the popping gaslight. Sitting by the fire in a red easy chair was Andy's father, the empty leg of his trousers folded and fastened by a large blanket pin.

"Hello Dad."

"Hello, Son. We weren't expecting you. Why didn't you write?"

"There wasn't time. I didn't know I'd got leave until the day before yesterday. If I'd sent you a letter I'd have got here before it."

Gerald Palmer had aged far beyond his forty-eight years. Always lean and athletic, he now showed a slack paunch that sagged over his unbuttoned trousers. His collarless shirt was crumpled and undone to show a buttoned undershirt from which a few wisps of grey hair protruded at the neck. White stubble dusted his cheeks; his eyes were shadowed and yellow. His mother was rifling the beer crate in the kitchen.

"Dad, you should see what Andy's brought!" She came back into the sitting room. "You must have spent a fortune, love."

"It's just a box of stuff from the Co-op. Sorry, I didn't have chance to get presents."

"This is the best present you could have brought us," said his mother, rubbing his arm.

Andy was still looking at his father, uncomfortable in the old man's silence. He gestured at the blanket pin. "So, how is… it? How are you getting on?"

Gerald looked dully at the empty trouser leg. "Could be worse. Could have shot my balls off."

"Gerald!"

He looked up at Andy. "They tell me to look on the bright side, then she shouts at me when I do." He picked up a pipe from the ashtray at his elbow fumbled in his pocket for matches. "You going to sit down, or aren't you stopping?"

Andy perched on the chair opposite. The sitting room was somehow unfamiliar, the camp bed a jarring incongruity. There was a faint unidentifiable smell, not unpleasant but alien and strange. His mother had returned to fussing over the box in the kitchen and the silence between him and his father became a low, insistent background hum in his ears.

"Have you got a… you know, a peg-leg or something?"

"It's out in the brew'us. Can't get on with it.," replied his father, scouring his pipe with a matchstick.

"Why not?"

"They said keep practising and it won't hurt so much. Well it does, so I don't."

Cupboard doors banged from the kitchen and Andy's mother called through, "I'm cutting some cake. Or do you want something proper to eat?"

"No, cake is fine, Mom, thanks."

"Be a love and put the kettle on to boil, will you? Or do you want a sherry?"

"I'll have a sherry actually. I'll get it." He stood, glad of the diversion, and walked to the sideboard. "Dad?"

"Ah, alright."

"You having one, Mom?"

"Well, it is a special occasion isn't it? Open the Bristol Cream."

Andy poured the deep brown wine, glugging into small conical glasses, each decorated with a painted cockerel. He recalled being allowed to finish his father's glass when the liquid just touched the rooster's feet.

"So how do you get about, Dad?"

"Got crutches, but mostly it's a chamber pot and the hip bath on Saturdays." He took the glass from Andy and flicked a smile that lit his face for a moment. "Thanks, son. You don't know how good it is to see you."

Andy clicked his glass against his father's. "You too, Dad."

Andy's mother returned to the room, buttoning her coat. "I'm just going down to Min's. She'll want to see you, so I'll bring her back and we can all have supper together."

"No, I'll go, it's getting dark," said Andy, jumping up. "I want to make a telephone call before Bailey's closes anyway."

"You haven't drunk your sherry, love. And who do you know that's got a telephone?"

"I'll tell you when I get back." He picked up his coat from the back of the chair and hurried out.

He recoiled from the relief that settled on him and his guilt pursued him down the steep Grove. In the brief months since he'd left everything had shrunk. The neat, modern houses were toy-like behind their privet bastions; the lamplighter's chains on the lamp-posts, once a vertiginous, ankle-grazing climb away, seemed almost within reach of his outstretched hand. Even the sky was closer, bellying oppressively on the chimneys.

Mrs Bailey at the post office was tiny, frail and elderly. Eight months had aged her thirty years and the kindly smile that had beamed down at him over the counter now turned up, pale and powdered, to welcome him. Left alone in the back of the shop he lifted the telephone receiver and requested Stainton's number. He heard clicks and snatches of conversation before a low whirring told him that, somewhere in Sutton Coldfield, a telephone was ringing. He waited nervously.

"Sutton 208."

Andy recognised Connie's voice. "Hello, Connie? This is Andy Palmer."

"Heavens, hello Andy. Where are you?"

"I'm in England. Is Stainton there?"

"No, I'm sorry. But where in England are you?"

"I'm in Erdington."

"Really? Then you must come to see us! Come to dinner, please!"

"Of course. When?"

"Come Saturday. Seven o'clock. Stainton will be thrilled. Do you have the address?"

"Yes. Thank you. Er, when will Stainton be in?"

"Oh, she's out a lot with her friends, so it's awfully difficult to say. She'll be here on Saturday, though, for certain."

"Oh. Alright. Well… give her my love, won't you?"

"Of course I will. We'll look forward to Saturday, then. Goodbye Andy, thank you so much for telephoning."

He held the phone long after Connie had hung up, laying it in its cradle only when the operator came on line to ask if he wanted to make another call. Wednesday. *Three more days.*

Out a lot with her friends.

He thanked Mrs Bailey and paid for the call, exiting into the deepening dusk.

*

Min was overjoyed to see her youngest brother so unexpectedly and paused only to turn out the lights and find her coat before joining him for the short walk back to the Grove. She took his arm, holding her coat closed over her swelling abdomen.

"How long now before I'm an uncle?" he asked.

"Six weeks. Stan's hoping he might get leave in time."

"You heard from him recently?"

"Yes. I don't know where he is, but the letters take a lot longer to arrive than yours do, so I think he must somewhere far off."

"He's still on the *Aster*?"

"Yes. He says it's not big or fast, but it's got a triple hull or something, so it's safe from mines and torpedoes."

"That's good."

They walked in silence for a short while, the bright pools under each streetlight stretching their bobbing shadows ahead of them.

"What's it like, France?" asked Min.

Andy considered. "Different," he said after a while. "It's two different countries, really. Behind the front line it's not that different from England. Fields going on for ever and houses scattered here and there. And the odd church. Not so many hedges, but otherwise it's like here. When you get over to the German's side it's the same. But in between…" He paused, thinking how to describe the hell of churned earth.

"In between it's like a brown soup, with bits of food rising to the top. Only it's not food, it's tree stumps, wire and stuff. There's craters full of water: green, bright red, or even blue sometimes. And some of them have bodies lying around them like… like petals on a daisy. All in a ring, with their feet pointing at the centre."

He shuddered, surprised to feel revulsion rising in him, far greater than his experience while flying daily over such horrors. "It stinks. You can smell it in your cockpit over the exhaust and the oil. It's sweet and stale, like dustbins."

Min hugged his arm. "My God Andy, how do you stand it?"

He shrugged. "You just sort of ignore it. Anyway, I'm lucky; I go back to a warm, safe bed every night, unlike the poor bloody infantry."

"Yes. Dad said it was horrible."

"How is Dad?"

"You've seen him; what do you think?"

Andy pulled the lapels of his coat tighter, suddenly cold. "I don't know. It was hard to be in the room with him. He's like a stranger. I don't think I've ever seen him unshaven and without a collar, and he looks a hundred."

"I know. Mom and I try to chivvy him up but nothing seems to work. He just sits in that chair, looking at the fire." She looked up at Andy. "I think he's given up."

"What about his false leg?"

"Won't wear it. Says it's too tight."

"And can't he get it fixed? Or get a wheelchair?"

"He's been back to the hospital I don't know how many times. They say it's meant to be tight, and that he'll get used to it in time. And he doesn't qualify for a wheelchair because he can use crutches. They need the wheelchairs for people who really need them." She looked up again, feeling his arm tighten. "Their words, not mine."

It started to snow as they turned into the Grove and the white dusting made the blue bricks that floored the side entry slick and treacherous underfoot as Andy pushed open the gate and helped Min solicitously into the back yard. Dad's shed loomed silently in the darkness, smelling as always of paraffin and French polish. Andy opened the door of the brew house as they passed and collected his father's false leg. Their mother had set the table and replenished the fire, giving the room a slightly festive air. Two full coal scuttles sat inside the fender, steaming slightly. Their father was still in his chair, a white napkin tucked into his collar. He looked up as Min and Andy entered and saw the leg.

"What you brought that bloody thing in for?"

"I'd like to see you wearing it."

"Well you won't. It's too tight."

"Can I see?"

"No."

"Dad, I just…"

"No."

*

Andy lay awake for a long time. The feeling of being a giant in Lilliput was more intense than ever, and the cosy, familiar room he'd shared with Rob had become claustrophobic and stifling. He opened the window and the cold air freed his lungs enough to let him relax in the faintly creaking bed.

"Hush, dear, you'll wake Dad."

He became aware of his mother bending over him, her hand on his shoulder. "What?"

"You were shouting, well, screaming really. Bad dream?"

Andy blinked, trying to focus, trying to understand where he was, and how his mother could be there. A dim memory of falling fluttered across his mind, and his hands and face tingled with half-remembered pain.

"No, I don't think so. Can't remember, really. Sorry, Mom."

She sat on the bed. "That's alright, Love. It's not the first time I've had to come in to you at night. Go back to sleep, you're alright now."

"Yes, I'm fine. Sorry." He closed his eyes and began to drift immediately. As sleep took him he was dimly aware of his mother's weight on the foot of the bed, her hand resting gently on his leg.

CHAPTER 35

Andy paced the house the next morning, restless and unable to settle. He pulled the tarpaulin off his Lea-Francis and cleaned and oiled it. Three kicks of the starter produced an encouraging backfire, and five minutes of plug-cleaning soon had the bike chugging happily. Friday. One more day...

He went back inside to collect his gloves, flying helmet and coat. "Just going to give the bike a quick run. Anything you want?"

"No, Love. Gerald? Andy's going out, do you want anything?"

A rumble came from the sitting room and his mother interpreted, "He says can you get him an ounce of Navy Cut?"

"Will do."

He wheeled the motorcycle out to the road, mounted and set off. The chill air cleared his head as it had the night before and he opened the throttle, relishing the wind's bite. Fifteen minutes' ride brought him to the sweeping curves of the Chester Road and he crouched behind the headlight, willing the bike faster. Whether by coincidence or some denied purpose, he found himself at the Monmouth Drive crossroads. He turned in and drove slowly along the tree-lined avenue, looking at the large houses to his right, finally seeing a sign proclaiming "Gorse Park" swinging from a bracket on an ancient oak. Stainton's house was an imposing white-painted building that commanded a sweeping lawn from a rise above the road. A highly polished maroon Daimler was parked on the drive in front of the open front door. A dark-haired man came out, calling something over his shoulder, and closed the door. Andy looked away quickly and accelerated.

He stopped at Bailey's to buy his father's Navy Cut, his mind churning possibilities, most of them dark. He paid for the tobacco and opened the door, pausing as the bell tinkled over his head. He turned back. "Mrs Bailey, do you mind if I use your telephone again?"

"Of course not dear."

He looked at the instrument for a long moment before lifting it to ask for Stainton's number. The remote telephone chirred several times and he was already replacing the receiver when he heard a voice. "Hello?"

"Hello? Who's there?" It was Stainton.

"Hello, it's Andy."

"Andy!" Either the volume of Stainton's yell or its pitch were too much for the earpiece, which clicked angrily. "Andy, I'm so glad you phoned! Where are you?"

"I'm at home. In Erdington."

"The address, you idiot. What's the address? I can't just drive to Erdington and shout your name."

"What? You mean today?"

"Of course I mean today! Why, would you rather I made an appointment?"

"No, I mean, it's just that your mother said you wouldn't be in until tomorrow."

"Well if you listen to my mother you really are an idiot. Give me your address and I'll be over in, what, would two hours suit you?"

"But... well..." Andy became aware that he was making incoherent noises. "It's number 8, Abraham Grove. Do you want directions?"

"No, I'll get an AA route. There's always a patrolman at the park gate. I'll hang up now so that I can get ready. I can't wait to see you, Andy."

"Nor can I." he replied, realising that it made no sense as he laid down the receiver. He looked at it, all black Bakelite and shining metal, and murmured, "See you in a couple of hours."

Grinning hugely, he flicked one of the bells with a fingernail as he pushed back the curtain to re-enter the front of the shop.

*

Andy's mother was delighted to learn that an extra place would be needed for tea and she fussed over the contents of the pantry, tutting and clucking as she inspected packets and tins. Even Gerald showed a glimmer of interest at the prospect of a visitor and quizzed Andy as he fettled his pipe.

"So, this is a posh nurse you met in France, then?"

"Well, she was a volunteer at the time – FANY. She was there with her mother."

"And you're courting?"

"I suppose you could say that." The image of the unknown man at the front door played in his mind.

"So how is it you kept her a secret, then?"

"I haven't. It just never came up."

"Wouldn't have, neither. Probably wanted to keep us secret from her and all."

Andy was saved from an angry retort by the entry of his mother in hat and coat.

"Gerald, pack it in." She turned to Andy, "I'm just going down the Coop to get some lettuce and stuff. Shan't be long."

"No, I'll go."

She patted his chest. "No, you get upstairs and get in the bath, you're all oil and grease from that motor bike. I've lit the Ewart. Gerald, you behave yourself this afternoon or…"

*

Andy opened the tap on the geyser, tensing slightly as the gas popped into life. He remembered its installation six or seven years before, when he'd been convinced it was about to explode. He sat on the toilet seat and watched the bath fill. His father's interrogation had brought back his doubts about his relationship with Stainton; was the man on the drive one of the friends she was out with every night? But there was little denying her enthusiasm to see him when he'd telephoned, so… He thought of Connie, sexually insatiable and predatory. Were such traits hereditary?

The bath was barely visible through the steam and he leaned forward to run in cold water, seeing the stained enamel where the cold tap dripped. What would Stainton think of the house? He'd always been slightly proud of their modern little semi-detached home behind its trimmed hedge, the domain of a reasonably prosperous office manager. Now it seemed tiny and dowdy compared to the grandeur of the houses overlooking Sutton Park. He swirled the bath water, testing the temperature. Thoughts of Stainton's visit brought him to his mother's warning to his father. How would he behave? How had the funny, light-hearted and athletic man who'd climbed trees and ridden bicycles with him turned into this glowering, unhappy cripple? The evening he'd viewed with joyful anticipation stretched ahead as one of dread and discomfort.

He turned off the water and began to undress.

*

Andy was leaning on the front gate when he saw the Daimler turn into the Grove. Stainton waved from the driving seat, shifting the gears expertly as the car began the steep climb. By the time she'd parked, set the brake, switched off and jumped into Andy's arms there was already a sizeable group of impressed onlookers. He pulled her feet off the ground and suddenly it was alright.

Andy's mother was standing by the front door, one hand bunching her apron. She bobbed as she shook hands with Stainton, coming perilously close to a curtsey.

"Hello, Miss. It's very nice to meet you. Did you drive that car by yourself?"

Stainton clasped both of Mrs Palmer's hands and leaned forward to kiss her cheek. "Hello, Mrs Palmer. Andy's told me so much about you. I've been dying to meet you."

Mrs Palmer flushed, unnerved by the greeting. "Oh, well, that's lovely, er, do come in, Miss."

"Please, call me Stainton. You're making me sound like a school ma'am. I do like your house."

Andy's father peered around the back of his chair as they entered the sitting room. Andy winced as he saw the artificial leg propped by the fireplace, where he'd left it the previous night. There was something grubby about its brown smoothness and dangling laces, about the off-white padding showing around the top like soiled underwear.

"Gerald, this is Stainton, Andy's friend."

Stainton took Gerald's hand in both of hers, holding it as she greeted him.

"Hullo Mr Palmer, Thank you so much for letting me visit." She smiled at Mrs Palmer, raising her eyebrows for permission as she pulled a dining chair over to sit close to him. "Do you mind if I sit here?"

"No, of course not. Call me Gerald. Gerry if you like."

"Gerry it is then. Andy says you had a terrible time at Ypres."

Andy and his mother exchanged agonised glances. The unmentionable had been mentioned.

"Ah, pretty bad. But there's some came off worse than me." He patted Stainton's hand. "But you'd know about that, being a nurse."

Stainton stood and retrieved the leg, standing it by her as she sat down. "Yes, and I've seen a few of these. I bet it hurts like nobody's business."

"It did. I don't use it now, though."

Stainton examined the lacing. "Can't say I blame you, Gerry. These things hurt more than losing the leg did. I'm amazed that anybody puts up with it for a day, let alone keeps going long enough to learn to walk." She began removing the laces. "I knew one chap who said that it's because everyone gets the lacing wrong. Let me see if I can remember what he showed me."

Mrs Palmer turned towards the kitchen. "I've got some nice ham in the boiler, dear. Would you have tea with us?"

"Thank you, I'd love to. Andy, why don't you help your Mum while Gerry and I get to know each other?"

Andy obediently followed his mother out to the kitchen. As he cut bread he heard quiet conversation from the sitting room, his father's voice a low rumble.

"As God's my witness, that's the most I've heard him say since he came home," said Mrs Palmer. She looked up at the sound of laughter. "That's a special one you've found there, Andy."

"I think you're right."

"I can't believe she drove that great big motor car."

Stainton appeared in the doorway. "Mrs Palmer, would you mind helping Gerry put his leg on please? I'll take over in here if you like. Andy can show me where everything is."

"Yes, surely," she said faintly, wiping her hands on her apron. She returned to the sitting room muttering, "Two minutes and she's done this!"

The room was crowded with the table extended to seat the four of them. Gerald's camp bed had claimed the space under the window, pushing them against the sideboard, huddled in elbow-brushing promiscuity. Gerald, aided by Andy and Stainton, had staggered uncertainly but gamely to a ladder-backed chair and now sat straight, his collar done up and an unaccustomed brightness in his face.

Stainton shared a complicit grin with him and said, "After tea, we were thinking of maybe going for a run in the car. What do you think, Mrs Palmer?"

"In the car?" It was obvious that she found the idea irresistible. "But it'll be dark, is that alright?"

"Perfectly. It has lights and everything. And you'll both be warm in the back with the rugs over you."

"Well, it would be an experience. You'll be warm enough, Gerald?"

"Course I will." He tapped his false leg, laughing. "And I've only got the one lot of toes to get cold."

"I'll just get… Shan't be a minute." Mrs Palmer stood and hurried out to the kitchen.

Gerald overbalanced as he manoeuvred into the back of the Daimler, sitting down heavily on the running board. Andy and Stainton tripped over each other as they tried to help, adding to the confusion. He leaned forward, wheezing breathlessly.

"Are you alright, Dad?" asked Andy.

"No I'm not. I've left half a pair of bloody good boots in Belgium." His laughter grew stronger as his breath returned.

Andy watched the lights striking their descending bars across Stainton's face as she drove confidently through the fast-emptying streets.

"This reminds me of a ride in an ambulance."

Stainton glanced at him, smiling. "Not too much I hope. I'd hate to think of your Mum and Dad getting up to what my Mum and Cubby were doing."

"You'd hate it? How'd you think I'd feel?"

He looked back at his parents, sitting regally in the plush passenger compartment, their legs swaddled in tartan rugs. His mother waved a pale hand to him in the darkness. His father was sitting forward, watching the passing houses with interest. He pointed, drawing his wife's attention to some fleeting diversion as it flicked past the window.

"I don't know what you did in there, but I can't believe what you've done for him."

Stainton shrugged. "There wasn't much to do. I've seen that look he had before." She drove quietly for a moment. "We had a matron at the field hospital. She told me that you have to give a tiny bit of sympathy before you completely ignore that there's anything wrong. Then they pull themselves through."

"It seems to work."

"It did this time. Never has before." She smiled across the driver's cab. "I didn't do anything. He just wanted someone to tell him to try."

"Ah, if only we'd thought of that."

They drove in silence for several minutes. Andy fought for inspiration, unable to think of what to say next. His imaginings of their reunion hadn't included sitting on a leather bench, separated by levers, with his parents watching through a glass partition.

Stainton changed gear to climb a hill. "It's hard to concentrate with you staring like that."

Andy started. "Sorry, was I staring?"

Stainton laughed. "I seem to remember the conversation was quite similar the last time we went for a ride together."

"I rode past your house today."

She looked across at him in the darkness, not understanding.

He was still looking at her, an unreadable expression on his face. "On my motor bike. I rode it past your house."

She looked back at the road. "And you didn't come in?"

"No. There was a man coming out."

"A man?" She thought for a moment. "Oh, that would have been Malcolm. So why did that stop you coming in?"

"Who's Malcolm?"

"He's the man from the garage. He'd just brought the car back. So why didn't..." She looked at him again. "Oh no, surely not."

"Your mother said you're out with your friends most nights."

"And what did you take that to mean?" Her voice had hardened.

"I didn't take it to mean anything," said Andy, feeling suddenly ridiculous.

"Oh, Andy, neither of us is stupid. Well, clearly one of us is." She shook her head, trying and discarding at least three responses before continuing. "I go out with my school friends once or twice a week. And it was a girls' school, before you ask. Is that what you want to hear?"

"I'm sorry. But you can't blame me for wondering."

"Yes I bloody can!" Her voice was quiet, but she thumped the steering wheel in frustration. "It's at times like these that I realise we hardly know one another."

"Don't say that. Of course we know each other."

"Well you don't know me, that much is clear."

Andy fiddled with his thumbs, looking down at his lap.

"Look, I'm sorry. I didn't mean any of this." He rubbed his forefingers along the bridge of his nose. "They chucked me out of France for causing fights. I can't believe I've picked one with you."

"You haven't." She sighed, tilting her head back. "Not quite anyway. Look, bring your night things tomorrow and stay the night." She saw him glance back at his parents. "Don't worry, my mother will be in, so how could anything unrespectable happen?"

Andy's mother tapped on the glass behind them and Andy turned to slide it open.

Mrs Palmer leaned forward to say, "I can't believe this, but Dad says could we stop at a pub? He wants to buy us all a drink."

CHAPTER 36

A small crowd gathered again in the Grove to see Andy board the Daimler as an immaculately-liveried chauffeur held the door. Connie Hamilton's driver was in his fifties, powerfully built, and probably hired for skills other than his driving abilities. He'd introduced himself as Mortimer, which could be first or last name, and had deftly shepherded Andy when he tried to sit in the front passenger seat. Andy's mother had laboured with brushes, cleaning fluid and fuller's earth to bring his uniform to a reasonable semblance of respectability. Now, his cap badge polished and boots shining under layers of Cherry Blossom, his cavalry breeches sliding on the brown leather, he spread his arms across the seat back and contemplated his changed circumstances.

The drive in front of Stainton's house already held two cars, from which elegantly-dressed couples were alighting. The front door was open, spilling light out onto the gravel; music and chatter wafted from inside. Connie met him at the door, reaching up to kiss his cheek with Bohemian abandon.

"Hello Andy, it's lovely to see you again. I hope you don't mind: I've invited a few friends to make a party of it. Come with me and we'll find Stainton."

She led him through a patrician dining room, where candelabras lit a dozen place settings, to a green-smelling orangery. Stainton stood near the end, chatting to a young man in cavalry dress uniform. She saw Andy enter and came to meet him with slightly undignified haste.

"Hello. You look a proper toff yer honour!" She kissed him fleetingly, took his hand and led him back to her perfectly-tailored companion. "Andy, let me introduce Forbes Chisholm-Frost. Forbes, this is Andy Palmer. He's a pilot."

Forbes inspected Andy's shoulder pips as he shook hands. "Lieutenant, eh? Seen much action?"

"A little. You?"

"Heavens, no!" He was tall, maybe an inch or so shorter than Andy, but with a stocky breadth to his shoulders. His scarlet jacket was expertly cut to disguise a slight paunch. His pale, pencil-thin moustache adorned a full-lipped mouth. "Can't wait to get out and have a go, obviously, but I'm stuck in a staff job for the time being. So, you've downed some Boche, have you? How many?"

"Hard to say. You end up with shared kills, a quarter here, an eighth there. No one really knows how many they've got." Andy wondered at his own unwillingness to enumerate his victories.

"Oh well, stick at it. I dare say they'll make an ace of you in the end."

"Forbes, be a dear and get us some drinks, would you?" Stainton handed him her empty glass.

"Of course. What'll it be, Palmer?"

"Oh, anything, thanks. Whisky if there is any."

Forbes departed in search of refreshment and Stainton led Andy from the orangery into a small sitting room.

"It won't take long for him to find us, but at least this will buy us a few minutes. First things first, come here."

She put her arms around his neck and they shared their first real kiss since Andy's homecoming. "I'm sorry about this; it was supposed to be a quiet dinner, but Mummy's turned it into something of a hoo-hah. She invited 'people you ought to meet.'"

"What, like Forbes Ponsonby-Vaseline in there?"

"Oh, he just turns up anywhere he hears a cork being drawn. He's harmless enough."

"At least he's dressed for the part. I feel like the scruff of the party."

"Don't be silly, you look marvellous. You scrub up rather well, you know."

"Thank my Mom for that. But it's hardly a dress uniform."

"Have you got a dress uniform?"

"Of course I have. It's the same as my normal one, but with the oil stains cleaned off. See?"

"Perfect." She looked past his shoulder. "Oh-oh, lobster approaching."

Forbes returned, bearing three glasses. "I say, Palmer, are those cavalry breeches?" he asked, "What regiment are you."

"Royal Warwickshire actually. I was infantry. Wouldn't do to turn up at a dinner party in puttees though, would it?"

"Hmm, could be right." He sipped his drink. "Still, out of uniform, not completely the thing, eh?"

"We don't go in much for uniforms in the RFC," said Andy, fighting his quick temper. "Once you're bundled up in a leather coat and fug boots, you might as well be wearing pyjamas."

"Well, each to his own, each to his own." Forbes finished his drink and looked disappointedly at the empty glass, which he handed to Andy. "Your round, old chap. Pink gin, please, and have one yourself, won't you?"

"I'll get them." Stainton intercepted the glass and escaped the room, grinning over her shoulder at Andy's silent cry for rescue.

"Hunting man are you, Palmer?" asked Forbes.

"Not really, no."

"Ah. It was the jodhpurs. Made me think you were a horseman. More of a shooting type then?"

"No. I mean, on the range before I transferred obviously, but…"

Forbes shook his head. "You see, that's where we go wrong. A proper fighting man knows how to use his weapons." He stroked the hilt of his sword. "I was regimental fencing champion. This beauty here is like a musical instrument. Would have been musketry champion too, but I missed the final." He tapped Andy's shoulder with a pointed finger, "Shooting aeroplanes down is all very well, but it takes skill to kill a Boche face-to-face."

"I'm sure it does. I hope you'll have the chance to prove your skill very soon."

Forbes was deaf to the irony. "No doubt about it. I'm sure your German is an excellent fellow, but let's see him stand against a sabre charge."

Stainton returned with a grey-moustached colonel in tow. He was ramrod-straight and carried a tray of drinks for her as though presenting arms. His uniform was similar to Forbes's, though more grand and adorned with gold braid on sleeves and shoulders.

"Uncle Edwin, may I present Lieutenant Andrew Palmer of the Royal Flying Corps. Andy, this is Colonel Chisholm."

"Ah, so this is the heroic young aviator, back from the war," said the colonel, chuckling faintly as he shook hands.

"Pleased to meet you, young man. Heard about the legs. All healed now, I trust?"

"Yes, thank you sir. It was nothing much."

"Pranging a kite is never 'nothing much'. I piled a Caudron in and was in traction for seven months."

"You're a flier, sir?"

"A failed one. Turned out I had the ability of a blind pigeon with a sprained wrist. The world's a safer place since I packed it in. I trained with Boom Trenchard and at least while I was there, he wasn't the worst."

Andy looked from the Colonel to Forbes. "Chisholm, did you say? Are you related?"

"Sadly, yes," replied the Colonel, with another whisky-breathed chuckle. "Forbes here is my son as well as my aide. We thought it unfair to expose our noble enemies to his fighting prowess."

Forbes glared at his father but stayed silent. The Colonel took Andy's arm, smiling at Stainton. "Miss Hamilton, would you be so kind as to find Forbes someone to talk to? I'd like a brief chat with your young man."

Colonel Chisholm led Andy back to the hall and into a small study; he seemed well-acquainted with the house's geography. He opened a polished partners' desk and produced a half-full bottle of amber liquid.

"Just what we need. Top-up?"

He waved Andy to a green leather chair and seated himself regally behind the desk. "Poor old Harry was a chum of mine," he said, waving his glass at the African memorabilia around the walls. "Hard to believe he's been dead nearly twenty years." He sipped reflectively. "What do you think of fighting in France?"

"I'm not sure what I think of it, sir. You just do it, I suppose."

"I can see you do." He tapped his breast pocket and sloshed his glass in the direction of the Military Cross ribbon on Andy's tunic. "Frighten you, does it?"

"I'm not sure what you mean, sir."

"How many Hun have you downed?"

"Nine and a few fractions."

"Plus a balloon, I hear. They're the target nobody wants to attack, aren't they?"

"You do get a bit shot about, but they're not that different."

The colonel nodded. "Hmm. So, does it frighten you?"

Andy shifted uncomfortably, unsure how to answer. The Colonel leaned forward to pass him the whisky bottle.

"Blood River Poort was my first and only action. I was thirty-two and damned terrified from beginning to end. Harry Hamilton and I had been at school together, both joined the cavalry, and joined Gough's mounted infantry to have some laughs in Africa. When Botha slashed us to ribbons I thought the world had ended. Stainton's father, my best friend, died right next to me."

"It must have been terrible, sir."

"There were twenty-odd of us killed. By comparison with what you chaps are going through in France it was a playground scrap." He tapped his own medal ribbons and laughed coldly. "I got this one for commendable courage in the face of the enemy."

He put his glass down and leaned forward. "What I'm trying to say, young man, is that feeling fear is not the same thing as cowardice. Now, honest answer. Does it frighten you?"

"Every day, sir."

Chisholm nodded, satisfied. "I think you've done enough. You're a brave young man who's performed admirably in the service of his country. You're a more than competent pilot, and we can make better use of you in England than we can by letting you get yourself killed in France."

"I'm sorry, sir, but I don't understand."

"Mr Palmer, I have a certain influence, and one of my colleagues desperately needs experienced pilots to take on training duties. He would count it a favour were I to introduce him to one of your calibre."

"Sir, you must excuse me, but has someone been speaking to you about this?"

The Colonel rocked his head. "It's been mentioned, but the training post is real, and you would be providing a considerable service to the war effort were you to accept it."

"I don't know how to answer, sir."

Chisholm stood, returning the depleted bottle to its drawer. "Then don't. Think it over. Here's my card; let me know your decision in a few days' time." He opened the study door. "Shall we?"

Andy found himself seated for dinner between Stainton and a purse-lipped dowager who was introduced as Mrs Hampton and who belied her demeanour with a wicked sense of fun.

"Call me Clarice, Mr Palmer," she intoned in a warbling contralto. "Mrs Hampton sounds too like a description of my deprived widowhood." She winked coquettishly at Andy's discomfiture.

"Well you'd better call me Andy then, for broadly parallel reasons," he grinned, recovering his composure.

She frowned for a moment, then laughed unrestrainedly, her head thrown back, her thin eyelids closed behind tortoiseshell-rimmed spectacles. "Oh, Stainton, thank you for finding this one for me. I think we'll both enjoy this dinner more than we expected," she gasped, dabbing her eyes with a lace handkerchief.

In fact at first the dinner was considerably more enjoyable than Andy had expected. Clarice maintained a flow of near-profane banter while discreetly guiding Andy's uncertainty over the correct selection of tools for eating lobster. Stainton was monopolised by Forbes Chisholm, seated on her other side and holding forth loudly and opinionatedly on topics as diverse as war strategy and industrial relations. She stemmed Andy's testiness by means of whispered asides appended to her more audible responses.

"Oh, I'd never have thought of that solution, Forbes," she sighed, fluttering the eyelashes of the vapid female, "Because it's moronic, you horse-toothed imbecile," she appended for Andy's benefit from behind her wine glass.

He began to drift. The wine was dark and velvety; probably more alcoholic than the thin, bitter, rural brews to which his palate had become accustomed. The dinner noise blurred and he found himself beginning to doze, coming awake as a sudden silence fell. He looked around at expectant faces.

"I'm sorry, I was gathering wool. What did you say?" He looked generally at the company, unsure who had spoken.

"I asked what you thought of the display at Highcroft Hall." Said a middle-aged woman whose name Andy vaguely recalled as something double-barrelled.

"I'm sorry, which display is that?"

"The cripples. They allow them to sit outside by the fence. You are from Erdington, aren't you?" Her tone implied this as some form of communicable disease.

"I have seen them, yes. I'm not aware of any display."

She narrowed her lips at his obtuseness. "That is the display. Hardly what one wants to see when passing by. I'm sorry for them, of course, but some of them are quite hideous."

Andy heard Stainton whisper a faint "Oh no." He felt her hand squeeze his knee and saw the slight shake of her head.

"I'm sure that must be terrible for you," he said tonelessly. "I'm sure they'll lock them away for you if you write to them."

"Heavens! I'm not suggesting they should be locked away! Just put somewhere out of sight."

"Let me assure you that that's almost exactly what happens. My father happens to be one of those cripples, and he's been spirited away to where no one has to see him or think of him again."

She bridled at his tone. "And where would that be?"

"A small house in Erdington, where he's expected to live on a quarter of what he was paid while he still had all his limbs. While he could still fight for the people around this table." His voice cracked. "Before he became a sight to be hidden from polite view."

A white-moustached ancient, stick-thin and bloodshot, intervened. "Just a moment, young man. I regret that your father was injured, of course, but the country doesn't have the money to throw away on people who cannot work or fight."

"And which do you do?"

"What?"

"Do you work or fight? How do you justify the money the country spends on you?"

The old man looked around, confused and angry. "What? What's he saying? I've done my work. I've earned my pension. What's he trying to imply?"

Colonel Chisholm intervened. "Jonathan, I suggest you pipe down. Mr Palmer is understandably upset." He turned to Andy with a placating smile. "Andy, I agree with you that it's unjust, but sadly the state can't afford to support all the thousands of wounded we now have."

"No, Colonel," Andy's voice was bitter. "But it somehow managed to find the money for a fucking war." His eyes clouded and he stood suddenly, throwing his napkin into the centre of the table. He turned and blundered from the room.

Stainton found him on the front drive, looking out across the park. Black clumps of gorse dotted the grass, silver in the moonlight. She pushed both arms inside his right elbow and held on tight, her forehead against his shoulder. They stood in silence. After a while Andy turned to wrap his arms around her, feeling the goose pimples on her bare arms.

"Hey, you're frozen."

"I know. Never mind. I'm sorry you had to hear those two old idiots."

"No, I'm sorry I let them get me angry." He laughed humourlessly. "Me, angry. It seems to be my only mood these days. If I'm not threatening to hit someone I'm swearing at them."

She pulled closer inside his arms, beginning to shiver. "It was a bit ripe for a casual dinner." She laughed softly. "Oh well, they'll get over it, I don't see them leaving in a huff."

As she spoke, the door opened and the woman appeared, supporting the cadaver-like old gentleman.

Mortimer eased past them to hold open the door of the Daimler.

"Oops, spoke too soon," whispered Stainton.

*

Andy's room was large and comfortable, boasting a willow-patterned wash basin with hot and cold running water. He brushed his teeth, undressed and stood at the window in his pyjamas, looking out across the road to the shadowed park. Lights glimmered from the training camp in the distance. The wine had given him a slight headache and he pressed his forehead against the cold glass. *What the hell am I doing here?*

He regretted what had happened at dinner; recognised the inappropriateness of his behaviour, but found it impossible to accuse himself for reacting badly. He felt trapped by this world to which the other guests belonged. A world where the unattractive inconveniences of life could be tastefully hidden behind respectable drapes. Connie had laughed off the incident, saying that it would do Audrey Housman-Jones good to hear a verb that her old man could no longer put into practice. But then she'd sobered quickly, counselling him not to antagonise the Colonel, who was in a position to do him a great deal of good.

"He's great friends with Trenchard, and he and my husband were in parliament with Lord Cowdray, who's an absolute dear. With people like that on your side you could have any posting you want."

And what posting did he want? He hated the joyful lurch he'd felt inside when the Colonel intimated that he need never again fly in combat. But the attraction was undeniable. He thought of Colin, Cubby and Page, imagined their responses had he been able to consult them, knew that the words "lucky bugger" would appear in all of their advice to seize the opportunity. *That's me. A lucky bugger.* Here, in a patrician's house, expecting to hear Stainton tiptoe into his room any moment, he was alive and prosperous, medal-decorated and selected for preferential treatment.

Why me?

Colin, the bishop's son, who laughed at his oecumenical upbringing, yet could be heard whispering prayers from his cubicle each night; Page, who had already sacrificed the flesh of his face to the flames of war; Cubby, who gave up his son and his dignity to satisfy the hunger of a foreign government; where was the benevolent providence to protect them from harm? He beat his head gently against the glass as he acknowledged that any or all of his friends might already be dead.

"Trying to escape?" Stainton closed the door quietly behind her and came to the window, putting her arms around his waist and pressing her face against his back.

CHAPTER 37

Corbett, the new squadron adjutant, motioned Colin and Page to seats. He'd fitted in rapidly, flying patrols whenever possible, and his relaxed and resilient nature provided an excellent foil for Barrington Holt's regimental irascibility. He'd also introduced the squadron to the energetic pleasures of bumble-puppy, thus reducing the degree of boredom drinking among the pilots at the same time as improving their fitness.

"What can we do for you, Tom?" asked Page, leaning back in his chair.

"I think we need a bit of a rethink and a reshuffle. This Richthofen fellow's playing silly buggers up and down the front, and he's cut a couple of squadrons to bits. We've been lucky so far, but I dare say our turn will come."

"So what's the plan?"

"First, patrols by flight need to pretty much stop. When we go, we go in force. The Huns keep jumping us in bloody great packs, and we can't fight back when there's only four of us."

"But if we go over in a bloody great pack ourselves, they don't come anywhere near us."

"Then we shoot up their ground forces until they've no choice." Corbett stood and began to pace. "I'd like you, Humphrey, to command A-flight, Colin, you take B-flight, and I'll take C-flight until Andy Palmer gets back. When we're patrolling as a squadron, Humphrey leads. That sound fair to you chaps?"

The two airmen muttered and nodded their approval and Corbett continued, pushing aside desktop clutter to unroll a map.

"First squadron show will be at two pip emma today. There's a suspected artillery battery in these woods southwest of Grevillers. A- and B-flight to attack with bombs while C-flight covers from above. If the Huns leave us alone, all well and good, but if they decide to come and play they'll have a dozen of us to cope with."

*

The eight Pups, sluggish under the weight of the 50lb bomb under each lower plane, arrived at the target at 4,000 feet. 2,000 above them, Corbett, with Cubby as his deputy leader, watched a distant spiral of dots that orbited somewhere near Havrincourt. Colin, 100 yards behind and 500 feet above A-flight, leaned over his cockpit rim, searching for the reported artillery battery. Archie put up a token complaint at their intrusion, but hardly the fury to be expected had he something important to protect. He saw Page lead A-flight lower and dived to keep formation. As they dipped below 2,000 feet, figures could be seen running from the woods and the muzzle flashes of small arms fire began to spark against the straw-coloured meadow. Still there was no sign of heavy guns and Page, having fired a few ill-tempered rounds at the grey shapes, began to climb to the east in search of a worthwhile target.

From his position high above, Corbett saw the turn to the east and led C-flight to follow. They were now flying directly towards the distant cluster of aircraft. The temperature began to drop rapidly and wisps of cloud started to form below them, occasionally hiding A- and B-flight as they laboured upwards. Haze formed rapidly to the east.

By the time that A- and B-flight reached the outskirts of Bapaume, the weather had deteriorated profoundly. The clouds had amalgamated into a solid wrack at 2,000 feet, from which a drifting drizzle floated down. The eight aircraft droned onward, each with its pilot leaning out to see past his misted windscreen; each pilot squinting to see beyond the hoop of rainbow that preceded him. Page selected an important-looking building, surrounded by parked trucks and guarded by Archie emplacements at each corner. He fired a flare and dived to the attack.

C-flight was patrolling just above the cloud-tops. Cubby knife-edged his Pup to look down, searching for a break in the rolling white. He looked to the east, willing his straining eyes to pierce the haze, to reveal the location of the German patrol. Movement caught his eye: for a second, something black had flicked through the cloud a mile away. He stared again but saw only spiralling, rising vapour. But he was certain that he'd glimpsed the top plane of an intruder, sneaking in through the mist. He dived in alongside Corbett, waggling his wings and pointing. Corbett looked down, then back at Cubby, shaking his head and shrugging elaborately. Cubby pointed more emphatically and Corbett reached a rapid decision, nodding and signalling to descend. The four Pups winged over and dived into the cloud.

They broke through into a grey mist of drifting rain. Diving ahead of them was a group of seven or eight aircraft. Beyond them, low, slow and unsuspecting, A- and B-Flights were strung out in line astern, delivering their bombs to the large house. Ground fire could be seen flashing and sparkling from gun pits to each side.

The German aircraft, heavier and more powerful than the Sopwiths, easily out-distanced C-Flight, and were already flattening out to choose their targets well before the Pups were anywhere near close enough to intervene. The last machine of B-Flight, still lining up for its bomb run, was knocked out of the sky in the first rush, diving engine-on to explode in a great cauliflower of flame. Warned by the detonation, the remaining aircraft scattered left and right.

Still diving, and urging his machine faster by straining forward, Cubby glanced behind him, just in time to see the Germans spring their second trap. A dark red Albatros emerged from the cloud, its twin guns already flaming. To his right he saw a Pup pin-pointed by the two lines of tracer. *Break away! Break away!*

He caught the flash of goggles as the pilot looked back at him. It was Prebble, still seemingly ignorant of the threat. Cubby kicked his Pup violently towards him, trying to force the inexperienced pilot to break away. Prebble appeared to start in surprise and was rolling away when the first bullets struck the fuselage behind him. He jerked forward in his cockpit, striking his face on the coaming, then bunted into a vertical dive. Cubby saw the blood on the back of Prebble's coat as a line of bullets stitched his own right upper plane. He rolled into a corkscrew dive and felt rather than heard the crash of the red Albatros clipping his right wingtip as it dived past.

CHAPTER 38

Dear Andy,

I hope your leave is going well. We did a squadron show yesterday, bombs. Now we do not really have a squadron. We got jumped by a pack of Albatri and lost, six-nil. Cubby, Humphrey and I got back alright, though Cubby had a mid-air that nearly did for him. He lost a starboard aileron and two feet of his right upper plane, so it's anybody's guess how the thing stayed together.

Prebble was killed by this chap in the red DIII who everyone's talking about, so I appear to have inherited his idiot dog. Corbett, the new Recording Officer, came with us and seems to know what he's doing. He led your flight, with Cubby, Prebble and a new chap who arrived the day you left on leave. Damned if I can remember his name.

So there's six of us left until we get some replacements. We can run rings round the Hun when we're up high, but when they catch us nearly on the deck they can dance all over us. It feels disloyal to the Pup to say it, but we really need some new aeroplanes. There are rumours that the Americans are finally coming in, and we are all hoping they'll bring something spectacular. There is talk of a 200mph scout, but I shall believe it when I see it.

We have a couple of days rest scheduled, with no flying until replacement pilots and machines arrive. So you should arrive back here just in time to miss it! Cubby, Humph and I are off to sample the joys of Amiens, and Corbett is joining us. He seems a highly decent chap; I'm sure you'll like him.

Must go now as I have to take the Idiot for a walk or he will probably eat what's left of your hearth rug while we are out. Give my love to Stainton and Connie.

Hurry back before we get up to full strength again and the old grind returns.

Affectionately,

Colin

Andy sat at the sitting-room table, Colin's letter beside him and a blank sheet of notepaper lying accusingly in front of him. He stared for several minutes before writing "Dear Colin," then set his pen down again and stared out of the window. He read the letter again, smoothing its creases with his thumb. Why should it be so difficult to reply?

"Dear Colin, just a line to let you know I'm not coming back as I've accepted a training job at Castle Bromwich. Hope you all do well, Andy."

He watched a blackbird hopping across the leaf-strewn lawn, tilting its head to look for wriggling prizes. It flew off, chack-chacking, as Stainton appeared round the corner of the brew house, arm-in-arm with Andy's father. Gerald Palmer stepped gingerly, his left hand against the wall, and winced each time he transferred his weight to the artificial leg. Andy looked again at the letter, picked up another sheet and wrote "Dear Cubby". Accepting the training post had seemed natural and morally irreproachable. Why now did it feel like desertion?

He fiddled with his pen until Stainton and his father struggled, laughing, through the kitchen door. She guided him to his chair and collapsed onto the sofa, fanning herself with her hand. Her face was pink and glowing from the cold air.

"This man's a prodigy!" she said, waving at Gerald. "I swear we'll have him off crutches and onto walking sticks within the week."

"And this wench is a flipping slave-driver!" laughed Andy's father. "I need to get walking on my own before she kills me!"

Andy looked at his father, transformed in a few short days by Stainton's enthusiastic coaching. He'd shaved and his tie was knotted tightly under a starched white collar. Sitting relaxed in the fireside chair, the artificial leg in place and a grin on his face, he was indistinguishable from the man he remembered before the war. The man he'd feared gone forever, lost in a Belgian trench.

Stainton looked over his shoulder. "Writing to Cubby?"

"Cubby or Colin. I'm not sure what to put, or who to send it to."

"To say you're not coming back?"

He nodded.

"Just write it and stop worrying. They're good enough friends to understand. Send them one each; they'll be delighted for you."

"I suppose so. It feels as if I'm deserting them, though."

"You're not, but I understand how it feels to you." She gently rubbed the back of his neck. "You'll feel better once you're in the air again, especially with no one shooting at you."

*

The Chief Flying Instructor was in his thirties but already grey-haired. A livid scar was slashed across his face, fading to blue-grey where it crossed the bridge of a broad and crooked nose, in whose shadow his toothbrush moustached still showed flecks of reddish-brown.

"Herbert Gregory," he said, extending a hand. "Call me Bertie."

Andy shook hands. "Andy Palmer. Pleased to meet you Bertie."

"Glad to have you on board, Andy. Come along and I'll introduce you to the other poor souls."

He led the way outside, where a battered collection of Avros and Farmans stood dejectedly in the rain.

"Here's the fleet. No flying today, thank God. Amazes me that some of them can drag themselves off the ground." He patted the wing of the last Avro 504 they passed. "This one's the pick of the litter. Don't let students near it until you're convinced they won't break it."

Andy looked at the machine, noting the stained, creased fabric and the pool of black oil below the cowling.

"Lovely."

Gregory pushed open the door of an Adrian hut. "Here we are. Staff room."

Inside was stiflingly hot and filled with dense smoke. It was a small room containing a motley collection of moth-eaten sofas and easy chairs. A large stove roared near the back wall. Three men in a mixture of uniforms and flying gear lounged in the chairs, puffing silently on billowing pipes.

"Shut the bloody door, Bertie, will you?"

The speaker looked like a deflated football, wrapped in a voluminous leather flying jacket under which could be seen layered sweaters and cardigans. He was sitting close to the stove, holding his hands towards it. He saw Andy and stood up.

"Ah, the new chap. Ron Blay, come on in." He advanced to shake hands. "This here is Spotty Holloway." He indicated a cadaverous youth with a profusely peppered complexion. "And this is Worms. Avoid getting between him and food."

Andy shook hands with Worms, a short, rounded pilot in a gabardine RNAS coat. All of the instructors were muffled and padded, despite the airless heat of the hut.

"You certainly like to keep warm."

"You wouldn't say that if you were here at night." Worms indicated a curtained door at the back of the room. "Sleeping quarters are through there. Colder than a cabbie's arse and when it's raining like this it's dryer outside."

"Doesn't the stove keep it warm?"

"Won't stay in all night, chum. You'd be getting up every half an hour to feed it. You're alright though, Bertie says you're a local boy. You'll be going home each night?"

"Yes, I'm only a couple of miles away."

"Lucky sod."

Andy sat for a couple of hours with the instructors, drinking multiple cups of tea from a rotation of tin mugs. Only Bertie Gregory had seen action, achieving two victories and some fractions before a bad landing brought together his face and the windscreen. Six months of facial reconstruction had left him looking no worse than an under-talented prize fighter, and he'd eagerly taken the opportunity of a training post. Spotty and Worms were both recent students who'd been selected as tutors.

Riding home that evening on the Lea-Francis he thought about his new posting and wondered what his friends in France would be doing. The afternoon had dragged pointlessly by in a featureless exchange of flying stories and complaints about student idiocy. His new companions were pleasant enough but their flames were somehow dim and smoky; they sputtered like untrimmed lamps, flickering behind sooted glass. It struck him that he'd spent an afternoon without laughing, and tried to remember the last time that had been true.

CHAPTER 39

Andy leaned forward and patted the top of the student's head. He felt the stick waggle in his hands and sat back as the Avro meandered left and right as inexpert hands tried to hold course in the brisk crosswind. He leaned forward again to shout in the student's ear.

"Nose to the right of the airfield. About there." He indicated with an outstretched arm. "Use rudder, not stick."

By the time he'd sat back again the aircraft was pointing directly at the airfield and drifting once again to the left. A pale flash close to the aerodrome caught his eye and he looked harder, seeing the unmistakeable flutter of a spiralling aircraft. He lost sight of it for a second, then saw spreading fire under a ribbon of oily smoke. His student, unaware, continued doggedly on his course, turning ever to the right as the wind drifted him towards the pyre.

After a landing that had tested even the cast-iron undercarriage of the Avro, Andy hurried to the stifling Adrian hut. He found Bertie Gregory standing by the stove with Worms, who was fussing with a cracked teapot.

"Who was that?"

Gregory looked round. "Williams. First solo."

"He was one of yours, wasn't he?"

Gregory nodded. "Yes, no surprise really; he didn't know the stick from his dick."

"So how many hours dual did you give him?"

Gregory shrugged. "About the same as always. Four or five I suppose. It'll be in the log. What's your point?"

"That's two killed this week."

"Woa, hang on, the other was one of Spotty's. Not my fault. Not that this one was, either."

"You're the CFI. They're all your responsibility."

Gregory exchanged glances with Worms and turned, nodding sourly, fully to face Andy. "You know, I just knew we'd be having this conversation sooner or later. So you don't like the way I run things?"

"I don't like the way we lose more pilots than a combat unit, and our aeroplanes are in worse shape."

"What do you expect? They don't know how to fly. Are you telling me nobody crashed when you were training?"

"No, I'm not telling you that," Andy strained to keep his voice level. "But we shouldn't just accept that that's the way it is. I've been here four weeks, and we've lost, what, six trainees?"

"Seven. And if you check you'll find that's not far off the average."

"Great. And how many of them were my students?"

Gregory applauded slowly. "Oh, congratulations. You've kept the poor lambs alive." He walked over to scan the status board on the wall.

"F7443, broken undercarriage, instructor: A. Palmer. F7169, wing damage, instructor: A. Palmer. F3071, broken undercarriage, instructor: A. Palmer."

He turned back to Andy. "Shall I carry on? You've caused more damage in a month than a plague of bloody locusts."

"Do you know why that is, Bertie? Because, every time, the student was actually flying the plane when it landed!"

Gregory pushed roughly past him and opened the door, pointing out to where a plume of smoke was still visible in the distance. "Do you want to end up like that? That's what students do! When they're with me they can put their hands on the controls and feel what I'm doing. Then, when they try it themselves, they're only going to kill themselves. You expect me to risk my life for a brainless trainee? Well fuck that for a game of soldiers!"

He stumped out, slamming the door behind him. Worms looked at Andy. uncertainly. He held out a dented tartan tin.

"Want a biscuit?"

*

"I don't know if it's all just me. I'm arguing with everybody these days, and there has to be a common denominator."

Andy and Stainton were walking in the park. The trees were showing a faint green-yellow haze on their stark branches. There was a suggestion of warmth in the sunlight that flashed off Powell's Pool, turning the fishermen into hunched silhouettes. Stainton's dogs, a pair of Irish setters, quested ahead, occasionally chasing one another between the distractions of siren rabbit scents.

"But it sounds to me as if you were right."

"Well, it would, wouldn't it? It's me telling you about it." He threw a stick for the nearer dog, who bounded after it and inspected it for a moment before returning to his objectless hunt.

Stainton was quiet for a few steps. "You don't fit in there, do you?"

"Not sure I fit in anywhere. I can't stand being in combat, and I hate being out of it." He shrugged. "At least in France we cared about the fact that people were dying."

"Really? Doesn't sound like it. Colin's letter sounded as if he was more bothered about inheriting a dog than he was about your hut mate being killed."

"You get that way. It's not that you don't care about it. It's like..." he cast about for a simile. "...like scar tissue. Like the callouses on Dad's leg. It's a hard shell you build to stop it all hurting so much."

They walked in silence, arms linked. A bench near the lakeside beckoned and they sat down to watch the fishermen. Andy leaned forward, inspecting his hands.

"Stainton, the best friends I've ever known could be killed every day I'm here. I dread the post every day."

Stainton shook her head, breathing out impatiently. "Welcome to England, 1917." She gestured to the houses, visible in the distance. "Knock on any of those doors, and you won't find one person who won't be terrified of what you've come to tell them."

Andy sighed and nodded. "That's true, but most of them aren't in a position to do anything about it." Stainton waited, knowing what he'd say next. Eventually he looked up at her.

"I think I have to go back."

"So you want to leave me?"

"No! Of course not, but..."

"But...?"

"But... I don't know. Just 'But'."

"Andy, it might not even be possible to go back. You can't just pick and choose your posting."

"I could ask the Colonel."

"Uncle Edwin? You could I suppose." She thought for a few moments. "Maybe you should talk to him. Maybe he can suggest something else. If he could just get you away from these morons you're stuck with at the moment, you'd feel differently I'm sure."

"Yes, probably."

CHAPTER 40

Andy gave his name to the uniformed attendant in the foyer of the Army & Navy Club and was relieved to see immediate recognition on the man's face.

Colonel Chisholm, sir? Yes, he's waiting for you in the coffee room. Please come this way."

Andy followed the attendant, trying not to match his military stride. In London for only the second time in his life, he felt overwhelmed by the tall Venetian-looking building with its marble floors and flowered ceilings. The Colonel sat near the back of a long room decorated with potted plants and lined with paintings. A low buzz of conversation rumbled and the air was fruited by coffee and cigar smoke. He stood as Andy approached.

"Ah, Palmer. Good to see you again." He glanced at the attendant. "Thank you Croft. Let them know we're ready for lunch, would you?"

He sat again in a white rattan chair, gesturing Andy to its companion. "So, how are my good friends Connie and Stainton?" He pointed to a silver pot. "Coffee?"

"Please. They're fine, thank you sir. They send their regards."

"Of course, of course." He poured coffee into a tiny white cup. "And what do you think of Castle Bromwich?"

"It's fine too; thank you for putting in a word for me there, sir."

Chisholm flapped a hand. "Nothing to it. But I'd far rather you were honest than tactful."

Andy laughed quietly, dropping sugar into his cup. "I'm sorry. Let's say it's not quite what I'd hoped for."

"And what did you hope for?"

"To be honest, sir, I don't really know. But not students who nobody can be bothered to teach, flying aeroplanes nobody can be bothered to maintain."

A liveried waiter glided to their table. "Lunch is served, Colonel Chisholm."

*

The dining room was smaller and quieter than the echoing coffee room. White starched tablecloths hung down, their corners pointing regimentally at the Indian carpet. Here and there an elderly officer dozed over his brandy. The Colonel flapped his napkin before spreading it across his knees.

"I'm sorry, the food's rather unimaginative, but the place fits like a pair of old slippers. As long as you like Brown Windsor, trout and roast beef you'll be alright. Avoid the puddings at all costs. Care for wine?"

"Thank you sir," replied Andy, immediately wondering whether he should have declined.

"Good. Can't stand all this lunchtime temperance." He waved the wine waiter over. "Afternoon Riggs, bottle of my Margaux if you would."

He broke a bread roll, spreading the pieces liberally with butter. "Name Smith-Barry mean anything to you?"

"No sir, I don't think so."

"Interesting chap. Friend of mine is his commanding officer. They've set up a flight training school at Gosport, if you know where that is."

"Vaguely. On the south coast isn't it?"

"Believe so. Anyway, this Smith-Barry chap has been bending ears all over the place about the deplorable state of our air training."

He broke off as the waiter brought and uncorked the wine. Chisholm glanced at the soupçon in his glass and nodded his approval without tasting it.

"As it happens, my chum Waldron was of similar mind and the two of them persuaded the Ministry to give them a shot. There'd be an opening there for you if you were interested."

Andy toyed with his soup spoon, watching the light from the chandeliers flick across the tablecloth. "That's very kind of you, sir."

An escutcheoned bowl of soup was placed in front of him, a sprinkling of parsley floating in its centre. He swirled it gently with his spoon. The Colonel tucked in with relish, looking up after a few spoons and dabbing his lips with his napkin.

"Yes, it is very kind of me since you mention it. Which makes me wonder why you are about to decline the offer." He returned to the soup.

Andy sat in silence, formulating and rejecting replies. Chisholm continued eating soup, finally tilting the bowl to scoop out the dregs. He leaned back, looking at Andy. "You're not eating your soup, then?"

"I'm not feeling terribly hungry, I'm sorry."

The Colonel regarded him for a few moments longer, then spread his hands. "So, where do we go from here? Your silence confirms that I am correct. But you agreed to a meeting; what is it you want me to do, send you back to France?"

Andy reddened, disarmed by the Colonel's astuteness. "I... Yes, sir, that is in fact what I was hoping to ask you."

"You put me in a difficult position, Palmer. Two people of whom I'm extremely fond have asked me to use whatever influence I may have to help you. I'm more than happy to comply, but if I do as you ask, then I am betraying a long and important friendship."

Andy pushed back his hair with both hands and leaned forward, resting his elbows on the table, hands clasped, forefingers peaked under his nose.

"Colonel, I do understand what I'm asking you, and I apologise for putting you in this position." He looked down at his cooling soup. "But staying here in England feels to me like betraying friendships that are equally important to me."

Chisholm raised his eyebrows. "Oh, so it's not a patriotic duty to King and country, then?"

"To be perfectly honest, sir, no. I do understand that I could help the war effort by helping to train new pilots. And I know that if I go back to France I could be killed in the first ten minutes and that that would help nobody. I suppose, if it's duty, then it's duty to people who I owe a lot to. They've kept me safe and alive, and I owe them the same."

"So you want me to try to get you posted back to your squadron?"

"Yes, sir."

The roast beef arrived and they sat in silence while the waiter filled their plates with vegetables and gravy. After he left, Chisholm savoured his wine, sniffing the glass and inspecting its contents with attention.

"If I were to do this, how do you think Stainton would react?"

"Not well, sir"

Chisholm sipped his wine. "No, not well. What are your intentions toward her?"

"You mean marriage?" He cut a slice of beef and held it on his fork. "We've spoken of it." He looked up at the Colonel. "It is what I want, sir. But not until the war's over. If I survive, then, yes, I hope we'll marry."

"And what's her view on that?"

Andy smiled ruefully. "She wants to be sure that I do survive."

The Colonel nodded. "And she introduced you to me in the hope that I'd do just that. And now you are asking me to do exactly the opposite. You see the dilemma, I'm sure."

Andy chewed a morsel of roast beef and nodded. "I do, sir, yes. And I'm sorry to put you in such a position."

"I should think so. Eat your lunch; it may not be up to your French cuisine, but that's not a bad slice of Scotch beef you have there. Eat up and tell me about these friends of yours."

Andy talked about Cubby, Colin and Page, recounting the larks and scrapes of four young men away from home. The Colonel listened attentively, laughing frequently and questioning often. He'd known Arthur French briefly and was visibly moved by Andy's account of his death. As he talked, Andy felt a dam break somewhere and the words crowded one another on his tongue. For the first time in weeks he heard himself laughing freely and without restraint. They were sipping port and nibbling the crumbs of their stilton by the time the stories ended. Andy felt a cold but pleasant emptiness in his nose and head, like the aftermath of childhood tears. The Colonel looked at him with an assessing gaze.

"Andrew, I can see what the Hamiltons see in you, and possibly even a bit of me when I was your age. Stainton's father and I were just as bloody stupid as you and your friends appear to be. And I know that, terrified as I was when Botha attacked us, I'd never have deserted him." He extended his right hand, clasping Andy's in both of his own when the younger man reached to shake it.

"Leave it with me, I'll do what I can. And good luck breaking the news to Stainton. I don't envy you that job."

*

Stainton was waiting on the platform at Streetly station as Andy stepped down from the train. He acknowledged the salutes of three suddenly-respectful squaddies who had clearly been importuning her, turning his head away to hide a grin. The Daimler was waiting at the top of the exit stairs, its engine ticking faintly. Mortimer held the rear door open for them to enter. Once inside, Stainton slid under his outstretched arm.

"So, how was Uncle Edwin?"

"In fine spirits. He sends his love."

"And is he able to help you?"

"He thinks so." Andy hesitated fatally, trying to frame his confession. By the time he'd persuaded himself to speak it was already too late.

"Oh, he's marvellous isn't he? Of course, we probably won't be able to see each other quite as often if you're posted to another training squadron, but I can come and stay. When will you hear from him?"

"I don't know. He didn't say."

The Daimler turned into Sutton Park and Andy watched the holly bushes slide past the windows. Stainton leaned back to focus on his face.

"Something's wrong," she said quietly.

He looked at her. "What?"

"It was a question. What's wrong?"

He looked out of the window again. Rabbits lolloped at the roadside, stopping, hunched and chewing rapidly, to watch the car glide past.

"We have to talk."

"About what? Where is this posting?" She looked at him harder. "Oh no. Tell me I'm wrong."

He sighed, shaking his head. "I don't think you are." He tried to put his arms around her but she slid away from him.

"Not France. You can't be thinking of going back."

"I've got to. I thought you'd understand."

"Of course I don't bloody understand! And why have you 'got to'? Who's forcing you to go?" Her voice was angry and her eyes wet.

"I've got to because I owe it to my friends. I feel as if I've abandoned them."

He knew, even as he said the words, that he'd made another mistake. "So in a choice between abandoning them and abandoning me, they win, is that it?"

"No, of course not. It's…"

"How not? Please explain how not, because that's the way it seems to me."

"I don't know if I can explain. I don't really understand myself. I just know that I don't belong here." He reached out again and this time managed to catch her hands. "I wish to God that wasn't true, but it is. I want to be with you, honestly I do. More than anything else in the world, but I just can't do it."

"But why?" She angrily wiped away tears.

"That's what I can't tell you, because I don't know."

"I don't understand that. I don't understand a word of what you're saying."

"Nor do I. That *is* what I'm saying."

"So that's it, then? You'll go back to France. Do I have no say in the matter?"

"Stainton, love, *I* have no say in the matter."

She laughed bitterly, pleased that anger was overruling her grief. "Oh, please don't give me that. You have all the say. You've made a decision and it's goodbye Stainton."

"No it's not! Not goodbye at all. I'll be back, I promise."

"And how can you make a promise like that, Andy? Are you bullet-proof all of a sudden?"

"I'm a flight leader. Flight leaders hardly ever get shot down."

"No, of course not. How's your friend French?"

"That was a landing accident."

"What difference does that make? He's dead isn't he?"

Andy found his own temper beginning to rise. "I'm a bloody sight more likely to die in an accident if I stay here and train pilots."

"Oh, I apologise. You're going back to the front line because it's safer there. Thank you, I understand perfectly now." She pulled her hands from his and retreated to the far side of the seat, staring fixedly out at the parkland.

*

In the weeks that followed, Andy found himself hoping that the Colonel had decided not to ask for the combat posting, or that his influence had proved unequal to the Air Board's hunger for experienced trainers. Stainton had thawed gradually over three or four days and he found even the mindless drudgery of the flight training school and its Lilliputian instructors becoming bearable. His relationship with Bertie had settled to a tolerant cease-fire, and Worms and Spotty even began to allow some flight input from their students.

Stainton's regular visits to Abraham Grove continued their transformation of Andy's father, and she and he became inseparable friends, chatting long and animatedly about his experiences and his passion for musical comedy. The doilies and china ornaments were removed from the piano in the front room and impromptu musical soirées were held once or twice a week. Min was usually present, perched on the pristine, unused chairs and providing the harmonies she and her father had shared before the war. Stainton's musical talent was applauded, as was Gerald's enthusiastic and spirited vamping. Life, in short, was good. And when Rob arrived unexpectedly for three days' leave, the family was complete. They went for drives in the Daimler, with Andy and Stainton enjoying the sharp spring air on the front bench while Mr and Mrs Palmer sat in regal magnificence in the rear compartment, their legs entangled with Rob's and Min's, seated opposite them on drop-down seats.

The newspapers told dire stories of the air war over the Western Front. Allied losses were becoming unsupportable, as their outdated machines were ripped apart by vastly superior German scouts with twin guns and 200hp engines. This and the scourge of Von Richthofen's squadron had spawned a chilling media name-tag: Bloody April. Andy daily scanned the lists of the dead, feeling a cold lurch every time he saw 128 Squadron listed.

Stainton's 20th birthday, on the ninth of June, was to be marked with a small party at Monmouth Drive, to which Andy's parents were invited. His mother fussed and panicked over suitable evening wear, and his father's best suit was despatched to the cleaner's in readiness.

Andy, at last ready to make the life-changing decision, stole a dress ring from Stainton's jewellery box. He took it to Orzel's in Erdington High Street, using it as a size guide to select an engagement ring that substantially impacted his savings.

He woke early on the Saturday morning to the sound of the door knocker and went downstairs in his dressing-gown. A telegram delivery boy on the doorstep handed him a buff envelope, hovering expectantly, as though expecting a tip, as Andy signed the chit. He tore open the envelope before the gate clanged shut, sure that it contained news of the death of his brother or one of his friends. Instead, in clipped, official language, it pronounced the outcome of his lunch with Colonel Chisholm, months before.

+LT ANDREW D. PALMER+
+YOU ARE DIRECTED TO REPORT TO 128 SQUADRON, BEAUVAL, FRANCE TO TAKE UP ACTIVE FLYING DUTIES+
+REPORT FOR DUTY, MAJ B. J. HOLT, OFFICER COMMANDING, NO LATER THAN 18:00 HRS, 15THJUNE, 1917+
+TRAVEL ORDERS FOLLOW BY POST+

That evening, as they waited for Mortimer to arrive in the Daimler, Andy sat on his bed and thought, the ring sparkling in its open box as he turned it in his hands.

The birthday party would have been a pleasant, family affair had Andy not been harbouring a dreadful secret. Presents were conferred by Connie and Andy's parents to suitable delight on their opening, and Andy felt Stainton's questioning eyes on him as he stood, awkward and empty-handed. After dinner, he stepped close to Stainton, taking her elbow.

"We need to talk."

They walked quietly through the orangery and through the French windows to the garden. The night was chilly with the young summer of early June. She turned to face him, her eyebrows frowning and her lower lip caught in her teeth.

"What's wrong?"

He was silent, seeking for a way to begin, and finally removing the folded telegram from his pocket. He handed it to her wordlessly. She held it to the light from the orangery and read, then crumpled the paper and held it in both hands, her head bowed and her thumbs dug into her eyes.

They stood like that for long minutes before Andy finally stirred and drew a deep breath. "Stainton, I…"

"Shut up. Please."

They stood in silence again, close but not touching. Andy ventured a hand on her shoulder and she pulled away with a faint cry. Then she pushed the crumpled telegram into his hand and rushed inside. She didn't appear again that evening, and the party passed uncomfortably without its guest of honour. The wisdom of Andy's choice was reviewed and considered without resolution and the suitable moment for polite withdrawal was awaited with anticipation.

Mrs Bailey's telephone being unavailable on a Sunday, Andy rode the Lea Francis to Monmouth Drive, only to find the house locked and the doorbell unanswered. He toured Sutton Coldfield, sipping tepid tea in Lyon's on the High Street, and looking constantly for the red Daimler.

After returning three times to Monmouth Drive to find the house still deserted, he rode disconsolately home.

His travel orders arrived on Monday morning, detailing him to entrain at Snow Hill on Wednesday. He telephoned several times through the day but, by Tuesday, it still remained unanswered. With less than 24 hours left before his departure, Andy set off again for Monmouth Drive.

This time, the Daimler was parked on the drive and the door was answered by Mortimer, who informed him that Mrs and Miss Hamilton were both out. As Andy turned away, the chauffeur called after him,

"Miss Hamilton went for a walk. You might, try the park, Mr Palmer."

He made for Powell's Pool, hoping to find Stainton on the benches, but found only governesses with prams and noisy children, being eyed resentfully by the fishermen. As he wandered aimlessly across the meadows, a flash of wings caught his eye. Baffled for a moment by the silence, he realised that the aircraft was a rubber-powered model, being watched by a small group on the ground. He walked closer and stood, hands in his pockets, watching as a second machine was launched into the air. He stayed for a few minutes before turning away. There, fifty yards away and standing alone, was Stainton. She nodded slightly and they walked towards each other to stand, both uncertain, six feet apart.

"I was looking for you." Andy said.

"I know, I saw you down by Powell's Pool and followed you up here."

"How are you?"

"Confused."

Andy withdrew his hands from his pockets. "Would it help if I said I am too?"

"Not really." She looked at him, standing with his hands half outstretched, as if uncertain of their function. "A bit." She stepped forward into his arms.

They stood, clasped tightly together for minutes. Finally, Andy found his voice. "I'm sorry. I've really ballsed it all up haven't I?"

She looked up into his face, seeing that his eyes were wet. "Pretty comprehensively." She glanced over to the aero modellers, "Come on, let's find a bench before we bring on delayed puberty to that bunch."

He smiled at her attempt at levity and dared to hope. They found a simple plank bench on the edge of the wood and sat, squinting at the brightness of the sunlit meadow. Andy's right hand was in his pocket, his left around Stainton's shoulders.

"Not much of a birthday then, was it?"

"It was fabulous. Your present was a complete surprise."

He fumbled in his pocket. "Not the one I'd planned to give you."

"I had rather hoped for something else. Maybe the other earring to match this one."

He noticed for the first time that she was wearing the single earring he'd bought, centuries ago, in Le Touquet. "Well if I'm back in that hospital again, I'll see what I…" he stopped lamely. "Sorry, that didn't come out the way I planned it."

"When do you leave?"

"Tomorrow, early."

She shivered slightly, despite the mildness of the morning. "So soon."

"That's why I needed to see you. One of the reasons, anyway. I'd planned to give you this on Saturday." He withdrew his hand from his pocket and looked at the tiny blue box. "I'd rehearsed exactly what I was going to say, and how to say it. Now I don't know what to do."

She looked at the box, frozen in the lengthening moment, before reaching to take it. She held it, unopened, in both hands.

"Do I want to open this?" It wasn't clear to whom the question was addressed.

"I want you to open it. Then I can ask you… what I'd planned to ask you on Saturday."

She stroked the gold satin embroidery with her thumb. "On Saturday I'd have opened it. That was when I thought you'd finished with the War."

"I know. That was why I couldn't do it." He took a deep breath. "Stainton, I love you, and I want to ask you to marry me."

"That's what you'd rehearsed was it? " She opened the box a fraction before letting it snap closed again. "Andy, I'd love us to be married, but…" She fell silent, still looking at the box. "Yes, you've really ballsed it all up."

"Does that mean no?"

"Why is it I always seem to be telling you that I don't know?" she asked, "Well, here I am again: I don't know what it means."

"You could at least open the box."

"I could. But it's like a superstition. I feel that if I look at the ring before I'm sure, we'll never be married."

"So you do want to?"

She leaned into his shoulder. "Of course I do. More than anything. I even understand why you feel you have to go back. But right at this moment I don't know if we can make those sorts of plans. Call that superstition too if you like."

She gave him back the box. "Keep it safe. The time will come when I can open it, I promise."

*

The platform of Snow Hill Station was noisy with men in a medley of uniforms. Standing still among the roiling throng, Andy and Stainton stood locked together. In isolated clearings of the milling soldiery, similar tableaux were played out by other couples, some of them with frowning children clutching their free hands. Stainton had insisted on rising early to drive him to the station. A train pulled in, hissing and chuffing, its green-painted carriages squeaking as it came to a halt. A porter skirted along the platform edge calling, "6:50 to Paddington. All aboard, please ladies and gentlemen."

Stainton suddenly gripped him tighter. "Have you got the ring in your pocket?"

Andy felt inside his overcoat and produced the box. She almost snatched it from him, opening it and pushing the ring fiercely onto her finger.

"Yes, I will. Please stay safe and hurry home."

She kissed him and turned, hurrying towards the exit.

CHAPTER 41

Andy was glad to jump out of the sweltering fug of the tender into the mildness of the June afternoon. The aerodrome's ramshackle aspect of a weather-punished farm appeared unchanged as he flicked an acknowledgement of the gate sentry's salute and coaxed the sagging five-bar gate into twisting, grass-scraping movement. He stood in the cobbled yard, looking around him. Beyond the far gate he could see that few aircraft were on the ground. Presumably, an afternoon squadron patrol was underway. A stranger emerged from the Squadron Office, preceded by Prebble's dog, panting and straining at the end of a length of rope. The stranger was broad-shouldered and athletic, with a moustache so pale as to be almost white. He waved to Andy and turned towards him, revealing equally pale eyelashes in a pink-cheeked face.

"Afternoon, Andy Palmer is it?" He came close, extending his hand. "Tom Corbett, Adjutant. Welcome back; I've been looking forward to meeting you."

Andy shook the hand while warding off the dog's assault on his groin. The dog whimpered and drooled in an ecstatic welcome, its tail thrashing and claws skittering on the cobblestones.

"Sorry about the Idiot. You've probably met him before?"

"Yes, he ate most of my furniture."

Corbett nodded. "That's why he's with me. I keep the brainless mutt while Colin's flying so that he's still got a bed to come back to." He bent to pick up one end of Andy's trunk. "Grab t'other end and I'll take you to your hut."

Andy picked up the other handle. "Thanks. I know where it is, though."

"Ah." Corbett hesitated. "I'm afraid I can't get you back in with Colin at the moment; his hut's full. Each flight bunks together now so that they don't wake each other up when we're not doing a squadron show."

"Fair enough." It made sense, but for the first time it struck Andy that things might have changed in four months.

"Sorry, about that, I know it's probably not what you'd like. Still, shouldn't be too bad, you'll be sharing with an old friend." Corbett pushed open the freshly-painted door of Cubby's hut. Inside was as neat and orderly as Andy remembered, but the rear of the hut was now divided by a new wall in which two doors were set. The one on the left was adorned with a hand-painted banner emblazoned, "Welcome Home".

Corbett lowered the trunk just inside the door. "I won't come right in; Cubby'd kill me if the dog messed anything up." He looked around, nodding appreciatively. "You're highly honoured; Cubby's scotched every attempt to get another bod in here with him."

He reached to shake hands again. "Glad you're here, Andy. You must be knackered so I'll leave you to it for now." He glanced at his watch. "Patrol should be back in half an hour or so. I'll see you at tea."

Andy sat on his trunk, reluctant to encroach on either of Cubby's easy chairs. *So, here we are again.* He looked around the room, noticing that the photograph of Cubby and his son was still in place on the sideboard. Intrigued, he stood and stepped over to pick it up and examine it by the window. While the similarity was undeniable, Danny McConnachie was broader in the shoulders than Andy, already showing signs that his skinny frame would soon fill out to equal his father's. His grin was as broad as Cubby's, but Andy fancied he saw a quiet sadness in the yes. He shook his head and laughed silently at his own imagination; the photograph was burnt to detailless black and washed-out white by the Egyptian sun. Danny could have been cross-eyed for all the detail that was visible. Andy replaced the picture and went to inspect his new sleeping quarters.

He woke to the sound of aero engines. He'd lain down intending to test the bed, and fallen asleep almost immediately, worn out by two days of rail, road and sea travel. The unfamiliar surroundings puzzled him for a moment before recollection broke through and he walked outside. The last Sopwith was bumping along the strip as he arrived at the flight line. Others were zig-zagging across the field, their wingtips controlled by running ack emmas. He inspected the machines anxiously, seeing no obvious damage, and relaxing further as he identified Colin's red spinner, Page's chequered fuselage band and Cubby's obscure antipodean marsupial.

His three friends assembled in a laughing group and started towards the farmyard. Colin was the first to see Andy standing by the gate; he nudged his companions and Cubby's whoop sounded over the rattle of engines. They closed the gap quickly and he received handshakes and shoulder-thumps from Colin and Page, followed by the expected engulfing bear hug from Cubby.

"Welcome to the Young Men's Holiday Camp. Come on, there's time to get a drink in before the community singing." He draped an arm around Andy's shoulders and the four of them pushed through the gate, heading for the mess.

The mess had changed little, though few of the names on the tally board were familiar to Andy. He saw that Page still led the kill total, now with twenty-four victories. Colin was second, with seventeen. Cubby was joint third with an unknown named Hargreaves, both of them tied on eight.

Cubby caught his look. "Yep, you need to look over your shoulder, son. The Tasmanian Devil's right behind you."

"I can see I've got some catching up to do," Andy replied.

The mess servant placed four pots of beer on the table. Andy raised his glass. " Grats on the third pip, Humph. What's it like out there? The papers make it sound pretty bloody."

Page glanced at the new captain's pips on his shoulders and shrugged. "We lost a lot for a while. You missed the worst of it, though. The SE5s are coming through in dribs and drabs and they've levelled things up a bit."

"I'd been hearing that the engines are no good."

"'Bout what you'd expect from the R.A.F., but they go like stink. They're all over the DIIIs when the fan's turning properly."

"Any for the squadron?"

"No such luck. But they crop up now and again and put no end of wind up Fritz. Fifty-Six have them up at Liettres and for a while it was raining Germans. Until Ball went down last month, anyway."

"Yes, I saw it in the papers. Nobody could believe he'd bought it."

"Only a matter of time, old chap. You can't keep going up on your own and tweaking the Kaiser's whiskers forever. Especially with a big red nose on your kite." He looked significantly at Colin.

"It's probably because of that nose I don't get more kills," Colin answered. "Hun see it and run a mile, thinking it's Albert Ball, come to have his wicked way."

"They won't think that now, unless they think you've come to haunt them."

"Hey, that's not a bad idea. I'll get my kite painted white and go up in a sheet. That'll put 'em off their cabbage." Colin sipped his beer. "How was the Sceptred Isle?"

"Hard to describe," said Andy, "It was great to be home and to see Stainton nearly every day, but the training school was a nightmare. The instructors leave their personalities at the door, the 'planes are wrecks, and the casualty rate's unbelievable."

"And how's the lovely Stainton?"

"Not very pleased with me. When I told her I was coming back here I thought I was off the team."

"Not surprised."

"Yes, bit of a bumpy flight for the last few days. But, er, I've asked her to marry me, and she said yes on the station platform."

Cubby stood up. "Fair enough, that's as good an excuse for a smash-up as I can think of." He banged his glass on the table and the general buzz of conversation subsided.

"Gentlemen, for those of you who don't know this lad here with his hair falling in his eyes, allow me to introduce the redoubtable Andrew Palmer MC, a highly experienced plane crasher, just returned from teaching his unique skills to England's young idea, most of which won't be joining us as a result."

There was a general round of welcoming noises and one or two claps. Cubby silenced his audience with patting hand motions. "Mr Palmer would like you all to join him in drinking the health of his new fiancée, the delightful Miss Stainton Hamilton, who I'd cheerfully have a crack at if I wasn't already interfering with her mother."

The applause was more enthusiastic, and calls of "Good luck!" and "God bless her!" were interspersed with catcalls and whistles.

Cubby raised his glass. "Gentlemen, the bar, and Lieutenant Palmer's tab, are open." He drained his glass and sat down.

"Why is it, every time I see you, I end up poorer?" asked Andy, grinning, knowing that the tab would be shared by his friends. It felt good to be home.

*

Corbett joined them as Andy and Cubby were bracing themselves as the base of the human pyramid for a game of Bok-Bok. He was accompanied by an officer with dark, intense eyes under heavy brows. He waved and sat at the table with Page and Colin, who preferred to save themselves for less dangerous pastimes, like being shot at by Germans.

Andy sat down ten minutes later, flushed and dishevelled. Behind him, Cubby was still in full charge, assaulting the enemy's pyramid by using one of its members as a battering ram. Corbett introduced the dark-eyed officer. "Andy, I'd like you to meet Eric Hoffe. He's C-Flight commander. I'd like to put you with him. Cubby here is deputy as before, and I'll introduce you to Harry Hargreaves when Cubby's finished using him to hit people."

Andy shook hands with Hoffe, trying not to react to the fact that he'd been replaced as flight commander. Hoffe seemed to sense the discomfort.

"Good to meet you, Andy. Sorry, I know you were FC before I arrived. I feel a bit of an interloper."

"No, not at all. They could hardly keep the job open on the off-chance that I came back. Glad to fly with you."

It was more than logical, and Andy genuinely felt no slight at the loss of responsibility. What had jarred him was the loss of the comparative safety of a flight commander's position, with his tail and flanks always covered. He suddenly confronted another companion from his earlier days in combat, one that he'd missed not at all. Throughout his months at home, Fear had been waiting patiently for his return.

*

Andy was on the 8 o'clock job the following day, a mixed-flight line patrol with Colin, Hargreaves, Cubby and Hoffe, with Page leading. It was already warm and Andy sweated uncomfortably in his layered clothing as he waited for his engine to warm up. A-Flight had been up at 05:00 and returned to report poor visibility and an absence of enemy activity.
They began the long climb to 18,000. The sweat cooled rapidly and Andy was soon shivering in his icy cocoon. He stamped his feet and flew with first one hand and then the other clamped between his thighs. The morning haze finally fell away from them at 10,000 and they emerged into brilliant sunshine. The sky to the east remained misty, turning the sun into an indistinct but dazzling blur capable of concealing the entire Luftstreitkräfte. Andy glanced at

the dashboard watch. *Fifteen minutes gone. Another hour and a quarter to go.* His flying in England had rarely exceeded 10,000 feet, and he was amazed how quickly he'd forgotten how it felt to be truly frozen.

They plodded up and down their patrol area in the splendid isolation of a blazing sky. The haze layer, 8,000 feet below them, was a motionless horizon of milk in front and behind. To the left, the English Channel showed dark blue, with England a faint, tantalising purple stain fringing it at the edge of sight. Andy dropped briefly out of formation and turned to the east to warm his gun, firing twenty rounds towards the solidifying wall that was building more rapidly now, and beginning to billow into genuine cloud. As he turned back his brain nudged him from his shivering thoughts. As he'd scanned the sky, his eyes had registered a black speck in the sun. He craned his neck back to look, wincing as the muscles protested; another vital discipline had been neglected during his training sojourn. The white, towering haze was featureless, the blazing yellow ball in its centre seeming to stare back at him with eyebrows raised in innocence. He zoomed ahead to pull alongside Page and pointed to the right, rocking his hand to indicate his uncertainty. Page nodded exaggeratedly and led the flight in a wide turn to face the possible threat.

They flew east for five minutes, undisturbed, six winged pairs of eyes that scanned and probed the brightness for movement. Hargreaves waggled his wings enthusiastically for a moment, but then waved his hands in contradiction, probably having been alarmed by spots on his windscreen or his dazzled vision. They turned back to the north and continued their patrol, watching the cloud bank intently. The haze below began to burn away as the day warmed.

The castle-battlement zig-zag of trenches appeared through the white veil, details becoming sharper as the tendrils of mist receded.

A cluster of black puffs caught their eyes and six heads leaned out from their cockpits to squint more intently. Far below them, a pale crucifix flickered in and out of view: a British artillery spotter plodding its perilous way south had attracted Archie's attention. The salvo was not repeated, suggesting that this had been a signal to nearby German aircraft, and the scrutiny from above was intensified, searching for the suspected enemy patrol. Andy saw them just as Page fired a flare and winged over into a dive. Four, possibly five, Huns were sweeping in rapidly from the spotter's left.

Andy was still banking into the dive when he heard the crackle of machine guns. He looked up and back and the sun was full of wings.

CHAPTER 42

Connie showed no maternal disapproval at Stainton's suspicions of pregnancy, but she was surprisingly conventional in her concerns about the infant's future. They were pottering in the orangery, snipping and fussing around the plants when she first approached the subject. Stainton had returned from the doctor's to announce that suspicion was now certainty, and that an outcome was to be expected near Christmas. Stainton was quietly thoughtful as she misted water around a Chinese orange. She glanced up to see her mother studying her.

"What?"

"How do you feel?"

"I'm absolutely fine. None of this sickness and misery I've been hearing about."

"No, I mean, how do you feel? About the future?"

Stainton returned to spraying the plant. "Not sure. Frightened, I suppose. Not about the birth... well, yes, about the birth, obviously. But mainly about what it all means. It sort of changes everything, doesn't it?"

"Have you told Andy yet?"

"Not yet, no. I wanted to be certain."

"And now that you are?"

"Well, of course."

They looked at each other for a few seconds. Connie raised her eyebrows.

"I'll write and tell him soon, of course I will," said Stainton finally.

Connie nodded slightly. "Just not quite yet." Her tone fell equally between a question and a statement.

"Just not quite yet." Stainton walked to the wall tap to refill the mister.

That night she lay awake for long hours, trying to arrange her emotions and plan the future. She loved Andy, of that she was sure, but the rejection of his return to his friends cast doubt on his feelings for her. And that brought her own sentiments into an unwelcome spotlight. Her rush of certainty on the station platform now seemed less persuasive as the practical impossibility of marriage drove it into its monochrome glare. Unless the war ended unexpectedly, she was unlikely even to see him before the baby's birth. The deadlock between the Allies and Germany was an irresolvable stalemate, bleeding the youth and the resolve from both sides, stretching into an infinitely cold future. She found herself imagining her opening the letter telling her of Andy's death, and shuddered to find feelings of relief among the anguish.

Connie noticed her daughter's increasing withdrawal over the following days, but it was some time before she succeeded in bringing the matter to discussion. She persuaded Stainton to join her for a shopping trip to Birmingham, and it was while riding home, the fold-down seats at the front of the Daimler's passenger compartment piled with sliding boxes and packets, that Stainton finally relaxed her guard. Connie looked closely at Stainton, who had just leaned forward for the hundredth time to prevent a hat box slipping to the floor.

"You look pale, dear. Are you feeling alright?"

Stainton smiled. "Fine, Mum. I told you, I feel absolutely fine."

"And you're sleeping?" Her daughter gave a slight guilty start. "No, thought not. Your eyes are black. What's troubling you?"

Stainton leaned back and closed her eyes. "Before this happened," she gestured vaguely downwards. "Before I knew it had happened, I've never been so sure of anything in my life. Andy and I would be married and we'd live happily ever after." She opened her eyes and looked at her mother. "Now it has happened, and it's a good job we're planning marriage. And now I don't know if I can do it."

Connie stroked her daughter's hair. "I know. I do understand, I promise. But it's important now that you do do it."

Stainton looked up in surprise. "I can't believe you, of all people, are saying that."

"Oh, don't get me wrong. In or out of wedlock means absolutely nothing to me. And I'm rather enjoying the notion of being a grandma. But this child will have to make its own way in the world. I can provide, but if it's to prosper, then the label 'bastard' has to be avoided. You see that don't you?"

"I do see that, but I never thought to hear it from you."

Connie pulled Stainton into the crook of her shoulder and kissed her hair. "It's a complicated world, dear. My opinions don't matter, only yours and the future of this child here. If you're not sure what to do now, then do nothing and wait until you are sure. I know you'll be right."

CHAPTER 43

Andy was already turning towards the enemy when he heard the guns. He pulled the stick back hard and right, slamming in full right rudder. The Pup flipped onto its right wing, into a diving near-spin and shot through the enemy formation. An Albatros flicked past him and was gone.

Straightening, he looked around him. The Huns had ignored him, pitching after the diving Sopwiths and closing in seconds to killing range. The British machines scattered and the duels began. He sensed a presence close by and looked to see another Pup pulling alongside. Cubby, from his position at the rear of the patrol, had seen Andy's swerve and followed him through the attackers. Now he pointed urgently downwards and pitched his nose into a dive. Andy pushed the stick forward and followed.

There were eight or nine German aircraft harrying the Pups. They were performing a deadly change-partners dance: an Albatros would engage in a turning battle until the Pup, more wieldy and responsive at this height, managed to turn inside him. He'd then break away and dive as a second Albatros took up position on the Pup's tail and the pattern repeated. In this way the British aircraft were constantly defending, while steadily losing height. As their altimeters wound down, so their manoeuvrability advantage diminished, and the faster German machines slowly gained ascendancy.

Andy selected his target; a zebra-striped Albatros was twisting after Page, who was pulling for a kill shot on a green machine ahead of him. He closed in to within fifty yards before firing, kicking his rudder left in anticipation of the Hun's swerve towards the Pup's poorer turn direction. The Albatros twisted into his tracer stream and rolled onto its back. Andy pulled back on the stick to avoid a collision and felt a shadow pressing on him from above. He looked up at the descending belly of another Albatros, its wheels only feet from his upper plane. He rammed the stick forward and felt a sharp blow on his cheek; his head jerked back and he saw a bar of chocolate, its wrapper torn and three squares broken off, sail upwards out of the cockpit. Even as the German's shadow receded, he grabbed it and thrust it back into his pocket.

Another shape flitted across his view and he grabbed for the trigger before registering the roundels on its top wing. As he shot through the space it had just vacated he felt his machine shudder as bullets hacked through it. He felt his seat sag slightly and something tugged at his back. Rolling to the right he looked down to see an Albatros, no doubt the one that had been pursuing the Pup he'd just narrowly missed, hanging from its prop and firing up at him. As it stalled away, a Sopwith came in from the side, impaling it on a lance of tracer.

Andy rolled level and looked around again. The enemy aircraft were clearing back to the east, trailing into formation as a white recall flare died slowly below them. He turned back towards the west, his eyes scanning for friendly aircraft. Cubby was first to drop onto his wing, soon joined by Page and Hargreaves. They formated behind Page's streamers, Andy on the right, Hargreaves left, and Cubby in his customary mother hen position above and behind. All four aircraft had received damage. Hargreaves signalled a dud engine as they crossed the lines and dropped out of formation. The remaining three limped home, Page's undercarriage collapsing on landing and depositing his machine to slump drunkenly at the side of the cinder strip.

Andy's aircraft was found to have one longeron almost completely shot through. The back of his seat had received at least two bullets, and the back of his coat proved to bear a matching vertical score. Corbett met them as they walked back to the farmyard. He reported that Hargreaves had landed at 46 Squadron, next to Colin's machine, which had been forced down by a ruptured fuel line, and that both were waiting for repairs. Hoffe had telephoned from White City to say that he'd crash-landed safely and was being entertained well by the Royal Artillery.

Cubby was credited with a "driven-down" victory over the prop-hanger that had hosed Andy, while Andy's zebra-stripe was disallowed when an artillery battery reported seeing it pull out, apparently undamaged. It was observed attacking a BE2 ten minutes later. No one else had managed to get any significant strikes.

The unavailability of airworthy aircraft washed out the rest of the day, and Cubby, Andy and Page received permission to go with the Crossley to help Colin and Hargreaves. Eschewing the services of a driver, Page and Andy slid from side to side on the front bench as Cubby swung enthusiastically through the bends, in time with the Strauss waltz that they roared, banging the dashboard in unison with their fists. "Ta daa daa daa da, Pom-Pom Pom-Pom!"

Andy's story of the floating chocolate bar was greeted with considerable hilarity and some respect. As Cubby put it, "You've got Fritz's tyre marks up the back of your head, and all you're worried about is losing your Dairy Milk. Now that's what I call a cool head!"

For the first time it occurred to Andy that, throughout the frenzied encounter, he'd forgotten to be afraid.

46 Squadron's aerodrome huddled in a cramped field near Izel-le-Hameau. Another Pup squadron, they greeted the three as kindred spirits and guided them to the mess, where Colin and Hargreaves were ensconced comfortably with a group of pilots. A barrage of introductions left Andy trying to relate names to faces and he gave up after memorising three. The enthusiastic talk was of the arrival of the new Sopwith, the Camel, with a high-powered le Rhone engine and – at last – twin guns, with a new design of interrupter gear. A tall, thoughtful looking fellow with a Sherwood Foresters cap badge, Andy hazarded his name as Lee, had flown the machine that afternoon.

"It's a bloody rocket. Goes like stink and turns even faster than a Pup. Loops by itself – you just stop pressing forward on the stick and over she goes. No need to dive first either. Can't wait to try the guns!"

His companion, a strikingly good-looking pilot in an immaculately-pressed uniform, disagreed. Andy recalled his name as Courtneidge, and wondered whether he might be related to the actress, Cicely.

"Lee, you're talking piffle as usual," Courtneidge smiled at the newcomers. "Don't believe him. It's a damned nightmare. Full right rudder when you take off, or you're going back the way you came, and your right arm aches like a trappist monk's with a Kirchner catalogue. Only good thing about it is the guns. It fires as fast as an Albatripe, none of that pop-pop-pop you get from the Pup."

"So when d'you get the full complement?" asked Page.

"Any day now, should be." The speaker looked barely old enough to be out alone. He was in shirt-sleeves and khaki braces. On his lap was a scrofulous Scottish terrier, whose name Andy recalled as Jock. He tried and failed to remember the boy's name. "I'll let you know what I think when these miserable sods let me try one."

"When you've grown enough to see over the gun butts, Odell, then we'll see."

Andy accepted a whisky from Lee and mused on the differences from squadron to squadron. These chaps might use surnames rather than Christian, and their dog appeared possessed of superior intelligence to 128's Idiot, but the conversation was probably identical in every mess across the world. He imagined a similar scene being played out the other side of the lines and the idea startled and slightly unsettled him. He wondered again what any of them, English or German, were doing here.

They drove back more sedately, containing as they did several of 46's whiskies. Colin and Hargreaves, their machines repaired, had taken off without incident. The assistance delivered by their friends consisted of waving from outside a hangar before returning to ogle the brand new Camel being prepared inside.

They arrived back at Beauval as dusk fell. The mess was buzzing with the latest news: orders had arrived from Wing to prepare for a move eastwards, to a new aerodrome near Gomiécourt. Rumour suggested that they'd be living under canvas, and the atmosphere fulminated with quiet mutiny. Andy found a letter on the table when he returned to the hut. Recognising Stainton's handwriting, he tore it open eagerly.

Dear Andy,

As you will have noticed, I haven't written for over a week. As you have probably already concluded, things are not exactly as we planned them. I'm sorry Andy, but I have to end it, at least for now, until I have worked certain things out. I hate to do this by letter, but if we were face to face I know I couldn't say it. I do love you, but not in a way that makes sense to me anymore.

I hope you'll write back, though there may be some delay in my replying; Mum and I have decided to leave the country for some time.

Do take care of yourself and stay safe.

All my fondest love,

Stainton.

He was still sitting at the table, staring sightlessly at the letter when Cubby came in an hour later. The Australian seemed to sense something wrong and was unusually quiet as he entered. He looked over Andy's shoulder at the letter and understood. He put his hand on the younger man's shoulder and Andy turned suddenly towards him, burying his face in Cubby's tunic. Cubby clasped him tight, feeling the shuddering, silent sobs.

CHAPTER 44

Gomiécourt fulfilled most of their misgivings. Instead of the thoughtfully cubicled huts, on which they now looked back with affection, the aviators now found themselves in sagging tents that baked in the sun and leaked in the rain. The landing field, between an ominous array of craters, was an uneven veneer of cinders over soup-like mud. The officers' mess justified the term; the previous incumbents had left little of the furniture with its original complement of legs, and the kitchen was pungently close to the latrines, to which it bore a distressing resemblance.

Andy had taken to spending most of his free time walking alone with the Idiot who, alone among the newcomers, seemed to approve entirely of his new quarters. Today he was questing ahead with a diligence that would have identified him as an experienced hunter, had he not repeatedly failed to notice the rabbits that watched his erratic approach with minimal concern. The dog disturbed a large hare, whose nerve had failed it when the Idiot's nose almost pushed it over. It exploded from cover, terrifying the dog and causing him to yelp and gallop back towards Andy. Half way there he was distracted by a butterfly and stopped to watch it with myopic fascination. The hare slowed to a walk and tried to give the impression that it had suddenly felt the urgent need to be 50 yards to the east.

Andy had written several letters to Stainton but, now a month later, had still received no reply. He'd even tried to telephone from the squadron office on two of his days doing orderly dog, but the connection process had proved too complex for the telephone operators.

His flying had become concerning to Hoffe, who had spoken softly to him only this morning. They'd returned from the early job, on which Hoffe and Andy had shared in downing a Halberstadt two-seater that stayed a fraction too long on its spotting patrol. Hoffe had fired fifty rounds from below its tail and the German observer had thrown up his arms and fallen back inside the fuselage almost before firing a shot at Andy who was approaching from above and to the right. Andy fired and walked his aim forward from behind the pilot up to the engine. A white mist of fuel sprayed from in front of the cockpit and the Halberstadt bunted into a steep dive. Andy had followed it down to below 1,000 feet, firing continually. The mist turned to flame at the same moment that the wings folded back and Andy ran out of ammunition.

Hoffe had been typically reserved about his dressing-down. He'd congratulated Andy on the kill, insisting that it was Andy's alone as he'd only disabled the gunner. "I think you could have assumed he was a goner without following him all the way down, though." He'd patted Andy's elbow, smiling. "Admire your diligence, old chap, but I don't want to lose you because some Hun on the ground gets lucky with a Spandau."

The Idiot selected the usual tree for his morning evacuation. His routine for defecation baffled everyone and amused nearly everyone, Colin being excluded from the latter group as cleaning the dog afterwards was generally regarded as his job. The dog reversed carefully up to the tree, peering backwards with the care and diligence of an ack emma manoeuvring the Crossley towards its trailer. Alerted to his arrival by the gentle bump, he then walked his back legs vertically up the trunk until he was virtually doing a handstand, his backside hovering unsteadily approximately above the first fork of branches. He then extended his neck forward, narrowed his eyes, and deposited an impressive turd on his own scrotum.

Andy kicked at the orange clay. The sun was hot on the back of his neck and he noticed the warning chafing around his collar that presaged sunburn. Fear, his constant companion in the cockpit, had departed to leave nothing but a cold numbness, dispelled only by the maniac lunge after a falling enemy. June had seen him down six enemy aircraft, bringing his total to sixteen with today's confirmed kill, just two behind Colin. He joined in the celebratory binges with convincingly feigned enthusiasm, consuming impressive volumes of alcohol before retiring to his tent, where Fear crouched patiently in the shadows, waiting for the almost nightly visit of the German bomber. There he'd lie, sweating among the whining mosquitos, and listen to the thumps and crashes as the unseen enemy above probed for him with grey tins of death.

Lying in the dark he suddenly realised it was his nineteenth birthday.

*

The mizzling rain that had made the morning D.O.P. a white-cloaked and miserable waste of petrol eventually found sufficient traction to accelerate to a lashing, blustering downpour that slapped the returning Pups to and fro as they groped to find the airfield. After a series of bouncing, swerving landings that resulted in one broken wheel and a ground-loop, the pilots huddled in the clammy, sagging mess tent to warm up with gulps of hot

Bovril. Around them, empty soup and jam cans clanked dully under the irregular drips that oozed from the cold canvas. Page smacked his lips appreciatively. His scars stood out crimson against the pinched, shivering blueness of the rest of his face.

"Bloody July? I reckon Scott would have called it off if he'd had to sit through cold like that!"

Colin nodded, looking out through the tent flap at the horizontal torrent. "Still, not all bad. What I'm seeing out there looks very like an afternoon off," he looked back at his companions. "Shame to waste it; fancy a run down to Achiet?"

Corbett endorsed their request for the trip to the extent of joining them, regretting only that the Crossley was away collecting a downed aircraft. Fortunately, one unexpected benefit of the move had been the discovery of a cache of half-a-dozen serviceable bicycles in the only solid building on the aerodrome, a decaying barn. So it was that Page, Colin, Corbett, Cubby and Andy found themselves wobbling hilariously south through the rain, towards the cosmopolitan delights of Achiet-le-Grand.

They pulled to a halt outside an estaminet near the northern edge of the village. Colin, whose machine lacked brakes, accomplished this manoeuvre by means of a tricky cannon shot off Cubby's bicycle into the hedge. The building looked respectable, and considerably less shell-damaged than its neighbours. However, Corbett was reluctant to settle on the first hostelry they'd encountered and prevailed on his companions to explore further. Arriving at a junction a few hundred yards later, he turned resolutely left, leading his bicycle patrol towards Cambrai.

"Oi, Tom, you do know you're going the wrong way, don't you?" enquired Cubby.

"Just exploring. Bear with me." Corbett replied, pedalling onward.

"Well discover something soon, mate. I'm bloody soaked."

The houses became sparse. After a mile those on the right disappeared completely. Those on the left showed increasing signs of war, with windows replaced by oiled cloth or boards. Many were in ruins.

"Where, in God's name, are you taking us, Tom?" asked Colin, puffing as they pedalled up a long hill.

"Just bear with me. I've got a feeling we'll find a good pub along here soon."

"Well you'd better be able to order the beers in German." grumbled Cubby.

The dissent threatened to escalate into outright mutiny when the houses died out completely. Still Corbett pressed on through the rain, insisting that he sensed the perfect estaminet just around the next turn. He finally halted next to a short flight of stone steps leading to an iron gate in an imposing brick wall.

"Here we go, this'll do nicely."

Colin's cycle crashed into Andy's, causing the latter to swerve into Cubby, who consequently brought down Page. Even Page's immovable equanimity was shaken and he complained loudly as he picked himself up.

"Corbett, we're more likely to get a twelve-bore down our throats than a beer. It's somebody's bloody house!"

"No, it's a pub, trust me."

"It had better be, because if I have to cycle back with buckshot in my arse, I'll be very disappointed."

It was an imposing building, undamaged other than splinter scars on its yellowed stucco walls. The windows were hidden behind heavy shutters, and the door was a massive black affair, studded with rough-wrought bolts. Corbett rapped the knocker and a small barred Judas hole opened; a voice from inside shrieked, "Tommi!" and there was a sound of bolts being withdrawn. The woman who ushered them inside could have been any age between fifty and seventy. She was expansively, rather than expensively, dressed in a Lautrec-style bustier and flared skirt, and her – or probably someone else's – hair was stacked high, with copper coils snaking down each side of a chinadoll face. She greeted Corbett rapturously and curtseyed elaborately to his friends, inviting them to enter her establishment.

Inside was a large room lit by red-shaded oil lamps that gave off a heavy, soporific fragrance. A small group of French officers was clustered around a dimly-lit table, speaking in whispers as they glared intently at their fanned cards. They nodded politely to the five Englishmen and returned to their game. Madame led them to a table, seating each of them individually with a welcoming pat and rub on the shoulder. A pleasantly pneumatic and similarly-dressed girl brought a carafe of wine and poured generously into five oversized glasses.

"*Sans doute, vous avez faim, messieurs? Voulez-vous la nourriture pour commencer?*" asked Madame.

"*Oui, merci madame. Nous somme affamés!*" replied Page, who was grinning hugely and clearly barely controlling his laughter.

As she left them, Page finally relaxed, roaring with laughter and pounding Corbett on the back. "You fly old bugger, you! How the hell did you know about this place?"

Corbett shrugged, grinning. "Pure stroke of luck, old chap. Never been here in my life. Sometimes I just get these hunches."

Cubby sipped his wine appreciatively, raising his glass to salute a gaggle of women inspecting them from the shadows at the back of the room.

"Well, good on you for bein' a bleedin' clairvoyant." He darted his eyes towards Colin, who was staring at the women with open-mouthed wonder, and winked at Corbett. "My guess that somebody's going to dampen his dipstick tonight."

The food was surprisingly good. A peppery fish soup was followed by mutton with baby peas, still in their pods, garnished with generous shavings of truffles. Pudding was a moist, shiny torte with yellow cream. When the cheese and port arrived, the five were sufficiently drunk to stand and toast the French officers then, caps held to their breasts, to de-dum their way through the Marsellaise. The French responded indulgently, singing *God Save the King* with considerably more accuracy and returning the toast in cloudy pastis. Then cognac and cigars were brought by the girls. There were four of them, dressed in dark, floating diaphany, and flickering black-pencilled eyes and lips that glinted like spilled wine in the smoky lamplight. They draped themselves artlessly on chairs that they dragged from other tables and made absurdly formal introductions to the Englishmen. After a few minutes, two more detached themselves from the Frenchmen's table and floated over to perch on the hard wooden arms of Page's chair, their arms behind his neck. The French officers seemed too absorbed in their game to object, or even to notice their departure.

The youngest-looking girl leaned close to Colin, asking, "You buy for me champagne, yes?" in a soft, high voice.

"Yes, yes, of course," answered Colin in the voice of a choirboy colliding with puberty in the middle of Allegri's *Miserere*.

Madame arrived immediately with six large sundae glasses, half-filled with a pale, fizzing liquid; possibly champagne, but probably some sort of sherbet. The girls downed them with lip-smacking appreciation and, with Colin's head-bobbing approval, called for another round.

"*Spof!*" cried one of the women, "*Nous devrions jouer spof!*"

Cubby looked around the table for enlightenment. "Any ideas? Anybody know what the hell 'spof' is?" He started as he felt a hand in his pocket. The girl nearest him was fishing out coppers and spreading them on the table.

"*Spof! La parodie! Vous devinez le nombre de pièces, vous savez?*"

"I think she means 'spoof'," offered Corbett.

Cubby accepted three sous from the girl, while she selected three francs for her own use. "I've got a feeling this is going to get expensive."

The rules were quickly explained to Colin and Andy, neither of whom had encountered the game before, and play commenced. Each player would conceal up to three coins in his or her hand and each would guess in turn the total number of coins in play. A correct guess allowed the player to drop out of the ensuing rounds. The last man standing was to buy a round of drinks. It quickly became apparent that last man standing was the accurate description; the girls clearly had some arcane system of signals that ensured uncanny accuracy in their guesses. Colin's estimates, by contrast, started off inaccurate and deteriorated rapidly as round after round was consumed.

"So, come on, Tom," Page prodded, leaning back from the table, "How did you find out about this place?"

Corbett looked up from explaining to Colin yet again that eleven people with a maximum of three coins each did not permit a total of forty. He grinned at Page.

It was five minutes' walk from my old airfield. We had to move out when the Jerries pushed forward, but the place is too popular for anybody to drop anything nasty on it." He nodded towards Colin, "I think we need to intervene while young hasty here's still got a working con-rod."

Colin was leaning back in his chair, smiling vacantly at the young girl who was whispering to him, her head on his chest. Page leaned forward and pressed something into her hand, giving her a conspiratorial wink and nodding gently towards the stairs. She smiled back at him and gently led Colin meekly from the room.

Andy, who had sat silent and glowering throughout the evening, stood suddenly. The bored girl who had tried unsuccessfully to engage him in conversation looked up as he took her hand. He beckoned her with a jerk of his head and walked with her to the back stairs.

CHAPTER 45

The Idiot had thrust his head into a rabbit hole in order to consume the freshest available droppings. His back legs kicked up stones and grass stems as he snaked his shoulders, trying to insinuate a fifty-pound canine into a hole purpose-designed by a two-pound herbivore for the specific purpose of preventing him from succeeding. So far, evolution, natural selection and the rabbit's vastly superior intellect were prevailing. Andy watched his windmilling tail absently. He looked up as an aircraft lifted off the cinders. Colin had taken delivery of the squadron's fifth Sopwith Camel and, pronouncing it an ill-tempered bitch, was now taking every possible opportunity to tame its worst excesses. He pulled his new machine into a steep climb that would have stalled a Pup into a fatal spin, then knife-edged into a clockwise turn, flattening out into a full-revs blast along the perimeter hedge. Reaching the edge of the field he converted his speed into a vertical climb and half-loop, rolling out to dive onto the far perimeter, his wheels skimming the crimson willow herb. The newly-painted red spinner flashed in the sunlight.

Andy's own Camel stood, minus its cowling, outside C-Flight's hangar. His opinions of the new fighter were coloured by his machine's reluctance to give full revs. He'd experienced its notorious tail heaviness and the massive gyroscopic twist of that spinning Clerget an arm's stretch ahead of him, but so far hadn't enjoyed the compensation of that same Clerget's power and speed. His new aircraft lacked his old Pup's good manners, and barely exceeded its speed. So far, progress was not providing a good bargain.

He'd taken the Camel up that morning to try the twin Vickers guns on the target range. Here at least there was recompense. Instead of the pop-pop-pop of the Pup's single gun, slowed to one shot per passage of the propeller blade by the Sopwith interrupter gear, the Camel emitted an extravagant and highly satisfying *bwaap* that kicked the whole airframe back against his hands and feet. Pulling out from the dive was more a question of relaxing on the stick rather than actually pulling up.

Colin's machine roared along the near hedge, its engine blipping a hello as it passed Andy. The Idiot ceased his attempts to shoulder aside northern France and reversed his skittering claws to extract his head from the hole. The Camel was climbing again at the end of the field by the time the head came free and was raised, in exactly the wrong direction, to yap at the empty sky. Quiet descended again on the shimmering field, apart from the insane twitter of larks and the ever-present rumble of distant artillery. Andy threw a stick to attract the dog's attention and started back towards the hangar.

A sweating fitter straightened as he approached, his salute leaving a black smudge on his grimed forehead.

"Morning, Wheeler. Found anything?" asked Andy.

"Clutching at straws to be honest, sir. We're going to try lapping the valves in, but she's got loads of compression, so it'll probably make bug... hardly any difference."

Andy nodded. "Any other ideas if that doesn't work?"

Wheeler scratched his head. "Well, we can change the valve springs; if that doesn't work, it's an NBE, and we'll have it out as soon as the spares arrive."

"When will that be?"

"Hard to say sir. Couple of days, maybe."

"Great. We've got a trench-strafe this afternoon. A nasty bloody engine's just what I need." He turned as Colin's Camel taxied to a halt outside the next hangar. Thanking Wheeler with a nod he strolled over to meet him.

Colin was out of the cockpit and talking to Hughie, who had guided his wingtip as he taxied, when Andy arrived. He deflected the Idiot's meteoric greeting with a turned knee and fondled the dog's ears as he looked up at his friend.

"Any good?" Colin nodded towards Andy's machine.

"Not much. I think I've just picked the runt of the litter. How's yours?"

"I think we're reaching an understanding. Can't say I like it, but it's bloody fast, and that right turn is outrageous. Hughie here's managed to get rid of some of the tail-heaviness, so my right arm can have a bit of a rest."

"Yeah, it probably needs it."

"Not since Tom Corbett introduced me to the delights of *la petite* Nicole. He's buggered my savings, but probably saved my eyesight."

*

Andy tinkered constantly with fuel and air settings before giving up and resigning himself to limping lamely along behind the other four Camels. On full power he could hold formation, but anything beyond the cruise was impossible. Fortunately they were patrolling at 5,000 feet, saving him the necessity of pulling out of line to warm his guns and the ensuing impossibility of catching up. He considered signalling a dud engine and pulling back, but the lure of blooding his new machine kept him in formation. Page was leading, his new Camel already bearing the trademark chequered band he'd inherited from Arthur French. Next was Corbett, flying behind and to the right of the leader. The remainder of the flight flew in echelon: Colin, then Andy, with Cubby in his preferred position as rear guard.

Andy looked back over his right shoulder and caught a flash of teeth as Cubby grinned through his windscreen. The big Australian was crammed into his cockpit with a snugness that presaged ill for his elbows, but Cubby had taken to the new Sopwith with unalloyed delight. He saw Andy's glance and pointed down at his machine before kissing his fingertips and gesturing skywards. Andy laughed silently. At least someone was happy. Archie found them as they crossed No Man's Land and Page led them into a sharp dive to get below his effective height. They crossed the enemy lines at 50 feet and one hundred and fifty miles per hour, a near-impossible target for accurate ground fire.

Their target was a camouflaged ammunition dump that had been reported that morning by an RE8. As they approached, Andy saw artillery bursting around the area. He hoped for efficient cooperation between divisions as the distance closed. Then it occurred to him to wonder why, if artillery could reach the dump, they had been detailed to attack it with their Vickers peashooters. Page fired the attack signal and led them into a steep climb to gain height for their attacking dive. As the five Camels emerged from ground cover and lost speed, the previously sporadic and inaccurate gunfire zeroed in and concentrated. Hunland came alive with machine guns. Andy felt his machine shudder under the impact of several hits. Page's aircraft winged over into his attack, spiralling through inverted into an upright dive, using the gyroscopic effect of the engine to pull the nose down. Corbett, immediately behind him, twisted right to follow Page's streamers downwards. Then both aircraft broke apart into fluttering fragments.

Colin pulled up sharply to avoid the debris, just as the ammunition dump erupted in a volcano of pink-orange flame.

Andy's sick engine worsened as they headed home. First one, then two cylinders stopped firing and he slowly dropped behind as Colin and Cubby pointed their noses for the airfield. As he turned onto his final approach he saw the other two machines already taxiing to the hard standing outside the hangars. They both jumped immediately from their machines and marched purposefully towards Barrington Holt's office as Andy touched down.

The tableau that met him in the OC's office was tense and highly charged. His friends were standing in front of the desk, Colin with hands in pockets and downcast eyes, his head shaking slowly in disbelief. Cubby was leaning over Holt's desk, his big hands spread on its cluttered top. Holt himself was standing up, the telephone pressed to his ear. Cubby looked back as Andy rushed in. He too shook his head as their eyes met, before he returned wordlessly to watching Holt.

"General Feeney?" Holt straightened slightly. "Well bloody well get him for me as I asked! Now!" He listened for a moment before barking again. "Yes, I am perfectly aware whom I'm addressing. Yes, H-O-L-T. Major Barrington Holt, Officer Commanding 128 Squadron, by all means make a note. But do it after you've got me General Feeney!"

Holt turned to the window, his fist pounding on the misted glass. "General? Good, Holt here, 128 Squadron.

Two of my pilots have just been killed by shellfire from one of your batteries. Ammunition dump at Bois de Récourt? Yes sir, I am perfectly aware that a direct hit was achieved. My question is: why were your men still firing when you had been properly notified of the presence of my patrol?"

He listened for a few moments. The three airmen could hear a faint high-pitched protest from the other end. Holt's eternally mask-like face was flushed with anger and he paced back and forth behind his desk.

"Sir, such threats have little meaning to me, but let me assure you that my last action as an officer will be to ensure a full inquiry into the incompetence that has resulted in the deaths of two irreplaceable officers. My report will be filed this evening. Thank you."

He threw the receiver at the cradle. It bounced and shattered on the uneven stone floor. Holt sank into his chair, massaging his closed eyes with his right forefinger and thumb. "Gentlemen, I am deeply sorry for the loss of your very good friends." He looked up at the three silent airmen. "General Feeney insisted on an airborne attack over my protests. The dump was well within artillery range, so I have no idea why."

Andy looked on in disbelief. Holt had never been known to question or criticise an order or superior. His palpable fury testified to his feelings over the loss of Page and Corbett.

Holt stood, reaching for his stick. "Please come with me to the mess. The squadron has been shot through the heart; the men should know as soon as possible."

The wake was subdued, with unusually little furniture damage, and when the group around the piano began singing sentimental ballads, Andy escaped to the clean air outside. He walked between the lines of tents, kicking dandelion heads ahead of him. The sky flickered and rumbled to the north east, and a matching flash and grumble to the south west presaged a summer storm. Arriving by the hard standing outside A-Flight hangar, he sat down on a pile of tyres to light a cigarette. Page was dead. Of all the deaths he'd experienced in his year of combat, this was the least understandable. It was inconceivable that this scarred, constantly joking immortal could ever do anything as serious and ordinary as die. Holt would emerge from his office any moment to announce that Page had crash-landed safely this side of the lines and was being cared for by a lonely, beautiful French widow. He found himself looking at the light from the OC's window, almost jumping up when the door opened.

But no such telephone call would come. Andy had seen the fragments of the two aircraft, fluttering in the wake of the shell that had shattered them both on its way to destroy its intended target. *No bodies though. Perhaps...*

He shook his head. He'd seen the ground swallow entire aircraft; that he'd not seen either of the falling pilots meant nothing. And if, by some miracle, they'd been conveyed safely to the ground 200 feet below, it would only to be blasted to vapour by the exploding munitions. Page and Corbett. Corbett and Page. Humph and Tom. He lit another cigarette and threw it away after two puffs.

Stainton.

The sense of loss and abandonment was crippling and he slid forward off the tyres until his knees hit the cold concrete. He caved in on himself, his knuckles grating on the rough ground, his palms open and turned upwards. His shoulders came down until he rested on elbows and forehead. He knelt there for several minutes. A mist of rain pin-pricked his palms and neck, and then a faint noise brought him back to the world. He sat up and looked around. After a few seconds he heard footsteps and a dark shape moved to the tyres. A rustle of clothing, and then the sound of a match striking. Cubby's face was lit by the flame, two cigarettes between his lips. He puffed them to life and handed one, a red spark in the darkness, to Andy. They sat in silence, smoking.

CHAPTER 46

The morning was cold enough to mist their breath as Hoffe led Andy, Cubby, Colin and Hargreaves out to the five Camels that stood on the concrete, their engines warming. The sky was still dark velvet-blue, shading to purple and crimson to the south-east.

Andy climbed into B4620, wondering if today it would finally decide to deliver full revs. The ack emmas had lapped in the valves, changed plugs and leads and valve springs. The result was definitely an improvement, but still he sensed a harshness, and a feeling that something was holding the machine back. Perhaps he was expecting too much from a machine that, while much faster than the Pup, was nevertheless far slower than the latest SE5s and Albatros DVs.

They took off into the wind before wheeling around to climb in echelon into the eastern sky. It was 4.00am.

They patrolled a line between Cambrai, Douai and Lille for ninety minutes, seeing nothing. A large formation of Huns flicked in and out of sight well to the east. They had probably spotted the Camel patrol, but seemed content to keep their distance. Andy was watching Hoffe's machine expectantly, hoping for the wash-out signal to herald the end of this shivering boredom. Sporadic bursts from Archie were a diversion almost to be welcomed and once, when a shell burst right in front of his aircraft, Andy actually felt comforted by the warmth of the acrid smoke. A red flare from Hoffe's machine brought him back to the present and he realised guiltily that he'd been gathering wool. Ten thousand feet below them, a cluster of black explosions had alerted the flight leader to an impending scrap. He led his four charges down to investigate. The intruder who had drawn Archie's protest was an RE8 plodding along above Douai, its observer leaning out of the rear pit to work his complicated camera. The single anti-aircraft salvo had to be a signal to a nearby Hun to remove this prying eye from the Germans' airspace.

They saw it as they passed 4,000. A two-seater Halberstadt was approaching the RE8 from the north, on an almost exact reciprocal. It was well below the British spotter, hidden from its pilot by the Harry Tate's long engine. Andy wondered if the German observer had seen the five Camels diving on him from behind. Prompted into caution he looked over his own shoulder, scanning the sky for enemies. Hoffe signalled for a split attack, and Andy peeled away, following Hargreaves. He glanced behind to see Cubby curving after him. Hoffe and Colin would attack from the other side in order to divide the German observer's fire.

The Halberstadt had closed within range of the RE8 and opened fire from its front gun. The Harry Tate's pilot reacted quickly and twisted his unwieldy machine down to meet the German head-on. As the Halberstadt swerved to avoid a collision, the British observer managed a short burst from his gun. The Halberstadt was at no more than 1,000 feet when Hoffe moved into a killing line on its left. Hargreaves' group was slightly behind, restricted by the wider left-hand turning radius of the Camels. From position two, Andy saw Hoffe pull sharply away without firing. As he turned, Andy saw the flight leader hammering his cocking levers. *Gun jam*. Colin was already in position for his attack, and tracer spouted from his twin Vickers. A two-second burst, and then Colin's guns also fell silent. His machine dropped sharply and began a wide spiral to earth. His propeller was turning slowly and unevenly, and something pale fluttered from his right upper plane, catching the sun.

Hargreaves, in attack range at last, fired a five second burst at the Halberstadt. Its observer, no longer threatened from his port side, sighted deliberately before replying. Undistracted by the necessity of flying his aeroplane, his aim was better than Hargreaves'. The deputy leader's machine suddenly spiralled sharply to the right, diving out of Andy's field of view. Andy leaned into his Aldis sight, ruddering right to lead his target, then pulled his trigger. He walked his bullets along the midline of the Halberstadt's fuselage from engine to tail. The observer disappeared below the rim of the rear pit as Andy dived below, close enough to see the varnished planking of the fuselage. He winged over, searching the ground below for Colin's machine. He saw it descending, apparently under control, its propeller now still and one aileron flapping in the slipstream. He looked back up in time to see Cubby dispatch the Halberstadt with a point-blank burst into its engine. Fire erupted immediately and the German plane tipped into a vertical dive.

Andy returned his attention to Colin's descent. The stricken Camel appeared almost stationary. From 500 feet, Andy could see its shadow, long in the early sunlight. The ground was peppered with shell holes, and Colin's machine was fishtailing nervously as its pilot searched for a safe landing spot. It was impossible to see at what point the Camel touched down, but Colin must have held it off right to the point of stalling. Suddenly it was bouncing, then it swerved violently left before coming to a rocking halt. Andy breathed again. *Survivable*.

He looked up again to see Cubby and Hoffe circling above him. The Halberstadt was a column of dirty brown smoke a couple of miles to the south. Suddenly he was gripped with an insane idea. He'd land next to Colin's machine, and escape to freedom with his friend clinging to his cabane struts. *No prisoner of war camp for you, me old mate.* He flew by the wreck, his wheels skimming the craters and tree stumps. Colin was out of the machine, apparently uninjured, waving as the Camel flew by. Behind him, the broken aeroplane had begun to burn. Andy noticed a small figure standing near. *What the hell's a girl doing here?*

Further away, Andy saw a patrol in field-grey approaching the crash site. His rescue plan evaporated; by the time he'd turned, slowed and found an escapable landing spot there'd be no time left to take off again before they were both captured. He applied full power again and kept the nose low to build speed for a zoom climb. As he pulled up to gain height he glanced back to see Colin running in the other direction, waving his arms and pointing. Andy guessed the reason and looked higher up. Diving from well above, the stalking Germans were tumbling out of the sun on the three Camels, still scattered after their attack on the Halberstadt.

Andy was climbing, but with only 70mph of airspeed he would arrive too late to hunt the hunted. Not that his two guns would shift the balance against such an overwhelming swarm. There were at least 20 single seaters, Albatros and Pfalz, closing on his companions. They would be in firing range in seconds.

Hoffe, identifiable by his leader's streamers, was separated from the other two. He appeared to be almost standing up in his cockpit. Andy had seen him hammering his cocking levers immediately after the attack, and guessed that Hoffe was now trying to free the feed belts. Successful or not, he needed to react to the threat within the next ten seconds to stand any chance of diving under the enemy swarm and bolting for safety.

The single streamer on Hargreaves' machine fluttered as the aircraft pitched up and down, staggering erratically. The Camel flying in close, solicitous attendance must be Cubby's, offering moral encouragement to the deputy leader, who must have been wounded by the Halberstadt's gunner. But if Hargreaves intended to return to base he was heading exactly the wrong way. Everyone was too preoccupied to look up.

Andy grabbed the Very pistol clipped to the side of his cockpit, cocked it and fired a red flare towards the three Camels. Cubby was first to see the threat. He pulled into a climb to meet the attackers head-on. Hoffe dived sharply, trying to slip under the enemy. Hargreaves seemed oblivious and continued in his stuttering progress to the north-east.

The German leader had neared to firing distance on Cubby and tracers snaked from both aircraft as their separation closed. They passed, seemingly within inches of one another, neither with any visible damage. The two next Huns, both lozenge-patterned Albatros, swerved in from left and right to gain a firing line. Their wings overlapped, touched and entangled. Cubby's Camel rolled sharply inverted to pull under them. The two interlocked Albatros ballooned suddenly upwards, opening a clear space for him to swoop through.

The tangle came apart as Cubby completed his escape roll. One Albatros pulled into what looked like a controlled descent, showing no damage discernible at distance. The other tumbled end-over-end, shedding upper and lower wings as it fell. And the still-spinning airscrew severed the entire tail section from Cubby's Sopwith.

Andy's screamed protest tore his throat. With 500 feet vertically and 500 yards horizontally still to cover to bring him in range, he screamed again in impotent agony as the Camel flipped nose-high and hung from its propeller for what seemed minutes. Then it rolled over onto its back and tumbled to earth.

The Germans had closed on Hargreaves and his aircraft was already a flaming meteor when Andy tore his eyes away from Cubby's fall. Hoffe was nowhere to be seen. Andy looked back, searching for Cubby's Camel, but unable to locate it against the patched brown earth. Then a fireball bloomed in a cratered field half a mile away. A black, perfectly formed smoke ring rose to heaven.

The enemy aircraft had wheeled and were quartering, looking for the remaining two Camels. A white flare curved from one machine and a few seconds later, a score of wings flashed in the sun as they turned towards him. Andy became aware of the tackety-tackety sound that had been nagging the edge of his consciousness for some time. His foul-hearted engine had chosen its moment to demonstrate its mastery of his fate. And suddenly the blood lust revenge evaporated. The dull, disinterested acceptance of a worthless life that had buffered him from the world for the last weeks disappeared in its wake.

Suddenly he wanted, above all else, to live.

EPILOGUE

The Ford Escort was a Godfrey Davis rental. Angie was used to more room and fewer pedals and, even after the two-hour drive from London, her gear changes still provoked a dip of the nose and a whine of protest from under the bonnet. The woman next to her opened her eyes with a start and Angie glanced apologetically at her.

"Sorry, Mum, did I wake you?"

"No, I wasn't asleep. I was resting my eyes while I listened to the radio."

"Oh, OK. I'll switch it on then."

Angie's voice betrayed a faint Australian accent. She was a pleasant-looking woman in her mid-sixties, slim and with hair that was still predominantly dark. Her mother was stick-thin and upright, with a clipped, finishing-school accent untainted by any hint of the Antipodes.

Angie leaned forward in her seat. "I think that's him. Do you think that's him?"

A balding man in his eighties was leaning on the wing of a green Hillman Hunter that was parked by a telephone box a little way ahead. He stood and waved as they slowed. Angie parked and opened the door, getting out to meet him as he crossed the road to them.

"Pleased to meet you, Mrs Halford. I'm Colin."

Angie shook his hand. "Please, call me Angie. It's good to meet you at last, Colin."

The passenger door closed and her mother stepped around the car, proudly upright, but leaning on a polished mahogany cane. Colin turned to meet her and put out both hands.

"Stainton. I can't believe it. After so many years."

He stretched to kiss her cheek. He was half a head shorter than she, rounded and compact.

"Why don't you leave your car here and we'll go on in mine?" he said to Angie.

His car was six or seven years old, but polished inside and out. Angie sat in the back watching the Suffolk countryside glide by, listening to him chattering enthusiastically to her mother. She leaned forward, resting her elbows in the gap between the front seats.

"You flew with my father then, Colin?"

He glanced over his shoulder. "Yes. We started together. Joined the squadron on the same day."

"And you were shot down I believe?"

"Shot myself down, actually. My interrupter gear failed and I shot half my propeller away. I landed my aeroplane, set fire to it, and while I waited to be taken prisoner I chatted to a little French girl who was scavenging the field."

"You must have been terrified."

He thought for a moment. "I suppose I must. I can't really remember how I was feeling. I was watching the fight above me."

He drove in silence for some time, shook his head slightly and resumed. "Cubby was hit by one of the German planes and crashed half a mile away." He glanced over his shoulder. "He was your grandmother's particular friend." He looked back through the windscreen and added quietly, almost to himself. "And mine. He was my friend."

His hand was resting on the gear lever. Stainton covered it with hers.

"We never knew what happened to him. I needed to get away from England, and Mum took us to Australia. She had this fixed notion that he'd come and find us when the war ended. But he never did. She was very fond of him."

"We all were," said Colin. "He was huge. I mean, not just big. He was like a giant. He and Andy were inseparable."

"I'm so glad that you and Andy stayed friends."

Colin smiled, nodding. "Me too. That day, when I saw him belting for home at zero feet, with half the German air force after him, I thought he was dead already. I had a letter from my parents not long before the war ended, saying that he'd made it back to the lines with a couple of bullets in him and a couple of dozen in his kite. A bunch of SE5s spotted him running for home and joined in. That attracted a French patrol and they all had a merry time split-arsing around while Andy slipped away and crash-landed just behind our trench line."

Colin took off his glasses and wiped them on a cloth he pulled from the door bin, his hands together on the bottom of the steering wheel. Stainton looked through the windscreen for a long time before asking, quietly: "How is he?"

Colin frowned, searching for his words. "Frail." He was quiet again. "Stainton, he might not know who you are. I'm sorry." He turned the car into a tree-lined drive. "Here we are."

It had probably once been a handsome house, built some time in the eighteenth century, but brick-built extensions with metal-framed windows had proliferated, and the stone portico had been subsumed by a modern double-glazed porch. They signed in at a high reception desk and were led by a blue-uniformed attendant along series of identical, creaking corridors with bewildering intersections and right-angle turns.

Stainton started and stood stock-still for a moment outside an open door from which came a quiet voice droning, "Oh golly, no. Oh golly, no."

The attendant led them to a large room with windows on three sides. A scattering of upright easy chairs of various designs and colours was populated by old men and women. A few were reading but, with the exception of a couple chatting animatedly in one corner, the rest sat motionless, either asleep or gazing straight ahead. The overheated air was heavy with the scents of boiled food, pine disinfectant and an indefinable sour-sweetness of floral scents overlaying corruption. A tiny woman in a pink shawl raised a hand as they passed. She frowned and her mouth opened as though trying to frame a vital question.

A high-backed chair at the far end of the room was turned outwards to face the French windows. A bony hand on the armrest was all that could be seen of its occupant. The attendant leaned over and spoke in a jolly, over-loud voice, "Hello, Andy. Some visitors for you!" She turned back to Colin, Stainton and Angie. "I'll get you some chairs."

Andy's face was skull-like, the skin stretched translucent over ivory-yellow cheekbones, shading to purple in the hollows around his eyes. He was wearing a heavy-knit cardigan with done-up leather buttons, despite the heat of the room. Angie noticed that an extra buttonhole next to the hem was matched by a superfluous button near the collar. Colin patted the nearer hand.

"Hullo my old chum. How are you today? I see they've lost your glasses again."

Andy's eyes remained fixed on the garden. His left hand trembled slightly on the armrest. Colin beckoned Stainton and Angie into his field of view.

"Look who's here to see you. This is Angie; she's your daughter. And this is Stainton."

The old man blinked and his eyes flicked between the women, his brows furrowing slightly. His jaw moved as though he was about to speak, then the eyes returned, unfocused, to the garden. The attendant brought chairs for the three of them and Stainton took Andy's right hand as she sat down, her knees touching his. Angie sat alongside him, her eyes fixed on the side of her father's face.

Stainton leaned forward and spoke quietly. "Hello Andy, it's so good to see you again."

The dim eyes flicked to her face again and the frown returned. After a moment he turned his head fully and looked at her. His head tilted back until it rested against the cushion and he sat, considering her. He took a long, slow breath through his nose and released it equally slowly, puffing his thin lips slightly apart. The corners of his mouth tightened slightly.

"Is that a smile? Mum, is he smiling?" asked Angie.

"I don't know." Stainton laid her hand on his leg, just above the knee. "Andy, do you remember the hospital? The bandages here? We bought each other presents, do you remember that?"

The eyes clouded again and drifted back to the empty garden.

Stainton looked over at the pale wooden upright piano against the side wall, donated by some relative who preferred its space to its melodies. She patted Andy's leg and stood up, leaning on her stick.

Angie looked up. "Mum, I don't think…"

Stainton silenced her with a shake of her head. She lifted the lid of the piano and began to play. Several of the residents looked up and a few even began to sing softly.

Keep the home fires burning,
Though your hearts are yearning.
Though our lads are far away, they dream of home.

She looked over her shoulder. Andy was sitting slightly more forward in his chair, looking at her as she played. A few of the staff heard the sound and clustered, smiling, in the doorway. Andy blinked, trying to clear his blurred vision.

The girl at the piano was playing a song he'd always hated, but tonight its gentle poignancy soothed and reassured him. She looked over her shoulder at him, flashing a smile from dark eyes and bright teeth. He grinned back and winked conspiratorially, happy to see her there. He blinked again, looking around at faces that shifted and faded, familiar, then strangers once again. His thumb stroked the bowl of the briar pipe she'd bought him. He chuckled silently, thinking of the sound of their soles clattering in the corridor as he and Stainton ran, giggling, from Nurse Wilkes's knowing smile. Janice had said there'd be no bed check tonight...

The song finished and the staff in the doorway applauded politely. As Stainton stood she saw Andy's lips move. Angie was leaning close to catch his words.

"Did he speak? What did he say?"

Angie leaned back and looked up, noticing that her mother seemed to have lost an earring.

"I think he said, 'I loved the larks,'" she replied.

******

GLOSSARY

Ack Emma WW1 phonetic for A.M. - Aircraft Mechanic. Also A.M., as in morning.

Albatros Usually applied to the German scout, though the Albatros factory produced many types before their famous shark-nosed fighter. From the DIII onwards it was commonly called the V-Strutter because of its main strut layout. The single-spar lower plane meant there was only one anchor point at the lower end of the interplane struts. This led to weakness in the lower wing, sometimes leading to collapse in a high-speed dive.

Archie Anti-aircraft fire. Spoken of as a person by pilots: "Archie's got a bee in his bonnet today!" Reputedly named after the refrain of a popular song: "Archibald, certainly not!"

Baby Elephant Spotter aircraft, term mainly used by Australian infantry

BE2c	Also known as a "Bloater", or more frequently simply "2c", the BE2c was yet another questionable product of the Royal Aircraft Factory. The Germans called it *"kaltes fleisch"* – cold meat, while the British press dubbed it "Fokker Fodder".
Belgium	Apart from the country, Australian slang for a fatal wound
D.O.P.	Deep Offensive Patrol. Patrol several miles behind enemy lines intended to impose air superiority.
Effel	Popular name for the windsock – short for "French letter"
Eindecker	German Fokker monoplane, responsible for the "Fokker Scourge"
FANY	First Aid Nursing Yeomanry: A voluntary organisation which provided first aid and medical evacuation, frequently close to enemy action.
FE2b	Another, more successful, creation of the Royal Aircraft Factory. A large two-seat pusher biplane used mainly for observation and bombing duties.

Flaming Onions	Incendiary flares fired in rapid succession by rotating-barrel guns. They were a feared and effective anti-aircraft weapon, believed (incorrectly) by many allied airmen to be joined by wires. Their simple design was not discovered by the allies until late in the war.
Fokker	Any aircraft made by the Fokker factory. Early on, usually referred to the Eindecker; later in the war to the excellent DVII. Could also apply to the Fokker DR1 Triplane, though this was usually referred to as "Tripe" or "Tripehound"
Flying Sickness D	The RFC's term for what the infantry called "shell-shock." Now viewed as post-traumatic stress disorder, it was little understood in WW1.
Harry Tate	See RE8
Imshi	Go, leave, from Arabic: Yalla imshi
Linseed, Linseed Lancer	Field medic
LMF	Lacking in Moral Fibre – official term for cowardice. An arbitrarily applied and draconically punished transgression.

Maghrib	Islam prayer said just after sunset.
Mihrab	Wall niche used to indicate the direction of Mecca.
Ocean Villas	Intentional mispronunciation of Auchonvillers.
P.B.I	Poor bloody infantry.
Pitot	Primitive method of indicating airspeed by means of a column of liquid on the dashboard, pushed up by the air pressure in a forward-facing pipe (still called the pitot tube), usually mounted on the wing outboard of the propeller wash.
R.A.F.	Until April 1st 1918, this invariably referred to the Royal Aircraft Factory, manufacturer of aircraft like the BE2, FE2b, RE8 and SE5. The "E" in all designations stood for "Experimental". Few of the experiments were successful.
RAP	Regimental Aid Post: A first-aid and triage station positioned near the front line.
RE8	Designed and built by the R.A.F. as a replacement for the unloved BE2, the RE8, often known as Harry Tate, provided unforgivably little improvement.

Tickler's Artillery	Improvised grenade made from empty food tins. Named after Tickler's Jam, which was available in two flavours: red or green.
Tripe, Tripehound	Usually refers to the Fokker DR1 Triplane, though – confusingly – may also be applied to the Sopwith Triplane.
V-Strutter	See Albatros
Wipers	Intentional mispronunciation of Ypres

ACKNOWLEDGEMENTS

My brother Martin created the germ that grew into a story. As in life, so in this book: he's been the lighthouse that saw me safe to the journey's end. We inherited a love of aviation from our father, to whom the book is dedicated.

I've been lucky enough to have a small bunch of patient readers who've been generously brutal and unforgiving. Steve Ball and Roger Mitchell were as ready to punish as applaud, but they've kept going through to the end. The family's been there too, so thank you to my son Adam for tidying up Andy's thoughts, and once again to Martin for giving realism to my dialogues.

Thanks as well to Renegade Writers, a group of talented – and hugely entertaining – authors who've let me get away with murder, but chastised me for letting my participles dangle. Malcolm Havard's encyclopaedic knowledge of WW1 aviation has kept me re-writing, correcting and deleting far beyond any test of reasonableness No other living man knows by heart the valid serial numbers for a Sopwith Camel.

The characters in this book are fictional. Any similarity to persons living or dead is largely coincidental, though a few real people have snuck in to become animae living inside an invented world. If the cap fits, thank you for your performance; you were wonderful.

Made in the USA
Charleston, SC
04 April 2016